❧ ISLANDS ❧

A director of an agency devoted to the welfare of children, Anny Butler has never had a real family. That changes when she marries Lewis Aiken, an exuberant surgeon fifteen years her senior. And with her new husband comes the Scrubs, a group of inseperable Charleston friends, who become Anny's devoted surrogate family.

Growing ever closer at the old beach house on Sullivan's Island, which they co-own, the group vows that eventually they will find a place by the sea where they will retire to live and care for each other. But the ravages of time soon take their toll: a hurricane, a fire, deaths. Yet the remaining Scrubs cling together, overseen by Camilla Curry, a healer who has always been their heart and core.

And when they finally move to a new island retreat—the beginning of their long-awaited life together—Anny will learn that everything is not as it seems, that some loves carry a secret and a terrible price.

A poignant novel of the love that unites us and the secrets that drive us apart, ISLANDS is Anne Rivers Siddons at her lyrical best—a glorious evocation of the people and the place she knows so well.

Praise for
ISLANDS
and
ANNE RIVERS SIDDONS

"As always, Siddons writes with a graceful
lushness, evoking the wild salt marshes of the
coast and Charleston's candlelit-drawing
rooms with equal ease . . . Good reading."
Orlando Sentinel

"Excellent . . . wonderful, lyrical prose
that sweeps and sings and soars."
Publishers Weekly

"Readers [will] linger over *Islands*."
Commercial Appeal, Memphis, Tennessee

"Like Faulkner and Conroy, the author
calmly manipulates the reader,
unfurling familial horrors with
just the right degree of psychic tension."
Miami Herald

"Anne Rivers Siddons is a master at
constructing a concrete framework and evoking
a mood, particularly when her milieu is her
beloved Low Country of South Carolina."
The Tennessean

"Siddons fans will applaud this latest effort. It's everything you want in entertaining, escape reading . . . *Islands* perfectly captures the magic and atmosphere of Charleston. Many readers will identify with her characters, or, at the very least, be fascinated with a lifestyle that they may not experience but to which they aspire."
Chattanooga News-Free Press

"Anne Rivers Siddons establishes herself in the front ranks of Southern writers . . . While there are hints of Truman Capote and Tennessee Williams . . . Siddons is her own woman."
Los Angeles Times Book Review

"Anne Rivers Siddons' settings and characters help readers fathom the [South's] people and pockets of uniqueness that have survived an overlay of sameness. At the same time, she delivers riveting reads. *Islands* continues that tradition of offering readers the equivalent of leaving the lookalike interstate highway exits for human-scale rural roads of the mind."
Denver Post

Books by
Anne Rivers Siddons

SWEETWATER CREEK
ISLANDS
NORA, NORA
LOW COUNTRY
UP ISLAND
FAULT LINES
DOWNTOWN
HILL TOWNS
COLONY
OUTER BANKS
KING'S OAK
PEACHTREE ROAD
HOMEPLACE
FOX'S EARTH
THE HOUSE NEXT DOOR
HEARTBREAK HOTEL
JOHN CHANCELLOR MAKES ME CRY

ATTENTION: ORGANIZATIONS AND CORPORATIONS
Most HarperTorch paperbacks are available at special quantity
discounts for bulk purchases for sales promotions, premiums,
or fund raising. For information, please call or write:

Special Markets Department, HarperCollins Publishers, Inc.,
10 East 53rd Street, New York, New York 10022-5299.
Telephone: (212) 207-7528.   Fax: (212) 207-7222.

ANNE RIVERS SIDDONS

ISLANDS

HarperTorch
An Imprint of HarperCollins*Publishers*

This is a work of fiction. Names, characters, places, and incidents are products of the author's imagination or are used fictitiously and are not to be construed as real. Any resemblance to actual events, locales, organizations, or persons, living or dead, is entirely coincidental.

❦

HARPERTORCH
An Imprint of HarperCollins*Publishers*
10 East 53rd Street
New York, New York 10022-5299

Copyright © 2004 by Anne Rivers Siddons
Author photo by Jack Alterman
ISBN: 0-06-113723-5

All rights reserved. No part of this book may be used or reproduced in any manner whatsoever without written permission, except in the case of brief quotations embodied in critical articles and reviews. For information address HarperTorch, an Imprint of HarperCollins Publishers.

First HarperTorch special printing: June 2006
First HarperTorch paperback printing: January 2005
First HarperCollins special printing: April 2004
First HarperCollins hardcover printing: May 2004

HarperCollins®, HarperTorch™, and ❦™ are trademarks of HarperCollins Publishers Inc.

Printed in the United States of America

Visit HarperTorch on the World Wide Web at www.harpercollins.com

10 9 8 7 6 5 4 3 2 1

If you purchased this book without a cover, you should be aware that this book is stolen property. It was reported as "unsold and destroyed" to the publisher, and neither the author nor the publisher has received any payment for this "stripped book."

For Larry Ashmead—

save the last dance for me.

Only where love and need are one,
And the work is play for mortal stakes . . .

—ROBERT FROST

After the first death there is no other.

—DYLAN THOMAS

PROLOGUE

EVEN IN THE MIDDLE OF IT, I knew that it was a
dream, but that did not spoil the sweet reality of
it. Reality is often more vivid in that kind of
dream because the dreamer knows he must soon
leave it whether or not it is a happy dream. This
was a very happy one.

I was in the beach house. Not the one we've
rented in the past few years, but the one we all
owned together, the big, old, rambling 1920s cottage on stilts down at the un-chic western end of
the island. It was the first one that I knew; Lewis
brought me there the summer we were married,
and I loved it as much in that first instant as I did
in all the years we went there. I never said that to
the others, because it sounded somehow presumptuous, as if an outlander were laying claim
to something he had not yet earned. And even
though they enfolded me and took me in as one
of them from the first, I knew that I was indeed an
outlander. It was Lewis they loved, at least then.

In the dream it was winter, and there was a
cold wind howling down the beach and scouring
the gray-tan sand into stinging swirls. I knew
how they would feel on my skin if I went out on

the beach: like particles of diamonds, almost bringing blood. I usually did not mind that, but this time I was glad to be inside the big living room. It was warm and lit and almost tossing in the wind, like the cabin of a ship. All the old lopsided lamps were yellow with light, and a fire burned in the fireplace at one end, spitting because the shed out back never quite kept the wood dry. At the other end where the staircase angled up over the junk closet, the big old space heater whispered and glowed deep red. The air in the room smelled of woodsmoke and kerosene and damp rugs and salt. In my dream it seemed the palpable breath of the house to me, and I breathed in deep draughts. It gave life.

"I know this is a dream, but I don't have to wake up yet, do I?" I said to Fairlie McKenzie, who lay on the couch under a salt-stiff old blanket by the fire, reading. Her bright hair spilled over the tattered sofa pillow in a cascade as red as the embers. Fairlie always seemed to me a creature of light and fire: she shimmered with it, even lying still.

"No, not yet," she said, smiling at me. "There's no hurry. The guys won't be back for hours. Sit down. In a minute I'll make some tea."

"I'll make it," Camilla Curry said from her card table beside the space heater at the other end of the room. She was copying something from a big book onto a yellow legal pad, her face and hands in a pool of light from the bridge lamp. I seldom saw Camilla without a pad and pen. She always had projects that seemed to engross her utterly, and the rest of us never quite knew what they were.

"This and that," she would say in her soft

drawl. "I'll let you see when I'm done." But her projects were always works in progress, because we never saw one.

"Let me," I said, grateful to be a useful part of the tapestry of the dream. Camilla, even in the dream, was bowed with osteoporosis, as she had been for a long time. Somehow it did not distort her fragile, fine-boned handsomeness: I always thought of her as ramrod-straight. Lewis said she always had been, until the cruel disease began to eat her bones. We never spoke of it, but we all tried to spare Camilla undue physical stress when we could. She always saw through us, and always hated it.

"You girls stay still. You get so little time out here, and I'm here most of all," she said. "I like to fiddle around in the kitchen."

Fairlie and I smiled at each other at the "girls." I was nearly fifty and Fairlie was only a few years younger than Camilla. But Camilla was mother to the group. She always had been the one to whom you went to find something, learn something, confess something, receive something. We all knew her role was self-chosen. Even the men followed the unspoken rule. Camilla made you want to give her the most you could of what her heart needed.

She got up and floated straight as a hummingbird into the kitchen. Her shoulders were erect and her step light as a girl's. She sang a little song as she walked: "Maybe I'm right, and maybe I'm wrong, and maybe I'm weak and maybe I'm strong, but nevertheless I'm in love with you. . . ."

"Charles says it's a sappy song, but I love it,"

she called back over her beautiful shoulder. She
had on a sheer blouse and a flowered skirt, and
wore high-heeled sandals. Because it was a
dream, it made perfect sense for her to walk like a
girl, to be dressed in the clothes of her girlhood,
for Charles to be alive. All of this made me even
happier.

"Camilla, even if it's a dream, I want to stay," I
called back after her. "I don't want to go back."

"You can stay, Anny," her plummy voice called
from the kitchen. "Lewis isn't coming for you
yet."

I curled up on the rug in front of the fire beside
Fairlie on the sofa, pulling soft old cushions down
to make a nest. I wrapped myself in the faded
sofa quilt. The fire burned blue with damp, but
gave a steady heat. Outside the wind gusted and
rattled the winter-dried palms and peppered the
windows with staccato sand. The panes were
crusted with salt. I stretched out my arms and
legs to their furthest length and felt my joints
pop, and the heat seep into them. I looked over at
Fairlie to watch the firelight playing on her face.
Twilight was falling fast; the men would come
stamping in soon, letting cold, wet wind eddy in
with them, rubbing their hands.

"Don't bring those smelly fish in here," Fairlie
would say from the sofa. "I'm not cleaning fish
today or any other day."

And because it was a dream, Lewis would be
there along with Henry, as he always had been,
and would say, as he always said when he came
back from an expedition on which I had not
accompanied him, "How's my lazy girl?"

I closed my eyes and slid toward dream-sleep before the dying logs, happiness prickling like lights behind my lids. In the kitchen the teakettle began to whistle.

"There's plenty of time," I murmured.

"Yes," Fairlie said.

We were quiet.

The fire came then. . . .

part one

1

I met Lewis Aiken when I was thirty-five and resigned to the fact that I would not marry for love, only, perhaps, for convenience, and he was fifty and had long been married, until fairly recently, for no reason other than love. For a long time after our relationship began, I thought we had turned ourselves about; that I was the one who loved, clumsily and foolishly, with the passion of one who has never really felt passion before, and Lewis was the one who found in me comfort and convenience. By that time I did not care. He could name the terms. I would be whatever he wanted and needed me to be.

We met on an afternoon in April, humid and punishing as spring can often be in the Carolina Low Country, when the air felt like thick, wet steam and the smell of the pluff mud from the marshes around Charleston stung in nostrils and permeated clothes and hair. I was bringing a frightened, clubfooted child to the free clinic Lewis operated on Saturdays, and we were running late. My old Toyota was coughing and gagging in the heat, and I had turned off the air conditioner to spare its strength, and was running sweat. In the backseat, buckled into her car seat, the child howled steadily and dismally.

I did not blame her. I wanted to howl myself. Her feckless mother had dropped her off in my office the afternoon before and faded away for the second time running, leaving me to scramble around for a place for her daughter to spend Friday night and then pick her up the next day and take her to the clinic myself. Back in my office the paperwork that was the effluvia of desperate need mounted steadily.

"Sweetie, please stop crying," I said desperately, over my shoulder. "We're going to see the nice man who's going to help get your foot fixed, and then you can run around and jump and . . . oh, play soccer." I had no idea what movement would tempt a five-year-old, but it obviously was not soccer. The howls mounted.

I pulled into the lot next to the beautiful old house on Rutledge Avenue that housed Dr. Lewis Aiken's Low Country Pediatric Orthopedic Clinic. I knew that Dr. Aiken had long done free diagnostic and referral work with handicapped—physically challenged, I could not keep up—children from all around the region. He was regarded in my agency as one of the city's greatest child resources, one of our constant angels. The agency I managed was a part federally, part privately funded sort of clearinghouse for services for needy children and adolescents, and by that time I knew where all the angels were located.

I had come to work at the agency just out of the College of Charleston when I was twenty-two, when my duties consisted of manning telephones and running out for emergency meals and diapers for our clients, and somehow had never left. I was head now, and my duties were more often those of an administrator and fund-raiser and public relations director, but I had not lost my primary passion for the children we served; indeed, I had come to think that that was where all my scant supply of passion went. I had not yet met Dr. Aiken or many of our other care providers, though I knew all their office people on the phone. My small staff of cynically idealistic young men and women did most of the hands-on work now. But it was Saturday, and when the child's silly mother did not appear at the foster home that had taken in her daughter, the foster parents called me and I had no recourse but to go. Oh, well, I had no plans except the stack of books that had been piling up beside my bed and maybe a Sunday-afternoon movie with Marcy, my deputy.

Marcy and I spent some time together on weekends, not so much out of deep friendship, but more out of simple expediency. We liked each other, and it was nice to have someone else to go places with, but we came nowhere near being best friends, and certainly not the settled lesbian couple that I knew some of the junior staff thought us to be. Marcy had a sometimes-boyfriend in Columbia who came over every third weekend, whom she assumed, rather lackadaisically, I thought, that she would eventually marry. I had some men friends, all from the ranks of the vast medical complex that bloomed like kudzu in the center of Charleston, though none were doctors. I seemed to attract the administrator type. My mother could have told me so, and had: I could hear her voice as I struggled with the straps of the wriggling child's car seat: "If you don't fix yourself up some and get your nose out of those books, no interesting kind of man will have you. You don't know anything about anything but wiping noses and doing wash. How sexy do you think that is?"

And whose fault is that? I would think, but it would have been futile to say it aloud. She was usually drunk when she started in on me—she was usually drunk, period—and would not have remembered. I could never quite fathom what kind of man my mother thought was interesting; it seemed to me that all of them filled the bill. She'd certainly had a diverse stable. By the time alcohol became her constant lover, I was regularly taking care of my two younger sisters and brother, and overseeing housework and meals, too. Oddly enough, I rather liked it. It made me feel important, needed, and I had a talent for nurturing that was perhaps my strongest gift. And I did and do love my sisters and brother. My mother has been dead for many years now.

"Okay, toots, here we go," I said to little white-blond Shawna Sperry, who was mucus streaked and fretful but had stopped crying. I picked her up in my arms—with the steel brace she was heavy, but I could not bear to see her lurching walk—and carried her into the lobby of the center. There was no one about. The receptionist's desk was empty and tidy in a way that meant no one had been working there, and there was a stillness and silence in which ambient sounds rang. An air conditioner thumped fretfully in the window. Dust motes stood in the slant of sickly light from the windows. It was a greenish, thin light that I knew meant a storm. You didn't have to live long in the Low Country to be able to read the skies and seas and marshes. Perfect. I would have the inestimable joy of trying to get a steel-ballasted child through a rainstorm and into my moribund car. The windshield wiper on the driver's side had died a couple of weeks before, and I had not gotten around to having it fixed.

We sat down in the lobby and I smoothed Shawna's wispy hair and dabbed at her nose with a tissue. I ran my hands over my own hair; curly at its best, humidity and heat sent it into an aboriginal tangle of near-black frizz. With my dark eyes and olive skin, I often thought I looked at least partly African American. This had not pleased my mother either; in high school she had tried to get me to have my mop straightened and lightened, but by that time my unadorned appearance had become my one rebellion, and I was halfway through college before I even bought a lipstick. I chewed at my lower lip. It felt grainy and papery; I knew that the color I had swiped on that morning was long gone, leaving only a ragged outline on my mouth. Sticky underarms and sweat-dampened legs completed the effect. I hoped that Dr. Lewis Aiken was seventy-five and uncompromisingly unattractive.

The silence spun out. Shawna leaned against my arm and napped. The air-conditioned air began to chill me in my sweaty clothes. Finally I

called out, "Hello? Is there anybody here? I'm
Anny Butler from Outreach. I'm here with the little girl who was to get an evaluation this afternoon?"

There was more silence, and then a man's voice
from somewhere beyond the reception area said,
"Oh, shit. Excuse me. What time is it? I'm sorry.
How did it get so late? I'm Lewis Aiken."

He came into the reception area and we looked
at each other, and I laughed, helplessly. He was
short and compact and, somehow, red all over,
and his ginger hair was so wildly disheveled that
it looked as if he had had his finger in a light
socket. His steel-rimmed eyeglasses were
mended with tape. He had a heavy growth of
orange beard through which his white teeth
flashed piratically, and he wore the most scurrilous scrubs I have ever seen. He was barefoot. If
I had not known who he was, I would have picked
up Shawna and run. As it was, she stared at him
and began to wail again.

He shuffled over and picked her up and slung
her expertly on one hip, and looked into her face.

"I don't blame you," he said solemnly. "If I had
just met me, I'd yell, too. I bet I look like Ronald
McDonald, don't I? All my lady patients say that."

And miraculously, Shawna stopped howling
and looked at him and smiled, an enchanting,
three-cornered kitten's smile. I had never seen it
before. She put her finger on his nose and pushed.

"Not Ronald," she said, and giggled.

"Right," he said. "I don't have my big red nose,
do I? Well, I forgot I was having company. Come
on back and I'll see if I can find it."

He scooped up a folder from the desk on his way back, and looked at it, still holding Shawna on his hip. She was pulling his hair and laughing. He looked up from the file. "Mmm-hmm. Club-foot referral. Shawna Sperry. And you would be Mrs. Sperry?" he said, looking over his shoulder at me.

"No," I said irritably. Had he not heard me, then? "I'm Anny Butler. I run Outreach. You've done some work for us before. We had an appointment . . . "

"So you did," he said, reading from the chart. "Though it says here that the child's mother would be bringing her. Well, I'm glad to meet you, Anny Butler. You folks do good work."

"The child's mother has done a flit," I said, wondering from where on earth I had dredged up that expression. It sounded like one of those flip, cloying English murder mysteries that I particularly loathed. Murder should not be funny. "She may never be seen again. You do good work, too. Thanks for working us in on your Saturday afternoon. What am I keeping you from? Golf?"

I was babbling, which did not please me, and besides, it was patently obvious that this man had never played golf in his life. He would have been forcibly removed from the course at the country club.

"As a matter of fact," he said, not looking back this time, "I was cutting my toenails."

"Yuck," said Shawna, and we all laughed. There was nothing else for it.

The office he took us into was small and clean and white and untidy. He sat Shawna down on the table and began to unlatch her brace and remove her buckle-up shoe.

"Let's see what we've got here, sweetheart," he said. I stood awkwardly in the corner, because there was no chair, and busied myself with studying the diplomas and photographs on the walls. Duke, Johns Hopkins, certified by several boards, licensed to practice medicine in the state of South Carolina, fellow of several colleges of this and that. I assumed from the dates on the diplomas that he would be about fifty, though he looked a Mickey-Rooneyish thirty or so, with the turned-up nose and the blur of freckles on his face and arms.

One of the photographs was of a stunningly beautiful dark-haired woman and two equally beautiful young girls, daughters almost certainly, from the resemblance, on a beach that could be any beach anywhere. They wore sun hats and smiled into the camera. Teeth flashed. A movie family. Another photo was of the woman, in white pants and a striped T-shirt, and a much younger Lewis Aiken, on the deck of a sleek, low sailboat. I recognized the low pile of Fort Sumter behind it; the Charleston harbor, then. A third photo was of a tall, narrow, pink stucco house, with round white columns and sheltering palm trees. It was placed end to end on its walled lot, with matching up- and downstairs verandas and an iridescent tin roof. A Charleston single house, it was called, because it would be a single room wide and no telling how many rooms deep. I had heard that the earliest denizens of the city turned their houses with their ends to the street to catch the stray breezes from the harbor, and also that they did it because the early houses were taxed on the number of windows visible from the street. I supposed that, Charleston being Charleston, either or both explanations were correct. From its air of floating in space, I thought that the house was almost certainly on the sea-fronted Battery.

Lewis Aiken got the child's massive shoe off, and her sock, and began gently to rotate her foot. Shawna frowned and jerked her foot back, and then screwed up her face preparatory to more weeping, and reached out for me. I moved to go to her, but he said, "It's maybe better that you're not in the room. I've found that they settle down quicker if the parent or guardian or whatever isn't here. Would you mind too much waiting in the office out there? This shouldn't take long."

Feeling ridiculously rejected, I went back into the silent outer office. He shut the door between us, so that I could not hear them. Sudden visions of child molestation bloomed in my mind, but they did not last long. Somehow it was impossible that this smiling, tousled man would harm a child. And we'd worked with him so often before. . . .

I wandered restlessly around the little ante-room. More photographs hung on the walls, and I bent to examine them in the purpling cloud-light.

A big studio portrait of the dark woman, in her wedding dress, dominated the wall behind the receptionist's desk. Close up, she was even more stunning than in the smaller photos: there was spirit and a sort of imperious pride in the tilt of her head, and her smile teased. Her groom had apparently not made it into the photo.

"We did it! Love, Sissy," a sloping backhand said across the bottom corner of the photograph. It was dated twenty years before. So, the girls were teenagers, probably. He did not look old enough for teenage daughters, but there was no doubt that they were his and the dark woman's; they flanked the big portrait, and there were photos of them at all ages, from grave, beautiful toddlers through graceful preadolescents on horseback to the ones I took to be the most recent, clustered about. Always they smiled identical white smiles; always they were photographed together.

Twins, I thought. They're twins. This is a magical family. Dr. Lewis Aiken and his beautiful wife, Sissy, and his twin daughters—I leaned closer— Lila and Phoebe. I'll bet they've been in every magazine and Sunday supplement in the Low Country. Why does the man who has everything spend his Saturdays struggling with leg braces and crying children, not to mention mothers like Tiffany Sperry?

But I knew the answer. "Lewis Aiken is an absolute saint," I had heard other foundation workers say. I had snorted, because so few people really are, but perhaps this square red man was, or something close to it. There was assuredly nothing of the holy martyr about him, but I knew that meant nothing. St. Francis was profoundly ugly. Josef Mengele was an elegant man.

Thunder cracked outside, and the hot, straight-down rain of the Low Country sizzled onto sidewalks and sluiced off car roofs. From the looks of the dense sheet of water, this was no passing shower. I had, of course, no umbrella, mine having been sent home a week or so before with a tired black woman carrying her grandson. Cerebral palsy, I remembered. In all probability, not so much could be done for him as for this child. Some of the cruelest and most random-seeming afflictions had no cure. We could find, at best, palliative care. I sighed, hoping that the grandmother and her charge had made it home safe and dry. Shawna Sperry and I would not.

"Shit," I said under my breath. "No good deed goes unpunished."

Presently Lewis Aiken came out of his office holding the hand of little Shawna, who stumped happily along beside him, a lollipop stick protruding from her mouth.

"It's a little linty, but it was the best I could do," he said. "I feel pretty optimistic about Shawna. This is fairly straightforward. I want her to see another pediatric orthopedic man . . . Clive Sutton; I'll write it down for you, and call him. I don't do the surgeries on the children I see. Conflict of interest, and all that shit. But Clive's done them for me before, and he'll adjust his fees according to your budget and the mother's ability to pay. Probably do it for nothing, but don't tell him I told you that. Will you call me after he's seen her?"

"Of course," I said, taking Shawna into my arms. No way was I going to let her slog through that downpour. "Thank you for waiting for us."

"No problem. God. Look at that rain. When did that start? You want to wait here until it slows up a little? I'm not going to close up quite yet."

"No, they're expecting her back at the foster home. And I've still got to track down her mother before tonight, if I can. Our budget doesn't run to too many nights on the town."

"Well, at least let me give you the office umbrella. We used to have several, but they're not like coat hangers; they don't screw in the closet and breed more. They disappear."

"I'll bring it back," I said gratefully.

"Don't bother. My receptionist will love the chance to bitch at me for letting our last one get away, and I'll love sending her out for new ones. We have a sort of complicated arrangement, but it suits us."

I laughed. "Thanks," I said, and opened the umbrella and held it awkwardly over the heavy child, and ducked out into the storm.

The umbrella provided a little shelter for Shawna, but virtually none for me. Just as we reached the Toyota, the umbrella died a violent death by turning itself inside out, and before I could get Shawna into her car seat and get back around to my side, I was as wet as if I had dived into a pool.

"Shit, shit, *shit*!" I muttered, wringing my skirt and twisting the water out of my sopping hair. It was stifling in the car, but I knew that if I turned on the air conditioner, the child and I would both soon be shivering violently. The foster mother was the belligerent sort who delighted in finding errors and outrages in our handling of her charges so that she could report them to social services. I was already in her book for failing to find the child's mother. A soaked and shivering Shawna would provide her with fuel for months.

I cracked the window to let in some of the rain-freshened air, and dabbed at Shawna's face and hands with the towel I kept in the car after one of my children threw up her Happy Meal.

"We'll get cool when the car starts," I said.

"Bath," Shawna said happily, taking in my wet clothes and hair and face.

"Bath is right," I told her. "Let's get you and me both home and into some dry clothes."

I hoped fervently that the aggrieved foster mother had some spare children's clothes on hand—most did—because Shawna had nothing but what she'd had on when her mother had faded into the bush. Otherwise, if she had not returned—and I had no hope that she had—I would have to find clothes for Shawna, and toothpaste and such. I cursed Tiffany Sperry, not for the first time. What on earth could matter more to her than her handicapped child? But it was a useless curse, and I knew it. To the Tiffanys of the world, almost anything could matter more.

"Here we go," I said, and turned the key in the ignition. Nothing happened. I turned it again, and again. Nothing but a kind of ominous metallic burring. Outside, the rain racheted up its intensity a notch.

"I'm hungry," Shawna whined. "I want to go to the bathroom."

I put my head down on the steering wheel and closed my eyes. Lightning forked, and thunder boomed. Shawna began to howl.

There was a rapping on my window, and I looked up to see Lewis Aiken standing there, scrubs and hair plastered down with water, still barefoot.

"What's the matter?" he mouthed.

"Car won't start," I yelled back. I felt ridiculously guilty, as though he had caught me in some monstrous ineptitude, or even worse, thought me engaged in a ruse to get his attention.

"Come on," he said, opening my door and letting fresh rain gust in. "I'm parked right behind you. I'll run you both home, and we can get your car taken care of later."

"There's no need," I began, and then stopped and blushed. Of course there was a need. If he did not take us home, we would plainly sit in his parking lot all night.

"Thanks," I muttered ungraciously.

He plucked Shawna out of her car seat with a deftness born of practice and covered her face and head with the towel I handed him. He ran with her to a big, mud-spattered green Range Rover and popped her into the backseat and opened the door for me. I climbed in and sat there, shivering and puddling water on his upholstery. From the looks of it, it had been dampened with far worse.

He ducked into the driver's side and sat shaking the water from his head, and then grinned at me.

"This could be the beginning of a beautiful friendship," he said.

"'Of all the gin joints in all the world, I had to walk into yours,'" I said, and we both laughed. Suddenly things felt okay. All right. This situation, which a moment before had been a catastrophe, was . . . not.

Later, after the rain had abated to a sullen drizzle and Shawna had been settled for the night under the righteous roof of the foster couple, he took me home to my apartment. I rented a small one in a redbrick building on the corner of East Bay and Wentworth, with nothing of the charm of surrounding Ansonborough to recommend it. But it was cheap and close to my office, and I had gradually made it into home. I had, I realized every so often with a slight shock, been living there for nine years. The building had changed owners four times in that space of time, and I really did not know the current ones, a youngish couple who lived in the bottom apartment and kept an eye on things. The former owner had been a thin, heavily made-up woman whose sole passion seemed to be attempting to catch me and the fussy old retired College of Charleston professor across the hall in riotous living. That she never succeeded did not lessen her efforts. I had been glad to see the new owners. They seemed pleasant enough, in an anonymous sort of way, and we nodded amiably on the stairs. I did not plan to change my habits, which were as abstemious as ever, but I was grateful that the landlordly perception of them seemed to have changed.

"I can't thank you enough," I said as Lewis Aiken brought the Range Rover to a stop. "I'll call the garage about my car, and they can take it from there. You've done enough for me and Shawna."

He stretched and pulled his wet shirt away from his body.

"Will you make me a cup of tea?" he said.

I stiffened. What was this? Not, surely, what was euphemistically called in my mother's day a pass—"Did he make a pass at you? You tell me the truth—" but if not that, what? Surely he knew that I had seen the photographs of his beautiful family and house. Obscure disappointment rose in my throat.

"Isn't your family expecting you at home?" I said. "You've spent the entire afternoon on Shawna and me. For goodness sake, go home and get dry and have a glass of wine or something. It'll be better than my tea, I can promise you that."

"My family is in California," he said. "My wife and I divorced several years ago, and she and the girls live in Santa Barbara now. Her family is there. And I'm cold and I've got a fifty-mile drive ahead of me. I really wish you'd give me something hot to drink. I promise that your virtue is safe with me."

And I believed him. For one thing, he was the sort of man you simply believed. Period. For another, what man in his right mind would put the moves on a woman who looked like a drowned marsupial?

"It's a long way from the Battery, but I'll be happy to make you some tea," I said. "I don't have anything dry you can put on, though."

And I blushed furiously. He grinned.

"I'll sit on a towel and be fine," he said. "I really do just want a shot of something hot. I've got to get back to the country before long."

"Where's the country?" I said, getting out of

the Range Rover and slogging up the steps to the veranda of my apartment house.

"Edisto Island," he said. "My family has always had a place out there on the river. It's too big and too empty, and I rattle around in it, but it's one of my favorite places on earth. I stay there part of every weekend."

He came around the car and put his hand under my elbow and we went up onto the veranda. I thought, with laughter rising hysterically in my throat, of how we must look, a short, wet, red-haired, barefoot man and a short, wet, round, spaniel-eyed woman. I wished the former owner could see us. She would finally be vindicated.

"I'll bet you came in just to see Shawna," I said, fumbling with the big old key in my lock.

"No, I spent the night in town last night. I've got a little carriage house behind a big house on Bull Street. I'd have been here anyway."

"You don't use the big house in the photo?" I said, blushing again at my own effrontery. It was total.

"My wife wanted it and I didn't want her to have it, so I deeded it to someone else," he said matter-of-factly. "It was in my family, not hers. That's when she lit out for Santa Barbara. Mama and Daddy sprang for an adjoining casita."

"I'm sorry," I said. I was. He had, it seemed, lost almost everything.

"Me, too," he said. I could hear nothing of pain in his voice, but it must be there, under everything.

"Tea coming up," I said, and opened my door.

"This is nice," Lewis said, looking around my minute living room, and I saw that in his fresh eyes, it was. It is easy, in Charleston, to think of rooms being beautiful only if they are centuries old and rich with moldings and mahogany and portraits and silver; it is the curse of living downtown, where such rooms are the norm. But there are other ways of pleasing the mind and eye, and I had to aspire to them, because the first was forever beyond my reach.

I had painted the small, high-ceilinged room a soft butter yellow—"Tuscan Gold," the paint swatch said—and done the high moldings and windowsills in white. I had bought the two wing chairs from a secondhand shop in West Ashley and the beautiful, gut-spilling camelback sofa at an estate sale on Tradd Street. I had laid over them soft throws and shawls and pieces of old fabric I had found over the years in the shops on King Street. King Street was the provenance of my favorite things; in its antiques shops, as fabled as Aladdin's cave, I had found small oriental rugs so thin and fine that they rippled like silk; mismatched pieces of porcelain, bits of old silver, prints and lamps and mirrors with their ornate frames all gone to tarnish. Over my tiny white fireplace mantel I had one original painting, one of Richard Hagerty's surrealistic tropical scenes, with a wonderful primitive leopard peering through such foliage as had never bloomed in an earthly jungle. I had saved for a year to buy the big painting, afraid each day that someone else would snatch it, and when I brought it home and hung it, the room swam into a kind of focus and sophistication that saved it absolutely from being the fusty lair of a spinster. The painting anchored and lit the room. I added ficus and palm trees and a few treasured orchids. The result was part Cotswold cottage, part family parlor, part seraglio. I never came into it without feeling its arms come around me.

I got towels from the bathroom and gave them to Lewis, put on the kettle, and went in to change into dry jeans and one of my brother's old shirts. I toweled my hair and combed it with my fingers and turned on the thumping window air conditioner whose stale, powerful breath would soon turn my three rooms into an igloo, and went, as barefoot as he, back into the living room. Outside, the rain had started again.

"It's a wonderful nest," he said, wandering around the room and looking at my clutter of things. "I hate spare, cold, 'modern' rooms. They look like the furniture should have price tags on it. Are these mainly family things?"

He had taken off his wet shirt and hung it on the back of a kitchen chair and had a towel draped capelike around his shoulders. It struck me that there was no capacity for embarrassment in him. He would say and do whatever he wished with no thought for decorum. I wondered how Charleston had produced such a man.

"Yes, but they're other people's families," I said. "We always rented, and my mother didn't leave much but some clothes and photographs and a set of Melamine dinnerware. My sister has that. But I always wanted a place like this, that looked as if it had been a part of my family for ages. So I borrowed other people's."

I had not meant to sound pathetic; I was proud of my room and thought myself lucky and clever to have it. But he turned and looked at me soberly.

"You're pretty much alone, aren't you?" he said.

"Why do you assume that?"

"People who spend their lives looking after other people often are," he said. "I see a lot of it. Is that why you do what you do? Because taking care of people fills you up?"

I looked at him.

"I do what I do because I like it and because I do it well," I said. I was annoyed with him. How dare he come into my space and drape his wet clothes on my furniture and presume any sort of insight into me? It spoke of a familiarity I allowed very few people, certainly not people I had met three hours before.

"I'm sorry," he said, grimacing. "I've always been that way. Into my head, out of my mouth. My mother always said I was a throwback to some pirate or criminal or something on my father's side. She certainly raised me better. I apologize. I have no right to any of your life except what you choose to share."

The teakettle sang out, and I went in to it gratefully. They were not the words of a casual acquaintance; they assumed a relationship that did not exist. I did not particularly want a relationship of any sort, and did not know how to handle this man.

We drank the tea in silence, watching the rain fall and listening to its monotonous spatter on the veranda railing outside. It was almost full dark now. I wondered when he would go home. I felt crowded and irritable.

"Listen, would you like to order a pizza?" he said. "I'm hungry, and I don't want to stop after I get on the road. I promise I'll be out of here right after that."

"Are you buying?"

"You bet," he said, and went to the phone in the kitchen. I heard him dial almost immediately; he did not have to look up a number, then. This was a man who had a long familiarity with take-out pizza. Well, he was alone, too. People who have memorized take-out numbers usually are.

The pizza came and we ate it in the living room before my empty fireplace, drinking the half bottle of merlot I'd found. I thought it had been left over from a dinner I'd cooked for Marcy and her boyfriend months before. It was on the brink of going sour, but the warmth of it felt good going down. Predictably, the air conditioner was chilling the apartment.

I went into the kitchen to turn it down and Lewis followed with our plates and glasses. The window above the unit had frosted with its breath, and he went to it and wrote on it with his finger, *Annie*.

I moved up behind him and reached over and crossed out the *ie* and drew a *y*. *Anny*. He looked back at me, smiling slightly.

"When I started first grade, I wanted a nickname more than anything," I said. "Everybody else had one. My first name is Anna, so I told the teacher that everybody called me Annie, only I couldn't spell it, so I just added the *y*. Somehow it's stuck all these years."

"That's one of the saddest things I ever heard," he said, turning to me. "Why didn't your parents give you a nickname? Why didn't you tell them you wanted one?"

"Oh, for pity's sake, don't make a poor soul out of me," I said. "I like my nickname. It's not like every other Annie you meet on the street. But since you ask, nobody was around much to give me one. My father left us when I was eight and my sisters and brother were younger, and by that time my mother was pretty much a drunk. I took care of us, and I liked it, and I was good at it, and I think I was as much parent to them as they needed. They've all turned out really well."

"I'll bet they have," he said. "Is your mother still alive?"

"No. She died my first year of college. We lived in North Charleston. I was able to stay at home and go to school, too."

I took the last swallow of the merlot in my glass.

"I don't know why I'm telling you this," I said. "It makes me sound like an orphan of the storm, and I'm not; I have a very good life. It's the life I've chosen. I wouldn't change it."

"Wouldn't you?"

"No. Listen, don't you think you ought to get started? The rain's letting up and you've got a long drive."

He did not answer. Instead, he said, "You never

had a childhood, did you? You never played, you never had anyone who took care of you."

"I had a grandmother who loved us all very much," I said. "She lived in Myrtle Beach. We saw her often. She was always there if we needed her. She sent us money regularly; it kept us in the house and fed us when I was in school. And I did play. I used to lock myself in my room after the kids were in bed, and I'd dance all over the room, and act out stories, and play the lead in every movie I'd ever seen. I must have read every adventure book in the library. I wrote stories, too, in my diary."

"I'll bet nobody ever saw them," he said. "I bet nobody ever saw you dance. You know what? I'm going to take you dancing. I know just the place. It's out on the river. We'll eat oysters and play the jukebox and dance up a storm."

"Lewis, why did you get divorced?" I said. I did not even feel strange asking it, not in the midst of the extraordinary conversation we were having. Turnabout was fair play.

"I think she finally just didn't like living with me," he said slowly. "I'm not a very social animal. Sissy was—is—social to the nth degree. I guess I missed one too many galas. I couldn't change. Even if I could I wouldn't have."

"Do you still love her?"

"I don't know. I certainly did for a long time. I just don't like her very much. She's not really a very nice person. I hate thinking she's raising the girls to be just like her, clothes and lunches and parties and all that. They were such funny, good little kids. They've left holes in my heart."

"Do you see them?"

"Well, it's a long way to Santa Barbara. Sissy doesn't come back here. I get the girls whenever I can manage the time and she feels like it. It's not enough."

"No," I said, still looking out my frosted, calligraphed window. "I don't imagine it is."

He came up behind me and put his arms around me and rested his chin on the top of my head. I didn't think he had to stoop much to do it.

"Your hair is still wet," he said. "I'm not kidding about the dancing. I'm going to call you every day until you say yes."

I thought of his world; I imagined the rich tapestry of friends and cousins and sweethearts from out of his childhood; the dense, baroque network of connections that was so uniquely Charleston. Lewis Aiken would not lack for women to eat oysters and dance with. Women of his own set. Smart, beautiful women. Downtown women.

"Lewis, why me?" I said into the window.

"Why not you?" he said, and kissed the top of my head and went out my front door. I listened to the soft growl of the Range Rover's engine until it lost itself on East Bay.

That night I turned the radio to a soft-rock station and I danced barefoot, in my brother's shirt, danced and danced until I lost my breath and fell into bed, and slept through the wet night without dreams.

2

MONDAY WAS ALWAYS a slow day in our office; I
never could figure out why. Marcy and the others
always maintained that our clients were nursing
weekend hangovers, and in many cases I suppose
that was true. Whatever the reason, I welcomed
the lull. It gave me a small space in which to try
and catch up on the ever-present paperwork that
is the sodden anchor holding all philanthropies to
the earth. And it gave me a chance to meet with
my staff and see where we'd been the week
before, and where we wished to go in the following one. We also sometimes treated ourselves to
lunch out of the office. Monday was almost the
only day we ever did that. The rest of the week
one of the junior staff grudgingly ordered in and
went and collected our lunches, and we ate at our
desks. Often I brought my own yogurt and fruit.

On this Monday Marcy and I had no takers, so
we went out to lunch alone together to the funky,
enormously popular Hominy Grill, which was
close enough for the staffs of the medical complex
so that the restaurant and courtyard were usually
dotted with white coats. The food was innovative
and wonderfully cooked, and there was usually a

sprinkling of downtown women and one or two proper Charleston dowagers, being treated by their daughters. The Grill was nothing if not eclectic.

Marcy, who is as tall and thin as a crane, ordered the fried-oyster salad. I had the vegetable plate. I knew that I never got enough vegetables; yogurt and frozen pasta are the staples of a single's refrigerator. The Grill's collards and squash casserole were sublime. The macaroni and cheese made you weep for your childhood.

We ate under an umbrella in the tiny courtyard. After we finished our lunches, we sat for a while watching a pair of green lizards seep slowly down the white stucco wall of the restaurant. You could never catch them moving, but if you looked away, you would often find them inches or feet away from where they had been. Lizard watching is hypnotic. We were reluctant to leave our sunny courtyard and go back to work.

"Let's go over some of the office stuff," I said. "Make believe we're working. We'll stay . . . oh, until that smallest lizard gets to the drainpipe."

"So how did it go with the Sperrys?" Marcy said. "Did Tiffany show?"

"Nope. I don't know why I even hoped she would. I ended up taking Shawna to Dr. Aiken. I had to put her up with the Boltons, and so far as I know, she's still there. It's going to cost us a fortune, not to mention giving Adelaine Bolton enough ammunition to keep social services busy for a year."

"She can't just leave her child there indefinitely," Marcy said in exasperation. Tiffany Sperry was a recurring thorn in our sides.

"Oh, she'll show today or tomorrow with some excuse or other," I said. "The last time it was that her ovaries were swollen and she couldn't get out of bed. She didn't say whose. If she's not back by this afternoon, I'll call social services myself. She's flirting with bad trouble."

"What did Dr. Aiken say about Shawna?" Marcy asked, stirring her second glass of iced tea.

"He thinks she can be helped. Said it was pretty straightforward. He's going to send me a memo on the consultation, and the name of a surgeon who just might do the operation for free. I'm prepared to beg. Shawna's a sweet child. She loved Dr. Aiken. As well she should. We got caught in that downpour and my car wouldn't start, and he took her to the Boltons' and me to my place. I ended up giving him a cup of tea, and we ordered a pizza."

Marcy stared, and I flushed. I had no idea why I was telling her about the evening with Lewis Aiken. I almost never discussed my personal life, even with her. All I knew was that it gave me a surge of pure pleasure to talk about him. I liked saying his name.

"My Lord, you and Lewis Aiken alone in your apartment eating pizza! What was he like?"

"Wet and hungry," I said. "Barefoot. What should he be like? He's a nice, funny man who likes kids and misses his own. He's divorced, and she's got the children in Santa Barbara. I gather it wasn't a very amicable divorce."

"Don't you know anything?" Marcy breathed. "Amicable! It was the scandal of the year; everybody knows about it. I still hear people talking about it. Everybody knows what a bitch she was; I don't know anybody who doesn't love Dr. Aiken. Literally, I hear. I think he's gone with a lot of women since she left."

Obscurely, my heart dropped.

"Where do you hear this stuff?" I said. "Have you been hanging around the yacht club?"

"Just eat lunch in the hospital cafeteria sometime," Marcy said. "There's not a nurse in there who doesn't know all about it, and who wouldn't give a month's pay to go out with him. I don't think he dates anybody in the medical community, though. His family's been here since the Huguenots; he's strictly a downtown guy."

I had known that, of course; it was implicit in the photographs in his office. But I still felt a small curl of desolation, like smoke. I was, of course, quite literally only a port in a storm to Lewis Aiken. The rest—the talk and laughter, the invitation to go dancing, the kiss on the top of the head—were obviously simply spillovers of Lewis's charm. He would have bestowed them on any woman as easily as he gave his smile.

"Was she a Charleston woman?" I asked, as casually as I could. "I saw her pictures in his office, and the twins. They're all beautiful. It looked like a movie family."

"No, she's from Baltimore. He met her when he was at Hopkins. She's beautiful, all right, but her family wasn't anywhere near as rich or wellborn as his. Everybody says she never really loved him, but she did love that house, and the boat, and the club memberships, and the place in the country, and the money. I think he was a goner when he first laid eyes on her. Apparently, he stuck with her for a long time after she started running around on him. I hear she had affairs with half of Charleston, and a lot of them were his friends. She was really something; I saw her at a hospital thing once. You couldn't look away from her."

"It can't be all that easy to have affairs in Charleston," I said. "You'd be bumping into everybody you knew all the time."

"From what I hear, you'd be surprised by how easy it is," she said. "Either that, or lots of people don't really care who's diddling around with who."

"So why didn't he leave her?"

"The girls, I'm sure. And then I hear he was totally in love with her. I think the divorce almost killed him."

"Why did he finally divorce her?" I asked. I was ashamed of myself, but I could not stop probing for facts about Lewis Aiken. He had seemed so open with me the night before, but I saw now that I had not caught the sense of him at all, and I wanted to know him. I hurt for his hurt.

"She did, not him. They were renovating the house on the Battery—not fancy enough for her, I guess—and she had a really steamy affair with the architect. He wasn't a local guy, but he was a real stud and he had a good practice here. I don't think the poor guy had a chance. They were all over the place with it; everybody was talking. Dr. Aiken moved to the country with the girls and

she filed for divorce. He just let her. She was
going to marry the guy and they were going to
live in splendor in the Battery house—on the
Aikens's money. Of course, his family loathed her,
and hadn't spoken to her for ages, and she retali-
ated by not letting them see the girls. I hear he
was going to contest the divorce, but when she
went after the house, that was it. The architect
didn't marry her after all, and she hightailed it
home to California, where her parents had
moved. I hear they bought her a house next door
to theirs. I think she got a generous settlement,
but it wasn't what she had had with Dr. Aiken. I'll
bet she regrets that little fling. She had it all, and
blew it."

"What happened to the architect?"

"He went back home to his wife in Orange-
burg."

"What a comedown," I said, laughing. "Marcy,
it's incredible to me that you know all this."

"Everybody knows. He's a catch."

Lewis Aiken called the next day and asked me
to dinner.

"I hear you're a catch," I said.

"Blue-plate catch of the day," he said. "Wear
your jeans and your dancing shoes, and bring
some bug spray. This place doesn't have much but
mosquitoes and a jukebox and the best oysters in
the Low Country. Pick you up at six."

Booter's Bait and Oysters lies at the end of a
flimsy dock that stretches out over the marshes to
Bohicket Creek, which separates Wadmalaw
Island from John's Island. I never could have

found it on that evening. It seemed to me so deeply embedded in the wild heart of the marsh and swamp country, so far from even the sparse filling stations and cinder-block stores and garages we passed on the way, on the little country road, that we were in another country, one that lay a continent away from Charleston. And in a sense it did. This wild, swamp-cradled, salt-infused country had far more to do with alligators and rattlesnakes and eagles and ospreys and the occasional bobcat than it did with men and their doings. The houses we did pass were shacks and trailers sliding slowly into the tangles of vines and encroaching live oaks. Rusted cars decorated dirt yards; old gut-sprung sofas sat on porches. Skiffs and rowboats had pride of place in what passed for most driveways.

"I guess you're sure about this," I said.

"Oh, yeah. Booter and I grew up together, summers. Our place is not so far from here. We ran wild all over the place. There isn't an inch of Bohicket Creek we haven't fished or hunted. He's a better shot than anybody I know, and he's the best fisherman in the Low Country. He keeps boats for some of the guys at his dock, and it got so that people just hung around when they came in, and chewed the fat and drank beer, and finally he put a roof over the end of it and a couple of tables and benches, and got a jukebox and a beer license . . . though I've never been so sure about that. People come from all around here for the oysters. Oh, not the town crowd that thinks roughing it is the Wreck on Mount Pleasant. But folks around here. The oysters come out of the water the day you eat them, and there's only two ways that you can—roasted and raw. Junior Crosby, an old black man who used to work for my father on the Edisto place, does the oyster roasts. He's got a gallon drum and a sheet of iron and he builds a fire and gets it just right, and then plunks a croker sack full of oysters on it and yanks 'em off when they're ready, and you take the clumps and open them yourself. Somehow I didn't think you'd have one, so I brought oyster knives for both of us."

"Well, I certainly know what an oyster roast is," I said. "I've been to them at some pretty fancy places, at benefits for the foundation. But you certainly didn't have to open your own oysters. There were people to do it for you."

"You'd get thrown in the creek at Booter's if you asked somebody to do that," Lewis said. "But I'll show you how. And if you slice your finger off, there's a doctor in the house."

We bumped down a dirt road so thickly overhung with moss and branches that it was like driving through a tunnel and abruptly came out into a clearing. I gasped. The creek here was just widening out into a sea of marsh grass, silvered by a small breeze and flushed pink by the setting sun. The line of the trees against the far edge of the marsh was black. Over it all a high white ghost moon rode.

"It's beautiful," I said.

There was a long dock and the promised pavilion at the end, roofed with tin, and a cluster of fishing boats waddled back and forth on their tethers at the platform below. Trucks and old sedans and motorcycles crowded the rutted parking lot. Jukebox music thumped into the quiet twilight, over the whine of insects and the slap of water on pilings.

"Let's do it," Lewis said, and we parked and went inside.

There were no walls, but a central island held a bar and a sink and an old red Coca-Cola cooler the likes of which I had not seen since I was a child. It looked fully that old. Men in dirty jeans and T-shirts and a few women in tight jeans and cutoffs and midriff-baring tees stood at the bar or clustered around the picnic tables on the open deck. They were all laughing and some were doing little cut-up dance steps to the jukebox, and most were drinking beer. Everybody looked up when we entered. My heart dropped. I thought with shame of my ironed jeans and new pink T-shirt, and my new, blinding-white sneakers. I had slumming written all over me as surely as if I had worn satin. Lewis, who wore rumpled scrubs again, and sandals, somehow did not stand out. You could tell by the way he walked in that he was at home in this place.

A chorus of greetings rose to meet us—"Hey, Lewis!" "How you doin', boy?" "Been cuttin' up any more kids?" "Where you been? Thought you'd gotten yourself into that movie they're shootin' downtown!" Fondness and equality swam in the air like the swarm of mosquitoes that had already found my face and arms. No one looked directly at me, but I could feel eyes on me like little pits of fire.

A grizzled, red-brown man at the bar grinned,

showing a gap in his tobacco-stained teeth, and pulled a Budweiser out of the cooler and opened it and thumped it down in front of Lewis.

"Hey, Booter," Lewis said. "This is my friend Anny Butler. She takes care of sick kids and we work together sometimes."

Apparently, it was important that I be qualified. Set into the scheme of things. Booter turned his grin on me.

"Get you something, ma'am?"

"Please call me Anny. I'd like a Diet Coke."

The crowd at the bar snickered and I flushed.

"Got Mountain Dew and beer," Booter said. "I could make you some coffee, though."

"Beer's fine."

It was. It was cold and sweating in my hand, and drops of condensation fell onto my arms and hands, cooling them. It was airlessly hot under the canopy of tin. The squadrons of mosquitoes were vicious and relentless. I had lathered myself all over with the strong, piney-green liquid Lewis had given me, but apparently I was fresh meat. No one else at the bar or tables seemed to be bothered. I drank another beer quickly and the bites seemed to sting less.

Junior Crosby came in toting his paraphernalia then, and the steaming of the oysters got under way. The crowd descended on them like locusts, piling the great clumps of adhering shells onto tin plates and attacking them with oyster knives to pry them open and pop the roasted oyster into their mouths. They tasted wonderful, the few that I managed to get open. By the time I had finished my first plate, everybody else had gone back for thirds and fourths, and the beer flowed. Night fell, thick and black and moon haunted. The creek water was silvered with it out into the marsh.

Lewis finally relented and opened the oysters for me, and bought me another beer, and another. I did not even like beer, but this tasted wonderful, somehow, all of a piece with the salt of the marsh and the scent of the faraway mimosas.

"I'll be drunk," I said.

"Well, I should certainly hope so," Lewis said. "Because I promised you dancing, and dancing out here is far better accomplished drunk."

He went up to the jukebox, a battered old Wurlitzer that looked to me the same vintage as the cooler, and made a selection. All over the dock people were dancing; I had scarcely noticed them, but now I could not look away. Apparently, the only songs Booter had on his jukebox were the old rock-and-roll and country-and-western songs of the fifties, which I barely remembered from my childhood. All around me, burly, light-footed men and willowy, big-haired women were stomping and swaying and undulating to the Platters, Bill Haley and His Comets, Frankie Lymon and the Teenagers, Little Richard, Gene Vincent and the Blue Caps.

"It's a time warp," I said. "Where's Elvis?"

"Too upscale for this crowd," Lewis said, grinning. "Fats Domino doing 'Blueberry Hill' is about as highbrow as it gets."

He swung me up and out onto the dance floor, and the music caught me as surely as his red-freckled arms, and I was dancing as I had never danced before, intense, sweating, as sure and light of foot as any of the other women present, utterly lost in the beat and the vibration of stomping feet on the wooden boards. They sounded hollow, as wood does over water; it was all a part of the magic of the night. I have never been so sure, before or since, that I was as seamlessly good at anything as I was that night dancing on Booter Crogan's dock.

Finally, when I was panting and laughing and wilting into his arms, sticky with oyster juice and sweat and wild haired with creek humidity, Lewis put on another record and pulled me against him. This time, it was not rock and roll, but Percy Sledge wailing, "When a Man Loves a Woman." The beat was slow, insinuating, heartbreaking. I put my face into his shoulder and he rested his chin on the top of my head and we swayed close together, hardly moving. I was lost in him, the feel of him, the smell. I did not want the song ever to end.

When it did, I moved back and shook my head as if I was coming up from underwater.

"Let's get a beer and go sit on the end of the dock and put our feet in the water," he said. And we did. My head was spinning so that the moon seemed to double itself, and swim back together before splitting apart again.

"I've had too much to drink," I said. The water was still warm from the day, but just under the surface was the chill of the past winter. It felt wonderful on my burning feet, like bathing them in champagne.

He put his arm around me and I rested my head on his shoulder.

"Why don't you have a boyfriend?" he said. "Why aren't you married?"

"I don't know," I said honestly. "It just never came up. For a long time the only kind of men I knew about were my mother's 'friends,' the ones who came to the house all the time. We had to go to our rooms when they visited, and one night when I was sixteen or so one of them came after me when my mother had passed out on the sofa. It was no big deal; he was too drunk to do anything to me, and I hit him with a tennis racquet. My mother woke up and threw him out, and promised me it would never happen again, and it didn't. She drank after that, but she didn't have any more friends, that I know of."

"You hit him with a tennis racquet?" Lewis said, beginning to laugh.

"I'm certainly not helpless," I said. "And I do have boyfriends; I always did. I dated a good bit in school. But I had the kids then, and up until they went away to school, and after that . . . I don't know. I just wanted to be still and quiet. It got to be a habit."

We were quiet for a while, and then I said, "I heard about your wife. About the divorce and all. I'm really sorry, Lewis."

He didn't speak, and I thought that I had gone to a place where I was not allowed. But then he shook his head and sighed.

"For a long time it was good, at least for me," he said. "She was enchanting. She still is. I wouldn't have let her go if there had been anything left of me in her life. But I couldn't let . . . all that . . . go on in front of the girls. And besides, there was always something about our life . . . it was a picture-book life. It never did seem quite real to me. And I guess it wasn't. Real felt like those kids I saw every Saturday. All that pain and despair, no money . . . not that I wanted that for my family, God, no, but there was just never any . . . darkness to us. Any contrast to all that light. Somehow I just couldn't trust that."

"I know," I said. I did. I had it in me, too; I needed it, that interior shadow where I could hide myself sometimes, a cavelike protection against the blinding world. I think it was what drew me to the work I do. I understand darkness.

"Look," he said. "When we get back, I don't guess I can come in?"

"No," I said.

"I didn't think so. So would you like to come out to the island with me one day this weekend? I'll cook dinner for you; I'm a good cook. And I'll show you everything that I love. I'd like you to see it all. There's an alligator nursery you'll flip over."

"You sure know how to show a girl a good time," I said sleepily.

The Ace Basin lies in a great, 350,000-acre wilderness centered by a shallow bay created by the confluence of the Ashepoo, Combahee, and Edisto Rivers. It harbors an estuarine ecosystem so rich in layers and layers of life, so fertile and green and secret, so very old, so totally set apart from the world of men and machines, that there is literally no place on earth remotely like it. It is as far removed from the beautiful, mannerly, infinitely civilized grid of Charleston south of Broad

Street, with its verandaed old houses in pink and
ocher and yellow and taupe wood or stucco, the
colors of soft heat, as Tashkent would be, or
Antarctica. Other areas in the Low Country that
were once as pristine have irrevocably gone over
to man now, and cannot be reclaimed, but a combination of public and private agencies and indi-
viduals have set their teeth and shoulders to
safeguard the Ace, and now protect sizable
swatches of it. In that vast and succoring basin,
one third light, one third water, and only one
third earth, life in all its abundance has evolved
almost unseen for millions of years, infused twice
a day by the great salt breath of the tides. I had
never really seen it, never really known that it lay
there to my south, a dreaming continent, a separate lost world. When I first went there with
Lewis, it almost frightened me.

We came off a scabrous paved road onto a dirt
and gravel track that seemed to go on forever.
There had been no mannerly sign announcing
Sweetgrass Plantation, the property's name, as
there were for the big stately plantations open to
visitors to the west and north—Magnolia Hall,
Middleton Place, Boone Hall, Medway. There was
not even a mailbox. It was eleven o'clock on a
Sunday morning, and already the heat was shimmering off the road and insects were buzzing in
the vast stretches of marsh grass and occasional
flashes of black tidal creeks. Lewis did not turn on
the air-conditioning in the Range Rover, and my
neck and back ran sweat under my shirt.

"I hate air-conditioning," he said, catching me
pulling my shirt away from my body. "People

ought to sweat in the summer. Makes it real. Makes you slow down and smell the swamp and the pluff mud. Makes you kind of sleepy and sexy. What do you think?"

"I think it makes me sleepy and smelly. And cross as a bear. I don't want to smell the pluff mud," I said, swatting a mosquito that had ridden with us all the way from Charleston. "Where do you get your mail?"

"I don't, out here," he said. "Everything goes to the house or the office. There's nothing anybody needs to tell me that can't wait till I get back to Charleston. I don't even have a phone; I use my cell phone, and I wouldn't bring that if I didn't have patients."

"So you really rough it out here," I said.

"Well, not really."

The road curved, and I looked down a long alley of live oaks hung with gray moss to a gentle bluff on the river, where the house stood. I drew in my breath. Set into the maritime forest of live oak, cedar, loblolly and slash pine and palmettos, the house looked as if it had risen from the damp earth so it could look over the blue river in front of it. It was beautiful.

"I thought it would be. . . . I thought there would be columns and things," I said stupidly. This rambling, stilted, pavilioned gray cypress house spoke to my heart like no columns had ever done. "This is wonderful."

"Yes," he said matter-of-factly. "I had it built after the divorce, when I knew that I would be spending so much time here. We had the whole column thing before that, a hundred and fifty

years worth of rotting stucco and peeling walls
and enough mold to keep the Low Country in
penicillin for years. My mother adored it, and
wouldn't even let me make repairs; she said she
wanted it kept as Daddy had before he died. By
the time she went to live with my sister in Connecticut, it was downright dangerous, and it
would have cost more to repair it than to build
fresh. So I had it torn down and built this one. I
think it's what a marsh house should be—silvery
gray like the marsh grass, raised so the breezes
off the water can come in, cool and shaded inside,
high ceilings, lots of glass in every direction. And
a good kitchen. The old one was a horror. I've
loved living here, though most of Charleston
thinks I've desecrated the family name. My
mother doesn't even know the old house is gone."

"Doesn't she come back sometimes?"

"No. She doesn't seem to want to be anywhere
she and Dad lived together. After he died she
didn't want the Battery house, either. I think she
may be going into Alzheimer's. My sister says
she's awfully vague and forgetful now."

"How sad, not to want to be in your home anymore. Are you sad?"

"No. This and Bull Street are home now. You're
not home, not really. Are you sad?"

"No. But I didn't leave places like a plantation
or the Battery house, either. Almost anything else
would be an improvement over where I lived. I
love my apartment."

"You're going to love this even more," he said,
and swung the car into a berth beneath a live oak
that literally swept the ground with its branches. I

looked up; it was like being in a cathedral. No
rain could penetrate that canopy of leaves and
moss. After the noise of the car, the water silence
was soft and palpable. I could hear the river running a good hundred feet away, at the end of a
canopied dock over the marsh.

We went up the steps and into the house. The
door was not locked. Inside, I caught my breath
again. Beautiful. Simple and light washed and
beautiful. The water and the marsh grass and the
air and the sun seemed a part of the fabric of the
house. This was a house for light hearts.

He had, I was sure, brought many things from
the Battery house here to this one. The wide, polished pine floors were pooled in places with thin
bonfires of old orientals. A damask sofa, rump
sprung and fading but still grand, sat, opposite a
pair of buttery, worn-leather Morris chairs, in
front of a great stone fireplace. Airy Scandinavian
and French provincial pieces melted seamlessly
into the whole stew, along with a delicate inlaid
escritoire, a formidable partners' desk before one
of the river windows, before the other a chintz
chaise showing the unmistakable stigmata of cat
scratchings on its leg. I don't know why it all
worked, but it did. The house lifted you up. It
would be hard to stay unhappy here. Maybe, I
thought, the sheer fact that you love things makes
them fit together.

We walked through a cool, dim central hall and
into the enormous stone-floored kitchen. There
were a professional gas stove, refrigerator, and
countertop appliances among the clutter of dried
flowers and hanging herbs and cooking utensils.

Something wonderful simmered in a big pot on the stove. A thin brown woman stood stirring it, a caramel child capering about her. The rug before the fireplace was strewn with toys.

"Thought I heard you clomping around in there," the woman said, smiling but not turning from the stove. Lewis went to her and hugged her fiercely from behind.

"Lindy, my love," he warbled. "Come away with me, Lindy. . . ."

"I'm not going anywhere with you, you sorry hound," she said, and did turn then, and offered me her hand. I took it, smiling back at her warm smile. Laugh lines fanned around her eyes, but other than that, the severe brown face was unmarked; she could have been any age at all.

"I'm Linda Cousins," she said. "I'm a nurse at the county clinic on Edisto, but I help Lewis here keep himself decent on weekends. This is my son, Tommy."

"I'm Anny Butler," I said. "I'm a friend of Lewis from my work."

"I hope you're a friend from more than that," she said, the smile widening. "This one needs a good stout friend more than anybody I ever saw."

I felt myself redden, wondering how to reply to this, but at that moment little Tommy Cousins came around his mother's legs and grinned at me. He was an enchanting child, melted chocolate eyes, much like my own, pure, beautiful features. I saw that he wore a slightly built-up shoe, and looked back at Lewis.

"Yeah, he's one of mine, aren't you, champ?" Lewis said, knuckling the child's close-cropped curls. "I fixed him up, oh, maybe five years ago. Before he could walk. Now there's no stopping him."

"You gon' marry her?" Tommy said, looking at me with assessing eyes.

"Why? You think I should?" Lewis said. My face burned brighter.

The little boy stared at me for another space of time.

"Yeah, I think you ought to," he said finally. "She's soft, like a pillow. I bet she can sure cook."

Lewis threw back his red head and roared with laughter, and the child joined in. Linda Cousins came over to me and touched my shoulder.

"Don't listen to either one of them," she said. "They're so full of themselves they stink to high heaven. I'd walk right out on them except one belongs to me and the other one would drown in his own sloppiness if I did."

Lewis swung the wiggling child up into his arms.

"Linda and her husband, Robert, and Tommy live on the place, down the river a little farther. Robert's father helped my folks out some, and Robert and Linda do the same for me or I wouldn't be able to keep this place. Linda also makes the best she-crab soup I ever ate, even better than mine. She's making some for us. I asked her and Robert to join us, but she's got some idea that I'm going to seduce you with she-crab soup and wine and I don't know what all, and so they'll take a rain check."

"Lewis, my Lord," I began, red to the roots of

my hair, and he laughed and gave me a quick, hard hug around my shoulders.

"Sorry," he said. "But I'm serving you notice right now that she's right. I have never met the woman who could resist Linda's soup . . . and me, of course."

He was teasing, but his words burned. Linda saw it.

"I haven't noticed any women out here clamoring for either you or my soup," she said severely. "You be nice to this one. She looks too fine for the likes of you, anyway."

"I'll be nice to her," he said soberly. "I'll be nicer to her than anybody I've ever known. I run my mouth too much, but I mean that."

He looked at me steadily with his narrow blue eyes. I turned away. I felt off base and tight around my heart. I did not want a flirtatious, shallow physical relationship with this man, but I did not know what I did want, and did not think that there could possibly be any other relationship with me that he would choose. There were simply too many others of his own world.

"Do I get the tour?" I said.

I did. From his Boston Whaler on the river and along the narrow tidal creeks, and in the jerry-rigged tractor affair he used in the brush and hummocks of the swamp, I saw his world of shimmering earth and still water, of cordgrass and bald cypress and overarching live oaks and pines. I saw the life that lives in that incredible water world: water snakes and once or twice the big, brutish rattlesnakes of the Low Country; alligators large and small, submerged like logs near mud-slicked banks, only their eyes saying that they were not made of wood.

I saw the nursery that he had mentioned, a small, sunny pond fringed with reeds and cordgrass where the mothers brought their young to mature, safe from whatever preyed on small gators. The young were beautiful, striped yellow and green and black, with cold amber eyes, and they lay in the water like little branches of the same tree, though they were all ages of baby. One or two big, lazy, malachite-and-obsidian mothers lay immobile on the banks in the sun, seeming to sleep rather than to guard. But, Lewis said, make a move toward one of the babies and they would be up on the bank and after you in a heartbeat.

"We lose a good many stupid dogs that way," he said. "Along with the wild pigs and the raccoons and whatever else prowls around here. You'd think they'd learn. I hear that over on Kiawah and down at Hilton Head the shelf life of poodles and shih tzus is not long."

I felt the hair rise on the nape of my neck. They were simply so old, so primal, so implacable, the color of stagnant water, of muddy death. I did not think I would ever learn to love the alligators of Edisto.

But the other live things—my heart lifted up to meet them. An eagle took off from its nest on a dead pine and swooped down over the water. Ospreys wheeled and whistled in the arch of the sky. Turtles sunned themselves on reed-grown banks; a white-tailed deer flashed his ensign far off on a lightly forested hummock; the explosions of cinnamon and resurrection ferns burned brilliant green; the green seas of cordgrass rippled in the light, clean, fish-smelling wind; the great, primeval towers of the bald cypress dwarfed all else. By the time we got back to the dock, in the late afternoon, the sun was dropping rapidly over the line of trees across the river and a small chill was stealing into the air, along with the phalanxes of mosquitoes.

"Let's eat inside," he said. "I'd thought we might put up a little table on the end of the dock; the stars out here are incredible, and the night sounds are something to hear. And there's somebody I want you to meet. But we'll come out later, about eleven. The wind picks up about then, and the mosquitoes will be gone."

"That's pretty late, isn't it?" I said. "It's at least an hour back to Charleston."

"I hoped you'd stay," he said simply.

I took a deep breath and turned to face him.

"Lewis," I said, "why me? There must be a hundred women in your life more interesting than I am. There must be fifty who'd sleep with you in the middle of Broad Street if you asked them. I don't . . . I can't just have some kind of fling with you, and then be crumpled up and tossed away like a Kleenex. I don't have time for that, and it would hurt me badly because I like you a great deal. So this simply cannot go any further than it has. Let's be friends. I make a wonderful friend. I think you would, too."

He leaned over and pulled me up out of the Whaler and into his arms. He rested his chin on the top of my head, a favorite resting place, obvi-

ously. I could not even think of the glossy heads
that had felt that pointed weight.

"I don't want a fling with you," he said. "I want
you to be part of my life. I don't know how; that
depends on you, but I *will* know. Why you?
Because you're good, Anny. You're a good person
through and through; I knew that about you the
minute I laid eyes on you. I love what you do. And
you're funny and sweet and you're not one of
those hundred women, or the fifty. I've been
there. I've done that. That's not what I need; it
never was. I need this. I need to work and talk and
laugh and be laughed at, and dance, and hold on
to somebody soft and round and smaller than me.
What I need is you. What will it take to make you
believe it? I'll do whatever it is."

"Then let me take it slow," I said. "Don't talk
about staying the night with you. Don't talk about
seducing me, even if you're teasing me. I'm new
at this, Lewis. I know it sounds ridiculous, for
somebody thirty-five years old to be new at anything, but this is . . . not like anything I've done
before. You must be fifty; you know so much more
than I do. There's so much more in your life than
there is in mine. If it turns out that you still want
me around after some time has passed, we can
think about what comes next. But tonight, I want
to go home."

"You got it," he said. "But I still want you to
hang around till about eleven. You've got to meet
this friend of mine."

We ate sweet, rich she-crab soup in front of the
fireplace, where pungent cedar and pine burned,
and drank a wonderful white wine, like flowers,

and mopped the soup up with homemade bread from Linda Cousins's oven, and followed it all with Ben & Jerry's ice cream.

"I make good pies, but it don't get any better than this," Lewis said. He ate three bowls of Chunky Monkey. I ate two.

We listened to music before the fire—Pachelbel, Otis Redding—but we did not dance, and he did not touch me. I felt drowsy and calm and cosseted, shut away, somehow, from my own life. He had to shake me awake when eleven o'clock was near.

"Out at the end of the dock," he said, pointing me toward the door. "I've brought a blanket and a sweater for you. We may have to wait a little while."

"Who is this friend who can't just come in the damned house?" I groused. I was chilly and sleepy.

"You'll see."

We sat out at the end of the dock on the blanket he had brought. I wore the big Shetland sweater gratefully, and wished for thick socks. We did not talk much. Overhead the stars wheeled, blazing and crystal; I have never seen so many. I thought of F. Scott Fitzgerald: "Stars like silver pepper." Where had I read that? Under the dock, water slapped, and the cordgrass on the solid little hummock just to the side of the gangway down to the Whaler rustled and whispered. I was drowsing again when he shook me lightly.

"Look," he whispered. I looked where he pointed, down on the hummock just beneath us. Yellow eyes stared back, and in the starlight great tufted ears were silhouetted. A cat, but no house cat I had ever seen; this was truly a great cat.

I held my breath. The yellow eyes held mine, and then they simply vanished, melting away in the darkness. There seemed a darker space where the cat had been.

"Bobcat," Lewis said. I could feel him smiling in the dark. "Comes most nights at eleven. I wait for him if I'm here. I don't know if he comes when I'm not here; probably, but I like to think he comes just to pass a little time with me. I've been seeing him for a couple of years now."

Something broke open within me, something knotted and deep that I had not known was there. So wild, the bobcat was simply so wild, and had made me such a priceless gift of his wildness . . . I began to cry. Lewis put his arms around me and pulled me against him, and when I finished crying he kissed me, a deep, complex kiss with nothing of flirtatiousness in it, and time, after all, did not pass, and what came next, came there in the starlight on the end of Lewis's dock, with, perhaps, a bobcat to bear witness.

3

THE NEXT WEEKEND Lewis took me to the beach house for the first time. It was a cool, clean-washed day with tender blue skies, and the water in the harbor, where the Cooper River met the sea, glittered like crumpled foil in the light wind.

The great, double-humped twin bridges arch like the skeletons of giant water snakes over the wide river mouth, dizzying in their stark suspension and swaying height. The older one, connecting the peninsula to Mount Pleasant, is a terrifying carnival ride with two narrow lanes and a vertiginous lack of side railing. There *is* railing, of course, but it seems, when you are in an automobile climbing its heights, that there is virtually nothing between you and the water's surface, nearly one hundred feet below. The newer bridge is wider and better railed, but it still leaves me dry mouthed and sweaty palmed when I cross it. The newer is the only one I can drive over. The older is a more direct route to East Bay and my apartment, but I always take the new one, happy to drive the extra looping curves to Meeting Street, in exchange for an ersatz safety. In all the times after that day that we went to the house on

Sullivan's Island, I never failed to breathe deeply only when we reached the level of the surrounding marshes once more.

"You're going to have to get over that," Lewis said as we swept down off the last height. "I can't stop and wipe your palms every time we go to the island."

"I'll try," I said, smiling at the implied infinity of visits stretching into my future. But I never managed to quell the fear. Perfect things must be paid for.

When I first saw it on a map, Sullivan's Island looked to me rather like an inflamed appendix. On its landward side it is wrapped in marshes and indented with cays and pierced by small tidal creeks. Coming off the Ben Sawyer bridge from Mount Pleasant onto the island, across the inland waterway, it always seemed that you were entering an enchanted, old-fashioned scene, like an impressionist painting. The great salt marshes, the broad ribbon of glittering waterway, the fringe of low-lying cottages studding the inner shore, with small docks and bobbing boats, and beyond it all, the great amplitude of the blue Atlantic . . . It was a Cézanne seascape. I had visited the island before, many times, but it was to make my way through the dunes on one of the few beach-access paths, to lie on the flat, tawny beach on a damp beach towel with one or another friend, looking out at the sea and back toward the row of old cottages that lay behind the dune line, sheltered from our view by waving, rattling sea grass. I would not be visiting any of those houses, I knew; they had, since the late nineteenth century, been the retreats of the old Charleston families who migrated there in search of sea breezes and rustication in the long, sweltering summers. Often, I heard, they brought their household goods and their servants, and sometimes the family cow. The houses were seldom rented, and there were no motels or inns on the island. It was clear to such as me that this was in the broadest sense of the word a private island. Plain and a little shabby, with only a few seafood shacks and a convenience-store gas station, the loudest thing on Sullivan's Island seemed to be the cries of children and seabirds, and the fastest thing the ubiquitous golf carts the summer residents used to putt up to the store to get the *New York Times*, often accompanied by children and large, tongue-lolling dogs. Lewis called it, that first day, a sandy-rumped, old-fashioned family place. But I knew who those families were.

If you wanted livelier, more egalitarian beaches and rowdier evening action, there was Folly Beach to the south and the Isle of Palms to the north, both of which teemed and boomed in summer. Or if you wanted gated insularity and a sea viewed through great, three-storied Palladian windows, there was always Kiawah or Wild Dunes, across the Breach Inlet on the east tip of the Isle of Palms. You could, if you had the wherewithal, buy into those places. You had to be invited to Sullivan's Island, and even then beach properties for sale were as rare as igloos. Sullivan's was the oldest beach resort in the Charleston area, and I was scared to death of it.

"Why?" Lewis asked when I told him once

again on that first day that perhaps it would be better if I waited a little while to visit the beach house where his six closest friends spent weekends and sometimes weeks at a time.

"I'm not one of you all. I'm not born to this. I'm not really a Charlestonian; I just live here. They'll undoubtedly be perfectly charming to me, but there's bound to be a wall of some kind, and sooner or later you're going to resent me for it."

"A, I'll never resent you for anything. Period. End of discussion," he said, ruffling my salt-stormed hair. "B, some of them aren't from Charleston, either, and nobody resents them."

"But they married Charleston people early on. You met some of them right after med school, didn't you? And you were brought up from your playpen with the others. You're really a family. It's such a downtown thing. I'm just not able to do that."

"Anny, what the hell is 'that'? What do you think we do downtown? What do you think we do out here? Druid rites? Animal sacrifices? Ethnic cleansing, to keep the gene pool pure?"

"It looks pretty pure to me."

"Then you've got either a big surprise or a big disappointment coming. You're better looking than most of them and smarter than any of them. They're going to love you."

"Lewis—"

"Put a sock in it," he said, grinning, and swung the Range Rover right onto the pocked, heat-shimmering middle road that ran the length of the island. I was silent for a space of time.

We passed the grassy swell of Fort Moultrie,

which I had seen before, but never investigated. It looked like an ancient tumulus containing the remains of a giant, or a great king.

"Sullivan's was a war island before it was anything else," Lewis said, gesturing at the fort. "Fort Moultrie stopped the first Charleston incursion by the British in the Revolutionary War. There are fortifications and bunkers all over the island; you can see them back in the middle rows, along the stations. Henry and I used to prowl through them all the time. We'd take off everything but our trunks—and sometimes everything, once we got inside—and stripe ourselves up with mud or shoe polish, and stalk each other through the tunnels with sharpened sticks. I don't know why we didn't kill each other. Once we stalked the McKenzies' dog Scout, and he got lost way back in the tunnels and we couldn't find him for two days. Henry's dad almost throttled us. I think he liked Scout better than us."

"You all must have been menaces," I said. "Did you just run wild on the island?"

"Oh, yeah. All the kids did. Back then there was nothing to hurt you except the tides at Breach Inlet and whatever snakes were around. Kids knew about those by the time they were two or three. Come to think of it, there still isn't anything much here to hurt you. I've been coming out here since I was eight years old, and this island hasn't changed essentially since then."

"It sounds idyllic," I said. It did. A gentle, sunny kingdom of surf and sand and creeks and inlets, an island fiefdom ruled by children.

"Did your family have a house here?" I asked.

"No. My mother was scared to death of open water. Waves made her crazy. I don't know how she survived on the Battery; she'd go into the very back of the house when the surf was high, and close the shutters. My parents always went to the Edisto house. I loved messing around out there, even when I was small, but there was nobody much but my sister and a few of the hands' kids to play with. So I spent weeks and sometimes months on Sullivan's at Henry's folks's house. He had two older sisters who spent most of their time doing their nails and parading by the Coast Guard station, so I think I was like another younger son to Mrs. McKenzie. She and the kids came out for the summers, like a lot of Charleston families then. I never remember her treating me any way except exactly like Henry. Kind of a fond, benign neglect. She knew we were safe, and we were mostly out of her hair. I really loved her."

"Did she know about the tunnels and all that?"

"I don't think so. Maybe a little. But I know she didn't know about some of the rest of it. Like diving off the Ben Sawyer bridge into the inland waterway—not that there was much boat traffic then. But it was deep and fast. We scared ourselves. And we did try to swim Breach Inlet once, and ended up halfway up the Isle of Palms. We had to walk home so nobody would know. And the time we took Mr. McKenzie's johnboat out on the cove in a thunderstorm, with lightning hitting all around us. Or the times we smoked behind the dunes, or took some of Mr. McKenzie's rum to the beach at night and slept out there because we couldn't walk home."

"Didn't she miss you?"

"Nope. We told her we were camping out. We did that a lot, in back of the dune line or over on Little Goat Island. Sometimes we wouldn't see her or Henry's sisters for a day or so at a time. She knew that if our bicycles weren't there, we were off somewhere in the neighborhood. We used to go over to Camilla's house on the beach a lot. Henry lived on the cove. We had the best sailing and crabbing, but Camilla had the beach and the ocean. We had to let her do whatever we were doing in exchange for the use of her beach, but it was worth it. Camilla was one of the few girls we could tolerate. She was a great tomboy; she could swim and sail better than we could. And her sister was much older, so her mother and grandmother were glad she had some company, even if it was us. I think they'd have drowned us if they'd known what sort of things we got her into. But like I said, Sullivan's was the safest place in the world then. And Henry adored her. Always did, from kindergarten on. They were a pair by the time they were ten years old."

"But he didn't marry her," I said.

"No. Charlie Curry came to the hospital right after her deb year, and she dropped old Henry like a hot rock and was married to Charlie by Christmas of that year. One of the biggest weddings Charleston had ever seen. Henry didn't go; he took off back to Hopkins early."

"Poor Henry."

"Yeah, well, by that time Fairlie had come along, and before long Henry was a goner. Man, she was something else. Well, you'll see."

"Where did she come from?"

"She came down from Kentucky to study dance at the College of Charleston. Henry met her at a party that his mother gave for the troupe. She was a good bit younger than we were, but Henry couldn't have cared less. Only his mother cared; she'd had her sights set on Camilla all along. Two of the great old Charleston families and all that shit. But even she bowed to the inevitable. Fairlie was gorgeous. Still is, but when she was that young . . . God, she was like a lit candle."

My mouth was dry. I was not like a lit anything, except maybe a squat emergency candle.

"Tell me about the rest of them," I said. "Tell me about the Scrubs."

"I have. A hundred times."

"Tell me again. Tell me why you call yourselves the Scrubs. Tell me how they look. Tell me what makes them laugh. Tell me what they love."

He stopped the car to let a small procession cross the road, toward the beach. A youngish woman in a man's shirt and sunglasses came first, followed by two towheaded, brown children in swimsuits and flip-flops. Bringing up the rear was a young girl in a modest bikini, her arms piled high with towels, a cooler, an umbrella, and beach toys. She was barefoot, and pranced skittishly across the hot pavement.

"They look like a family of ducklings," I said.

"Typical Sullivan's Island nuclear family," Lewis said, grinning. "Mama out from Charleston for the summer, while Daddy stays home on Tradd Street and works at the bank and comes out on weekends. The kids. And the nanny. You know the nannies by the number of things they carry, and the fact that they always bring up the rear. There weren't any in our time. I don't know if kids have gotten much worse since then, or mothers have gotten less able to cope. If Henry and I had had a teenager in a bikini in residence, we'd never have left the front porch."

"You sound like you were a juvenile sex fiend," I said.

"And never grew out of it," he said, putting his hand on my bare knee. I could feel the heat of it all over me. I thought of the weekend just past, and felt my arms and legs go slack and heavy. We had seen each other every night since then, but we had not made love again. I had waited for it, first in an embarrassed shyness, then in puzzlement, and finally with an impatience that I could feel in the pit of my stomach. Did he regret the night on the dock, then? But if he did, why did he continue to see me? Why did he bring me to this place that was, I knew, deep in one of the central chambers of his heart?

As if he had read my mind, he said, "I can't wait to get you on a sand dune. It's an unforgettable experience. The moon, the stars, the sand-spurs, the ghost crabs . . . "

"You'll be waiting a long time," I said, but something in me relaxed and stretched itself. There would be another time, then, even if it wasn't on a sand dune. And then I thought, What's the matter with me? Can you turn into a hot number at age thirty-five?

And I knew I could.

He started the car again, driving slowly west. On each side of Middle Street there were modest cottages and bungalows, many on stilts. They were well kept and many had flourishing gardens, but they were a long way from grand.

"Where are the big old cottages?" I said. "I know they must be along the beach, but I've never seen any."

"They are. They're on what we call the first row. That's the first row from the beach. There's a second row, and a third, and a fourth, and so on. The little streets that cut through them to this one are called stations, because they used to be stops on a trolley line that ran along the island. Things get a little rattier as they get farther from the beach."

"Not very democratic."

"We never thought it was."

"All right, the Scrubs."

"That's simply because all of us are, in one way or another, connected to medicine. Henry and I went to Duke and Hopkins together. Charlie's always been in hospital administration. Simms's father owned a medical supply business that served the whole South, and Simms has built it up into a national concern. Second or third largest in the country, I think. Simms and Henry and I were born here, and grew up together, along with Camilla and Lila. We had the start of a core group, and then Charlie and Fairlie came, and somehow we just . . . clicked. Over the years we got close, closer than with some of our families. In a way, you're right. They *are* my family."

"Your wife . . . ," I said tentatively. "Was she part of it?"

"No." He looked straight ahead. "Sissy was never part of it. She thought Sullivan's was sticky and sandy and shabby and she didn't like any of the women. Oh, maybe Camilla, a little . . . at least she liked her family tree, and it's hard not to like Camilla no matter what. But she really disliked Fairlie and Lila. Too good looking, I think."

"She didn't have any worries on that score," I said, thinking of the radiant young woman in her wedding dress.

"Sissy always hated having sand in her shoes and wind in her hair. And the accommodations at the house are less than palatial, to say the least. Mostly she stayed in Charleston and went to parties, and took the girls shopping and to their own parties."

"And they didn't like the beach?" I said, wondering what sort of children wouldn't love surf and sand and endless blue.

"Well, we all came out once in a while when they were very young, but Sissy didn't care for the other kids, thought they were rowdy little hoodlums who simply ran wild. And they were, just like their parents had been. And the girls got so sunburned one summer that we had to take them to the hospital, and that was that. She loved Sweetgrass, though, and we spent a lot of time out there. She liked being able to ask her friends to the family plantation, and later to the Battery house. When I came out here, I came alone."

"I think that's terribly sad," I said, dipping my head to his shoulder briefly. He reached over and touched my hair.

"Well, anyway, the rest of us finally worked out

a sort of system with the beach house. Camilla's mother wasn't interested in it after her husband died, so we all got together and pooled our pennies and bought it. It belongs to all of us. Whoever wants to come out every weekend, or spend longer here, can do it. And they can bring anybody they want to. Some of us have other places to go, like I have Edisto, and don't get here as often as the others. But once a month, we all meet here for a day and sometimes two. Nobody misses it. Children used to come, but now it's mostly just us again, like in the beginning. You asked what we laugh at? Everything. And what we love? Many things, of course, but high on the list is the ocean, and that house, and . . . us. It's odd, but the beach has always been the thing that held us together. The water is like blood to us, I guess."

I was silent. I thought that there was no way they were going to enfold me in that complex web of loves and laughter, no matter what Lewis said. I had never even known such friendship existed. Suddenly I wanted, more than anything in the world, to tell Lewis to turn the car around and take me home.

"We're here," he said, turning the car off onto a rough, sandy track that led through a forest of scrub pines and palmettos and an occasional stunted live oak, flanked by dunes. It seemed to me that we drove for a long time. There was nothing on either side of us but sand and scrub.

"This is definitely the inelegant end of the island," Lewis said. "Most of the fancy cottages are up toward the east end. But I've always been glad of that because we have relatively few neighbors. The beach along here is sort of skimpy, and the dunes are high and shifty. It's kept the property pretty wild."

And then we were through the undergrowth and out into a glaring, sandy space beyond which the dunes rose high, fringed with waving sea oats, and the sound of the hidden ocean boomed in my ears, and I saw the house for the first time.

It was a hybrid of a house, to put it kindly. It stood unshaded in the middle of the blinding-white clearing, and its peeling gray shingles threw off heat like a hot pavement; you could see the shimmering waves of it. The central portion was square and two storied, with many small windows where I could see curtains blowing in the sea wind, and startlingly, a widow's walk atop it, like a church hat on a dowager. Various shingled wings and ells had been added, obviously later, and a screened-in porch surrounded it. The house sat high on its pilings, and there was a pool of dense, dark shade underneath, where I could see a couple of cars and a lawn mower and what looked to be a volleyball net draped over a Ping-Pong table. Down in the yard, or whatever they called the scorching-white area surrounding it, the noonday heat must surely be close to unbearable. But I had seen the flutter of the curtains, and heard the snap of what must be a flag in the wind. All the living in this house would be done in the air.

"I need to be here," I said stupidly to Lewis, hardly aware that I spoke. The house sang to me as my mother never had.

"I know," he smiled. "And here you are."

A long flight of wooden steps led up from the sand to the porch in back. They were railed and stout looking, but needed paint badly. The rest of the house did, too. I loved every chip and gouge. This beautiful house was nevertheless a hoyden in torn clothes, and would demand nothing from you except allegiance. It had mine before we got out of the car.

"It's wonderful," I said to Lewis, trudging across the sand to the steps. Sandspurs pricked at my legs, and small, vicious insects homed in on me.

"Yes, it is," he said. "There's nothing about it aesthetically right; it started life as a New England saltbox because Camilla's father had visited Nantucket and fell in love with the old seafarers' houses there. Most of the other houses are low, behind the dunes, but he said that if he had a house on the beach, he, by God, wanted to see the beach. This house is on one of the highest points on the island, and it's raised another story by the stilts. He bought up all the land down to the primary dune line, because he said he didn't want to be looking into anybody else's bathroom window. Once you're in the house, it's like being on a ship at sea. You look straight over the dunes to the beach and the ocean; the tops of the palms are about level with the porch. Whoever added the wings and the porch didn't require anything but bedroom space and a place to sit outside. None of it's ever going to make *Architectural Digest*. But somehow it works. Even if the bedrooms are the size of a Legare Street closet and the walls are so thin you can hear your neighbors . . . snore."

He leered at me.

"Well, there's always the dunes," I said, and he laughed and took my hand and we ran up the steps and onto the porch and into the wind.

It hit us squarely when we reached the back door of the house, which was open. The front door was, too. A river of salt-sweet air rushed through it and I could see the entire big room and the front porch beyond it, and beyond that the lines of the dunes retreating down to the beach and the sea. The tide was coming in full, and white surf laced the blue-and-green water. I had a jumbled impression of old wicker and frayed grass rugs and a litter of newspapers and books, and coffee cups and crumpled napkins, and a huge, dead stone fireplace at one end. At the other, narrow stairs climbed up into the gloom of the second floor. A clutter of fishing rods stood propped beside the front screen door, and for some reason, a battered yellow sea kayak rested on the porch beside a rope hammock. There was no one in the house.

There was a note, though, pinned to the battered trestle table with a bottle of insect repellent.

"On beach," it said. "Bring more towels and some ice from the freezer and another umbrella. Welcome, Anny!"

It was signed simply "C." Camilla, I thought. My throat tightened.

"I don't have a bathing suit," I said in a small voice.

"There's bound to be one around here that'll fit you," Lewis said. "Go upstairs and look in the first bedroom on the right. That's Camilla and Charlie's. She's the keeper of the spare bathing suits. People keep leaving them; there must be twenty of them by now."

"I can't just go into their room—"

"Oh, go on. Nobody cares about that. Sometimes you'll wake up and somebody will be rooting through your dresser drawer or your suitcase, looking for a stamp or your car keys, or most likely an Alka-Seltzer. This is a pretty socialist house."

I crept up the dark old stairs and into the tiny bedroom overlooking the porch roof. There was a big old mahogany bed, a rice bed I thought, piled high with yellowed lace pillows and covered with an ivory cotton coverlet. Except for end tables and a couple of lopsided lamps and a massive old chest of drawers, there was little else in the room. It smelled of salt and camphor and generations. And then I saw a small alcove that held a slender writing desk and a lamp and piles and piles of papers and clippings and stamps and stationery, its envelopes undoubtedly stuck together with damp, and a beautiful green silk–covered book that I assumed was a journal or a diary of some sort. Beach roses wilted in a little bisque vase. Camilla's corner, the place where she truly lived.

In the bottom drawer of the chest I found the bathing suits, neatly folded in tissue paper and smelling of lavender. There must indeed have been twenty of them, and from the look of them, they spanned at least thirty years. I finally found a pink-flowered cotton suit with a little skirt that shouted Lilly Pulitzer, and put it on in the dimness, and crept back downstairs holding my shorts and shirt before me.

"It's perfect," Lewis said, grinning, pulling my folded clothes away from me to look. "It's you. If you'd put on a bikini, I'd have taken you straight home."

"The latest thing up there is one of those Rose Marie Reid things with the puffy legs and the fronts so boned that they stand a foot away from your boobs. I had one in high school. I looked like the front end of a fifty-three Studebaker."

He laughed and kissed me on the forehead, and we took the towels and ice and the big, skewed umbrella and went down the front steps and across the long board walkway over the dune and onto the beach.

The tide was full in, and the sun stood directly overhead, so the whole beach and sea were a sheet of blinding glitter. The light swallowed the world; it was as if I had been stricken sightless by light. It even sucked in sound. I could see groups of people down the beach, under umbrellas, and children whooping and splashing in the surf, and gulls wheeling overhead. But I could not hear them, nor the soft hush of the surf as it ran far up the beach to lose itself in a smear of glass, edged with foam. I could smell, though: the primal, amniotic smell of the sea; the scent of hot sun on the sea grass, somehow like hay; even the ghost of someone's coconut sunscreen. And something else: under it all, the sick-sweet, acrid smell of the pluff mud from the marshes along the inland waterway, Charleston's official smell.

Beside me, Lewis said something, but I could not hear him. He began to laugh. He pointed to the beach, but I could not see what he was indicating. I might as well have been smitten by Apollo.

I turned to look at him and he took off his sunglasses and put them on my nose, and the world snapped back again, clear and sharp shadowed.

In the damp sand along the beach, the words "Hi, Anny" had been incised, in letters three or four feet high. Behind the message, side by side like a chorus line, stood the Scrubs, waving and laughing.

I felt the wind lift the limp skirt of my ghastly bathing suit and explode my hair. If I could have turned and run, I would have. But Lewis's hand was firmly on my back, pushing me forward, and the Rockette line of the people who would be my friends, or not, came swarming up the dunes to greet us.

They were, I knew, all except Fairlie, about Lewis's age, brushing fifty and maybe edging beyond it. But they looked to me like those clever kids who came spilling out of a thousand movie barns, shouting, "Hey, gang, I know! Let's put on a show!" I got a confused montage of red-silk hair burning in the sun, white-blond hair over a narrow deeply tanned face, faded, utilitarian swimsuits, long brown limbs, and white teeth. Everybody was thin. How could so many middle-aged people look so gawkily, gracefully adolescent? There was one male shape that was thick barreled and broad shouldered, but he was so tall that he seemed a part of that thicket of slender trees. Lewis and I, standing there on the dune above them, were the only low-slung, earth-footed people in the group.

"I feel like a garden gnome," I whispered to him miserably, and he hugged me hard around the shoulders before they swallowed us up.

I was hugged and kissed on the cheek and borne down the beach to where a couple of sun-whitened umbrellas stood. Underneath them was a tangle of damp towels and rubber flip-flops and paper cups and a sweating cooler. Lewis dumped the ice and towels and the extra umbrella.

"Okay," he said. "Here she is. One at a time or she's going to run like a rabbit. Your fame has preceded you."

I sat down on a damp towel, feeling the chilly sand under it seep into the tights under the swimsuit's skirt. One by one, like supplicants to a queen, they came and sat or knelt beside me. Lewis presented and explained them. I knew that I would remember little of it, but I smiled and nodded like an idiot, thinking I must look like a black-thatched jack-o'-lantern in a too-small Lilly Pulitzer swimsuit.

Camilla Curry was tall and very slender, already stooped a little with the osteoporosis that would claim her body before too long. But her long legs and arms and her slender hands and feet were youthful, and her narrow, fine-boned face was as serene and beautiful as an effigy on a medieval tomb. She had thick chestnut hair that she wore in a loose chignon and brown eyes that glowed deep in a thicket of lashes. Her smile was a benediction.

"Well, Lewis," she said, "you finally got it right." And to me, "You must be something special. You're the only one Lewis has ever brought out here."

I felt a rush of love. In all the time I knew Camilla, that never changed.

Her husband, Charles Curry, was the tall, broad man I had noticed earlier. He was going bald, and his skin was weathered to the color of mahogany, and he gave me a hug that threatened to break my ribs. Charles was, I knew, the chief administrative officer at Queens Hospital, downtown, where Lewis and Henry McKenzie were attending physicians. Charles, I remembered, was one of the only two Scrubs, not including me, who was not Charleston born and bred. It did not seem to have hindered him in any way. He had married into one of the city's oldest and most distinguished families, and that did not appear to have hindered him, either. I thought I remembered Lewis telling me he was from Indiana, and marveled at the completeness of his assimilation. He was a bit overweight, and his skin was peeling like an old walrus's hide, and he had a hole in his trunks that just missed being obscene, but his gravelly voice and genial, honking laugh spoke of total self-confidence and I could see that his sheer vitality would have won him entry into more than a few pallid drawing rooms. I did not think that he cared, one way or another.

Fairlie McKenzie came next to be presented. I had the swift impression that I was being interviewed for a position as housemaid. Fairlie drew the eye like wildfire. Even in her late forties, it was nearly impossible to look away from her. I thought of what Lewis had said about the way she had looked as a young dancer just come to town, and I could see that girl in her as if in pentimento. Her heavy copper hair blew free in the wind and burned in the sun; she had sharp, foxes' features and astonishing blue eyes and she moved like a beautiful snake, coiled and utterly unaware of her body.

"Anny," she said, and Kentucky ran like rich sour mash through her voice. It was the Kentucky of thoroughbred farms, not coal mines. "We've all been waiting with bated breath to see what fabulous Mata Hari finally managed to get old Lewis to bring her onto sacred ground."

"Not much of one, I don't think," I said, and she laughed, but did not say anything else. I did not like Fairlie McKenzie, not then. She was sharp and sarcastic, and her dancer's body in her black racing suit fairly shouted "tacky" at mine in the Lilly.

Henry McKenzie came behind her. I loved Henry instantly. I thought most people would. Somehow, he radiated safety. He was the tall, fair-haired one I had noticed, and his brown body was as lanky and limber as a scarecrow's. He had hazel eyes that seemed half asleep, and a smile that you could only call sweet. Every girl's mother would have coveted him. It must have been a real loss to the Charleston gene pool when Henry picked the flamboyant Fairlie and moved her into Bedon's Alley. Lewis had told me Henry was a cardiologist, and spent much of his time, when he could get away, working with native doctors in such agonizingly poor places as Haiti and the wild green heart of Puerto Rico, and even Africa. I thought, spitefully, that there was probably no chance that Fairlie accompanied him.

"Lewis has told me about your work at the agency," he said. "It's wonderful work. I'd like to talk to you about it one of these days. All of the countries I visit need something like that desperately. Maybe you'd like to come with us sometime and just see how we might go about it—"

"Henry, for pity's sake," Camilla said in exasperation and affection. "I'm sure Anny's got a few other ideas about her life besides serving as an unpaid lackey for you in Hoo-Doo Hollow or wherever."

"Well," Henry said equably, "whatever she wants to do with her life, she sure is pretty."

Fairlie snorted. The rest of the Scrubs laughed. Suddenly, it was all right. For that moment, everything was.

Simms and Lila Howard came last, together. If you were familiar with the city, you would have thought "Charleston" immediately upon sighting them anywhere in the world. Lila was small and neatly curved, and had chin-length honey-blond hair anchored away from her face with sunglasses on the top of her head. She was only lightly tanned, and had a heart-shaped face and large, far-apart brown eyes. She wore a boy-legged blue seersucker swimsuit faded almost to white, and there were little gold hoops in her ears. Her voice was honey and smoke, with Charleston's peculiar broad *a* embedded in it. Her smile was sunny. I could see her on some crepe myrtle–shaded veranda, asking if anyone would like their drink freshened up a tad. Simms was neither tall nor short, and slightly built, with brown hair going gray. He had the sleepy eyes and slow voice of every downtown-born man I had ever met, and I could imagine, over his baggy, knee-length madras plaid trunks, the downtown uniform of khaki pants, blue shirt, and bow tie. He had the white lines of a sailor incised into his forehead and around his eyes; Lewis had them, too. Lewis had told me that Simms was probably the best sailor in the Carolina Yacht Club, and was a fierce and focused competitor. That must, I thought, be the side of him that ran the second-largest medical supply company in the country. Here, in the dappled shade of the beach umbrella, the only side I saw was the easy, slightly lazy man who was boyhood friend and adult companion. I imagined that Simms made a great deal more money than any of the others, and could add to that Lila's family's two-hundred-year-old largesse. But here on this beach, under this sleepy sun, he was first and foremost a Scrub. I liked him for that, and liked Lila for her generous smile. Lewis had told me that Lila sold real estate, rather desultorily, in a small firm of downtown women who knew every house south of Broad and when it might come on the market weeks before it was listed. He said they made a lot of money.

"You are a breath of fresh air in this bunch," Lila said, and hugged me. She smelled of lavender soap. Simms took my hands in his and smiled at me. "You are mighty welcome, Anny Butler," he said. "We were fixing to throw this boy here out of the house for not pulling his own weight."

"What he means," Lila said, "is that we take turns bringing the food, and of course the women get stuck with that, and Lewis's contribution, when he thinks of it, is to pick up some beer and boiled peanuts on the way out here. Prepare to help feed the multitudes, Anny."

"Will takeout do?" I said, thinking of my schedule of late nights and early mornings.

"We'd be happy to get takeout," Henry said. "We usually get tomato sandwiches and Kool-Aid because that's what we all ate when we were kids over here. I for one would consider takeout exotic in the extreme."

"You conveniently forget the gallons of she-crab soup and the tons of raw shrimp I lug over here," Lewis said, grinning.

"Yeah, but your Sweetgrass housekeeper makes the soup and I happen to know you get the shrimp at Harris Teeter," Simms said. "The rule is, we have to suffer for our feasts."

"What's this 'we' stuff?" Fairlie said from under the huge straw hat she had put on.

"Since when have you learned to cook anything but tomato soup and toast?" Henry teased her.

"I clean up. I wash dishes," she retorted. "While, of course, all you guys sit on the porch with cigars or go sailing."

Gradually the conversation slowed and faded, and everyone seemed content to simply sit in the shade and gaze at the sea. I was glad of the quiet, glad the initial ordeal was past me, and tried to slump as casually on the towel as everyone else while keeping my skirt tugged down over my crotch.

Silence soon fell, and people lay back on towels and stretched in the green-tinted umbrella shade, and gradually breathing deepened. Somebody coughed, and somebody else cleared a throat; outside the little kingdom of our umbrellas the sounds of children and radios and waves and gulls swelled and faded as sounds do when you are sliding into sleep. For the first time that day, I felt my muscles slacken and my breath deepen. I can do this, I thought, just before my mind flowed away with the hush of the sea.

"ALLEY-OOP! OOP! OOP-OOOP-OOP!"

A squalling, near-demented howl jerked me out of sleep, heart hammering, and before I could blink, hands on either side of me jerked me up off the towel and across the beach at a stumbling run. Blinking and gasping, I saw that I was at the center of a line of Scrubs, being hauled relentlessly and ingloriously toward the sea.

"Stop!" I cried. "Stop! I haven't been swimming in twenty years!"

But no one heard me, roaring and chanting as they were. Before I could get my breath, we were crashing through the surf and on out into rolling waist-deep water, and then a great swell took us and we all went under.

If you have not been into the ocean, really into it, in a very long time, you simply forget. You forget that to go deep, to let it take you completely, to bear you up on tides unseen in a green sun-shot stasis, is to roll and dive in weightlessness that is a sort of bliss. I think that it must be what those

lovely, endless saline days swimming in the
womb are like. That day, under the glittering surface of the sea off Sullivan's Island, I drifted, spinning slowly in the water, shadowy and cool in its
depths, brightening and warming as you looked
toward the surface. My limbs became free and
supple; my hair floated out like a mermaid's; my
ridiculous skirt flowed around me like silk gauze.
I was lighter than air and more supple than a dol-
phin, and I did not want to come up. I could see
why drowning might be seductive. When Lewis
grabbed my wrist and jerked me to my feet in
chest-deep water, I jerked back, frowning.

"Do you know how long you were down
there?" he said tightly. "We thought we'd
drowned you. Camilla has gone down the beach
to the lifeguard station. What was the matter?"

"Nothing," I said dreamily. "It was wonderful.
I'd forgotten how it feels to really be all the way *in*
the ocean."

"Well, you managed to scare the shit out of
everybody," Fairlie McKenzie said. "What do you
do for an encore?"

"Shut up, Fairlie," Henry said, and this time
there was no softness in his drawl.

Lila ran down the beach to divert Camilla, and
the rest of us gathered the towels and cooler and
umbrellas and trudged back over the dunes to the
house. The others bantered back and forth, but I
followed along, head hung in mortification, feeling the suppleness leave my limbs and the grace
seep out of my sopping skirt.

"I'm sorry," I whispered to Lewis as we came
up onto the porch.

"What for?"

"For scaring everybody like that."

"Forget it," he said. "Sometime I'll tell you about the time Lila and Fairlie took the Whaler out on the creek and ran it aground in an oyster bed, and we had to get the Coast Guard to tow them in. You're small potatoes to that."

"It's funny, then, isn't it, that it was Fairlie who got so mad at me?" I said.

"That's just Fairlie. She's prickly and outspoken, and she's jealous of anything or anybody who threatens to break up the group. But she's the most loyal friend I know. Once she's seen that you're no threat to the group dynamic, she'll take you in like a sister. Christ, you should have seen her with Sissy. She nearly flayed her alive with her tongue."

"Did Sissy mind?"

"I don't think she even noticed."

"You'd think that someone from outside wouldn't feel so strongly about the group," I said.

"I think that's precisely why she does," Lewis said. "Go get dressed and we'll start lunch. It's the main event out here. Lasts for hours."

I changed swiftly in the upstairs bathroom, the dim, underwater green of the old windows and mirror turning my puckered flesh fish white. I had locked the door, and when I came out, Fairlie and Camilla were walking around in the bedroom stark naked, towels wrapped around their hair, laughing and collecting dry clothes. Fairlie was smoking a cigarette. No one was hurrying.

"Hi, sweetie, are you okay?" Camilla said.

I nodded, vigorously, averting my eyes. I

turned and went out the door and down the stairs in my dry shorts and shirt, hearing, behind me, the wasp buzz of Fairlie's laugh.

Well, I thought, my boobs are bigger than hers. Next time I'll show her. I can get as bare assed as anybody.

We had lunch at the scarred old trestle table on the screened-in porch. The wind had dropped at the turn of the tide, and the lazy overhead fan stirred the thick air just enough to dry the sweat that stood on our faces. Cheeks and shoulders were flushed with new pink, and wet hair dried uncombed. Fairlie and Lila and Camilla had opened boxes and bags and brought out wonderful things: caviar on ice and little toasts, piles of fresh fruit, bread and cheese and cold shrimp and crab legs, thin slices of smoked salmon. Many bottles of wine sat sweating on a side table. Tomato sandwiches and Kool-Aid, indeed.

"I'm really sorry," I said. "I didn't know about the food. I'll bring double next time."

Fairlie's eyebrows rose: next time?

"Don't worry about it, love," Camilla said. "Lewis paid for the wine. Next time you can bring the entrée. Chinese takeout would be just fine."

"I can do a little better than that," I mumbled. I determined then to make something so incredibly elegant and difficult that it would be greeted with applause and cries of ecstasy, and bring it the next time we came.

We ate and drank wine and talked and laughed for three hours. Music from a cracked white plastic radio curled around us: the Tams, the Shirelles, the Zodiacs. Beach music. The talk was mainly of

their childhoods, or their first years together as a
group: this beach and this house were not, I saw,
about times and events outside it. All of them had
Charleston lives full to overflowing: work, other
friends, families, charities, boards, vacations, bad
times as well as good. But out here, among themselves, they could live for a bit in a time-stopped
parallel universe. I did not mind the stories of
people I would never know, jokes I would never
understand, references that I could never connect
until someone patiently did it for me. I knew that
over time Lewis would bring me into the web of
the Scrubs. For now I was content to sit, full of
shrimp and wine, and listen to the intricate verbal
tapestry of this group of friends. I had never
heard its like before.

At last the red heat went out of the sun and the
beach and the sea grayed, and the sky over the
inland waterway opposite the house began to
flush and then flame with sunset. Over the ocean,
now dull pewter, a young moon rode high. And
still they talked, and they talked, and they talked.
I did not ever want them to stop. This was the
new language that might define my life.

Nobody was in a hurry, or hungry. We sat until
the thick, sudden darkness of the Low Country
fell down over us, until the young moon
whitened, until the swarms of stars came out. We
sipped the last of the wine, and still they talked.
When someone finally turned to me and said,
"Tell us about you, Anny. Don't leave anything
out," I found that I had almost no voice.

"I think I've forgotten how to talk," I said, and
they laughed, even Fairlie.

"A not-uncommon syndrome out here," Lewis said. "I'll tell y'all about Anny Butler, because she'll leave the best stuff out."

And he did. He told them about my childhood and my mother and sisters and brother, and about the agency and what it was and what I did there, and about our meeting the bobcat on the dock at Sweetgrass. I held my breath, but he did not tell them about the rest of that night. I thought, though, that it might be implicit, for everyone smiled indulgently.

"You really are a nurturer, then," Henry said. "That's good. So is Camilla, but we've about worn her out."

"Not going to happen," Camilla said from the semidarkness of the old rope hammock where she had nested. "Speaking of nurturing, though, I've been through the most awful thing I'll ever go through this week. I had to move Mama into Bishop Gadsden. There was just no way she could stay on Tradd anymore, even with Lavinia there all day and me and Lydia taking turns at night. If you turn your back, she's out the door; Margaret Daughtry found her out beside their fish pond last week, and that's on Meeting, a couple of blocks away. She was wearing her fur over her nightgown. How she got that far without somebody seeing her and bringing her home I'll never know. Well, except that the streets are full of tourists, and I guess for all they know, all old Charleston ladies regularly run around in their nightgowns and minks. And last week she put a pot on the stove and turned on the burner while Lavinia was

in the bathroom, and the smoke alarm went off
and the fire department came. Lydia and I get
almost no sleep at all when we're there with her.
Listening for her to start that awful shuffling
around all over the house that she does at night. I
can't let her fall down those narrow old stairs and
I refuse to lock her in in her own house. And
there's just no way we can have her at the house,
not and keep on working, and Lydia has her
grandchildren full time after Kitty . . . well, you
know. So Charlie pulled some strings and got her
in, and I took her over there day before yesterday.
Oh, God, she thought she was going to a garden
club meeting; it was just horrible. And it's a lovely
suite, and a lot of her friends are already there,
and Lydia or I will go every day, but I'll never get
over feeling guilty. When I left she cried and said,
'When can I come home?' and I cried all the way
home. Because I know what she means. She
wants, by God, her own place, the place she's
made beautiful and welcoming all these years,
and her things, and her friends, and the street she
knows, and to live by her own rhythms and call
her own shots, and, most of all, not to walk down
a hall or into a dining room and see a sea of old
people who all look alike and smell like talcum
and pee, none of whom she can recognize. Of
course she wants that. And I just don't know how
to give it to her."

"Dementia," Lewis said. "It's a killer. I think I'd
shoot myself, if I was still compos mentis enough
to know I had it. Can y'all see Anny changing my
diapers?"

I could. I could do that, I thought. As if he had caught the thought, Henry looked at me and smiled.

"It's something we're all going to have to face, if our parents live that long. And I guess we'll face it ourselves one day, and our children will feel the same way you do, Camilla," Lila said. For once she did not sound cheerful and perky.

"I just damned well refuse," Fairlie said tautly. "I'll be a bag lady before I let somebody dump me in a place I don't know, with a bunch of people I couldn't care less about, and I'd kill anybody who came near me with diapers."

"It's not something anybody wants to think about," Camilla said. "I guess I never did, until it came up. But I'm going to start planning now. I don't know what the plan will be, or how I'll make it work, but my children are not going to have to go through that with Charlie and me."

Camilla's two boys lived on the West Coast with their families, and did something unimaginable in Silicon Valley. I did not think Camilla and Charlie saw them very often.

We were silent, watching the moon leave its silver snail's track on the water. I knew that all our thoughts dwelled in some painfully bright, sterile place far in the future, a place that was inimical to life. A little wind off the inland waterway sprang up, and all of a sudden sun-reddened shoulders felt chilled. People began to stir and stretch. I did not want this magical day to end in that cold place.

"Let's just all move out here together, and take care of each other," Fairlie said. "We have all the medical help we need, and God knows Simms could get us enough drugs to keep us happy until the Rapture. There are stores just over the bridge and the hospital is twenty minutes away. We could easily find somebody to cook and clean and run errands."

She looked at me. I looked back, levelly.

"It's an idea, isn't it?" Lila said. "Not necessarily here . . . the weather's just too uncertain and we could get blown over to West Ashley in one night. But somewhere really nice, with a lot of rooms, or even little villas, with a central living and dining area. There are a lot of resorts like that around on the islands. I could start looking tomorrow."

"No resorts," Simms said. "I'm not spending my golden years on Hilton Head."

"No, really, I'll bet I could find something in a month," Lila said.

"We don't have to decide where now," Charlie said. "But we can decide to do it when the time comes. We could even find something where we could spend a month or two together and see if we can stand each other. Later, of course. Right now this house is perfect."

The mood lightened, and the talk drifted to the bizarre and ridiculous things we might all do together. Form a geriatric outlaw band and steal toilet paper out of hotels and motels. Storm Wal-Mart and have a sit-in in our wheelchairs. Skinny-dip in whatever body of water was near—for water must be part of it all—and raise such a scandalous commotion that property values in a three-mile radius would drop.

"Play doctor on the beach," Lewis said.

"You can do that now," Charlie honked, and we all laughed.

The idea hung just over our heads for the rest of the evening, like ripe fruit dangling. One by one we lapsed back into silence. Then Camilla said, "Let's do it. Let's just agree to do it. If it doesn't work out, nobody's bound to it, but consider the alternative. Between us, we've got just about all the resources to make it work."

"And a new member who's a good fifteen years younger than the rest of us. What about it, Camilla? Haven't you always wanted a maid?" Fairlie said.

This silence was not contemplative, not peaceful. My ears rang. I heard Lewis draw a breath to say something in reply. I knew that it would be destroyingly angry.

"I have a maid," Camilla said. "But I would love to have a daughter." And she smiled at me, her archaic, V-shaped smile that so suited her medieval beauty.

My eyes stung and I smiled back, and the moment was averted.

"Call for a vote," Henry said, staring at Fairlie, who had the grace to look ashamed. "All in favor of the Scrubs fading into the sunset together, say aye."

And we all cried, "Aye!"

"Done and done," Henry said. "Now let's swear on . . . what? What's our most sacred thing?"

"The wine closet!" "The key to the big upstairs

bathroom!" "The fishing tackle!" Each offering was met with a chorus of jeers.

"What about the photograph in the hall, over the coat rack?" I said hesitantly. The photo was of them all, much younger and less worn, but recognizable, grinning by the front door of the house while Camilla held up a big, old-fashioned key. It had the look of beginnings to it.

"Perfect!" Camilla cried. "That was the first time we all came out together. Remember? How it rained, and the toilet backed up, and Lila got stung by a jellyfish?"

A chorus of approval rose, and I felt a ridiculous swell of pride, and Henry got the photo off the wall and held it out to each of us in turn.

"Swear," he said, and "I swear" we all said.

"What if some of us . . . aren't around when the time comes?" Camilla said. "Does the one left get to come, or what?"

"One for all and all for one," Lewis said. "If only two of us are left, or three, or whatever, we still do it. This is not about couples. It's about the Scrubs."

We gathered our things and filed out into the night. The last ones out—Lewis and I—locked the door. Lewis put the key into his pocket. They all had keys.

Fairlie hung back. When I came abreast of her, she said, "Good choice. I wish I'd thought of it."

"Thanks," I said, but she was already gone, with her dancer's flat-footed stride, and she did not hear me.

"Well done, Anny Butler," Lewis said, and kissed me on the back steps down to the dunes.

* * *

Lewis and I were married that September in the tiny white slaves' chapel at Sweetgrass. There were not many people: the Scrubs; his daughters, looking pleasant and closed into themselves; my sisters and brother; Marcy from my office; Linda and Robert and little Tommy, beaming. Linda made her she-crab soup for the wedding party. Everyone stayed late and drank a great deal of champagne.

When we were planning the wedding, Lewis had asked me where I would like to go on our honeymoon.

"Anywhere but Sea Island," he said, and I gathered that was where his marriage to Sissy began.

"The beach house," I said. "I want to spend it at the beach house."

And he laughed at me, but that's exactly what we did. The rest of the Scrubs came out for the weekend, bearing food and wine and tawdry, wonderful gifts, never for one moment considering that they might be intruding. I did not consider it, either. I was a Scrub. We were a unit.

Lewis had said that he thought perhaps we might want to open the big house on the Battery and live there, but on the last night of our honeymoon before the others came, I said, "Do you really want to?" and he said no.

"Me either," I said, weak with gratitude that I would never have to try and live up to that house. "I've been so scared of it."

"I've been so tired of it," he said. "We'll just live on Bull Street and Edisto and here, for the time being. You can take your time deciding where in Charleston you want to live permanently. Or even if."

"We've got to have some kind of reception or party for all your people—and that's half of Charleston," I said.

"Well, we will. After we're settled in. We'll use the Battery house for that. Its last hurrah."

But somehow we never did it.

I have always heard that marriage changes you, and, of course it does, but not always in the way the conventional wisdom would have it. With Lewis, the shape of my life did not change appreciably. The little house on Bull Street, though graceful and beautifully detailed, was not all that much larger than my apartment, so that from the very beginning I had no sense of rattling and creeping around in great spaces. I did not bring much with me to Lewis's house, so it did not bulge with furniture. What there was, he had brought out of the Battery house after the divorce, and it was old and beautiful and lustrous with care, but he had no great baroque pieces, no hive-like crystal chandeliers hanging over the small English dining table, not a fringe, not a tassel.

"Go over to the Battery anytime and pick out what you want," he said. "The hysterical society won't hassle you. Camilla's on the board."

But as lovely as the old house was, I did not want to go into it. I did not even like to pass it on my sporadic jogs. The Battery stank of Sissy to me, if not to anyone else.

"I don't want anything except what I have," I said, meaning it in all respects.

"Me, either," he said.

Our external lives did not change. I continued to work early and late at the agency, ferrying around the Shawna Sperrys of my world and attempting to corral their feckless mothers; begging discreetly and sometimes not so on the telephone for funds, services, homes, treatments for my flock, making speeches, attending grindingly tedious meetings with my board, accounting for paper clips and paper diapers instead of young lives anchored. As I always had, I fretted about it at home.

"Why don't you just quit?" Lewis said. "You don't have to work, you know. You could volunteer, or start a business of your own. We could have a baby."

I looked at him.

"I have about twenty of them right now," I said. "And you have two. Lewis, even if we started now, you'd be close to seventy when our first graduated from college. But you know, if you want to think about it . . . "

"I don't," he said, grinning. "I don't want anybody but you. I just don't want you to go all broody on me down the line."

"I've been taking care of children since I was eight years old," I said. "I don't want to go back to the diaper phase of it."

And so we did not have children of our own. Until very recently, I did not miss them.

Lewis continued to keep his hideous hours at the clinic. Dinner, if we could manage it together, was often at nine or ten o'clock. On weekends we usually left on Friday for Sweetgrass and stayed over Saturday night. On Sunday we went to the beach house. That seldom changed.

No, the armature of our lives was not altered appreciably. But at least for me, the interior changes were profound. I learned to laugh. I learned to play. I learned to lose my temper, yell, sulk, behave irrationally. I learned to cry. When we had our first fight, over Lewis accusing me, unfairly, of neglecting to pay Corinne, our cleaning lady, I shouted at him and burst into tears and ran upstairs. I lay on our bed, heart hammering with the enormity of my outburst, waiting for him to come coldly up and end our marriage. Of course he didn't; when I crept back downstairs hours later he was reading the *Post and Courier* and eating cold pizza.

"Did you take a nap?" he said.

"After all that stuff about Corinne?" I asked, incredulous.

"Oh," he said. "I found her check in the pocket of my lab coat. Want some of this?"

I realized then, for the first time, that marriage is about all of you, not just the best parts. Nothing in my child's or grown-up's world had taught me that. The liberation was like learning to fly.

We went to a lot of parties in our honor that first year, and I went to King Street and bought a few things that I thought would serve, though I never attained the elegance and brio that marks a downtown Charleston party, and when the first of the charity ball invitations came, I cried.

"Lewis, I can't," I snuffled. "I just can't. I can maybe do the smaller stuff but I can't do a ball."

"You don't have to. I gave them up when Sissy left. Nobody expects me anymore. We just won't."

"But we'll have to reciprocate for all the parties this year, sooner or later," I said.

"Why?" he said.

And so we became the Eccentric Aikens, who did not give parties, who did not do balls.

"I shudder to think what your mother would have to say about all this, Lewis," an old lady said to him once, at brunch at the Carolina Yacht Club. Those I could manage.

"Everybody's saying you're just turning your back on your whole heritage."

Her gaze skimmed me and bounced off.

"Come on, Tatty," Lewis said to the old lady, who was undoubtedly an aunt or a second cousin or a something-in-law. "You know I never went to parties much."

"Well, you did for a while," she said. "And it was lovely to see you out and about."

I knew she was referring to the Sissy era, and my face burned, but where once it would have been embarrassment, now it was anger.

The old lady tottered away on her Ferragamos, and Lewis said, under his breath, "'But that was in another country, and besides, the bitch is dead!'"

Every head in the dining room turned at our adolescent snicker.

We never moved out of the Bull Street house. Year after year, we went to Sweetgrass, and we went to the house on Sullivan's Island. We had occasional trips, some abroad, but somehow, wherever we went, I felt like a bird perched on a wire, ready for flight. I often had the feeling that the beach house was where my real life was, and that the rest was a sort of rich, endlessly fascinating half-life. I enjoyed, even loved, downtown Charleston, but it was where I went to wait to go to Sullivan's Island.

I did not see how the others could possibly feel the same way; it was the mind-set of the pilgrim, not the clan dweller. And yet, looking at us all on the beach or in the sea or before the fire, listening to us walking and laughing, listening even harder to what we did not say, I thought that perhaps they felt it, too, a little; that this place and its dwellers might truly be the reality, and all the rest its shadow. That in some atavistic way it was home, and we were family. I know that I felt that way all the years that we were together.

We few were a multitude.

When I think of the second summer I went to the beach house, I think of dogs and light.

There seemed to be dogs everywhere that year: on the beach; in the surf; bumping along with their owners in golf carts toward the little cluster of shops at the foot of the bridge; lolling in patches of shade under porches and cars; trotting in amiable phalanxes along Middle Street, noses searching the weedy roadsides for who knows what. They ran heavily to pointers and setters, working dogs for the many hunters who summered on the island, and small, scruffy, happy-looking mutts. The days of the glut of labs and goldens was still in the future.

We had our own tribe at the beach house. Charlie's two Boykin spaniels, Boy and Girl, came almost every time the Currys did, and spent a great deal of time sleeping on the porch and eating whatever they could beg. They got plenty. All of us spoiled the dogs.

"Best hunting dogs in the world," Charlie said fondly. "They're legendary. Mouths as soft as velvet. They've never messed up a single duck."

"That's because they've never retrieved a single duck," Lewis said lazily, from the hammock. "Charlie hates hunting. These are two of the most expensive lap dogs in Charleston."

"Well, if I hunted them they'd be the best," Charlie said, grinning. It was almost impossible to annoy or anger him. He remains one of the most amiable men I ever knew.

"They *are* sweet, but they poop more than any other dogs I've ever seen," Camilla said. "I never go anywhere without my scoop and my Baggies."

And that was true. It was Camilla who took the dogs on long daily walks down the beach. Her tall, slightly stooped figure and the manic dogs became a fixed thread in the tapestry of that summer. The dogs would careen crazily from the dunes to the surf and back, sniffing for crabs and turtle-egg holes. Camilla's chestnut hair blew back in the wind, and sometimes you could see her lips moving, talking to the dogs. She bent frequently to scoop the prodigious poop. Often she went out of sight past where the beach curved, far to the east. Occasionally she stayed gone for hours. We did not worry about her. She would come back eventually, still serene, her hair tangled, fresh pink glowing on her wonderful cheekbones. The panting dogs would collapse on the porch.

"You don't want to run them too far," Charlie said once, earnestly, and the rest of us burst into laughter. The idea of Camilla Curry running a couple of legendary hunting dogs to exhaustion was ludicrous. Sometimes she walked the beach without the dogs, and came back much later carrying shells in her cupped hands. She never seemed to want company, and we did not ask to go along. Camilla moved in a bubble of privacy.

Henry's springer spaniel, Gladys, came, too. Gladys lived summers at the old McKenzie island house, over on the inland waterway. Fairlie and Henry's daughter, Nancy, often brought her brood out to the house for the summer, and when she did not, Henry's handyman lived on the place and took care of Gladys. Gladys, Fairlie said, loved Leroy far more than she did Henry, but when she was with us at the beach house, Gladys stuck to Henry in an ecstasy of love. She was a pretty thing, and Simms said she was one of the best dove dogs he'd ever seen.

"I've been trying to get Henry to breed her so I can have a pup, but he wants her to stay a virgin. He sure knows how to show a girl a good time."

"Gladys is above matters of the flesh," Henry said from under the brim of his hideous fishing hat. He was sprawled in a folding chair, his long legs, golden furred, stretched out before him. He wore no shoes, and I noticed that even the hair on his long toes was blond. Henry, the golden one of us. Somehow, I was surprised that Henry hunted.

Simms's hunting dogs were kept in a kennel on

his plantation on Waccamaw Island, but Lila's ridiculous toy of a Maltese came with them to the beach. Sugar was yappy and erratic and winsome, and she had the heart of a lion. It was wonderful to see her dashing into the surf after the big dogs, her little legs beginning to pump and her chin held above water before the others were ankle deep. The men groused about stuffed toys, but Sugar spent a great deal of time in everybody's lap, especially mine. I loved the silly, great-hearted creature.

Lewis's hunting dogs, Sneezy, Dopey, and Sleepy, had a luxurious kennel and run out at Sweetgrass, shaded from the sun and larger than my old apartment. Lewis no longer hunted, saying that one day he just decided not to blow birds out of the air anymore. But he adored the dogs, and when we were at Sweetgrass, they lay before the fire with us, swam off the dock in the river with us, and slept with us on Lewis's grandmother's beautiful old rice bed. I loved the dogs, too, but they snored horribly, and I often gave up in despair and crept into the guest room when the whistling honks grew too loud. Lewis would find me there in the morning, and would shake his head and promise to banish the dogs to their kennel at night, but he never did. They did not come to the beach house.

"Enough is enough," Lewis said. "I don't want to spend my Sundays scooping setter shit."

So Sneezy, Dopey, and Sleepy stayed home, where Robert spoiled them with duck breast and lamb and hunted them in the woods and marshes of Edisto. It was as good a dog's life as I could imagine.

That was the first year I ever saw Sullivan's Island's celebrated Fourth of July parade. It was a ragtag, joyous, seat-of-the-pants affair, with decorated golf carts and a motorcycle or two from the Isle of Palms, and the island fire trucks and ambulance, sirens wailing, and many children. All with dogs. The island dogs, most of whom knew each other from their nocturnal garbage-can scoutings, pranced along beside their young owners, decked out in flowers and tiny flags and ribbons. There was every kind of dog imaginable, and they were all unified by the pride of the day and the joy of belonging to Sullivan's Island. Our dogs did not march, but when the fireworks display arced and spat into the blue night sky, they howled in uniform accompaniment, their anthem to our country's birthday. Some of them lived in Charleston homes older by years than that.

So, the summer of the dogs. And the summer of the light.

The island light that year was simply magical, at least to me, who had never seen it so before. It was honey gold and soft, and so clear that everything—Charleston in the distance, Fort Sumter nearer by, the great tankers and freighters that passed, the navy's eerie, death-silent black nuclear submarines that occasionally broke the water off the beach—seemed to be outlined in crisp, deep blue. I remember no heat shimmering from the beach, no mist, no fog at night. At least when Lewis and I were there, the moon and stars were as distinct as a night-sky chart in a child's classroom, and the black, white-creamed water often danced with phosphorus. Lewis and I went into it late one night, naked and shivering a little, and felt the silken water alive with the soft hiss of sea fire. Afterward, we made love behind the first dune line. There was nothing else for it.

"This is pure heaven," I said on the porch, after a long August lunch. "I've never seen such weather, not that lasted so long. No wonder everybody comes to Sullivan's."

"It's not like this often, not by a long shot," Henry said. "August is usually just as miserable out here as it is in Charleston. You can just get wet quicker. This is unusual. I don't remember a summer just like it, do you, Lewis? Camilla?"

"I mainly remember mosquitoes and sand-burs," Lewis said.

"I remember Daddy saying that the old-timers said a summer like this was a weather breeder," Camilla said, not looking up from her knitting. "But I never saw much weather bred out here except thunderstorms and heat waves."

"You'll know something's coming if you see the Gray Man," Simms said, grinning.

"What's that?" I said. Somehow I did not like the sound of the words.

"Nobody quite knows," Simms said. "A man in a long gray cloak is supposed to appear on the beach if there's a bad storm coming. When they see him, people know to prepare."

"If I saw him, I'd prepare to get out of here," I said, shivering.

"Simms, you know that's only on Pawley's

Island," Lila chided. "Nobody's ever seen him anywhere else."

I looked at her. I had expected her to dismiss the Gray Man as a child's ghost story, but her face was serious.

"Do you believe in him, Lila?" I said.

"Well, I don't *not* believe in him," she said slowly. "Daddy has a friend on Pawley's who claims to have seen him, and two days later there was a tornado there. Lots of people have seen him. I don't know if there have always been storms, though."

Driving home that night, with the silver pepper of the stars fading out as the lights of Charleston rolled up over the bridge, I said to Lewis, "Do you believe in him? The Gray Man?"

"Not really, but I don't want to give him up, either. I can't think of anywhere else but the Low Country that has a Gray Man."

We were all at the beach house that Labor Day, and while we were there, Henry finally persuaded me to go with him on one of his missions of mercy, this time to the mountains of central Mexico.

"It's not close to anywhere," he said. "It's a terribly poor and backward region, and for years the only health care has been a bankrupt government clinic in a town fifty miles away, with only a burro path connecting the two, and that covered by rock slides and cave-ins half the year. But there's a new road now, just opened, and it puts the village within range of a bigger national highway that leads to several larger towns. A Dr. Mendoza has established a little hospital there, or hopes to, and found a couple of nurses and some funding for equipment. He got in touch with our folks in Washington, and asked for help from whoever could come. I was up, so said I'd be there. Now that there's some access to other, more populated areas, a setup on the order of Outreach—not nearly so sophisticated, of course, but a start—would be salvation for the village. Anny, please come. I can't pay you, but I can guarantee you a clean bed and three squares a day, and all the backup I can give you. There'll be some other docs there; I don't know who, or what their specialties are. But we'll have company, and you might enjoy the native people. I always have. There's an interpreter along, too. How about it? You like burritos?"

I thought of my last board meeting, which had been consumed entirely by a discussion of our PR effort to acquire gifts and services. I had nearly drifted into sleep during the excruciating minutiae of our current fund-raising confection, a dinner dance at the Kiawah Island home of a board member who had just redecorated and built a large pavilion out over the dunes, facing the sea. The gala's working title was the "Outreach Beach Ball."

"I have some vacation time coming," I said to Henry. "I think I'll go. I'm being Kiawahed to death right now."

Only then did I look at Lewis, questioningly.

"I love burritos," he said. "You got space for an old bone man?"

Henry laughed and hugged me and pounded Lewis on the bicep.

"Did you know that the mountains of Mexico have more poisonous scorpions than any other region in the world?" Fairlie said, swirling wine around in her glass. She was smiling, though. Through some alchemy, she and I had become friends, to the point where we could tease each other without wondering if there was a barb embedded.

"No wonder they need doctors," I said. "Why don't you come, Fairlie? I could use somebody to go to the ladies' room with."

"They got no ladies' rooms," Fairlie said, grinning. "Besides, what would I do? Teach them to dance?"

We all laughed, and Camilla smiled at me.

"Good for you, Anny," she said. "I've always worried about Henry on these little sorties. I keep thinking he might run off with a fiery señorita or something, and we'll never see him again. You can keep watch."

"He's already got a fiery señorita," Fairlie said, baring her teeth ferociously at Camilla, who laughed outright.

"So he does," she said.

That evening, just after sunset, I walked down the beach with only Gladys for company. The day had been blisteringly hot, but there was fog coming in over the dunes from the waterway, which meant, I knew, a change of weather. All of a sudden the empty beach and the warm water swirling around my ankles felt poignant, elegiac. This summer was ending. It made me sad.

I turned to go back. The fog had reached the top dune line and blurred the beach house. Its lit windows burned cheerful holes in the mist. All at once I could not wait to get off the empty beach and into the house. I started across to the steps to the wooden walkway, whistling to Gladys. She came larruping happily behind me. Both our feet slipped in the dry, shifting sand.

I looked up to see Camilla on the top of the dune line, a little way from the house. She wore her old raincoat, and it blew about her. I wondered what she was doing out in the fog. She always said that it made her bones hurt.

"Hey!" I called. "What are you doing up there?"

She did not answer, and I cupped my hands to throw my voice farther.

"Camilla?"

Again, there was no answer. I turned to make sure Gladys was with me, and when I turned back, Camilla had gone inside. Gladys and I bounded up the steps and into the house as if pursued.

They were all sitting around the unnecessary but beautiful fire, drinking wine. I loved them suddenly. Loved them all with a weight that hurt my heart.

"You've got wet hair," Lewis said.

"There's a big fog bank out there, in case you haven't noticed," I said. "Camilla, what were you doing out there on the dunes? I yelled, but I guess you didn't hear me."

She looked at me.

"I haven't been outside," she said. "Not this whole afternoon."

"I was sure it was you. It looked like that old raincoat of yours, the one with the hood."

"I gave that to the Salvation Army last spring," she said.

There was a silence.

"You saw the Gray Man," Simms said, leering. "Gonna be a storm sure as gun's iron."

"Oh, I did not," I said peevishly. "It was probably somebody up there looking for a dog or something."

"Nope. The Gray Man," Charlie jumped in. "Come all the way down from Pawley's just to see you. We better batten down."

On the way home, the fog thick and white by now, I said to Lewis, "I did see somebody on the dunes. Somebody real. Why does everybody have to carry on about the damned Gray Man?"

"Teasing you," he said briefly. He did not say any more.

"Lewis, you can't possibly think . . . "

"I guess not," he said.

We did not speak again until we got home.

"Want cocoa?" he said.

"I think I'd just like to go to bed. I've got to get up early if I'm going to arrange to take two weeks off."

"Well, I think I'll read awhile," he said, and kissed me on the forehead. "Be up later."

I lay awake for a long time, even after he came up, even after I heard his breathing deepen into sleep. I had wanted amused denial, fond ridicule, and, I realized, reassurance. Their absence felt like hunger.

* * *

Ciudad Real means "royal city," and it is difficult
to imagine that any one of its 355 inhabitants
gives much thought to the irony of that. It lies in
the north-central state of Chihuahua, huddled in
a gap in the Sierra Madre Occidental range,
approximately halfway between the small city of
Madera and the sea. Until very recently, it was
connected by road only to the slightly larger village of Oteros, whose own road led to the spectacular Barranco del Cobre, or Copper Canyon, and
stopped. There were footpaths over the mountain
to small towns on the Sonoran coast, but it was
not possible to get goods and crops for trading
and selling over them, and the great Copper
Canyon Railway that connects the arid mountainous interior of northern Mexico to the Pacific was
beyond the means of most of the villagers. Few of
them harvested crops or fabricated goods anyway. It was a desperately poor little hamlet set
among stunted oaks and stubby cacti. A cloud of
dust hung over it perpetually. There was a small,
crumbling adobe church, a cantina with rooms
above it for the thin teenage prostitutes and their
guests, a sort of store/gas station affair that sold
fly-specked canned goods and American snacks
and sodas and the occasional gallon of elderly
gas. There was a telephone in the cantina and
store, but none of the horrendously dirty and
dilapidated houses seemed to have one, and the
only TV aerial I saw was on the roof of the cantina. In its sun-smitten little central square, the
fountain was dry and the market stalls all but
empty. A few merchants sold thin, dispirited

chickens and a skinny, cold-eyed goat or two, and
bits of lumpish pottery, and baskets of wilting
vegetables and fruit that grew in the gardens
behind the homes. English, we found, was spoken
only by the unkempt priest, the doctor who had
summoned us, and the bar mistress of the cantina, who was also its madam. To get there from
Charleston, you flew to Atlanta and from there to
Mexico City and from there to Chihuahua, took a
battered bus from Chihuahua to Madera, and
depended for the remainder of the journey to
Ciudad Real on the kindness of strangers.

We came into Madera at three in the afternoon
on September the eighth, dirtier and more tired
than I, at least, had ever been in my life, and were
met by the aforementioned Dr. Lorenzo Mendoza,
in a Land Rover that made Lewis's Range Rover
look like a Rolls-Royce limousine. He was a short,
stocky, swarthy man with the darting energy of a
Tasmanian devil and a gold-starred smile as wide
as his entire face.

"My Americans are here!" he shouted, and
hugged us all in turn. He hesitated when he came
to me, said, "You are a nurse, perhaps? Wonderful!" and continued his hugging without listening
for an answer. He smelled powerfully of stale
sweat, but so did we. I so badly wanted a bath and
a nap that I would have gotten into the Land
Rover with the world's gamiest Sasquatch.
Wedged in between Henry and a gastroenterologist from Houston, I found myself trembling with
insane, suppressed laughter. I felt Henry's shoulder shaking and knew he was desperately trying
to contain laughter, too. I did not look at him; that

would have been death for both of us. In the seat
ahead of me, Lewis slept. He could sleep anywhere. I hated him momentarily. The gastroenterologist stared straight ahead. Two general
surgeons from Fort Worth cowered in the front
seat with Dr. Mendoza, being bombarded with
shotgunned information.

The new road, the good doctor said, connected
Ciudad Real to Madera, from there to Chihuahua,
and then on to Highway 40, which wound its way
across the waistline of the country and entered
Texas at McAllen.

"Now we are in reach of many health care facilities, and we can receive supplies," he cried gaily.
"I put up my little hospital and some temporary
housing for the staff even before the bulldozers
rolled out. It is small, but it will grow, and it is not
uncomfortable, I don't think. With my new
friends to teach new techniques to me and one or
two new associates coming in, and even a nurse
to instruct my nursing staff, we will soon be a distinguished regional facility."

And he laughed, a trifle hysterically. The two
surgeons grinned desperately. Lewis snored.
Henry snorted.

"Don't you *dare*," I hissed furiously at him. The
gastroenterologist did not move his eyes from the
road ahead.

We caromed through deserted little Ciudad
Real, scattering dust and chickens and a few
skinny black dogs. A fat woman with impossibly
lush, lacquered black hair waved from a window
over the cantina—the madam, I learned later,

Señora Diaz. In the entire two weeks we were there, I never saw hair nor hide of Señor Diaz. He was very much alive, Dr. Mendoza assured us, though he was seldom seen.

"It is just that he is shy," he said.

We careened around a curve overhung by a huge boulder, and there was the hospital of Dr. Mendoza. The distinguished regional medical facility. It consisted of three brand-new double-wide trailers placed side by side in a meager grove of scrub oaks and connected by a wooden walkway. A low wooden barracks affair sat a little behind the trailers, with a few folding plastic chairs set about it in the dirt and an outside shower affixed to one end. I wondered, crazily, how he had gotten the trailers and the material for the barracks over the new road.

In front of me, Lewis woke up.

"Holy shit," he said.

"Yes!" Dr. Mendoza shouted in ecstatic agreement. "It is truly holy shit, is it not?"

It was a shell-shocked and surreal sort of evening. The American doctors would be housed in the barracks—"brand new, still smelling of sweet new wood!"—but no one had told him I would be coming. The nurses had lodging with a couple of villagers, but he did not think there was any more available. We would go and have our dinner at the cantina, and give thought to the matter of where I was to sleep.

"A clean bed and three squares, huh?" I glared at Henry. "Maybe there's a goat shed around somewhere I could share."

"I'm sorry, Anny," he mumbled. "I've never been on one of these things that didn't have some kind of hotel or motel or something."

"You damned well ought to be sorry, Henry, my man," Lewis said ominously. But I could see his lips twitching. It was clear to all three of us, even before the arrangements were made, that I would be sleeping upstairs over the cantina with the three adolescent prostitutes.

"But by far the best room," Dr. Mendoza assured me earnestly. "It is for the ones who stay three or four hours. There is a television set and flowered sheets."

"You could come out of this a wealthy woman," Lewis said. And we all burst into laughter. It was clear that the surgeons and the gastroenterologist did not get the joke.

Looking back, I can picture those two weeks in Ciudad Real as if I were watching them on a screen. They have the surreal vividness of a fever dream: details stand out as if limned in light. I can remember the sights, sounds, smells, tastes so clearly that I become lost in them. Almost anything can call them back: the brassy wail of cantina music, the taste of dust, the smell of new wood in the barracks and old sweat and perfume in my seraglio bedroom, the taste of warm beef and tacos. I do not wish to summon that time; in many ways it was ghastly in the extreme, and pales utterly beside some of the beautiful places Lewis took me in the years after that. Nevertheless, there it is, lodged in my subconscious like a bone in a dog's throat. I think it's because those weeks were so absolutely self-contained, so totally without context. Nothing—not time, not the world—seemed to intrude upon them. That hyperreality is still a source of both pleasure and pain to me.

Nothing, absolutely nothing, went as we had supposed it would. The first morning we went into the hospital's minimal little waiting room and found it boiling with the miserable humanity of Ciudad Real. Patient old men and women; wailing children; vastly pregnant women; stoic, sullen men with racking coughs or bloody rags wrapped around an arm or a leg; even a black dog, tail thumping under the receptionist's desk. If there had been a receptionist. The two promised doctors did not appear.

"I have had word that they have been detained in Guatemala," Dr. Mendoza said. "Some foolishness at the border, no doubt."

"Those docs can kiss their asses good-bye," Lewis muttered to Henry.

The three nurses, rubbing sleep from their eyes, were short and squat, with Indio blood apparent in their opaque black eyes and slightly flattened noses. They wore proper nurses' uniforms, none too clean, and did not speak a syllable of English. The interpreter had missed his plane to Chihuahua and was considering renting a car.

"We can kiss his ass good-bye, too," Henry growled.

"I didn't realize there would be a clinic," Lewis said as amiably as I have ever heard him. It was an ominous sound. "It's going to be hard to share techniques and suggestions if we're busy all day treating walk-in patients. I was prepared to show you some new orthopedic surgery, and I know that Dr. McKenzie has some new wrinkles in cardiology. Most of these folks look like a nurse or a family physician could handle them."

"Oh, but you will treat and I will watch, and then I will show the two doctors when they come," Dr. Mendoza said happily. "And as you see, we have nurses." He gestured at the three young women. They gazed back with blank, obsidian stares.

"But they have no English," one of the general surgeons said, in a tight, constipated voice. "And unless I'm mistaken, none of us has adequate Spanish. Who is going to interpret?"

Dr. Mendoza looked hopefully at me.

"No, I'm sorry," I said. "I'm not good at all with Spanish. I'm really here to help you set up a program of resources available to your patients."

Dr. Mendoza puzzled for a moment, and then spat out something in rapid-fire Spanish to a young girl who looked relatively mobile. She left the trailer and trudged back toward the town.

"I have just the answer," the doctor said. "Mrs. Diaz speaks wonderful English. She will help us out."

And so it was that the first day in the hospital of Dr. Mendoza, the madam of the local house of joy served as interpreter and sometime disciplinarian, and did it very well indeed.

"What will happen when you have to go back to your daytime work?" I said to her as we sat, wiping sweat from our faces, in the folding plastic chairs outside the barracks. I had been drafted to serve as receptionist and appointments secretary, and that is what I did until the day we left. Almost immediately I liked this big, vital woman with luxuriant dyed hair and enough lipstick to frost a cake. She was intelligent, industrious, matter-of-fact, and virtually unflappable. I thought she was sorely wasted as a small-town madam, though I did not say it.

Carmella Diaz grinned. She had a fine gold tooth.

"My no-account *esposo* can get his sorry ass out of bed and keep the cantina," she said tranquilly. "Work really doesn't start until nighttime, and it don't take much to keep those hyenas in line. By the time they want one of my girls, they're too drunk to cause trouble, anyway."

I felt my cheeks burn, and then laughed. Why not? It was the way of things in Ciudad Real.

We triaged and treated as best we could until past eight that evening. Fevers, diarrhea, broken bones, cuts from God knows what, endless coughs and colds, one or two real medical problems that, without facilities and assured nursing care, the doctors could not handle.

"You need to evaluate every case and get the ones in real trouble over to the nearest big town," Lewis said at the end of that interminable day. "I can't operate here without surgical nurses and equipment and no antibiotic except penicillin. There are many good new ones; I'll make you a list. And anesthetics, too. You can't use the same one for everybody. You'll need an internal medicine man immediately; he can tell you what supplies you're apt to need. And you'll need a highly trained head nurse. Nursing care is going to make the difference out here."

"But here they are," Dr. Mendoza said, indicating the three young women, who had not moved.

"But who's going to train them?" one of the general surgeons asked.

"You doctors?" Dr. Mendoza said hopefully.

"No. Out of the question," Henry said. "I wish you'd been more specific about your problems when you got in touch with our people in America. You don't need new techniques. You need trained clinicians."

"And here you are," the doctor said, beaming.

The next morning the silent gastroenterologist said curtly, "Boil the goddamn water," and hired the husband of Señora Diaz to drive him to Madera. The two surgeons lasted until Wednesday. At this rate, I thought, Mr. Diaz is going to be a rich man.

Somehow it did not occur to the three of us to leave. There was a staggering load of illness to handle, and we did our best, day after day. Henry and Lewis swabbed throats, lanced boils, listened to chests, sewed up lacerations, thumped pregnant stomachs, handed out aspirin and vitamins and what little penicillin they had left. I held babies for shots and wrote down appointments, and learned to give injections. The three nurses watched it all impassively.

In the evenings, so tired that it was hardly possible to stumble up the hill, we retired to the cantina. It was a rough, smoky place, with a kind of savagery not far under the surface, but the patrons soon became used to us, or too drunk to bristle like roosters at the usurping gringos, and the food was not bad. If it ran heavily to chicken and what I thought might be goat, but did not ask, it soon ceased to matter. After the first four or five offers for my services, Carmella Diaz's blistering tongue got the message across that I was not for sale. I don't know what the patrons thought when I kissed Lewis and Henry on the cheek and went up to bed at the ridiculous hour of nine o'clock, even before the *putas* came to work.

"The word is out that you're some kind of fertility goddess," Lewis smirked.

"God forbid," I said.

I seldom found it difficult to fall asleep, lying cocooned in my floral sheets. I had long since given up on the television. There was only one fizzing channel, and it was in Spanish. It seemed to be football. No English newspapers or magazines made their way into Ciudad Real.

"You can send them all your old office magazines," I said, and they laughed. We laughed a great deal in those two weeks, Lewis and Henry and I. Our time there had a kind of comrades-in-arms feeling to it, as I imagined must have been engendered during the blitz of London. I felt skin close to both of them, as if we were a single unit.

I was sitting with Carmella in the plastic chairs, toward the end of our stay, thinking that I would miss her very much. She asked me why I had come to Ciudad Real and I told her about Outreach, and what it did.

"But I don't think you're far enough along for anything like that," I said. "Maybe when the hospital is fully staffed . . . "

"So you need someone to find out what people need and then get it for free," she said, going straight to the heart of the matter.

"That's it exactly," I said.

"I can do that," she said dismissively. "Many wealthy men will be coming to our village now that the new road is open. People have heard of my girls. I will remind them that our people need many things they could supply, far more than their wives need to know about their evenings here."

It was a measure of my assimilation that I said, "Perfect. I couldn't have done better myself."

On our last night in the village, Lewis gave Carmella fifty American dollars and followed me up the stairs to my room.

"They'll be talking about it for years," he said. "Wondering what kind of woman you are to cost a man fifty dollars a night."

We lay in bed, my cheek against his heart, listening to the music drifting up from the cantina, and the thin howls of ersatz lust the three young women employed. They were invariably the same: a piercing "*Aye, mi Dios!*" followed by a series of yips, as from a small dog.

"Shall we?" Lewis said, pulling me over him.

"Yip-yip-yip!" I cried.

Before dawn of the day we were to leave, Dr. Mendoza wrung our hands and pronounced himself ready for any kind of medical emergency, and capered away into his hospital. Carmella came to hug us good-bye.

"I will let you know about this outreach," she said.

Henry and Lewis and I walked to the Land Rover with our arms around one another's shoulders.

"What was all that about?" Henry said.

"Blackmail," I said serenely.

When we roared out of the square, there was nothing left behind but a cloud of dust and Carmella, faintly visible through it, waving.

We slept most of the way from Chihuahua to Mexico City, and then to Atlanta. When we came into the Atlanta terminal, everything seemed too bright and too big and too loud, a sensory assault. I felt thickheaded, stupid. It was like coming up from underwater.

Henry handed the ticket agent our tickets to Charleston, and the man looked at us strangely.

"You're kidding, right?"

"No, why?" Henry said.

"Where have you all been? Charleston's closed down tight. Hurricane Hugo went through two nights ago and just flattened it. Part of it's under martial law."

It was September 23, 1989, and all our lives had changed.

4

LATER, PEOPLE CAME to call Hugo the most destructive hurricane of that century. Despite the fact that Andrew, which ground up and spat out the Miami area a few years later, was technically a more destructive and expensive storm, Low Country people knew in their hearts that Hugo, in an odd way their own hurricane, changed more than lives, it changed a way of life.

Oh, Charleston and the islands did eventually clean up and rebuild and paint and fix up, so that the casual visitor saw only what historians had always said about us: the most beautiful historic district in the country. The horse-drawn tour wagons rolled again, and the tour buses clotted the narrow downtown streets, and flocks of drifting visitors blocked driveways and streets, led by straw-hatted long-skirted mother hens of approved local guides.

But to this day, Charlestonians speak of "before Hugo" and "after Hugo." From the morning of September 22, 1989, vulnerability walked with us on our narrow, beautiful streets as it never had before. Beauty and gentility no longer protected us. No one forgot what Hugo had done. We knew another frivolously named monster could come unbidden to us out of the waters off Cape Verde, where the great Atlantic hurricanes are born. Everywhere, in those first days, people walked with the uneasy need to keep looking over their shoulders.

That day in Atlanta, at the Delta counter, we all stared at the reservations clerk blankly, as you do at one who has demonstrated some patent insanity. Then we began babbling at him.

"What's left?" "How do you get there if you can't fly?" "Are there many fatalities? Many hurt?" "What's the worst damage? What is it: wind? water?" He lifted his hands wearily. He had obviously answered this question before.

"That's all I know," he said. "That you can't fly in there. The rest is hearsay. About the National Guard and the looting and all. There's a newsstand over there. I'm sure some of the papers will have something about it."

We looked at each other out of white, empty-eyed faces. Then Lewis and Henry dashed for the bank of telephones across the concourse and I headed for the newsstand. As I ran, I muttered over and over to myself, a witless mantra, "Let the beach house be all right. Let the beach house be all right." And then, guiltily, "Let our families and our houses be all right. Please let us get through this."

Lewis came back and we sat in the waiting area devouring the *Atlanta Journal-Constitution.* It had little detail and much sensationalism. Devastation. No power perhaps for weeks. Gas leaks, downed live wires, severe flooding from a seventeen-foot storm surge that occurred with the high tides. Everywhere, trees down, windows out, roofs torn off, whole houses demolished. Looting in the downtown business area. Utilities workers from eight states pouring into the city. Food and water situations desperate. President Bush declares disaster area. Boats tossed onto highways and jammed among houses.

Whole beachfront sections obliterated.

I began to cry. Lewis put his arms around me and rested his chin on the top of my head.

"Wait," he said. "Wait till we know. Henry got the last free phone. Downtown has stood for three hundred years. We can clean up a few tree limbs and shingles. Just wait and see if Henry can get through."

Soon we saw Henry's tall figure, incongruously still clad in scrub pants and a wrinkled Hawaiian shirt and sandals, loping across the waiting area. People turned to stare at him. One or two drew back from him. My sobs turned to hiccups of insane laughter.

"He looks like Ichabod Crane," I choked.

"Got through," he said. "Apparently a good bit of south of Broad still has phone service. I think we're in the same grid as the hospitals, and their phones are up. I called Fairlie first, and then Charlie at the hospital. It could be worse, I guess."

We looked at him, breaths held.

"Bedon's Alley is pretty much okay. Fairlie didn't leave, but she said it was the most horrifying night she'd ever spent. Camilla stayed with her while Charlie was at the hospital. Tradd Street has some trees down, but their house kept its roof and the storm surge just missed it. Lila and Simms weren't quite so lucky. The Battery took a direct hit. But the house stood, even though there was about a foot of water in their downstairs, and they lost their windows. Lewis, I think you've got a mess on the Battery. Two live oaks through the roof, and the portico and veranda gone. I don't know any more than that."

"It's the historical society's problem now, not mine," Lewis said wearily. "What do you hear about Bull Street?"

"Nobody Charlie knows has gotten over that way yet, but the College of Charleston is pretty much okay, and you're right there. They got the storm surge on the ground floors, but your house is set pretty far up. A few trees down. That's all I know . . ."

"The storm surge . . . ," I said. I had never thought of that. I had always assumed that the great teeth of a hurricane would be wind.

"It went clear across the peninsula," Henry said. "Boats from the city marina are sitting on Lockwood Avenue. Low-lying streets are underwater. When it receded, the mud and debris left behind were unbelievable. I don't think any of us got that. But Lewis . . . Charlie thinks that maybe that basement operating suite of yours flooded. Everything along Rutledge did."

I looked at Lewis. He looked off into the middle distance and then sighed.

"There go my insurance rates," he said. "Well, that's what it's for, I guess. What about Edisto? And Wadmalaw?"

"I don't know. Charlie said he's heard that the

people over on the river side were safe, but the beach got blasted. You and Simms might be okay."

Finally, because no one else would say it, I did.

"What about the beach house?"

Henry looked down.

"I don't know. Nobody does. The Ben Sawyer bridge is completely out and the National Guard is not letting anybody onto the islands. But Charlie said there were some aerial photos in the *Post and Courier*, and it looked . . . like there had never been houses there. Just gone. Bare beach, with the dunes flattened out. But he said he heard that there were a few houses that were completely untouched. There must have been some mini-tornadoes, to flatten one house and not the one next to it. People are getting over to the Isle of Palms on a ferry, but Sullivan's Island isn't letting anybody on yet."

He paused, and then said, "Fairlie said that Leroy came walking up to the house the next morning in tears, and said that the police made him leave our place at the last minute, but that he hadn't been able to find Gladys, and they wouldn't let him look. That's not so good. The place lies low."

"Oh, Henry," I said, the tears flooding back. Beautiful, foolish, loving Gladys. The best dove dog in the Low Country.

Lewis said, "I'm sorry, Henry. She could be fine, though."

"Sure she could," Henry said, and turned away from us. "If the bastards would just let us go over there and check. I'm going when we get back. What are they going to do? Shoot me?"

"I'll go with you," Lewis said, in a roughened voice.

We went out of the waiting room then, and went down to rent a car and go home to Charleston.

We said little on the five-hour drive. There seemed to be nothing to say. The vivid, surreal past two weeks had no place where we were headed. And the place we were headed had no reality. What you are unable to imagine you cannot easily speak of.

It is warm, even hot, in the Southeast in September. Outside, no color had tinged the leaves; they seemed dusty and used looking. Truck traffic was steady and maddening. Inside the rental car, the air-conditioning labored mightily, washing us in stale, frigid air. I felt desperate for sleep, but could not rest.

Henry drove the whole way. When Lewis or I tried to relieve him, he said, "I need something to concentrate on." So did we all, but we sensed that Henry needed it most. Gladys was a piece of his heart.

When we got within fifty miles of the Low Country, we began to see Hugo's stigmata. At first, it was simply fallen branches and the litter of leaves, and water standing in roadside ditches. Then the first fallen trees, pines with shallow roots, mostly. On the flat plain that bordered the coast, whole forests were down, leveled as if by a giant scythe. Fifteen miles out of Charleston we began to see collapsed houses, caved-in roofs, blasted windows. Wet furniture stood in yards. Many houses were open to the sky. Everywhere, trees were down across the secondary roads, though the interstate had been cleared. We saw no evidence of people. There were few cars; the ones we saw were mostly mangled.

We had come down Interstate 26. Long before it curved into East Bay, we could see that the devastation was past our imagining. When we finally made the turn toward East Bay, at seven o'clock in the evening, it was to see phalanxes of National Guardsmen stopping motorists, streets littered with branches and debris, power lines swinging crazily from downed poles, silent storefronts with their windows boarded, if they had windows at all. Many were roofless. The harbor warehouse facilities on our left were empty. Everything was silent.

There were no lights anywhere.

A young guardsman stopped us and looked into the car.

"What's your business here?" he said. "Curfew is in an hour."

Henry handed him the physician's identification that most doctors keep in their cars, and Lewis pulled his out, too. The young man studied them and then said, "Where will you be going?"

"Bedon's Alley," Henry said. The guardsman looked at his clipboard.

"You can go all the way down East Bay," he said. "It's been cleared. Watch out for Calhoun, though. It's flooded. Looks like there's lots of trees and debris blocking upper Tradd and Church Streets."

"What about Elliot?" Henry said.

The guardsman looked again.

"Seems to be open. But watch out. There's emergency vehicles all over the place, and they don't stop for intersections. Plus you've got a lot of gawkers wandering around."

We said nothing. Those gawkers were our friends and neighbors grieving for the mutilation of their city.

It was in a still, eerie green dusk that we turned onto Elliot Street, crept slowly through a couple of turns, and drove down Bedon's Alley to Henry and Fairlie's house. On the entire trip we did not hear a sound, or see a light. All windows seemed to be boarded. Leaves and branches were everywhere. As we pulled up to the huge old stucco pile that dominated the alley, a pungent smell reached us.

"Christ, that smells like barbecue," Lewis said. "Has somebody gone nuts?"

Henry pointed silently. Plumes of fragrant smoke were rising against the milky sky. They seemed to be coming from the back gardens of several of the houses. Through the iron gates we could see people milling around.

"I know," I said. It was the first thing I had been able to say since we turned onto East Bay. "They're all cooking their meat. None of the freezers would be working."

"It smells very festive," Henry said tightly.

"Well, why not cook it and share?" I said.

"What else are you going to do with it? Feed it to
the dogs?"

He did not reply, and I winced.

"Henry, I'm sorry."

He made a don't-mention-it motion with his
hand and braked the car to a stop in front of his
house. It, too, was boarded up and silent like the
others, but in an instant the massive old door was
thrown open, and Fairlie whirled down the steps
toward us. Henry unfolded himself from the
driver's seat and took one long stride and gathered her into his arms. She buried her head in the
hollow of his shoulder, and they stood that way
for a long time. I could see the last of the sun
turning the crown of her head to flame. She wore
cutoffs and a halter and flip-flops. Even at seven-
thirty, the car's thermometer had read ninety-two
degrees. Behind them, on the top step of the
house, Camilla stood, her face pale and tranquil, a
little smile tugging at the corners of her curly
mouth. She, too, was in shorts.

We got slowly out of the car, our limbs
cramped, and felt the wet smack of the heat. It
was no hotter than in Ciudad Real, I thought, but
it was much, much wetter. And then I thought,
How could I have thought of Ciudad Real in this
moment?

Camilla pattered down the stairs and came to
Lewis and me and put her arms around us. We
stood silently, hugging. I could feel the lovely tensile strength of her long arms, the bird's ribs in
her slender torso.

She pushed us a little away and looked at us.

"Thank God you're here," she said softly. "And thank God you didn't have to go through this."

Her coppery eyes were wet.

She turned then to Henry and Fairlie. They had broken apart and were looking up the block, at the tattered roofs and broken tree limbs. Camilla went silently to Henry and put her arms around him and pressed her face into his shoulder as Fairlie had done. She said nothing, nor did Henry. He just held her, smoothing back the strands of hair that were pasted to her forehead with sweat.

"It will be all right, Cam," Henry said presently, and she stepped back and smiled up at him. Tears stood on her cheeks.

"It will now," she said.

We sat for a long time in Fairlie and Henry's back garden. It was larger than most of Charleston's pocket gardens and comfortably littered with mismatched chairs and a round wrought-iron table and a hammock on a stand. It was also littered with palm fronds and drying leaves stripped from the live oaks that sheltered it, and branches, and even a couple of shingles. Lewis and I had sat here many times before, in candlelight, with the Scrubs lounging contentedly around after one of Fairlie's amazingly awful cold-pasta suppers. Because it was so large, both house and garden had become an in-town rallying spot for the Scrubs. I loved the mossy, shaggy old garden. It would never be on a tour.

This night, we sat in the light of a dozen guttering candles and a kerosene lantern. There was no light anywhere but that of other flickering candles along the alley, and the huge white moon that rode above the wounded rooftops. Even without electric lights, we could see quite clearly in the drenching moonlight.

"It's as if God or whoever is in charge of hurricanes is trying to make it up to us," Fairlie said. She shook her fist heavenward.

"No dice," she shouted.

We had eaten perfectly grilled beef tenderloin and the last of Fairlie's John's Island tomatoes, and had drunk quite a lot of burgundy, brought over by Simms, who had a wine cellar in his Battery basement.

"Or did," he said wryly. "I found these floating in the basement. There were a couple more on the first floor, sitting on the sofa. The former sofa, I should say. The surge left them there. There's a lot more if anybody wants to snorkel for it."

"I hate even thinking about your beautiful furniture," I said. "Most of it belonged to your grandparents, didn't it?"

"Tyrell and a couple of the guys from the plant and I got most of it upstairs," Simms said. "We boarded up the windows, too, but we might as well have used Kleenex. We're luckier than most of Charleston. I have a crew ready to get to work in the morning. We ought to be able to get back in there in a few days."

Lila and Simms were staying with Henry and Fairlie. We stayed, too, that first night. We had no idea if we could get onto Bull Street, and I was suddenly and totally exhausted. Even as we spoke of damages and changes and nevermores, I nodded off.

"Poor sweetie," Camilla said. "You've come a long way today, haven't you?"

Lewis brushed my chaotic hair back and said, "This time last night she was asleep in the best room in a Mexican ho' house. Had a TV, by God, and flowered sheets. Pretty fancy, even if it didn't do to think where those sheets had been."

Camilla laughed her rich, throaty laugh.

"I can't wait to hear about that. In fact, I can't wait to hear about the whole trip. Come on, Lewis. We need something to distract us."

"Another night, I promise," Lewis said. "There's something we need to do, and it may take a while."

"What on earth can you do with no lights and all this junk in the streets?" Lila said. In her lap, Sugar woke up and gave a peremptory treble bark. It was answered from somewhere in the top regions by deeper barks.

"Boy and Girl are staying with us, too," Fairlie said. "It's what we talked about out at the beach, isn't it? All of us together under one roof. Maybe we could just stay here."

There was a sheen of tears in her eyes, and I knew she was thinking of Gladys, our missing family member. I gave her hand a squeeze, and she smiled damply at me.

Henry and Lewis and Simms stood up. Henry spoke. "I talked to Charlie, and he said they're going to need us two or three straight days and nights," he said. "People are breaking legs and having heart attacks all over the place, trying to clean up this damage. I told him if we came in tonight we'd drop dead of fatigue, and he said to take the night off and begin early in the morning."

"He's the one who's going to drop dead if he doesn't let up," Camilla said. "I haven't seen him since the night Hugo hit, and I know he isn't sleeping more than an hour or two at a time. His voice sounds awful, all breathless and faint. Send him home, hear?"

"We will. Now listen, y'all," Lewis said. "We're going over to the island and take a look at the damage. There's not going to be any other time for it. I think . . . we've got to know."

"You what?" Fairlie squealed. "How the hell do you think you're going to get over there? The damned bridge is out. The National Guard is patrolling regularly. The very least they'd do is arrest you. I heard they have orders to shoot looters. Have you completely lost your minds? What are you going to do, swim?"

"No," said Simms. "Sail."

Camilla and Lila and I simply stared at them. Then Lila said, "Have we still got a boat?"

"We have the old one," Simms said. "I moved the *Venus* way back up the Ashley River, and she should be safe. But the *Flea* is still bobbing around the yacht club dock. God knows why the club didn't blow away, but it didn't. They did a good job of securing the boats."

"The *Flea* . . . ," Lila said. "But it's so tiny, Simms. And anyway, how do you think you can

get onto the island without a patrol seeing you? I
don't like this at all."

"She'll hold the three of us," he said. "And if
you remember, we painted her red when we gave
her to the kids. Even got a red sail. At night it
shows up black."

"Well, y'all don't," Fairlie snapped. "What are
you going to do, go in blackface?"

"Yes," Henry said.

"But with no lights—"

"Fairlie," Simms said, "I've been sailing that
stretch from the yacht club to the island all my
life. I could do it blindfolded. And the moon is
almost as bright as day. We're just going to ease
up to Henry's dock and then walk over to the
beach house, and come right back. But we need to
know."

My heart became a lump of dirty ice. No,
Lewis, I said in my head. It doesn't matter. None
of it matters but that you're safe.

But when he looked over at me and raised an
inquiring red eyebrow, I smiled. It was what my
brother would have called a chickenshit smile.

"Boys' night out," I said, and they laughed a little. Presently they went upstairs in the big house
and came back down in dark pants and wind-
breakers. They wore dark deck shoes, too, and
dark socks.

We stared. They looked like a Mafia hit group.

"Simms brought them over for us," Henry said.
"I'm supplying the blackface."

And he held out a tin of black shoe polish. Fairlie
and Camilla and I began to laugh. Lila only stared.

"Well, go paint your faces, kemo sabes, and let us see our braves off," Camilla said.

"We'll put it on down at the dock," Henry growled, but she took the tin away from him and sat him down in front of her.

"Be still," she said. "I'm an expert at making up little boys for Halloween. You won't know yourself." And she began to smear Henry's face with shoe polish.

She did the others after that. Everyone stood or sat silently, not knowing what to say. They were Peter Pan's lost boys, of course, but they were something else, too. Something beyond the husbands and fathers and doctors and businessmen we had known all our lives, something harder than friends. Something wilder. They had drawn away into themselves, into the feral ranks of men, far away from the company of women.

"Well," said Henry. "Let's do it."

They turned to walk out of the garden and through the crippled streets toward the yacht club. We watched them go, pillars of darkness, moving silently. My scalp crawled. I did not know Lewis. I did not know these men.

"Henry, put something on your head," Fairlie yelled after him. "You can see that hair of yours a mile away."

He gave her the V for victory signal. We all laughed, and the little cold spell was broken. Still, when they had passed out of sight, we looked at one another silently, as if to try to read in each other's faces what we should do next.

We sat down to wait.

Dark fell in earnest, and the mosquitoes came

in bloodsucking squadrons, but we did not move to go into the house. As long as we sat in the candlelit garden, we could preserve the illusion of just another outdoor summer supper. There was a lot of wine left, and we drank a good bit of it. The heat and the silence and the wine dulled the anxiety, but it was still there, under the layers of succor. At first we talked a little.

"Remind me to try and get in touch with my office first thing in the morning," I said. I felt extremely guilty that I had hardly thought of the agency since we left for Mexico, two weeks and a hundred years ago.

"Oh," Fairlie said, "I forgot to tell you. Somebody called here from your office . . . would it be Marcy? And said that you've pretty much got no first floor, but the second floor and the files are okay."

My little office, a former town house in a moribund development, sat across Calhoun Street from the Veterans Administration Hospital, overlooking the Ashley marina. I could just imagine what the storm surge had done to it. I closed my eyes in profound weariness. All that work, all those fund-raising drives, all the scrounging and sucking up for money . . .

"We'll take Charlie's Navigator and go check in the morning," Camilla said. "In fact, we'll go check on everybody's places. Maybe nothing's as bad as it seems."

Later, I do not know how much, but the moon had begun to sink toward the South Battery, Lila said, "You know what this reminds me of? That scene in *Gone With the Wind*, where Scarlett and

Melanie and the other women were sitting around sewing, waiting to hear that their men had come back from the Klan raid safely. There were Yankees all over the place, just like the National Guard now. The women never mentioned any of it. They just chatted as if nothing was wrong. I always loved that scene."

"Which of them would be Rhett and which one Ashley?" Fairlie said. Fatigue blurred her voice.

After that the talk died, and we simply sat.

I don't know how much longer it was when I heard the sound. I had been drifting in and out of sleep, and the candles were burned down, and the moon had set. It was almost totally dark.

In the profound silence we heard a jingle. And then the scrabble of claws. And then Gladys, sodden and filthy and ecstatic, slid and skittered onto the veranda, the whole back of her waggling.

Fairlie dropped to her knees and simply held the wriggling dog. I could tell, over the slurping of Gladys's tongue on her face, that Fairlie was crying.

The men suddenly materialized in the garden. Camilla lit a candle. We looked at them. They looked . . . exuberant. They practically gave off sparks.

Goddammit, I thought. They were playing commandos, and we were sitting here simply dying. Sons of bitches.

I knew where my anger came from, though.

"Well?" Camilla said. She sat up straight, with her hands folded in her lap.

"The beach house is standing," Lewis said. "I don't know how in the name of God it could be;

there's literally nothing but rubble around it. But there it is. The space under it took the storm surge; we saw the Ping-Pong table across the street down near Stella Maris, and I think the lawn mower is out on the point. But except for the porch screens and the stairs and walkway down to the beach, it looks pretty good. It didn't even lose any windows."

I felt tears gather in my chest and sting in my nose.

"What about . . . our place? How is it?" Fairlie said.

"You mean where is it?" Henry said. "There's literally nothing left but the dock. We went in there. I couldn't begin to guess where the house is."

"Oh, Henry," Camilla began, but he shook his head.

"We didn't use it much anymore. Even the grandchildren are beginning to have other things to do here in town. I'll find something to do with the insurance money, you can bet on that."

"Gladys?" Fairlie said, still hugging the dog.

"You know, she was sitting on the porch of the beach house, as far up under the hammock as she could get. She was shivering like a leaf, but the minute she heard our footsteps she began to bark. Gladys spent the remainder of her time on Sullivan's Island with my shorts holding her jaws shut. The guard was out in force."

"Did they see you?" I said.

"If they did, they had other fish to fry. You aren't going to know Sullivan's Island. There's just . . . almost nothing left."

"But the house," Lila said.

"But the house."

"Then we'll be all right."

"Yes," Henry said. "I believe we will."

Later that night, as it slid into morning, Lewis and I lay sweating and intertwined in the narrow bed in the room Fairlie kept for her grandchildren. The drone of mosquitoes should have maddened me, but I had been sleeping with mosquitoes for the past two weeks. It seemed to me that Mexican mosquitoes could teach Low Country mosquitoes a thing or two any day.

We were both simply too tired to talk, but we could not quite drift into sleep either. Above us, on the third floor somewhere, Boy and Girl and Sugar were padding around and snuffling. I knew that Gladys, wet and stinking and home, would be sleeping on Fairlie and Henry's bed.

I looked over at the purple Barney that sat on the little chair beside the bed. Lewis looked, too.

"Which is worse?" he said. "A Mexican ho' house or Barney?"

"Barney, by a landslide," I said.

And then we slept.

It was perhaps six weeks before we could cross over to Sullivan's Island, though we could and did sail along the strangely scalloped shore, or took Simms's Boston Whaler. From the water, it looked, I thought, like some desolate, shell-pocked beach during World War II, its battles over but its casualties still strewn, motionless. The dune lines were gone, or had been reconfigured into another seascape entirely. When we finally jolted down Middle Street, we could see that the palms, crepe myrtles, and live oaks that had shaded the old houses lay uprooted, leaves long dead. Some lay across the shattered roofs of the few houses that stood. There were no standing trees. There was no sea grass. Most of the cottages were piles of rubbish. But some stood, bravely and inexplicably, like sentinels who had failed to foresee a war. Ours was one of them. It stood alone far down the beach, nothing around it, its oleanders and palms gone. The walkway to the beach and the stairs had totally vanished. We never did find them. The porch screens had been torn like wet tissue paper. Washed-up debris from who knew where jammed the backyard, and a claw-footed bathtub tilted against the deck, obviously someone's treasure. Shingles littered the sand everywhere. But the windows were still stoutly boarded, and the roof, though partially denuded of shingles, still sheltered, and miraculously the hammock still stood serenely on the front porch. The storm surge had obviously gone just under the porch and swept through the basement, if it could be called that, and boiled on across to murder the houses toward the inland waterway, Henry's included.

The first time we had come over, to reconnoiter, the island had been deathly silent. There was not even any birdsong. Just the flat wash of the waves on an alien beach and here and there the flutter of a shredded flag.

But a week later, when we came leading a caravan of pickups and SUVs laden with lumber and rolls of screen and shingles, the island had come stubbornly alive again. Everywhere, clearing and construction were going on. The air rang with the sound of hammers and power drivers and the growling of bulldozers. A good many cottage owners stood about, their bewildered dogs leashed beside them, watching the wreckage of their pasts come down and the tentative beginning of their futures rise. Some left and never came back, we learned later, but a surprising number of Sullivan's Islanders were rebuilding.

"Are we all insane?" Fairlie said that first day, watching Tyrell and a crew of men from Simms's factory begin to unload supplies and clear rubble.

"Probably," Henry said. "But don't you want it fixed up?"

"Of course, it's just that we never have anything worse than a few floods and muddy racetracks in Kentucky."

"It costs a good bit to live in paradise," Camilla said, smiling at the battle-scarred old house that had been her family's. "Daddy would have been tickled to death to see that the widow's walk is still standing, when St. Michael's steeple and those others took a hit. He was quite proud of being a practicing pagan."

The warm, still autumns of the Low Country linger long, sometimes until nearly Christmas. Simms's crew worked steadily through October and into November, and we worked along with them on weekends. Back in downtown Charleston our houses were pretty much in order, and the plantations on Edisto and Wadmalaw were whole and functioning, if still sodden. Our offices were being healed, though slowly. I eventually got

used to seeing downtown as it was in those first
months; you can get used to anything, or at least
fit it into the grid of your experience, so that it
does not shock and pierce you anew every time
you see it. Of all the sad wreckage around me,
only the decimated old live oaks in White Point
Gardens had the power to stab my heart and
bring brine to my throat each time I saw them.
Generally, I think, we knew that we were as okay
as we could be at the moment, though in other
parts of the city desolation was still unrelieved.
All our attention went, that fall, to the beach
house.

On the last weekend before Thanksgiving, we
packed food and brought wine and a bunch of
late zinnias from Lila's garden and prepared to
finish the roof and the porch painting, and then to
celebrate. Lewis brought champagne, and Simms
brought a sack of oysters he had dug the day
before from his creek bank on Wadmalaw. Henry
and Fairlie had saved driftwood from their long
walks on the beach that fall, and it was silvery dry
and ready to go into the fireplace. Camilla had
taken the bedding and quilts home and cleaned
and dried them, and brought them back, sweet
smelling and fluffed, and put them on all the beds
in the house.

"Just in case somebody wants to spend the
night," she said.

"I know who that somebody will be," Charlie
said, smiling at her. She shrugged and wryly
smiled back. It was fitting, I thought. Their bedroom had been hers as a girl. Let them be the first
of us to fall asleep to the wash of the waves and

wake to the clean, fresh smell of salt and seaweed.

It was a nearly perfect day, one of those gilded
ones you remember at odd moments for the rest
of your life. I see it most often just before I fall
asleep. The sun was lower now, of course, but at
midday it was warm enough to discard sweaters
and jackets. Indeed, Lewis was in shorts and a T-
shirt, and Fairlie changed into a bathing suit from
the drawer upstairs and swam, defiantly, for
about five minutes. The rest of us cheered her on,
but made no move to follow. The low angle of the
light turned the calm sea to a sheet of glittering
pewter, and she came dashing out of it like some
sort of gangling goddess. I saw Henry grin,
secretly, and Camilla, watching them both,
smiled, too.

We took the dogs out for the first time. It had
simply been too hectic to watch over them before,
and I thought that they would be nervous and
agitated by the alteration of their world. I need
not have worried about Boy and Girl; they were
off for the water, noses to the sand, before the car
door had closed behind them. Sugar followed,
bounding up and down like a little rabbit, the better to see over these new dunes. Only Gladys was
not happy. She had shivered and whined when
we drove up to the house, and in the end Henry
had had to carry her in his arms and settle her on
the newly screened-in porch. She stopped crying,
but she did not move from her spot under the
hammock, and I sat in it and swung gently and
patted her.

"She needs to get back on her horse," Henry

said. "She can't be afraid of the island for the rest of her life."

"If you'd sat out a class-four hurricane under this hammock, you'd be afraid, too," I told him.

Lewis and I and Simms and Lila finished painting the walkway and steps early in the afternoon, and Henry and Fairlie raked up debris and stray nails and scraps of screening and dried palm fronds, and dumped them into a huge lawn basket they had brought. Camilla and Charlie finished the last of the shingling. I remember sitting on the top step of the walkway, with the warm, tan sand and the blue sea stretching away beyond me and a sweet, light breeze on my face, watching them. Charlie was on the roof of the porch, tearing off damaged shingles and tossing them down to Camilla. He had taken off his shirt, and his big shoulders and barrel chest had pinked in the sun, and his nearly bald head gleamed red. Every time he loosed a shingle he called, "Heads up!" and Camilla, her chestnut hair loose and blowing around her face, her slender arms and hands flashing, would try and catch the shingle, or retrieve it from the sand, and toss it onto the mounting pile on the big tarp. She caught a good many of them, moving as lithely as the tomboy she had been when she was a child here. She was laughing up at Charlie, and he grinned back. It struck me that I had never seen them doing anything physical together. Even when we danced, Camilla danced with someone else. Charlie, as he protested over and over, did not dance. But in this coordinated ballet of toss and catch, you could see how good they might have been together, if they had danced.

Later that afternoon the air grew cool and the low sun set, and Henry laid the driftwood fire and lit it. It sputtered a moment and then flared and settled to a soft, hissing roar. We all applauded. The heart of the house had come alive.

We sat for a long time after roasted oysters and shrimp gumbo, reluctant to let the evening go. I felt as though I had slipped into a secure berth after a long, wild sea journey. I think we all did. No one spoke very much. But we smiled a lot.

Lewis opened the champagne and poured it, and I passed it around. He lifted his glass, standing before the fireplace.

"To the Scrubs," he said. "One for all and all for one. And to the house."

We all lifted our glasses and said, "To the house," and drank. I put my glass down and smiled over at Camilla, who was sitting on the hearth with her arms wrapped around her knees. But she did not look at me. She was watching Charlie, who sat opposite her in the old wicker rocker, with a faint line of puzzlement between her eyes. I looked, too.

Charlie sat very still, glass in hand, staring straight ahead into the fire, a look of mild amazement on his face. And then, as slowly as a melting snowman, he leaned forward, out of his chair, and slid gently to the floor. The champagne glass crashed and tinkled, and a small lake of fizzing foam spread around it.

Lewis and Henry were kneeling over him in a second, and I found myself gripping Camilla's icy hands as we stood staring.

"Help me get him to the Navigator," Henry said sharply. "It's the biggest. I'll get in back with him. Lewis, you drive."

"Wait . . . ," Camilla began in a voice with no breath behind it.

"No time," Henry barked. "Anny, bring Camilla in the Rover. Fairlie, go with them."

"Where?" I said stupidly.

"Queens. Emergency entrance. Leave the Rover out front. I'll square it with security. Come on, Lewis, let's *go*!"

The Navigator squealed out of the driveway and was out of sight down Middle Street before Simms and Lila and Fairlie and I got Camilla into the Range Rover. As they pulled out, I saw Henry in the backseat, pounding Charlie's chest with his fist. I could not see Charlie's face. Henry's was fierce, focused.

On the careening drive back across the two looming bridges, I said nothing, but Simms, in the front seat, turned to Camilla in the back and spoke softly and steadily, in an even, everyday voice. I did not hear what he said. I could hear Lila murmuring to Camilla, too, but not her words. When I looked in the rearview mirror, I saw that she and Fairlie had their arms around Camilla, and Camilla was sitting very straight and still and white, her eyes fixed on the road ahead. In all the maddening time that it took before we screeched up to the emergency entrance at Queens Hospital, I never heard Camilla make a sound.

It only occurred to me after I had braked to a stop that I had driven over the two horrifying bridges with no more thought to them than a four-way stop sign.

When we reached the coronary intensive care unit, Henry and Lewis were sitting on a plastic-covered couch in the waiting room. They were silent, slumped, heads back against the couch. Both wore green scrubs, with masks dangling around their necks. I could see from the doorway that Henry was soaked to the waist with sweat. Their eyes were closed, and their faces were gray with fatigue.

Henry seemed to sense us before we made a sound. He stood up. Camilla stood stock-still, staring at him, and he held his arms out to her, silently. Like a sleepwalker she walked into them, and he folded her against him, close and hard. Lewis went over and hugged them both. No one spoke.

The original Sullivan's Island three, I thought, and began to cry. Behind me, Fairlie and Lila did, too. Simms made no sound but a small, strangled choke.

Late that night, as we led Camilla out of the coronary care unit and toward the Range Rover, she stopped and looked around at all of us. It was, Lewis told me later, virtually the only time they had heard her speak.

"We finished the house, didn't we?" she said, in a child's wondering voice.

"We by God did," Henry said. She was clinging to his arm as if she was an old woman. He took her weight.

"You're coming home with us tonight, no questions asked," Fairlie said. "In the morning we'll deal with . . . everything. Tonight you need to rest."

"No," Camilla said. "Just drop me by Tradd Street to get the car. I'm going to spend the night at the beach house."

"Well, then, we're coming with you," Lila and I said together.

She looked around at all of us.

"No," she said, and her voice was low and rasping, as if she had been screaming. "It was my house first and it will always be my house, and that's where I'm going. Do you think I could spend one night on Tradd Street without him? That was our house. The beach house is mine. And if any of you try to come with me, or come checking up on me, I'll . . . call the police. I swear I will. Let me be, now. I have a lot to rearrange."

We stared, stunned.

She took hold of Henry's arm again, and he just nodded at us, and together they walked down the long white hall and into whatever would be the rest of Camilla's life.

part two

5

ON A SMOKE-GRAY AFTERNOON in late October 1998, we sat on the porch of the beach house, wrapped in sweaters and towels against the stiff little wind out of the east. Soon it would bring rain; you could smell it coming, and there would be a big wind, because it was born in the east where all the big changes get started. It would be the end of the lingering, muted colors of the few hardwoods, and probably the end of the long, sweet fall. Already we lit the fire earlier, and came in out of the purpling twilights ready for heat and drinks and hot food. But on this afternoon the sense of endings was powerful, and we shivered on the porch longer than we might have otherwise.

Something was gnawing at the back of my mind, something out of memory. I could almost see it glimmering in the depths there, like a goldfish. But I could not catch it in my hands. It seemed important, but I did not know why. It wore a sheen of unrest like scales.

I heard the wind pick up, and across the windows the spatter of sand from off the top of the dunes. We all lifted our heads.

"Summer's over," Henry and Lila said together, and we all laughed. I got it then.

"Do you all remember that time that I was down on the beach, and I thought I saw Camilla on the dunes? It was an afternoon like this, when you knew the weather was changing for good. And everybody laughed at me, and said I'd seen the Gray Man, and that a storm would be coming . . . "

And then I stopped. Not three weeks later Hugo had come. And Charlie had been one of those who teased me about the Gray Man. I looked over at Camilla.

She smiled from her rocker beside the fire. It had become her place since Charlie had been gone. Before, it was his.

"It's okay," she said. "It's been a long time. We talked about that, Charlie and I. He thought it was funny, even after Hugo. He said he was surprised it had been you who saw the Gray Man; he would have thought Fairlie, maybe. I don't think he thought you were given to . . . fancies. After Hugo I remembered it from time to time, but I never laughed at it."

I studied her in the firelight. I thought that of us all, the past ten years had changed her least. Of course, by now the osteoporosis had bowed her considerably, and there were streaks of silver in the thick chestnut hair. But her medieval face was unlined, and her brown eyes still glowed in their hedge of lashes. She still wore her hair tied back at the nape of her neck, and sometimes still let it blow free. She was still slender, still fine boned, still as serene as a white candle. She still walked the old dogs on the beach, albeit much more slowly, and she still laughed with Lewis and Henry about their early days on the island.

She spent a great deal of time at the beach house now. At first we all worried about it, about her being alone and lonely for Charlie, but we came to see that in some primal way it nourished her. There was color in her face now that had not been there for a long time, and she laughed more often than I could remember her doing. I thought that she was truly beautiful now, as a few women become when they reach their early sixties.

The rest of us had not fared so well. Henry was totally white haired, though still lanky and brown as a stork. Lewis had lost all but a tonsure of his red hair, and now his head was as freckled as the rest of him. Fairlie was still as slim and supple as a girl, and her red hair still flamed in the sun, but the skin of her face had wrinkled all over, very finely, like loved old organza. From a distance you did not notice it; Fairlie now was very nearly Fairlie then. But only nearly.

Lila had grayed and somehow shrunk a bit—Charleston women did not let themselves get fat—but she still wore her chin-length bob anchored off her face with a band or her sunglasses, and her long, flowered skirts, and her voice was still true and piping and sweet. It was hard to think of Lila as the coolly competent real estate magnate that she had become, but she owned her own firm now, and made, literally, millions. The old houses south of Broad were being bought up by the dozens by affluent newcomers, and renovated, and Lila sold a good number of them.

Simms was totally gray and had grown a mustache, also gray, that should have looked ridiculous on his round downtown face, but somehow did not. He had stopped, I thought, looking like the youngest one in the men's grill at the yacht club. When had that happened?

I had threads of white in my explosive black mop and a bottom that cried out for the panty girdle I would not wear. Thank God Lewis proclaimed it merely "cuppable." And there was a little more chin now. Forty-five was not thirty-five.

I felt a great flush of love for us all that afternoon. We were still the Scrubs. When I looked at us, my brain registered the changes, but my eyes still saw us all as we had been in those first summers. Our then-faces were imprinted on my retinas. The heart sees what it needs to see.

The house truly had not changed in any essential way. Even the porch railings and the stairway to the boardwalk that we had built in the weeks after Hugo were a little shabby now, and teetery. And the then-new roof shingles had weathered to the no-color of the old. There were a couple of formidable leaks on the stair landing and in the kitchen, and there was a lot of talk about getting them fixed, but somehow no one made the call. We set out pots when it rained and enjoyed the tinkle and plink of raindrops into them. I don't think that anyone wanted any more change.

"We'll have to do it sometime," Lila said worriedly, the real estate doyenne in her coming out. "It's going to depreciate a good bit if we don't."

"For God's sake, have you listed it?" Lewis said, and she flushed and laughed.

"Of course not. I just can't stand the thought of it . . . rotting away."

"It's always been rotting away," Camilla said comfortably. "Even when I was little, something was always wrong with it. If it was all fixed up and decorated, I don't think I could stay in it."

"Well, it's surely not that," Fairlie said, and we smiled complacently.

It surely was not. The house wore the same shingling and sported the same lumpen, damp-smelling upholstered and peeling wicker pieces that it had when Camilla inherited it. Lila had brought out a smart new flokati rug to replace the paper-thin old oriental that had been soaked when Hugo's rain came flooding down the chimney. It was thick and creamy and invited lolling, but no one lolled. Its very whiteness, in all that musty dimness, kept catching the corners of our eyes. Finally Lila gave up and dug the sour old oriental out of her attic and dried it in the sweet air and sun, and put it back down in front of the fireplace. We and the house all sighed together with pleasure, and Lila gave the new rug to Camilla for in town. Outside, the dune lines were not the original ones, and crepe myrtles had replaced the slain oleanders and palms that clustered around the porch, but that was outside. Inside was still us.

From the very beginning, I was surprised by how small a hole Charlie left in the fabric of the beach house. It was not that we did not miss him;

one or another of us would tear up regularly when somebody spoke of Charlie, and Boy and Girl, gray muzzled and lame these ten years later, still looked eagerly for him when they got out of the car and struggled up the steps and into the house. That alone moved us regularly to tears. When it happened Camilla would pet the dogs fiercely and then look away, out at the ocean. She hated for anyone to see her cry. Few people did.

No, it was rather that the sense of us as a unit was somehow unbroken, and the knowledge that somehow Camilla contained Charlie so completely that, even absent, he was comfortably here. I felt joy that the integrity of the group was not compromised, even when a loved member was gone, and once said so to Camilla.

"The center will hold," she said.

"It feels like he's still here," I said to Lewis shortly after Charlie's death.

"He's probably down around Cape Horn by now," Lewis said. For when Charlie died, Camilla had had him cremated, as he had wished, and we had scattered his ashes in the sea in front of the beach house.

Nearly everybody but us was furious with Camilla. All the older women in her life—and there were many, because, like Lewis, she was related to half of Charleston—were aghast.

"Your people have always been in Magnolia Cemetery," one of a bridge-playing flock of them said to Camilla when she had me to lunch at the yacht club, two days after Charlie died. "What on earth can you be thinking of? Cremation? Throwing him in the ocean like bait shrimp? What would your mother say?"

"Probably 'Is it lunchtime yet?'" Camilla said under her breath.

Her sister, Lydia, did not speak to her for days, and her mother, still living, if not sentient, at Bishop Gadsden roused herself from her succoring torpor long enough to spit out, "There is no place but Magnolia. Your father will be appalled. Who was it again you said you wanted to dump in the ocean?"

Her two sons and their strange California families came to stand silently on this unprepossessing eastern shore and watch their mother, in shorts and T-shirt, wade into the ocean with the Episcopal minister from Holy Cross, a family friend, and consign their feathery gray father to the white-laced water.

"Don't we have a plot at Magnolia?" the oldest said. "I thought we had enough space for everybody. We've always counted on it."

His tan surfer daughter and thin wife rolled their eyes. I could not imagine they gave a lot of thought to Magnolia Cemetery.

"I know Daddy by rights didn't really belong at Magnolia, but you sure do, and we do. Didn't anybody hassle you about it?" the younger son, who did something with food irradiation in a Silicon Valley town known only to technicians, said. I knew that he had left Charleston to go to MIT and had since not spent more than two weeks at a time at home.

Camilla lifted her head and smiled at her cuckoo child.

"You can take the boy out of Charleston, but you can't take Charleston out of the boy," she said. Her face was damp, whether with tears or seawater I could not tell.

"It's what he wanted," she went on gently. "Your dad always said he thought Magnolia Cemetery looked like the set for a grade-B vampire movie. He asked for the ocean. Come to that, I think I will, too."

"I may have to have you cremated," the son said grimly, "but I will not scatter you in this goddamned ocean."

"Dump me in an ashtray then," Camilla snapped, tiring of it all. "I'm surely not going to care."

We were all surprised, and I, for one, wanted to cheer. I had seldom heard Camilla raise her voice. It was good to know that she could get angry, and even better to know that she could be a very funny woman. I wanted to hug her.

The day of Charlie's ceremony was as clear and gentle as late summer, though it was the Sunday after Thanksgiving. Hugo had left an ironic legacy of sweet, luminous weather. The sky was a tender blue, and the sea, without rancor, creamed and hushed on the beach. Most of us had spent the night before at the beach house, and Lewis and I and Fairlie had gone swimming in the morning. The water was still as warm as blood, as amniotic fluid. At noon, while we were still sitting on the porch surrounded by bottles of flat champagne, with which we had toasted Charlie's handsome bronze urn, the first of the cars from Charleston came lurching and grinding into the sandy space around the back stairs. Fairlie had been dispatched to be the lookout for them.

"Holy shit," she called back from the kitchen, where she had been peering out the window. "It's a big old Lincoln town car with a chauffeur and about a million old ladies, and they're all wearing hats! What do I do with them?"

"Oh, God, it's Mother's garden club," Camilla gasped. "I didn't ask them; I sort of put the word out that it would be just us and some of Charlie's people from the hospital, but I should have known they'd come. That's Margaret Pingree's car and it must be Jasper driving. I thought he was dead. Maybe he *is* dead, and just doesn't know it. Listen, you guys, you'll have to go down and get them around to the boardwalk somehow. Two of them that I know of have bad hips, and Margaret is on a walker. We can't possibly get them up the back steps and then back down again. Fairlie, you and Lila and Anny help me get some chairs down there. We can put them along the top dune line and they can watch from there. Be careful, Henry, Lewis. They'll all have on their goddamned 'little heels.'"

I began to laugh helplessly, and after a moment all the women joined in. We were still laughing as we lugged chairs down the steps to the board-walk, clad in shorts and T-shirts, barefoot because we were all going into the water with Camilla and Charlie. Camilla brought up the rear bearing Charlie's urn; she was shaking so with silent laughter that I feared we would end up anointing the dunes and sandburs with Charlie, instead of the eternal sea.

Charlie's service was a stupefying mixture of
Episcopal and Gullah and rock and roll, and
should have been ludicrous, but was deeply moving, at least to us. I could not see the garden club
ladies or the sons of Charlie and Camilla; they
stood on the first dune line, and we were at the
edge of the surf, letting it lap our ankles. But I
could hear an occasional hiss of outrage among
the sniffs, and thought that whatever it might
mean to us, this moment by the sea could not
compete with St. Michael's. Fortunately for everyone, Camilla mostly, there would be a memorial
service at St. Michael's on the next Wednesday,
followed by a proper reception at Lila and
Simms's Battery house, which had been hastily
and thoroughly cleaned and repaired by Tyrell
and crew from Simms's plant. Even Lila's grandmother's cherished orientals had been restored
and were back in place on the newly varnished
wide pine floors in the double drawing rooms.
There was no more sign of Hugo there except
glaring sunlight where palms and live oaks had
once stood. The Howard name got a lot done
quickly.

But this was Charlie's day, and Camilla's, and
in a very real way ours, and we took Charlie
down to the sea he loved in our own way.

The tanned, balding minister from Holy Cross,
where Charlie had gone if he went to church at all,
stood knee-deep in the water, waiting for us, the
Book of Common Prayer in his folded hands, his
brown legs bare below his swimming trunks. He
wore, instead of a clerical collar, a faded Grand
Strand T-shirt. A plain metal crucifix hung around

his neck. I supposed it was to identify him as clergy in case anyone of an official status caught him flinging ashes into the ocean and asked for an explanation. The clergy would not, of course, lie, but could claim certain ecclesiastical immunities. But we were not worried. No official had ever been seen on the beach this far to the west. All the action was around the crossroads, and east toward the Isle of Palms.

Creighton Mills had been a childhood friend of Camilla and Lewis and Henry's, and he smiled when we walked into the surf and stopped in a ragged line. Camilla stood in the center, and Creighton gave her a little salute.

"I still can't get used to the idea that Creigh Mills can save my soul," Lewis whispered to me.

"Better one of our own," Henry said under his voice.

Creighton looked at Camilla for a long moment, and then read in a quiet voice, from the Book of Common Prayer, "'I am the resurrection and the life, saith the Lord: he that believeth in me, though he were dead, yet shall he live; and whosoever liveth and believeth in me shall never die.

"'I know that my redeemer liveth, and that he shall stand at the latter day upon the earth: and though this body be destroyed, yet shall I see God: whom I shall see for myself, and mine eyes shall behold, and not as a stranger.'"

There was a pause, and I heard an old lady say in the loud, flat voice of the nearly deaf, "Well, at least it's the 1928 one, and not that dreadful hippie thing they're doing everywhere now."

Beside me, I heard Lewis snort.

"Shut up," I hissed.

Creighton Mills gave a barely perceptible nod and Henry clicked on the small cassette player he carried. I had not seen it before. Over the soft hush of the surf, Bobby Darin's voice lifted up: "Somewhere, beyond the sea . . ."

I knew that Charlie had loved the song, and felt my eyes sting. Lewis squeezed my hand. Then the music segued into "Long Tall Sally," "Little Darlin'," "Whole Lot of Shakin' Goin' On," the Shirelles's "Foolish Little Girl," Charlie's personal favorite, and finally, "Sitting on the Dock of the Bay," to which we had all danced on the sand and the rough planks over the water, and the beach house's tired grass matting.

It was just right. Even as I felt tears start down my cheeks, laughter rose in my throat. I looked over at Camilla, who, with Lewis and Henry, I learned later, picked the songs, and nodded. She nodded back, smiling, her eyes wet.

Creighton Mills looked at Camilla again, and she inclined her head, and from behind us we heard the scuffle and scrabble of paws, and the chink of chains. We turned to see Simms leading Boy and Girl, exuberant and stretching their leashes taut, down to the surf's edge. They strained to get into the water, and looked up at Camilla in bewilderment when they were not allowed to run free.

"Stay, sweeties," she said softly. "Stay and say good-bye to Daddy."

I did begin to cry then, and so did Lila. Fairlie stared fiercely out to sea, her throat working. I did not dare look at Henry and Lewis. Gladys did not come down to the beach; she stayed on the porch, from which she never strayed now, along with Sugar, whose muffled yips rose over the sound of the waves and the seabirds. But they were with us. Our whole family was here.

Then down the steps from the boardwalk four women came, black women in long skirts and bright blouses and jewelry and feathers, women who walked like queens and sang as they walked. As they sang, they shook small tambourines and one carried a curious little drum with a voice like faraway thunder. I recognized Linda Cousins, Lewis's housekeeper, at the head of the procession. As she passed, she grinned over at us. Lewis gave her a great, leering wink.

Around Charleston and the Low Country, there are groups, mainly black women, who preserve and perform the old songs and shouts of the Gullah slaves who brought them from Africa long ago. They are magnificent; people travel many miles to hear them. I remembered that Charlie had been entranced by them, and often dragged whoever he could corral out to the old Moving Star Hall on John's Island, where, he said, the best of the Gullah praise singing could be heard. He was right. To hear them is to fly back on a dark wind to a time when fires burn in forests and drums speak, and magic walks. I did not know that Linda Cousins was a member of one of the groups, but I knew without being told that Lewis had arranged this for Charlie, and pressed his hand hard. He squeezed back.

At the water's edge the women sang, "Oh, hallelujah, hallelujah, glory hallelujah, you know the storm passing over, hallelu. The tallest tree in paradise Christians call the tree of life, you know the storm is passing over, hallelu."

And they sang, swaying and clapping, "Reborn again, reborn again, oh, reborn again. Can't get to heaven less you reborn again. Oh, Satan is mad, and I'm so glad, oh, reborn again. Lost the soul he thought he had, oh, reborn again."

After several more shouts and songs, some exuberant, some solemn and poignant, they slid sweetly into "Deep River." When the last notes faded away, the silence rang like a bell. It seemed to me that even the sea paused, and the wind that marked the turn of the tide.

Creighton held his hands out to Camilla, and she waded into the water, her eyes fastened on his face, bearing Charlie's urn, until she stood beside him. The slow, heaving green water broke around their legs, hers pearl white, his tanned. He took her free hand in his, and closed his eyes, and said something so softly that only Camilla could hear him. Her lips moved with his. I still do not know what Charlie's final prayer was.

He lifted his voice and said, "'Unto Almighty God we commend the soul of our brother, Charles Curry, departed, and we commit his body to the deep; in sure and certain hope of the Resurrection unto eternal life, through our Lord Jesus Christ; at whose coming in glorious majesty to judge the world, the sea shall give up her dead; and the corruptible bodies of those who sleep in him shall be changed, and made like unto his glorious body;

according to the mighty working whereby he is able to subdue all things unto himself.'"

He nodded to Camilla. She lifted the urn slowly to chin level, and pressed it against her cheek, and then she cast Charlie's ashes into the ocean. A band of jagged, running shadows flew over us just at the moment the ashes settled, before they were whirled away, and we looked up to see a flock of pelicans, perfect pterodactyls, flying so closely over the surface of the sea that we might have reached up and touched them. They were not afraid of us; the pelicans of Sullivan's Island have been here far longer than we have, and with far less intrusion. Charlie had loved pelicans. Camilla turned around to us, her face running with tears, and smiled.

"'The Lord be with you,'" Creighton Mills said.

"'And with thy spirit,'" we all murmured. Most of us were crying openly now.

Simms let Boy and Girl go then, and they dashed into the still-warm, creaming surf and raised their doggy voices into the sky in praise of water.

That evening I went up to the widow's walk atop the house. I don't really know why; somehow we had never gone there very often. From that height you could see the entire island, and over to the Isle of Palms, and back to Charleston, and the port docks and gas tanks, and the inland waterway. It was a remarkable view, but I think that we did not often want to be reminded that the beach house was part of a teeming, sprawling whole. Up here, that fact was inescapable.

But there was almost always a spectacular sunset, especially in the late autumn, and the post-Hugo ones had been breathtaking. The men often sailed at sunset, coming in out of the sinking sun to the dock on the inland waterway, and I think, looking back, that I went up to see if they, with Charlie, would come gliding in. The sun was a great dying conflagration, vermilion and purple, shot through with gold, and empty of humanity. No sails broke its skin, no Scrubs, no Charlie. The wind picked up, with, finally, late November hidden in it. I turned to go back down, but then Camilla's head appeared at the top of the spiral staircase and I waited.

She came out onto the little railed space and put her arm around my waist and laid her head on my shoulder. She had to lean down to do it. She wore a thick Fair Isle sweater of Charlie's, and had brought one for me. It was tattered and pilled and smelled of salt and smoke and Charlie. I put it on gratefully.

"Did you come up to see him off?" she said, smiling a little. I nodded. To try and speak just then would have been a disaster. She squeezed my waist.

"I guess they don't call it a widow's walk for nothing," she said.

Very clearly, and for the first time, I thought, Charlie isn't coming back. He died and I'm never going to see him again.

A great void opened inside me, and I felt myself sliding into. My knees buckled and I sat down abruptly on the rough boards of the widow's walk. I cried; I cried so hard that for a space of time I could not get my breath, and thought that I would choke. Through the great salt tide of grief, I thought, stupidly, This has got to stop. I never cry. Not like this. What will Camilla think?

"I want him back," I gasped. "I want him back."

"So do I," Camilla said.

She sat down beside me and pulled my head down to her shoulder, and rocked me gently back and forth. After a while I could catch my breath, and the tears slowed and then stopped. Still, Camilla held me.

"I've never seen you really cry," she said, and her voice was serene. "Charlie would be honored, I think, but he'd hate to think he caused you such grief. It's right to mourn him now, but I hope you'll come to think of laughter and foolishness when you think of him. I hope we all will. It's a better legacy than tears."

She kissed me on the cheek and straightened up.

"Let's go down and I'll make you some tea and put a good splash of rum in it. And I'll have some myself. We'll all have some."

I hugged her. Her bones felt as light as balsa wood.

"I should be comforting you," I said. "What was I thinking of?"

"You were thinking of Charlie, and that's a great comfort," she said.

The sunset was graying out and the air was chilling, and I got up to follow her downstairs, to where light and warmth and safety waited. Just then Lewis and Henry poked their heads out into the twilight, and came up onto the widow's walk. I pressed Lewis's hand.

"I'm going on down," I said. "You all stay with Camilla for a while."

I stopped on the third step down and looked back up. They stood together, Lewis and Henry and Camilla, as they had stood so often from childhood on, and the men had their arms around her. She was looking into their faces, one and then the other, and talking softly. Comforting them, as she had always done. We had all been greedy for her comfort, and careless with it. I wondered if she would ever accept succor from us. We would have to think of ways to offer it obliquely.

She was staying at the beach house until Thursday, the day after Charlie's memorial service and the reception at Lila and Simms's. No one could move her on that, nor would she let any of us stay the night with her.

"It gives me a breather," she said. "It's the last time in a long time I'll be able to just . . . be. There's too much to be done when I do come back to town. You can all come out in the daytime, if you want to, but not at night. I'm doing some writing, and that's when I write best."

When we pressed her to tell us what she was writing, she would say only, "Remembrances. Notes to people. Lists of stuff. The life stories of the Scrubs. Dark tales of passion and sin and redemption. Let me be or I'll make some of the great villains of literature out of all of you."

So we let her be. I do not think there was a one of us who, caught in the web of our everyday "outside" lives, did not think of her often that

week, seeing her, perhaps, in sunlight and firelight and in the close black of night, writing, writing, writing, always with the sound of the sea in
her ears. For myself, I could not see her doing
anything at all, merely sitting in the wicker
rocker beside the fire, her hands folded in her lap,
waiting, as if to be filled up.

On the day of Charlie's memorial service at St.
Michael's, cold rain lashed the city. Downtowners
accustomed to walking to St. Michael's drove or
had themselves driven, and traffic around the
intersection of Meeting and Broad Streets, always
slow, was at a near standstill. It is seldom that you
hear a car horn in downtown Charleston, unless
the car has an out-of-state tag, much less in the
vicinity of St. Michael's. But Charlie's big day got
under way to an anthem of exasperated horns.

"What can you expect from an outsider?"
Lewis grinned, as we ran through the rain from
an illegal parking space on King Street. Lewis had
brazenly put his physician's permit on the windshield. We were sheltered by an immense green-
and-yellow golf umbrella that had been left in the
Range Rover by a forgotten guest. It was all I
could find as we left the house. Somehow it
seemed all of a piece with the blaring horns.

Many Charlestonians, particularly downtowners, have had their coming ins and goings out and
all their great life rituals in between at St.
Michael's since 1752. It is a graceful and dignified
building, reminiscent of and perhaps inspired by
the London city churches of Sir Christopher Wren
and James Gibbes. Its glowing paneling and simple leaded windows let in a light that is warming

and somehow exalting. I have been to many services there, although we attend church, when we do, at Grace Episcopal, which is a short walk from our house. Weddings, christenings, funerals, and sometimes the chamber music concerts during the two weeks of Spoleto . . . I have sat many times with Lewis in the red-cedar box pew that his family has occupied for two hundred years.

"Who sits in it now that none of you come here much?" I asked him once.

"Tourists from Newark and Scranton," he said. "I specified it in writing. Costs them a bundle."

But in all the times I have been in St. Michael's, I have seldom seen anyone remotely resembling a tourist. Not at a service. If there are unfamiliar faces in the congregation, they are apt to be relatives or guests of the communicants. There are no rules about it, of course. That is simply the way it is. The few visitors who venture in for a service or a concert are generally viewed as the sort of people who will appreciate the beauty and resonance of the old church. The shorts and halters and flip-flops that are the hallmark of the wandering downtown tourist, even in St. Michael's churchyard adjacent to the church, are not often seen in the sanctuary. I think that St. Michael himself, who is depicted in a great Tiffany window slaying the dragon, would step down and smite them smartly.

I have always loved the sensory particulars of St. Michael's. Its steeple, slender and white and topped with a gilt ball, is visible from the places I frequent most: my office, the Bull Street house, the beach house. It is a presence in my life. It has a living history that I love. It was painted black during the Revolutionary and Civil Wars so that it would not be visible to the vessels bombarding the city from the harbor. It has survived earthquakes, fires, and, in my time, Hurricane Hugo. Once, at a party for the benefactors of Queens Hospital, I met an aristocratic old German who said, when I asked him if he had visited the city before, "Not precisely. But I have seen the steeple of St. Michael's through a periscope." Whether or not he was to be believed, it made my blood cool for a moment, the thought of that silent black leviathan lying deep in the harbor waters, its great-stalked eye fixed implacably on us.

The bells of St. Michael's have lifted my heart for many years, at noontime and sunset. Their bronze song can be heard all over downtown. They have been stolen by the British, buried in Columbia during the Civil War, shipped back to Whitecastle to be recast twice. On this day of autumn rain and wind, they rang sweetly for Charlie Curry. I knew that it must be a great comfort to Camilla and Charlie's family and friends, and I know that it was to me, that their voices lifted as truly for an Indiana outlander as they did for the departing souls of the original families. I remembered something that Fairlie had said once, in some pet or other over one of the hampering Charleston mores, "No matter where you go or who you are, and no matter where you want to fetch up, Charleston will get you in the end."

But it had not, after all, gotten Charlie. Perhaps St. Michael's held the city's collective memories of him, but the green Atlantic of the island had his body and essence. It was not, I thought, such a bad split.

The church was packed with quiet people who nodded and smiled politely at me and more warmly at Lewis, and gave Camilla small hugs and cheek-brushing kisses. They smelled of wet wool and lavender and somehow of incense, though I doubted that the church burned it anymore. An odor, perhaps, of sanctity. After the service, which was as beautiful and graceful as the old church and as anchored in years, the congregation moved up the aisles and out onto the Tuscan portico. Camilla and her sons and their wives and children stood there to receive their soft murmurs of sympathy and love. Camilla seemed a perfect part of them there in her black suit and pearls, taken back into the bloodstream of the city, moving, as if oiled, to the cadences and rhythms that, I knew, I would never hear. Somehow it made me uneasy. What if she simply stayed?

But as her sister Lydia's town car glided to the curb to pick them up for the short trip to the Battery, she turned and made a little circle in the air with her thumb and forefinger.

"One down," she said almost under her breath. We all smiled. We had her still.

Lila and Simms's house is a three-story brick Charleston single, with accents of the Greek revival that was popular in the early nineteenth century, when it was built. It has white-railed piazzas on all three floors, and a rose-arched doorway off the street and into the ground-floor piazza, where the official front door is. It is one of the most beautiful houses on East Battery, though not so grand as some built later and iced like wedding cakes with architectural details from two dozen centuries. The houses on the Battery, East and South, are a stunning sight, looking as they do over the great seawall or through the huge oaks of White Point Gardens, at the Ashley River or straight out to sea. The Battery is what most people think of when they think of Charleston, and it may be one of the most photographed streets in the world.

It is also one of the most tourist thronged. Even on this day of cold, sheeting rain, flocks of umbrellaed and anoraked visitors slogged along the broken old sidewalks, looking alternately at the sodden guidebooks clutched in their hands and up at the houses. People going into Lila and Simms's house had to park blocks away, or maneuver around knots of people standing still and staring as they entered the piazza door, hoping for a glimpse of the fabled garden and old Charlestonians in situ. For some reason, these sightings are greatly prized. I remember once, just before rounding the brick wall onto Bull Street with a load of clothes for the dry cleaner in my arms, hearing a small group talking on the other side of the wall.

"It's funny that you never see any of the natives," a shrill female Long Island voice said. Just then I came into the street and nodded as I put the clothes in my car.

"Oh, there's one," the same voice announced.

"*Nativus horribilis*," I murmured to myself, driving away and seeing them in the rearview mirror, staring after me.

One of the Howard house's unique features, much chronicled, is the double drawing room on the third floor. The two great receiving spaces are joined by doors that fold back to allow a ballroom-size vista, which is what I suspect it was originally used for. Simms and Lila had few balls, except for their daughter Clary's debut, and so, except for house tours, the third floor was rarely used. The Howards lived in the second-floor library and the little sitting room off the kitchen, where a fireplace and a TV hid. In warm weather, living was done on the first- and second-floor piazzas, shaded from the street by a brick wall shrouded in roses and Confederate jasmine vines.

I had been in the first- and second-floor rooms and on the piazzas and in the garden many times, but I had seldom seen the drawing rooms polished and glowing with candlelight and ablaze with flowers, or alive with people. It looked, in the dim light from the cascading rain at the tall windows, as it must have looked in the days of its original glory, during Charleston's golden age of balls and receptions and great, nine-course dinners. A long Hepplewhite table had been set up in the center of the second room, laden with Lila's grandmother's thin, translucent old Haviland and heavy Revere tea and coffee services. A huge ham glistened at one end, and at the other, a towered, tiered silver dish held little biscuits with ham and beef tenderloin and deviled crab. The enormous silver epergne in the center, which had belonged to one of their ancestors from the time of the lords proprietor, I forget which, spilled sugared fruit and magnolia leaves and pink and green poinsettias. Christmas, I thought. Of course. It was almost Christmas. There was every succulent dish that Charleston claimed as its own, including the ubiquitous shrimp and grits and the crab cakes and the platters of little roasted doves. Charlie would have loved the food, I thought. I didn't know how he would have felt about the gathering itself. It was studded with people who, I knew, had never thought him a suitable match for Camilla, but had been far too polite ever to say so. But Charlie had known, I was sure, who they were.

"I'll bet he's fuming right now," I said to Lewis.

"I'll bet he's not," Lewis grinned. "I'll bet he's hovering around the molding waiting for some old lady to choke on a dove bone."

"What are you two laughing about?" Camilla said, coming up to us and linking her arms in ours. She was smiling.

"Charlie," I said. "How are you holding up, sweetie?"

"Tolerably well," she said, and I thought she was. There had been many tears at the memorial service, but as far as I knew, none of them had been Camilla's. She shone like a beacon in the great gilded room, and people flocked around her as if to a fire.

We took cups of Simms's grandfather's light dragoon punch from a dignified waiter passing them on a silver tray and went out onto the piazza. From this top one you could see, as Lewis said, as far as Madagascar. The wind whipped the tops of the wet palms, and the mist from the rain stung our faces, but we did not turn to go in. We stood with linked arms, drinking punch and looking at the amplitude of the sea and sky around us.

"'Sea-drinking city,'" Lewis said. "Josephine Pinckney wrote that years and years ago. I'm never in one of these old houses that I don't think of it. I had it hanging somewhere in our house; I don't remember where."

Lewis's house was farther down the street, toward the turn onto South Battery. You could not see it from where we stood. I was glad. I really think he was, too. But still, to look at this warm sea every day, to breathe its breath, to hear its voice . . .

"Do you miss seeing the ocean every day?"

"I see a better one every weekend," he said.

"It's the same ocean."

"No, it's not."

"Let's go home," I said. "I have a great desire to watch TV in bed."

We took the elevator down to the first floor, where Lila stood greeting latecomers and saying good-bye to others. She turned to us, and all of a sudden I really saw her, saw Lila Howard herself outside the context of the island and the beach house, saw her as clearly as if I were seeing her for the first time. I almost gasped. When had she gotten so thin? Where had the hollows in her smooth cheeks come from, and the smudges under her eyes? She looked like a woman haunted. Somehow I knew that it was not merely grief for Charlie. Dear God, was she ill?

I put my arm around her.

"You okay?" I said. "It was a perfectly beautiful

send-off, and Camilla is so grateful. Charlie would be, too. But you look tired to death. You've done too much."

"No, I wanted to do it," she said, and smiled, and the sad sorcery faded from her eyes. She was Lila again, in her element, as I had always pictured her.

"Where's Simms?" Lewis said. "I want to say good-bye. I owe him a lunch."

Her eyes moved away.

"He's around," she said. "I'm going to light into him good for abandoning his guests."

"I'll go find him," I said. "I've got to go to the ladies' room, anyway. I'll never make it home through this rain and traffic."

"Anny . . . " Lila's voice rose, and it sounded flat and thin. I waved at her over my shoulder and dived into the crowd. It was really rotten of Simms to leave her with door duty.

The downstairs powder room was mobbed, and a cluster of dark-clad women stood around it.

I really can't wait, I thought, and then remembered that there was a tiny, dilapidated bathroom at the end of the piazza, next to the little house where the gardener kept his tools. I trotted toward it. The long sisal runner on the brick floor was sodden; my feet squelched as I went. I reached the door and put my hand on the knob to open it.

"Go ahead," Simms's voice, thick and slow, came from inside. "Nobody will see us. Nobody ever comes to this bathroom. Take them off, love. I want to see all of you. I want to touch you all over. . . . "

"Simms, wait, now . . . ," a woman's voice said. It was a young voice, small and thin. It did not have the downtown Charleston cadences, the little lilt. The woman was not anyone I knew. I did not think any of us would know her.

I stood stock-still, my ears ringing, my heart pounding sickly. I turned and fled back down the piazza and into the house, trying to arrange my mouth into a smile, feeling a rictus bloom there instead.

"No luck," I chirped. "Do tell him good-bye for us. And we'll see you soon. . . . "

I did not say "next weekend at the beach house." I could not make my mouth form the words. Lila looked at me silently.

"I'll tell him you said good-bye," she said. Her eyes were dark and flat. She knew, then. How long? How long had Simms been sneaking into bathrooms with this or other young women? I hated him suddenly. Grief poured in after the hate.

"Take care of yourself. We love you," I said, and hugged Lila, and we went out into the rain.

"Don't you feel well?" Lewis said to me on the drive home. I was huddled against the door of the car, my arms wrapped around me. Despite the roaring of the heater, I could not get warm.

"Just a cold trying to start, I think," I said. "I'm going to make some hot tea and lie down. You want some?"

He didn't. "But I'll bring you up a bowl of chili and we'll have it on trays," he said. "No wonder you're cold; we've been wet half the day."

I did not answer. Upstairs I skinned off my

clothes and got into a sweatshirt and pants and pulled the covers up to my chin, and turned off my bedside light. When he finally came up, I was asleep at last, drowned in the thick, hot sleep that grief or shock brings.

I woke in the dead of night, in that stopped, still place where nothing moves, time does not go forward, light does not come. I felt literally sick with pain and fear and loss. Charlie's death could not destroy the web of the Scrubs, I thought. But the acid of Simms's betrayal might. Finally I got up and sat in the wing chair by the window, and cried. When light finally crept in around the bottom of the blinds, I was done with crying.

I didn't tell Lewis what I had heard the day before. I never did tell him. Just before dawn I heard Camilla's voice as plainly as if she had spoken: "The center will hold."

And after all, through all the years after that day, nothing really happened with them, at least nothing you could speak of. If Simms spent more and more time away from the beach house, well, we knew that the business was expanding rapidly all over the country and even abroad. If Lila was quieter and thinner, if she spent a great deal of time sitting beside Camilla, who often squeezed her hand or teased her into laughter, well, they had been born on the same street, gone to school together, been in each other's weddings. The affection between them was nothing new. Only I knew, as surely as I have ever known anything, that Camilla knew about Simms, and had long borne Lila up, like a raft, and would continue to do so.

As she had said, the center held.

6

JUST BEFORE CHRISTMAS 1999, with one millennium sliding inexorably into another, we sat in the early dark before the fire in the beach house, reluctant to get up and begin to clear the redolent remnants of our annual Sullivan's Island Christmas feast. All of us had family celebrations on the day itself, and we would cherish their warmth and the familial chaos that was as much tradition as the smilax ropes on the staircase banisters, and the turkey or duck that was the provender of the family hunters. Few Charlestonians bought their Christmas bird.

The various downtown clans would gather, replete with great-aunts and imperial grandmothers and shrieking children and handsome young men and women home from Princeton and Harvard and Sweetbriar and in a few renegade instances, outposts such as Bennington and Antioch. Whatever living arrangements and leisure-time pursuits and body parts with rings and piercings occupied the collegial young during the school year, they were laid aside for the velvets and satins and blue blazers and bow ties of home. Christmas was the height of the debutante sea-

son, and some of the young women and their
families swept giddily from one party or ball to
another, often twice or three times a day. That
some of the young women would go back to stud-
ies of international law or particle physics or
forensic medicine in no way impeded the magic
of this hiatus.

Just for this time, downtown seemed to me
much like it might have been in an earlier, more
graceful century. The magnolia leaf and Williams-
burg wreaths on doors would not come down
until Twelfth Night, and white tapers would burn
in tall windows from dusk on. There was a feeling
abroad in this particular season that it was necessary and right to bring out the oldest ornaments,
the oldest receipts; to sing the oldest carols, to dip
in and out of friends' homes as had been done
since the nineteenth century, hugging and crying,
"Merry Christmas," and leaving a small gift or a
batch of benne seed cookies.

"Stay and have a drop of eggnog with us," the
visitees would cry, and the visitors would do so.
Charleston eggnog is hallowed and potent, often
made with the same Barbadian rum that great-
great-grandfather used. I often imagined that
Christmas morning in many homes south of
Broad might be a bit bleary.

Perhaps no one spoke of it, but I thought that
the new millennium threatened to change lives
and personal ecosystems here more violently
than in most places in America. There was simply
such a deep well of beautiful stasis. Many of us
knew full well and without question who we were
until midnight on the thirty-first of December.

Who would we be on January 1, 2000? Elsewhere they feared Y2K; here the demon was the necessity of making our way in a totally new thousand years. We did not know how to do that. That sort of change had never visited Charleston. It made no sense, perhaps, but the great, creeping shadow of the impending change stalked the old streets.

"Somehow I keep wanting to look over my shoulder," Lila said on the night of our Scrubs Christmas dinner. "I know with my mind that nothing will change, not really, but this is the only place that I feel will stay . . . like it's always been. Where we'll stay like we've always been."

"We're not that now." I smiled at her. "And I have the fanny to prove it."

"You know what I mean," Lila said. I did.

I got up and stretched and walked out onto the porch to clear my food-and-drink-smogged mind. The air was still and very cold for Charleston at Christmas. There would be frost on the spartina in the morning, and a hard freeze inland. Already the suicidal azaleas and camellias that always rush the season downtown wore mantles of sheeting and quilts. My own huge pink Debutante camellias back on Bull Street sported brittle, moth-eaten velvet draperies from Lewis's Battery house. They had been folded in the attic for many years; perhaps, like the animals in the legend, they would speak at midnight on Christmas Eve, and talk wistfully of the grand, candlelit balls and feasts that they had once presided over.

"Get real," I said aloud to myself, and looked up at the black, star-pricked sky. The stars seemed to swim so close and burning cold that you could reach up and touch them; the Milky Way was a luminous cloud. I breathed deeply. Over the smells from the house—wood smoke and cedar and wax myrtle from the tree and swags and wreaths we had put up, and Christmas dinner itself—a river of clean, cold salt poured off the sea and into my face.

I hope I die here, I thought, and then remembered that Charlie had, and wept a little, for the place that was never set at the table now, and the tottering old dogs who never ceased sniffing for him. But I still thought that it would be the finest place imaginable to end a life that had been so defined by it.

There was a sharp rap on the glass door, and I looked to see Lewis, gesturing me in.

"Come back in," his mouth said silently.

"You come out here," I mouthed.

"Are you crazy?" his lips said. And I smiled and went back inside. For a moment, the house was stale and stifling, but only for a moment. Warmth wrapped me again, and I sat down on the raised hearth, realizing only then that I was shivering. Over the layered aromas of roasted oysters and port-glazed goose—Fairlie's idea for a change from the turkey or duck we usually had, and a very bad one—the sharp tingle of champagne tickled my nose.

"Time for the toast," Henry said, handing me a glass and raising his. It was his turn this year. We all raised our glasses.

"To the Scrubs, which were, are, and ever will be," he said. "And to the next thousand years. To the great blessing of being present at the begin-

ning of the journey. And to Lila and Simms.
Merry Christmas. Happy anniversary. Happy
millennium."

We touched glasses all around and cried,
"Here, here," as we had always done, and drank
deeply. The crisp froth of champagne washed
away the lingering taste of goosey port. We all
moved up to hug Lila and Simms. Henry, tall and
tawny in the leaping firelight and suddenly so
like the Henry I had laughed with all through
Mexico that it took my breath away, poured
another round, and we drank that, too. Silence
fell. For a moment, there seemed nothing to say. It
had not been, all told, a comfortable day.

Lila and Simms had been married on the day
before Christmas Eve in St. Michael's, of course,
and this day was their fortieth anniversary. Lila
had told us in the fall that she and Simms were
repeating their wedding vows on this anniversary, and instead of St. Michael's, wanted to do it
here.

"What a lovely idea," Camilla said. "We should
all do it."

We were silent. There was no "we" for Camilla
anymore.

"It's the place we've really been happiest," Lila
had said, not looking at Simms. He said nothing.
He nodded. Lewis and I exchanged glances.
There was a strange note in Lila's musical voice,
one that I had not heard before. It seemed equal
parts iron and tremolo. But then it was gone, and
she went on sweetly.

"We always planned to do it on our fiftieth, but
I wanted to do it in the same century we were

married in. Who knows if we could still get up the church steps ten years from now? And all of a sudden, instead of the big hoo-ha at St. Michael's, and all the children and grandchildren and half of Charleston, and the reception and endless bad champagne, I just wanted to have it here. Just us. The family is not at all pleased, but we've promised them they can have a high holy mass with the archbishop of Canterbury for our fiftieth, if they want to. By then maybe we'll be too senile to care."

So we hung a few extra holly wreaths and banked the fireplace in green and white poinsettias, which most of us hated but had been developed in Charleston and had been massed at the altar on Lila and Simms's wedding day, and lit candles and turned off the lamps and, by fire and candle and tree light only, Lila and Simms Howard reaffirmed their vows.

They had chosen late afternoon, instead of seven o'clock, when the original ceremony had taken place, because Simms had a command performance later on at his company's Christmas party, and did not feel he should break tradition. His grandfather and his father had raised the toast and spoken a few avuncular words each Christmas of their times, and Simms always had, too.

"It seems like bad luck not to do it this time," he said. "I don't want to hex the company for the next millennium. I'll just stay an hour or so. I can probably be back for dessert."

We all nodded. Some of us smiled. The thought of Simms, stuffed full of goose and champagne and in his khakis and a crew-neck sweater, presiding over the vast, distinctly suburban holiday revels of a medical supply company was an engaging one. As if she could read our thoughts, Lila said, "He has his tuxedo in the car. He says he'll change in the rest room at the plant."

Simms grinned and most of us did, too. Lila did not. Neither did I. Would there be a little-used rest room in some tucked-away corner of the plant? Would a honey-haired, silky-skinned young woman with a flat upstate accent wait there for him?

I hated the thought and looked over, involuntarily, at Lila. She was looking straight ahead. I looked at Camilla. She was staring intently at Lila, as if to hold her upright with the sheer force of her gaze. I did not know if it was still going on, Simms and his women. But I knew that Lila, and the rest of us, were forever changed by it, even if most of us did not know it. Even if the center still held, there was a tiny crack now.

"Oh, Simms, who or what could be worth it?" I whispered just before Creighton Mills, more massive and commanding now, but still in his beach clothes, set down his sherry glass and moved to stand before the fireplace. The firelight leaped on his glasses and the cross on his chest, and he wore his clerical collar, but despite these he was still simply one of us.

"Church is in session," he said, smiling. "Lila, Simms. Will you stand together before me, Simms on my right hand and Lila on my left?"

They moved into their positions. From behind them I could not see their faces, but I could see the faces of those of us who could. Camilla watched, perfectly still, her beautiful face neutral. Henry smiled in simple happiness; pure Henry. Fairlie, beside him, her face smoothed into girlhood by the firelight, reached for his hand. Camilla's eyes moved briefly to them, and then back to Lila and Simms.

"'Dearly beloved, we are gathered together here in the sight of God, and in the face of this company, to join together this man and this woman in holy matrimony . . .'"

Creighton Mills's beautiful voice and the flickering firelight were hypnotic. Our days and nights in the place seemed to unroll before me like a strip of film. The Scrubs rushing me into the surf on my first day here, laughing. Fairlie and Henry doing the shag ankle deep in the rushing green and white water, to show me how it was done. Henry and Lewis heading out with their surf-casting gear while Fairlie, stretched out in the hammock, said, "Don't even think of bringing those fish in here." Camilla, alone and far down the beach with Boy and Girl. Lewis and me, naked in the phosphorescent surf, on fire with joy in our every atom. Charlie bellowing with glee as a long flight of pelicans grazed the water just beyond him, "Goddamn! It's the loan committee!"

Oh, Charlie.

All of us, on my first night, hands on the photo of the Scrubs on the first day they had come into the house as owners, swearing to share our lives forever.

Lila and Simms holding hands as they climbed the stairs from the beach at twilight, their heads bent together, talking earnestly. Talking, talking . . .

"'. . . let him now speak or else hereafter for ever hold his peace.'"

There was a silence; even the fire seemed to hush its breathing, and then Creighton said, "'Wilt thou have this woman to be thy wedded wife, to live together after God's ordinance in the holy estate of matrimony? Wilt thou love her, comfort her, honour, and keep her in sickness and in health; and, forsaking all others, keep thee only unto her, so long as ye both shall live?'"

"I will," Simms said. I could scarcely hear him.

When it was her turn, Lila's voice rang out as bright and hard as a diamond.

"I will."

"'Who giveth this woman to be married to this man?'" Creigh said.

Camilla got up from the rocker beside the fire, and stood, bent and fragile.

"I do," she said.

It was an enormously moving moment. Tears glimmered in more than one pair of eyes. In my mind I saw Camilla as she had been on the day I had met her, on the beach under the faded umbrella that we still used, glowing and beautiful, holding out her arms to me, saying to Lewis, "Well, Lewis, you finally got it right."

I did not really hear the rest of the ceremony, nor see it clearly. Tears blinded my eyes and the past in this place roared in my ears. I heard Simms say "'. . . to love and to cherish, till death do us part, according to God's holy ordinance, and thereto I plight thee my troth.'"

You'd better, you son of a bitch, I thought fiercely.

When Lila repeated the vow, her voice was nearly inaudible.

Simms slipped a ring onto her finger. It was an enormous sapphire, almost the color of Lila's eyes, and it looked like a great bubble of trapped seawater on her ring finger. She looked at it, and then up at Simms, a perplexed look, as if she had expected to see the small Tiffany solitaire with which he had married her. I wondered how much it had cost. Not enough. Not nearly enough.

"' . . . Those whom God hath joined together let no man put asunder,'" Creighton Mills said. Camilla was still in her fireside chair. Her eyes burned into the side of Simms's face. He did not turn. How could he not have felt those eyes?

"' . . . I pronounce that they are man and wife,'" Creigh said. And instead of the traditional benediction, he paused for a moment, and then said, "'Lighten our darkness, we beseech thee, O Lord; and by thy great mercy defend us from all perils and dangers of this night; for the love of thy only Son, our Savior, Jesus Christ. Amen.'"

"Amen," we all whispered. We looked around at one another. Creigh Mills caught the looks and grinned and said, "It's the old collect for aid against perils. Part of the traditional evening prayer. Lila asked for it. Come to that, it's not such a bad way to end a marriage ceremony, especially in this new millennium. I think I'll incorporate it in the future. Beats prenuptial counseling by a country mile."

Simms bent his face to Lila's and kissed her.

Both their eyes were closed. When they turned to face us, smiling, I saw that both their faces were wet.

A little silence held for a moment, and then Lewis said, "That ought to last you guys for a while. Let the games begin!"

We ate our feast then, murmuring compliments over the oyster-and-pecan dressing, drinking up all of the excellent Chilean wine that Lewis had brought, jibing at Fairlie's gelatinous goose, oozing fat and port and mired in prunes.

"Well, you should have known better," she said lazily. Fairlie was no better a cook now than the day I had met her. "Next year just assign me the booze. I can't go wrong. You guys will drink anything."

For the first time that I could remember, our beach house Christmas was an edgy and tenuous one. Everyone, not just I, seemed to feel the frisson, though I am not sure most of us could name it. Simms left just after the meal, and his absence seemed to leave a fissure in the skin of the evening that no one was eager to step over. Lila showed her new ring around, smiling at the compliments, but her eyes went every now and then to the door. Henry and Fairlie got up immediately and began to stack dishes in the pitted old white enamel sink, even though, over the years, Fairlie had been known to take long walks in bone-chilling cold or pouring rain to avoid the moment. Henry and I began to gather crumpled paper and ribbon. Camilla sat still, watching us, and then said, "Leave it, please. Everybody just sit down. I'm coming back out in the morning; I'll do it then. Right now I just want my people around me."

"You're coming out here on Christmas Eve?" I said worriedly. We were used to her habit of spending solitary hours and even days here, but surely now, at this season of homing . . .

"The children and grandchildren aren't getting in until tomorrow afternoon," she said. "I think little Camilla is dancing in the *Nutcracker* for the four-millionth time tonight. Just as well. My cousin Mary Lee is having one of her unspeakable brunches at noon, and I don't have to go to the airport until four. I'll do scalloped oysters for just us tomorrow night, and Lydia is having everybody for Christmas dinner. Thank God it's at five. That will give us all time to get drunk. I'd love the time out here alone in the morning. . . ."

Camilla rarely drank, but I knew that her battalion-like extended family harbored a few imbibers. Most Charlestonians's did. Lewis had said that when he was a child he had thought that carrying Uncle Joe Henry Cannon upstairs to sleep off the punch was as much a ritual of Christmas as the tree and the carols.

We laughed.

But still . . . but still. Tonight had always been our own Christmas ritual. None of us had ever come here on the actual festival days.

Lewis and I took the sacks of trash out to stow them in the big receptacle under the house. Everyone else settled themselves back around the fire and Camilla. The smell of perking coffee followed us out the kitchen door and into the cold. I looked back. It was a Norman Rockwell scene: the whispering fire, and the tree lights on the faces of old friends, drawn close at this season. But it felt like just that, an illustration.

We stood in the cold sand behind the house, holding each other close. I smelled the mothy wool of his sweater and felt his breath warm on my hair. We did not speak for a while, nor did we move to go back in. Overhead, the stars wheeled and burned, and the surf breathed on the beach.

"What's the matter with tonight?" I said into his shoulder. "I feel like when we go back upstairs it will all be different. It won't be us sitting there. Nothing will even look the same."

"'The times, they are a-changin','" he said. "Things aren't the same, Anny. They haven't been for a long time. They started changing when Charlie died. You just didn't want to notice."

I felt colder than I should have, there in the circle of his arms. I half-remembered studying entropy in physics in college. What had I remembered of it? That it was the nature of an organism to lose its structure and drift toward chaos? Was that happening to us, so slowly that we did not even comprehend it? That the entity that was us and the house and the beach was moving molecularly outward, like a dying star?

But there's a center still, I thought. Just like Camilla said. Maybe it's a little looser now, maybe a little flaccid. After all, we've lost Charlie, lost the sense of Lila-and-Simms, lost other things. But they were within the realm of the normal abrasions of time and life; they might hurt, but were not mortal. I was willing to admit that the whole organism that we were together could alter. That it might implode was more than I could contemplate.

"But here we are still," I said fiercely. My lips chafed against his sweater. "Still here, going into an entirely new millennium together. So many years, for most of you. After so long, after all we've lived through, what could possibly change in any of our lives that would move the . . . the focus of us anywhere else but to us and the house? I mean us, the Scrubs. I'm not talking about our lives outside."

"I've often wondered just what it was that held us together," Lewis said, hugging me hard. "It's not exactly normal, after all; not many school-day alliances last, not really. Did you know that some folks in Charleston call us the Lost Tribe, and the house Never-Never-Land? By all rights we should be just seeing each other at parties and weddings and funerals, and waving to each other at Sunday lunch at the yacht club. But you're right. Here we are still. I think everybody's feeling a little strange these days, not just us. Like things are beginning to change, to end. It must be millennium fever."

"But *we* really haven't changed much," I said stubbornly, feeling on the brink of peevish, childish tears.

"Look back, you'll see," he said, and kissed me on the forehead, and we dashed up the steps and back into the warm, dim room.

The strangeness persisted during coffee. People stole surreptitious glances at their watches, and cut their eyes worriedly toward Camilla. But she sat as serene as a Buddha, wrapped in the scurrilous old wedding ring quilt that we used for a picnic blanket, staring into the fire and rocking. She was smiling slightly.

She looked over at me.

"Have you been out of town?" she said. "I haven't seen you for three or four mornings now, and your car hasn't been there. I was afraid you were stuck somewhere awful like Scranton and might miss Christmas."

And I looked quickly at Lewis and blinked, as if I had just been shaken out of a long, deep sleep. There it was, then, the first great change, after Charlie's death, and almost that long ago now. Why had I never thought of it as that? I looked over at Lewis. He smiled and nodded.

Ten years ago, just after New Year's 1990, Camilla had had a late super with Lewis and me at Bull Street. All of us had been drifting into the habit of calling Camilla on the spur of the moment to share meals and short trips with us; we did not do it out of duty and Camilla knew that. She accepted or not, as she pleased. For the last weeks she had seemed more distracted than was normal for Camilla, even given Charlie's death. It was a calm distraction, merely a gentle otherwhereness. But it was noticeable, because Camilla had always been so perfectly there, so in the moment with us all. We did not exactly worry but we noticed it, and talked to each other about it.

"You think we ought to ask if anything's wrong?" I said on a Sunday afternoon at the beach house, just after that Christmas. Lewis and Henry and Fairlie were the only ones there. We were making a kind of bouillabaisse out of the small drums Henry and Lewis had caught that cold afternoon, and a few crabs Fairlie and I had netted off the dock, and some shrimp we'd bought at Simmons's on the way over to the island.

"Maybe we should," Fairlie said, dumping a whole bottle of chardonnay into the stew. She hated both the smell and taste of drum.

"If something was wrong with one of us, she'd have it out of us in a minute."

"Let her be," Lewis said. "She's always done this, kind of gone away somewhere every now and then. I can remember from when we were kids."

"Yeah," Henry agreed. "It usually meant some kind of Camilla bombshell guaranteed to alter the course of our universe."

"She was like that just before she got engaged to Charlie," Lewis said. "It was like she wasn't on the same physical plane as the rest of us."

Henry said nothing, only doused the broth with enough cayenne to lift it right out of the pot.

"Jesus, Henry," Fairlie cried. "That's going to scar our tracheas for life."

It didn't, though. But it did effectively kill the oily taste of the drum.

That night at supper with us on Bull Street, Camilla came out of her reverie just as I set a bowl of she-crab soup on the table, and said, "I just sold the Tradd Street house. A very nice woman named Isabel Bradford Thomas—she uses all three names—bought it for her daughter, Miss Darby York Thomas, for a wedding present. They're from Greenwich, Connecticut, and don't seem the sort who'll put flamingos in the garden.

I like them both. We close next Monday. I'm moving Tuesday morning. I'm telling you because you'll probably hear Lydia screaming all the way over here when I tell her."

"Jesus, Camilla, are you sure you want to do that? I always thought of that house as your insurance policy," Lewis said, putting his spoon down and staring at her. Now that she had come out of her reverie, her face and eyes shone.

She's actually happy, I thought. I'm so glad.

Aloud I said nothing.

"I can live very well indeed on what I sold it for," she said, grinning. "And I have a little money in a trust from my grandmother, and Daddy left both us girls a little more. Mother's got the balance of it, and she made another bundle when she sold off that big chunk of land on the Folly River, just across from Wadmalaw. Of course Daddy had promised the Coastal Conservancy to put it into a conservation easement, but if Mother knew that, she didn't let it bother her. It's that awful Folly Plantation development now. A cut-rate Kiawah. I hear it's struggling. I hope so.

"Anyway, I guess that that money and what's left of hers after Bishop Gadsden will come equally to Lydia and me. Though it would be just like her to leave it to the garden club or St. Michael's or somewhere. Whatever, with the sale of the house and this and that, I'm perfectly all right. More than all right."

"You didn't want to live there without Charlie?" I said.

"I really didn't want to live there, period. I'm sick of all the upkeep and the historic-house crap and the tours and people sticking their noses through the gate into the piazza. I have been for a long time. But for some reason, Charlie loved it. You wouldn't have thought it, would you?"

"I always thought it was you," I said.

"So where in the name of God are you going to live?" Lewis said sternly. I knew that he became stern when he was worried.

"Well, I've bought a little three-story house at the foot of Gillon Street. Completely renovated. The top floor is a very chic penthouse overlooking the harbor, with terraces all around. There's over four thousand square feet of living space on that floor alone, and the kitchen and baths are a dream. It's got three bedrooms, so the children can come when they absolutely have to, and I can have an office, and there's a two-car garage and an elevator from the parking garage. The dogs can run in the waterfront park, and I can practically see the widow's walk on the beach house from the terrace, and, best of all, I can keep it myself, with some help maybe once a week. It's easy to keep. It's essentially a loft, very open. Beautiful brick walls, and beams."

We were both silent. Camilla Curry in a loft? Doing her own housework?

I began to laugh. Camilla joined in, and then, after a moment, Lewis.

"You don't do anything halfway, do you, toots?" he said. "You do know that the historic preservation people are going to take a contract out on you, don't you? I thought they hated all that apartment and condominium development across East Bay like typhoid."

"Well, the building really *is* old," Camilla said. "And besides, I'm on the board, and I'm writing an interminable history of our good works that nobody else wanted to. They'd have to pay a professional a million bucks to tackle it."

"What are you going to do with the rest of it?" I said. "You said you had the top. Weren't there two floors below that?"

"There are," she said. "Already finished for apartments or office space. Parking and all. Listen, Anny. I'm going to make you an offer you can't refuse."

As it turned out, I couldn't.

In two months I had moved my staff and files and what furniture hadn't been ruined by Hugo into the two floors below Camilla, and Outreach became a downtown concern. The rent Camilla asked was a pittance compared to what she could have gotten, but she said it was worth it to her to have the space occupied by people she knew and who could keep an eye on her floor when she was away. She would not take a penny more.

"I will impose on you mercilessly," she said, when Lewis and I tried to persuade her to accept at least a little more money. I had gotten a small insurance payment on the ruined office on West Ashley, and my board would probably pony up a bit more. "It will be more than worth any rent you could pay me."

She didn't impose, of course, being Camilla, but it did end up that we spent a good deal of time together. Sometimes she asked me up for a bite of lunch in her sun-dazzled loft, and at other times she brought her sandwich and I brought mine and we ate them together while the dogs snuffled around the waterfront park overlooking the harbor. I often called and asked if she wanted me to pick up anything for her from Harris Teeter when I shopped, and she usually did. Even with the elevator, the advancing osteoporosis made carrying heavy grocery bags difficult for her. I insisted on carrying anything heavy from her car up to her penthouse; she would call me on her car phone, and I, or sometimes Marcy or one of the others, would meet her in the garage and hoist the burdens for her. No one minded doing it, because everybody in my office loved Camilla, who had us all for holiday drop-ins and sent down little treats now and then. But Camilla hated being fetched and carried for.

"It's one reason I moved here, with the elevator and everything on one floor," she grumped. "I don't need a young harem doing my bidding. It embarrasses me."

"Where would you be if you fell and broke a hip?" I said.

"Right up here with a live-in something or other," she replied. "There's room. I made sure of that. And then, of course, we'll all eventually be living together somewhere wonderful on the water; and the rest of you can tote things for me. I've got it all covered."

Since Charlie died we had not spoken of our plan to move in together and care for each other when we reached retirement age, and it gave me a flush of pure comfort to hear her refer to it. Things were still the same. Loss had not altered us. All systems were still go.

In the years since that time, my office had flourished and expanded its services, and I truly believe it was in part because Camilla's extensive network of well-heeled contacts associated Outreach with her, and opened their purses accordingly. She had no official connection to us, and I never asked her for one; she did not sit on my board and I would have died before I would have let anyone solicit her on our behalf. But there she sat, a floor above us in this pretty downtown house like a benevolent angel, and I had heard more than one of our supporters say, "How are things doing up at Camilla's?"

Sometimes she would bring a visitor or an associate on one of her endless projects—she was literally never idle—down to meet us on their way out, and often ended up holding a fractious child or grabbing a ringing phone.

"You see what they're coping with," she would say to her guest. "You remember Outreach at Christmas."

And many of them did.

I loved my small office on the second floor, with its arched Gothic window that looked into a little courtyard bordered with palmettos and flowering shrubs. There was a small wrought-iron umbrella table and chairs there where clients could wait and we could have a quick meal or a Coke, and a joggling board, which had come from Camilla's Tradd Street house, that enchanted our small charges. Lewis and Henry had built me a little raised brick fishpond and Lila and Simms had gifted me with four gorgeous, flashing koi, who grew sleek and spoiled and enormous from the offerings of the children. When a great blue heron had taken to perching like a gargoyle in the live oak overhead and glaring hungrily at the koi, Lewis fashioned an ornamental screened gazebo over the pool, and the heron soon flapped creakily off elsewhere.

But we did not lack for wildlife. Besides the koi, our garden was home to a tribe of pretty green lizards, and a family of fat squirrels, and once, in our first spring there, a pair of mallards had swooped down and spent two or three days looking us over and scrabbling about in the shrubbery as if they were making a nest. Eventually they left us for a much grander garden and pool, but I had been enchanted with the two wild visitors. They seemed a fortunate omen, part of the magic of the place.

I didn't see as much of it as I would have liked, however. For the previous two years, I had been doing something different, which I loved, that felt as if it might ultimately help change and heal lives. In the years since Outreach had moved into the new space, I had accompanied Lewis and Henry on more trips to scavenged places withering from lack of medical attention, and I had met many more doctors who gave their time, as Lewis and Henry did. Always it was my mission to try and set up a rudimentary community resource center for whatever village we were in, and I got pretty proficient at it. None of the doctors we worked with knew of anyone else who was doing anything similar.

"It would be a godsend if somebody like you was available to all the medical teams that go out," a stout, red-faced tropical disease specialist

said, one itching, steaming evening in the
Guatemalan jungle. He was swatting miserably at
mosquitoes and drinking vodka like water. I was
itching, too, but at least Lewis and I had a small,
bare, clean room with mosquito netting all to ourselves in the tottering little inn on the riverbank,
and there was actually a rusty fan, and a coughing shower. I was grateful. Rudimentary as it was,
it did not approach the sheer gaudy awfulness of
the upstairs of the whorehouse in the mountains
of Mexico.

Henry and Lewis looked at him, and then at me.

"Why not Anny herself?" Henry said, and
Lewis grinned slowly and nodded.

"Like a consultant, you mean," the red-faced
doctor said.

"Like that," Henry said. "Groups could hire
her as part of their teams; I think your national
organizations would spring for a fee if it wasn't
ridiculous. She could go wherever she was
needed most, not just with Lewis and me. She's a
pro at this now, and she doesn't take up much
space or eat much. She'll sleep anywhere, too."

I glared at Lewis and he leered showily.

"I couldn't leave Outreach that much," I
protested, seeing the idea form itself in my head
even as I demurred. "And I'd be away from home
a lot more than I want to be. I'm at the age when I
should be slowing down, not taking on a whole
new career and routinely slogging around in jun-
gles or deserts or wherever. It's a good idea,
though."

Lewis leaned back in his dilapidated chair and
swigged warm local beer, grimacing.

"Well, how about this?" he said. "How about you fly into one or two cities a month where they have medical volunteer programs like ours, and maybe a couple of times a year to Washington, and have seminars on setting up these programs? Teach the docs how you do it and how to recruit local talent, show them what and who's needed and how to locate them wherever the teams go. Maybe teach seminars for the nurses, too; they're probably the ones who'll end up setting up the programs. Make up brochures and a slide show or film or something showing what you've done in other places. Get some testimonials."

"I . . . how can I leave the office that long?" I said. "And who would hire me? I'd have to make at least enough money to cover expenses. I could donate my time, but airfare and hotels—"

"*A*," Lewis said, "Outreach can run itself by now. You know that. That Marcy of yours could head it and you could keep a little office space there if you liked, help out when things were slow for you. *B*, who'd hire you? Anybody sponsoring these groups, in a New York minute."

"But how would they know about me?"

"Are you kidding? This bunch tells their sponsors. They tell others. And so on. You'll be launched in a month."

"Right, by God," said the tropical specialist, swatting on his neck something large and evil that was not a mosquito, but no longer noticing. "I'm calling my bunch before we leave here."

I thought perhaps his promise would be washed away with the piss of the next morning's hangover, but it was not. I had an invitation in

Pittsburgh and one in Houston before we left the jungle.

It's what I have done ever since. I keep a cubicle at the office in Charleston, and pay Outreach a modest rent, and I help out every now and then when they're abysmally overloaded. But mainly I spend a couple of days almost every week in cities around the country, and the rest of the time I'm on the phone with clients, or in meetings when they come to me. I miss working daily with Outreach, but as Henry had predicted, Marcy is a superb director, and with our enlarged staff and Camilla's bridge pals's largesse, the office rolls smoothly on largely without me.

Sometimes I hated that. I would think back to the early days, of scrabbling for funds and holding wet, squirming babies and chasing down empty-headed teenage mothers and trying to coax another summer out of my disreputable old car. I would remember the day I met Lewis, in the steaming rain in his parking lot, clutching a wriggling abandoned child, and my heart would squeeze with love and wistfulness for that wild-haired young woman and outrageous red younger man.

But all in all, I loved what I did, and I knew that it was important work, and I still went home most evenings to the dancing wild man, who was, if less red-thatched on top, still a laughing, freckled dervish. Lewis, in his sixties, had lost little but hair.

We spent a lot more of our time out at Sweetgrass in the latter part of the decade. Lewis had acquired a rangy, dedicated young partner for his practice, and spent a great deal more time in the charity clinic. But except for emergencies, he kept his clinic hours to the first three days of the week, and came home to the Edisto house on Wednesday nights or Thursday mornings. When I came back home to Charleston now, it was in all probability to Edisto that I went. The slow, dreaming spell of the river and marsh, and the sweet whisper of the old oaks and longleaf pines in which Lewis had planted many of his acres for a cash crop to run the plantation, and the grassy hummocks and skeins of drifting gray moss soothed my airline-jangled nerves, and gave me back my young husband.

For Lewis flourished like the proverbial green bay tree at Sweetgrass, and I could see, in his freckle-splotched face and wide, sweet grin, the day that we would sell or rent Bull Street and divide our time between Sweetgrass and the beach house. We only kept the house now for a place to spend the night in town, or to put our feet up during a long, hectic day. I still loved my funny little Gothic cave, but more and more, Sweetgrass was mine and Lewis's real home.

The beach house was still our collective home, the home for the entity that was the Scrubs. Wherever we strayed, no matter what changes had come to us, we all came homing back to Sullivan's Island like pigeons, whenever we could manage it. It seemed to me to be even more precious now, with the years spinning faster away from us, than it had been in that golden time when time itself seemed to bubble like a bottomless spring from the sand.

Henry, too, was semiretired by now, and devoted a great deal more time to his trips out of town with the flying doctors. Fairlie, still darting and restless of mind and body, had largely given up her dance classes, and grew bored and snappish in Henry's absences. She finally surprised us all by taking up riding and then teaching equestrian courses to children and preteens at the big equestrian center on John's Island. She bloomed again in the long, sunny days on horseback, and even entered a couple of shows on the hunter-jumper she preferred. She won in her class both times.

We were all surprised; Fairlie had never before shown any interest in riding. We did not even know that she rode, or if she had told us, did not remember.

"But I always did at home, until I came to the College of Charleston," she said. "I was damned good. Ribbons and cups all over the house. It feels wonderful to be back at it, and Henry's gone so often. I'm thinking of buying my own horse. We always had them at home, though they were mainly flat racers."

"What does Henry think of all this?" Camilla said in amusement.

"He thinks it's great. Keeps me off his back."

"A horse will go great on Bedon's Alley," Simms said, grinning. "You can keep him in the kennel with Gladys."

For old Gladys, thin and patchy in her hide, and limping, was still alive and in relatively good health, and still fiercely and devotedly Henry's dog.

"The Japanese call it the one-pointed heart," Camilla said once, observing Gladys's devotion. "They talk about it in reference to artists who are consumed by their work, but I don't see why it shouldn't apply to dogs. I'm reading a book about sixteenth-century Japanese art."

"I thought you were writing a book," Lila said, smiling at her lifelong friend.

"That, too," Camilla said

Our old dogs out at Sweetgrass had long since died, and lay now in the dog cemetery under a live oak behind the house, in the herb garden Linda Cousins kept. There were many of them, the dogs of this place, back to the very first one, Lewis said. He often went to visit them in the cool of the evenings. Robert Cousins, who had been the master of many of their hearts, kept the graves clipped and mowed and the small head-stones upright. I thought that he grieved truly for them. He and Lewis talked of them often, as if they had been old friends, lost. Well, of course they had.

Lila's wild-hearted little Sugar was gone. It seemed to me that she simply and finally wore out her great, joyful heart and went to sleep. Lila cried for days, and I cried, too. I had loved the ridiculous little dog, who had never known her boundaries. Simms had given Lila another Maltese, a puppy, for Christmas that year, and she was a lovely little thing, petite and winsome and so feminine as to make you laugh. Lila swore she batted her long eyelashes at you. Her name was Honey. Lila doted on her. I could never really warm to her, after my love affair with the tiny tiger that had been Sugar. But she went everywhere with Lila, in her large Realtor's tote, to all appointments and to the office and shopping, to the beach house.

"You spend more time with that dog than you do Simms," Fairlie said once to Lila. Fairlie was not a fan of Honey. The little dog had bitten her knuckles sharply when Fairlie reached to pet her.

"Well, I wouldn't stick my hand right in your horse's face . . . if you had a horse," Lila had said, in defense and only half teasing.

"A well-trained horse wouldn't bite no matter what," Fairlie had snapped. "Maybe 'well trained' is the operative word here. Does she bite Simms? I'll bet she does."

"I don't think she really knows who Simms is," Lila said sweetly.

We shifted uncomfortably around the dinner table. Simms's trips away were escalating as he neared retirement age, and his career was not slowing, as the other men's had. Logically, we all knew why. The medical-supply company was represented on three continents now. Simms would want to see everything in order before he eased off and passed the reins. We all supposed it would be to his daughter Clary's methodical Rotary Club husband, by whom he had three interchangeable grandchildren. I wondered sometimes if he had not simply had his order for a son-in-law and successor filled early on. Timothy was perfect in both respects. It was difficult to tell how Clary felt about it. She was, as Fairlie said, the uncrowned soccer mom of the Western Hemisphere, totally immersed in her children.

Lila and Simms were very rich now, much more so than any of us were or ever would be. But very little had changed on the surface of their lives. They still lived on East Battery, in the beautiful old house they had always owned. They still came to the beach house, though Simms not so frequently as the rest of us. They had let the place on Wadmalaw go, and mostly Lila worked. Simms sailed often, ferociously and alone. Once in a while they spent some time with their daughter's family on Kiawah, but the children and grandchildren of Lila and Simms did not come to Sullivan's Island.

Come to that, none of ours did either, not really. Lewis's two daughters were both married, with children. They had fled California and their mother, and settled on Long Island and in Connecticut respectively, and went in the summers to Europe or the Caribbean or Point O' Woods. They called dutifully, and once or twice we saw them when Lewis or I had business in New York, for lunches with the grandchildren at the Russian Tea Room, or dinners somewhere stark and chic that the twins picked. They had brought the grandchildren to Edisto once while they sailed in the Greek isles, and the children sulked and sighed loudly, and refused to go out into the heat of the Low Country, preferring to watch television. They were unmoved by the ospreys and eagles and herons and wood storks, and refused even to accompany their grandfather to the wondrous baby alligator nursery. The bobcat, I supposed, had long ago gone to some black-water hummock in the sky, but on certain still nights when the river was silent except for the lazy slap against the pilings of the dock, and no moon rode the sky, we both heard, or thought we did, the faint rustle of spartina grass at the foot of the dock, and the slap-thud of heavy paws. The children did not come out to listen. The summer that they were with us, the Perseid meteor shower was closer and more spectacular than we could remember, extravagant fireworks in the sky, but the aggrieved children were glued to the hard-rock channel on cable, mourning the malls of Long Island and Connecticut. We were both exhausted and delighted when we decanted them from the ancient Range Rover at the Charleston airport.

"Truly the spawn of their grandmother," Lewis said. The children did not visit again.

Henry and Fairlie did spend a lot of time with their daughter, Nancy, and her brood of tall, skinny red-blond children. They were as gangling and sweet tempered as Henry and as quicksilver as Fairlie, and we all enjoyed them when they came out to the beach house. But they, too, had their own enclave at Wild Dunes, and Fairlie and Henry saw them mostly there or in Bedon's Alley.

"I wish they had a place like this to run wild in," Henry said to us when he and Fairlie had come out to Edisto the last weekend of the year and the century. "They're going to grow up with no sense at all of the plantation life that all their people before them lived. They already think a plantation is a place with guides in costumes, that you have to pay to get into."

"I always thought you'd maybe buy a place out

here or somewhere after your island place went
with Hugo," Lewis said. "I remember that for a
while you were talking about it. It's surely not too
late. The Crunches are putting Red Wing on the
market. I think Lila's handling it. We'd be neighbors."

There was an odd silence. Henry shoved his
hands into his pockets and kicked at a stump.
Fairlie looked off down the river.

"It just never seemed the right time," Henry
said finally. "Listen, there's something—"

"I need to get back to town," Fairlie said
abruptly. "The center has a new mare coming in
from Aiken. I want to get a look at her."

She turned and started back to their truck.
Henry looked at us helplessly, then shrugged and
turned and followed her. "See you guys New
Year's," he said over his shoulder. Lewis and I
stared after them. I thought they had planned to
stay for lunch.

I told Camilla about the little scene when I went
up to have lunch with her the next day.

"He had something he wanted to say to us," I
said. "But she just cut him off."

She looked out over the water.

"She's a force of nature," she said. "He could
no more stand up to her for very long than he
could to a category-five hurricane."

"You think there's something on Fairlie's mind
that she doesn't want us to know?"

"Has been, for a long time. She's been downright distant. Usually you can't stop her talking."

And she had, now that I thought of it. Distant
and even more restless than usual.

"Well, at least Henry seems pretty much the same," I said worriedly. "Or he did until yesterday."

"Bless his dearest heart," Camilla said, smiling. "It takes a lot to ruffle Henry. She can do it, though. I always wondered, in a way, why he married her, aside from the fact that he's crazy about her, of course. Henry needs a safe, sheltered harbor more than anybody else I know. He hasn't had a whole lot of that with Fairlie. Of course, he'd never say so, but I've known him all my life. I know when he needs his home port."

I had never thought of Henry as someone who needed an anchor, or a sheltered harbor. He went fearlessly and with relish into places few other men would go. But still, she was right; she had known him since kindergarten, at Miss Hanahan's Little School behind her home on Church Street.

"All of a sudden it feels like almost everybody I know is . . . somebody I don't know," I said unhappily. "I wish I knew what was going on with us."

"It's not all of us," she said, pouring me a last cup of the fragrant oolong that she knew I loved. "It's just some of us. Maybe we'll find out New Year's Eve. No better time to open people up. Don't fret, Anny. It will take more than a couple of burrs under our saddles to change us in any important way."

She got up to pull the drapes across the French doors to the terrace, where the dull glitter of low winter light on the water was blinding. I got up and went back downstairs to my office for the last time in the only century I knew.

7

THE NEXT MORNING, New Year's Eve, 1999, I got
up early and went over to the Queens Hospital
Wellness Center to do my stint on the treadmill
and the weights. I tried to do it every time we
stayed in town, which we'd done the night before
because we were going out to the beach house
around midafternoon. But I'd never liked it, and
only did it because Lewis insisted, and it did
make me feel better.

Henry did it religiously most mornings when
he was in town, and relished it. For one thing, it
kept his body compact and trim, and for another,
it was the hands-down favorite unofficial social
club of the downtown community—the men,
anyway. They all knew each other, and were easy
in the knowing, not caring a whit about sagging
stomachs or softening biceps. I envied them both
the effortless companionship and the careless
acceptance of their bodies.

For myself, I had no corresponding network of
exercise buddies, largely because I got there earlier than most women did, and was glad of that. I
hated the idea of jiggling and huffing and sweating under the eyes of anybody else, most espe-

cially the sleek women who came to the center on their way to lunch or committee meetings, carrying their street clothes in Saks bags. So I came early, muffled in sweats, and sought out the farthest treadmill in the room, and the weight bench farthest from the mirrored wall. Usually I had my corner of the gym to myself, but today there was someone striding vigorously on the elliptical trainer next to my favorite treadmill. Before I could sidle away, a high female voice cried, "Mrs. Aiken! Anny! Happy New Year!"

Oh, shit, I thought. Bunny Burford. Just exactly the note I want to end the century on.

Bunny was a legend in the downtown medical community. Once, when I first knew her, I called her an icon, and Lewis grimaced and said, "An iceberg would be more like it."

"But she's always giggling and trilling and hugging," I said. "I don't see any ice in that."

"That's because the real Bunny Burford is submerged so deep very few people ever see her. But way down there she's cold as steel and twice as hard. If you don't know how to handle her, she can be damned dangerous. Don't ever tell her anything personal, Anny. She won't forget it, and she'll find a way to use it."

"Then how did she get to be deputy administrator of Queens? Seems to me you'd have to have something more going for you than spite and ambition."

"Oh, she does. She's smart as a whip, and she runs a tighter ship than Charlie ever did. She was his secretary when he first came to the hospital, and she made herself more and more indispensable, until she really could run it almost as well as he could. Trouble was, not many of our big supporters liked her, and the staff certainly didn't. She was merciless to the nurses. Henry always thought she wanted to be a doctor, and made her position at Queens into the next-best thing. Her authority is almost unassailable. It would take someone years to learn as much about the hospital and the people there as Bunny knows. She fancies herself a sort of social hostess, too. She shows up at every party and fund-raiser and seminar as though she were an ordained part of it, and smiles and flatters and listens raptly until whoever's being courted is floating ten feet off the floor. In that sense, she is a good fund-raiser. It's one of the reasons nobody wants to challenge her."

"And the other reasons?"

"Well, like I said, she knows an awful lot about an awful lot of people. I don't know if she's ever used any of it or not, though I've heard she has, but everybody knows she could. Now *that's* power."

"She sounds awful," I said. "I don't see how an . . . an outlander could just come into Queens and get herself an inside track like that."

"Well," he said, "for one thing she's not exactly an outlander. She grew up on Church Street and went to Miss Hanahan's Little School along with most of us, and her brains got her a scholarship to Ashley Hall with a lot of the girls. I don't imagine she was ever really part of all that . . . she went to the Little School because her mother was a teacher's helper there, and they lived on Church dependent on somebody or other in exchange for her mother's doing the cleaning. I don't know where or if she went to college; I think I heard business school. I know she wasn't around Charleston for a while. And then, just after Charlie came in to take over, she appeared in his office and asked to be his secretary, and she was so smooth and assured and obviously smart, and she asked for so little money, that he hired her on the spot. You know Charlie . . . he was never a detail man. He was more than glad to have somebody competent to handle all that. And she was very, very competent. Good looking, too. That didn't hurt."

"Good looking?" I asked incredulously, thinking of Bunny's towering, blocklike figure and nearly vermilion hair, piled high in a lacquered coil that looked as if a mortar shell could not dent it. Her eyes were pale blue and narrow, and her mouth was large and lipsticked to the same shade as her hair, and all her features seemed to sit in the middle of her face, as in a child's drawing. She seemed absolutely impenetrable. She did have pretty skin, though, taut and pink and white, and virtually unlined. I wondered if the rest of Bunny, beneath the tailored Talbot suits she wore, was as smooth and soft and dewy. It was a bizarre notion.

"She was good looking, in a kind of Amazonian way," Lewis said. "She was tall, with a little waist and those incredible boobs and hips, and her hair was almost as red as Fairlie's, and she wore it in a long pageboy. And she always wore thick red lipstick that made her look like she'd just eaten a raccoon or something. She always seemed to me like Stupefyin' Jones in *Li'l Abner*. Oh, yeah. She cut quite a swath for a while. Charlie dated her some when he first came."

"What happened with that?" I asked.

"Camilla," he said. "There was no contest there."

So on this last morning of the last century in the millennium, I flinched as if I had been bitten by a blackfly, and said, "Hi, Bunny. You're up and at it early this morning."

She wore a neon-pink velour top and pants, and her astonishing bosom jutted shelflike and absolutely immobile in front of her as she strode on the elliptical trainer. It was hard not to stare at it. She wore matching pink pom-poms on her white exercise shoes.

"I've got plans for later," she said coyly. "I need to get started early. What about you all? Aren't the Scrubs going somewhere exotic like Hawaii or the Riviera to see the millennium out?"

I thought that her notions of exotic did not exactly coincide with mine, and I hated the familiarity of "the Scrubs" on her lips. Nobody else I knew but Bunny ever called us that, except us.

"Exotic in the extreme," I said. "Sullivan's Island, to be exact."

"Oh, yes, Camilla's beach house. It must really be something special; I heard enough about it from Charlie over the years. I've never seen it. We always went to the Isle of Palms."

I did not know who "we" was, and did not ask.

"Well, it's not very special, I'm afraid, except to us. It's practically falling apart. We all own it equally with Camilla now."

I was immediately sorry I had told her that; it was no one's business but ours. But something about the way "Camilla" also sounded on her lips put my back up; a sly sort of familiarity, maybe. I knew that Camilla would probably not even remember who Bunny Burford was.

She smiled broadly, her cheeks bunching up into tight little apples, and said, "How convenient for Camilla. Well, she always did know how to get what she wanted, even in kindergarten. I can remember her just standing and staring at a ball I was playing with, smiling and smiling, until I gave it to her. I never saw that smile fail. I'm surprised she hasn't smiled somebody else into taking care of her since Charlie died."

I felt cold rage spread in my chest, but would not give her the satisfaction of showing it.

"Camilla hardly needs taking care of," I said. "She usually takes care of us."

"Bet she does," Bunny said, grinning fiercely. "Well, have the Scrubs got all their supplies laid in?"

"Supplies?"

"For Y2K," she said as if to a backward child. "You know, water and food and kerosene for heating and cooking. Toilet paper, toothpaste. If the bridges go out, you all could be stuck over there for weeks."

"Sounds wonderful," I said. "I've always wanted to do that. What about you? Have you battened down?"

"Oh, yes," she said complacently. "My friend and I have reservations at a lovely hotel in Asheville, and my car is already packed with everything you could possibly need for a long siege. My friend is even bringing his gun."

"*Gun?*" I had a crazy image of Bunny stalking

through the woods in all her massive pink fuzziness, gun at the ready in case some woodland creature was unlucky enough to show itself.

"We don't anticipate needing it," she said. "The hotel is very secure, and it's a lot easier to defend yourself in the mountains. But we feel safer just having it. You never know who might break into your room in a power outage."

True, I thought. It's undoubtedly open season on room service waiters.

Aloud I said, "Well, good luck to you, Bunny. I hope you don't have to use any of that stuff. And have a happy new whatever."

"The same to you," she said as I got off the treadmill and started for the shower. I wanted to get in and out and dressed again before she came into the locker room. Bunny Burford naked and pink and dripping was more than I could handle. I turned away so she could not see the laughter starting in my eyes.

"You all get your supplies in, you hear?" she called after me. "Better to be safe than sorry."

"Right," I called back over my shoulder. "I'm just on my way to pick up sandbags now."

Before I got to the locker room I heard her say, "Sandbags?" in a worried voice. I was in the shower with the water roaring down on me before I allowed myself laughter.

In the car on our way over to the island, I told Lewis about my encounter with Bunny.

"She's even more awful than I thought she was," I said. "She actually implied that Camilla schemes and manipulates all the time, to get what she wants. I think Camilla took her ball in kindergarten, or something. Anyway, she's never forgotten it."

"She wouldn't." Lewis grinned. "Camilla is everything Bunny isn't, and won't ever be. By the way, did you know her name was Bernice, not Bunny? At any rate, she's had a thing about Camilla ever since Charlie met her. Thinks Camilla stole him from her. I've never heard her say anything, but some of the nurses have, and it gets around. Nobody pays any attention to her."

"I hope it never gets back to Camilla."

"Why? She'd laugh her ass off. You know nothing much ever bothers Cam. Who's the friend she's taking to the mountains?"

"I don't know, but he's packing a gun."

He winced. "So would I, if Bunny was my friend. What kind of supplies do you think they're taking?"

"Oh, you know. Bottled water. Toilet paper. Dress shields."

"Bad girl," he said, grinning.

The sky was lowering when we reached the beach house, although the air was soft and there was a hint of some flowery fragrance in the air. Whether it was blooming on the island or borne in from far away on the tide, I could not tell. Except for Camilla's old gray Mercedes, ours was the only car in the sandy parking space. There was an aluminum ramp now, up to the house, beside the steps. We had had it installed for Boy and Girl, who could no longer manage the stairs, and for Gladys.

"I use it sometimes, too," Camilla said ruefully. "The four of us old crocks crawling up it must be something to see."

We had all laughed. Camilla might be badly stooped now, but she was so ethereally lovely in her sixties that the word "crock" could not possibly apply. I was sure that she knew that.

We got out of the Range Rover and unloaded the back. Tonight was to be the feast of all our feasts. We had brought sherried she-crab bisque from Linda Cousins's kitchen, and both duck and quail, courtesy of Robert. I had bought some silken, hideously expensive truffled pâté from O'Hara & Flynn. Henry and Fairlie were bringing rare-as-black-pearls white asparagus, which we would have with a caviar mayonnaise. Lila had stuffed an imperial crown pork roast and Simms was bringing champagne of a vintage that the rest of us would have had to mortgage our homes for. Camilla was making the dessert. She would not tell us what it was to be. Even though we had hauled food up these stairs hundreds of times, it was hard not to be excited about tonight's dinner. Everything about the day and the night had the breath-held air of anticipation about it.

The turn of a century, the turn of a millennium . . . portent was everywhere. All of a sudden, midway up the stairs, I shivered, as if a goose had walked over my grave. I stopped and looked back at Lewis.

"What?" he said.

"This millennium thing feels like some kind of juggernaut bearing down on us," I said. "I don't want to live in a new millennium. I haven't used up the old one yet."

"Go on up before I drop this, my little Luddite," Lewis said. "When we're ninety the *Post and Courier* will hail us as the only generation to see the year and the century *and* the millennium turn. We'll be interviewed incessantly."

"You wish."

From the outset, the night was Camilla's. She met us at the door virtually shimmering with excitement, thrumming with a kind of palpable radiance. I had seen her happy before, and laughing, and exhilarated, but I had never seen her like this. You could almost see the dancing particles of light around her, feel her exuberance. We both smiled, and then laughed. It was impossible not to.

"You look like somebody plugged you in," Lewis said, kissing her on the cheek. "Share with the class."

"Oh, I don't know," she said, hugging us both hard. "All of a sudden I just thought how many years we've all been together here, and how I've loved it, and how I've loved you both, and everybody, and how glad I am that it's never changed."

An answering wave of love for her and us and the house and the island swept over me, and I hugged her back, and spun her around. I was shorter by five inches, but she was as light as a bird's wing, as a winged seedling borne down on the wind from a chestnut tree.

"Me, too," I said, tears prickling behind my eyelids. "I can't even imagine what all those years would have been like without you . . . without us. We're like family. No, better than family, because we chose each other."

"You know what Robert Frost said about family and home," Camilla smiled. "He said, 'It's where, when you go there, they have to take you in.'

We've taken each other in through everything."

"Till death do us part," Lewis grinned, teasing her for her crazy delight.

"Till then," she said, her eyes brimming, and I knew that she was serious. Somehow, the thought made me uneasy.

We had agreed for this one night to dress formally, over the groans from Lewis and Henry, and I went up to our bedroom and hung our evening clothes in the musty, mothy closet. Does anything else smell like a beach house closet? Out the window I could see scudding cloud shadows on the beach and water, and see the spartina bending down under the rising little wind. Little gusts of sand peppered the windowpane. Suddenly I was wild to be out on the beach to taste the wind, to let the blown sand sting and scour my face.

"Anybody want to go for a walk?" I said.

"Absolutely not," Camilla said. "I've worked all afternoon on my hair."

"Me, either," Lewis said. "I'd join you in a nap, though. If we hurried up and slept fast, we could get in a couple of good hours."

Even though he'd largely passed on his regular practice to young Philip Ware, he sometimes went in when a real surgical emergency presented itself, and one had last night. He'd been in the operating room at Queens until three. Most doctors I knew were chronically sleep deprived, and grabbed naps when and wherever they could.

"Go on and take one," I said. "I won't be long. I just want to take the last beach walk of the century. I'll be back way before dark."

"Take the dogs, will you?" Camilla called from

the kitchen, where something smelled heavenly.

And so the two grumbling old Boykins and I went out into the stinging wind, and walked down the wooden steps to the beach.

It was colder on the beach than I had expected. The wind was straight out of the east, raw and smelling of dank, salty winter water. I scrunched my neck farther down into the cowl of my hooded sweatshirt, and jammed my hands into my pockets. We crossed the corrugated ripples where the tide cut ran when it was full, and went down to the hard-packed sand just above the tidal slick. The tide was going out. Frothy lips of dirty white foam receded toward the water. Here and there a broken shell or a rubbery, glistening tentacle of seaweed lay half buried. Sometimes in the winter the beach was studded with sea glass and shells and wonderful, twisted limbs and logs of driftwood, but today the beach was nearly empty, of both its artifacts and its people.

Boy and Girl sat down on the sand at the same time and gave me reproving looks. They refused to get up when I whistled to them, so reluctantly, I took a last look at the tossing green-gray sea and turned back toward the dunes and the house. Complacently, now that they had achieved their purpose, they gave me doggy grins and waddled ahead of me toward the steps.

I looked up at the house, thinking that it was the last time in this century that I would see it like this, looming like a light ship over the beach and the sea, just at twilight, with the windows glowing. As always, my heart lifted.

My eyes went past the house to the big dune to its left, and my heart gave a great, fishlike leap and then seemed to stop. There, on the dune line, just as I had seen it on the week before Hugo so long ago, was a figure cloaked in gray, looking down on me. I stood still. The dogs whined at me reproachfully.

Then the fading light shifted and the figure became Camilla, in her old gray raincoat, waving to me and calling something.

"Lewis and I are going for more ice," she shouted through cupped hands. "Be back in a few minutes."

I waved back, standing still for a moment while my heart slowed its thundering. Somehow I thought I could not have borne another omen.

By the time they came in with the ice, dark had fallen. I had had a quick shower and was upstairs dressing. I felt, for some reason, as breath-held and tremulous as a young girl before her first prom. It was not, of course, the first time we had all seen each other in evening dress, but it was the first time on this island, in this house. Why that was important, I could not have said, but it was.

"You up there?" Camilla called out from the kitchen below. "I could use a hand."

"Yes," I said. "I'm coming."

I went slowly down the old staircase, trailing my fingers on the splintery banister, stepping over the perennially damp spot on the runner underneath the leak we had never had fixed. I took a deep breath, and then came all the way down into the living room.

"Holy shit," Lewis breathed.

"Anny, you look absolutely glorious," Camilla said.

I could feel myself, ridiculously, blushing.

The dress was black and fluid and long, thin-strapped and cut in a deep V in front and back. More of my modest, sun-speckled breasts showed than in anything else I had ever worn. I had bought it impulsively at Saks several years ago when they had marked almost everything down to nearly affordable, thinking that a plain black evening dress would probably last my lifetime and should come in handy one time or another. But in the intimate light of my own bedroom my breasts had seemed to protrude like overripe melons from the bodice, and the black silk cupped my ample behind like lascivious hands, and I had never worn it. But tonight it was just us. . . .

In the past two or three years, a thick silver streak had appeared in my hair, running from part to ends as if it had been painted there. I secretly liked it, though I often said I knew that I looked like a skunk, because it was the only distinctive thing about my still-untamable thatch of curls. Tonight I wore a pair of silver earrings I had bought in Arizona, when I'd gone there to work in the remote Four Corners area with Lewis and Henry. The earrings were ornately scrolled and pierced, and hung halfway to my bare shoulders. They and a pair of excruciatingly painful black satin high-heeled sandals that I could not remember why I had bought were the only accessories. I had practically no jewelry, and had never really wanted any.

"Is it immoral to ravish your own wife on the stairs?" Lewis said.

"No, just uncomfortable," Camilla said, laughing. "Go on upstairs and get dressed yourself, you goaty satyr. You've shot your chance for a nap."

"Open the wine and pour us a glass, Anny," she said as she followed him up the stairs. "And would you stick another log on the fire? No, wait, let Lewis do it when he comes down. Oh, and Fairlie called. Henry is stuck at the hospital with an emergency and will be here when he can. She's coming on out. She's furious with him."

I rummaged in the drawer we called the thing drawer for a corkscrew, thinking that it was late in the game to get upset when your doctor husband had an emergency. By the time Camilla and Lewis came down, the wine was poured and waiting and I had set out the pâté and crackers and a bowl of the benne wafers that no Charleston cocktail party is ever without.

I drew in my breath when Camilla appeared. I had expected her usual silvery-gray chiffon or dull-green satin, but she was dressed in a long slide of crimson velvet, cut low and caught under her breasts with a diamond brooch that I knew had been her grandmother's, long sleeves that came to a point over her slender hands, and a diamond and ruby necklace that looked a part of some fabled crown jewels, under glass in a tower across the sea. Her copper-and-silver hair had been brushed until it flew around her face with electricity, and, like Camilla herself, seemed to give off sparks. She could have been a woman on a tapestry in a great castle. She seemed utterly archaic, utterly of another time. I had thought so many times before, but Camilla tonight was a medieval effigy come to life.

"Excuse me while I go upstairs and set fire to my dress," I said. "It seems a shame to waste this on us."

"I wouldn't wear this except for us," she said. "I've had this dress since I came out, and the necklace was my great-grandmother Charlebois's. She's supposed to have smuggled it out when the Huguenots fled the persecution, but I think she nicked it somewhere. What persecuted Huguenot ever had anything like this?"

A car's tires scrunched in the driveway, and Lewis, looking scrubbed and correct in black tie, went to look out the kitchen window.

"Lila and Simms," he said. "All dressed up, as my old mammy used to say, like mules in buggy harness."

"You never had an old mammy," Camilla snorted. "You were the only kid in Charleston who had a white nanny."

"That never goes out of this house," Lewis said, and went down to help Simms with the case of champagne.

Like many downtown men, Simms wore evening clothes as if he was born to them—which he was. No matter how paunchy or jowly he got, nor how often we saw him in salt-stained sailing clothes or his hideous old college madras bathing trunks, Simms in black tie was formidable, so right that you thought, on seeing him, "Well, of course." Even Simms struggling through sand holding one end of a case of champagne was indisputably south of Broad.

How do they *do* that? I had wondered more than once.

Lila, picking her way through the sand in cobwebby silver sandals, looked, in the diffuse light from the old yellow outdoor bug light, as she must have looked on the night of her debut. Hers had been the St. Cecilia ball, I remembered, possible to you only if your father was a member of the society. She wore a simple white dress cut modestly at the neck, with cap sleeves and a princess waist, and her mother's famous triple-strand pearls. Her hair was put up, and her earrings were modest pearls, and until she turned around, Lila Howard might have seemed a dove among peacocks. But in back, her dress was cut to the waist or perhaps even a bit below, and had a skirt slit to the knee. She was so thin that the knobs on her spine stood out in bas-relief, but somehow, I thought, an extra ounce of flesh would have looked gross. Lila, like Simms, looked exactly what she was. Somehow they drew the eye like a light in darkness.

Fairlie had ridden out with them. I had seen Fairlie's sea-green silk before, a shimmery column that dipped up to the knee in front, and left one elegant shoulder bare. But whatever she wore, it was not possible to look away from Fairlie for very long. Her spectacular red-and-silver hair brushed her shoulders, and two hectic red spots stood out on her cheeks. I had seen those spots before. They were anger, not rouge. Fairlie looked . . . incendiary. I thought, moving to kiss her cheek as she came into the kitchen, that it could not always be comfortable being married to Fairlie. Exhilarating, beguiling, amusing, yes. But rarely simply comfortable. I had never thought Henry minded, particularly; he gave no sign of it. But I thought also that I would not like to get the full bore of those flaming blue eyes, as he would when he finally got here.

It could have been another tense evening, but Camilla's incandescent happiness simply banished tension. She sat beside the fire with happiness flowing off her like honey, and none of us would have spoiled the night for her any more than we would have slapped a child. We smiled at her reminiscences of our holidays on the island with as much glee as she did; when she laughed, we laughed with her, delightedly, as you do at a small child's belly laugh. Before long we were simply giddy on Camilla. She could have asked us to jump off the widow's walk and we would have rushed to do so.

I had a sudden thought.

Bunny Burford was right, I thought. She does get what she wants. And we give it to her gladly. She does it with sheer laughter and love; who could refuse that? If that's manipulative, it's also enchanting, a gift to all of us. It may even be what's held us together for so long. I always thought it might be the house, but maybe it's simply Camilla. It's like a spell, or sorcery.

And I smiled at my old friend with love and amusement. She smiled back, a smile that warmed and enfolded. You are the most special thing in my life, it said.

"I'm not going to wait one more minute for Henry," Fairlie said, getting up to look in on her asparagus. "He can just eat leftovers. The rest of us are starving."

Of us all, Fairlie was the only one who seemed impervious to Camilla's spell. She sat straight in her chair by the fire, her beautiful back totally upright, her legs crossed, one foot swinging. I was reminded of the lashing tail of a great cat. Her mouth was a straight line and her narrowed eyes were fixed on Camilla. I could not imagine what she was thinking; if she was angry, let her confine it to Henry.

She went into the kitchen, and we all stirred and looked at Camilla. She was looking after Fairlie with a sort of tender bemusement.

"Perhaps she's right," she said. "Henry could be held up for who knows how long."

We were getting up from our chairs, reluctant to lose the magic of the last hour, when there was a thundering of footsteps on the back steps, and the door flew back on its hinges, and Henry hurtled into the kitchen, grinning and breathing heavily, as if he had been running for miles.

"Tell me I didn't miss dinner," he said.

We all burst into laughter. He wore rumpled blue hospital scrubs and the clogs many surgeons wear when operating, and over them his perfectly fitted tuxedo jacket and a black tie, untied and hanging crazily down the front of him. His long face wore its customary beatific smile, and his silver hair was in his eyes. Suddenly I simply and wholly loved him.

Camilla ran to him and hugged him fiercely. Then she tipped her head back and looked up into his face.

"I love you, you idiot," she cried. "Who is more wonderful than you are?"

And the night lifted up and flowed on again, borne up by joy.

We sat late at dinner. Camilla had brought out her mother's huge silver candelabra, and in the middle of the table the ivory tapers burned steadily. The table itself was swathed in Lila's mother's silky white damask. The matching napkins, I thought, might have served as tea-table cloths.

"Mother always called them the double-damask dinner napkins," Lila said. "She always washed and ironed them herself. Eliza could out-wash and out-iron her any day, but Mother wouldn't let anybody else touch them. Woe unto whoever spilled anything on them, or actually used them to dab their lips. I have a great urge to dump red wine on every one of them."

"I know just what you mean," Camilla said. "Once, when I was about eight, I used Mother's napkins to make bandages for the hospital I was starting. The dogs were my patients. You can imagine what dog drool does to old damask."

"I carved my initials in our linoleum once," I said. "Mother never noticed it until she sobered up, four years later."

The table burst into laughter. My origins were part of our history now, my provenance ours. No one was ill at ease with it.

Dinner was glorious. We ate until about eleven, and drank a great deal of the lovely, fruity merlot Simms had brought, along with the champagne. In the living room the fire hissed and snickered, sighing as it settled into embers. Outside the wind rose.

Finally Camilla got up and went into the kitchen.

"No looking," she said. We had nearly finished another bottle of wine when she came out, bearing a baked Alaska on a silver tray. It was high and intricately swirled, and its meringue was delicately browned. She had surrounded it with the suicidal early camellias that bloom in Charleston gardens around Christmas. We drew in our breath in a collective gasp of pleasure. It was perfectly right.

"I haven't had baked Alaska since . . . well, I think it was your birthday party, Camilla," Lila said. "We must have been about ten. I remember so clearly Elsie bringing it out on the veranda where we were sitting at little tables, and telling us to eat it quick because it was going to melt in a minute."

"And it did," Camilla said. "Do you remember what Lewis and Henry and Simms did with it?"

"Had a snowball fight," Lewis said. "Only one I ever got to have in Charleston. God, your mother was furious with us. I haven't had baked Alaska since."

I felt a stab of, not envy, but loss, that I had not shared their rich collective childhood. I had never in my life had baked Alaska.

It was a night for memories.

"Remember the time we were going to some formal thing or other and none of you guys had black ties? I forget why," Lila said. "We had all met at my house, and Mother called Mr. Garling himself, and he went down and opened the store, and was standing out on the street corner when we drove by, and he handed in three ties. You put them on in the car."

"Princes of the city," Fairlie muttered. It was not said fondly. What was the matter with Fairlie? I thought again.

"It seems like yesterday," Camilla said, leaning back in her chair. "Time is funny. When I was young, I used to think it went in a straight line, from one place to another, but now it seems like it sort of curves all over the place and doubles back on itself. You can be anywhere at all, any time. What do they call that thing?"

"A Möbius strip," Henry said. "That's a nice idea. You could go back and visit your life anywhere and any time you wanted."

"It sounds like flypaper," Fairlie said.

Camilla sighed deeply, and looked at her watch.

"If I could freeze time, this is exactly where I'd do it," she said, smiling around the table at us. "I'd keep us and this night just like we are now. But since I can't, let's do the next-best thing. It's a surprise. We've got thirty minutes till midnight. I need you all to come out in back with me."

"You've got to be kidding," Fairlie said. "It must be thirty degrees out there. I didn't bring a coat."

"Wrap up in a blanket," Camilla said. "You can't miss this."

We bundled ourselves into whatever we could find.

"Give me five minutes," Camilla said. "And I need to borrow Henry."

"When didn't you?" Fairlie said, almost inaudibly.

I thought I was the only one to hear her. It was true. Camilla had asked Henry for help of one sort or another many times since Charlie died, and he had given it affectionately and without question. So what? The other men had come to her aid at times, too. We all had. We were, after all, the Scrubs.

I watched as she and Henry went out the back door and vanished down the steps. She had on her old raincoat and seemed to float on Henry's arm like a captive cloud. From the back you did not notice the cruel hump. As they vanished out of sight down the steps, she was saying something to him, and he was bent close to listen, laughing.

"Now," she called up presently, and we went out into the cold of the dying century.

Someone had put up the old tiki torches in a circle in the sand, and lit them, and the glow was both beautiful and unearthly. In the center of the circle they made sat a group of large tin boxes and cans, half sunk in the sand. Just outside the circle was an aluminum washtub filled with champagne on ice. Beside it was a tray of those ghastly plastic flutes that you can buy in grocery stores around the holidays.

We were silent, looking at Camilla and Henry.

"Fireworks," Camilla said, laughter caught in her throat. "Charlie absolutely loved them. Henry got as many of the fancy ones as he could find, and we're going to shoot them off at midnight. Light up the whole sky. Let Charlie and everybody else know the Scrubs are still here."

And we did. We filled the awful glasses full of the wonderful champagne, and held them up in silent toasts to one another, and as the bells of all the churches in Charleston and Mount Pleasant and Sullivan's Island rang out, and the great eruption of fireworks from the waterfront park across the bay in Charleston bloomed into the sky, Henry reached down and lit the fuses.

"Get back," he said, and we jumped back just as there was a great *whump* and the air exploded with the sound and light and color. Streaking arcs shot into the sky and became multiple showers of pure color, drifting slowly toward the earth. Great bangs produced green, blue, and red flowers, never seen in an earthly garden. Exploding stars seemed to shriek in midair, and died gently on the sand in tiny sizzles of yellow and silver. It was amazing, an aurora borealis that we had created for Charlie at the birth of this looming epoch.

No one spoke for a long moment, and then Lila whispered, "What are they, Henry?"

"Cherry bombs, screamers, Roman candles. Only not the old ones we used to shoot off when we were kids. These are the real deals. I got them at a stand on West Ashley. We probably needed a permit."

"If we didn't get a permit to launch Charlie," Fairlie said, grinning, "we sure as hell don't need one to shoot off a few firecrackers."

After the last spark had settled to earth and vanished like a snowflake, we all kissed. We had never done this at our other New Year's Eve celebrations, only with our husbands or wives, but this seemed the natural and indeed the only thing to do. Lewis kissed me deeply and long, his hands in my hair. Simms's mustache brushed and tickled as he bent down to me. Henry's kiss was soft, and as sweet and unaffected as Henry himself.

"Happy New Year, pretty girl," he whispered.

"Happy New Year, Charlie," Camilla said in a light, clear voice.

Mine were not the only wet eyes as we went back up the stairs and into the warm house.

"I brought brandy," Camilla said. "Let's have some in front of the fire before we go to bed. I hate to let this night go."

We sat before the dying fire, mostly quiet, sipping the old Courvoisier. My mind, lulled with brandy and firelight, did not alight on any one thing, but hovered back and forth over the years in this house, sipping at them like a hummingbird. Lewis sat on the rump-sprung sofa beside me and held my hand, his finger tracing soft scrolls on my wrist. For a long time no one spoke.

Then Camilla said, "There's one more thing. I've been thinking for a long time about how to end this night, and I think this is perfect. I hope y'all will agree. Let's renew our vows. Let's repeat the Scrubs's sacred oath to take care of each other forever, and swear it on the photograph, like we did way back when."

Her eyes and skin glowed, and her mouth curved in the soft smile she smiled when she had done something to please one of us, a smile of pleasure and gratitude at being allowed to serve. If she had asked me at that moment to swear to murder, I would have done it.

We all raised our voices in delighted agreement. Like the rest of Camilla's night, it was simply the perfect thing to do.

Simms had stood up to get the photograph
from its place on the wall when Fairlie said, "Oh,
let's wait till the next time we're out here. We've
really got to get back to town, and I don't want to
rush it."

We all stared at her. Her cheeks were flaming.

"You aren't staying over?" Camilla said. They
always did, on New Year's Eve. We all did.

None of the rest of us spoke. Strangeness
curled into the air.

"Well, I just wanted to start off the next thousand years in my own bed."

"Your own bed is upstairs, too," Camilla said
softly. She looked at Henry, who would not meet
anyone's eyes. Finally he raised his own to
Camilla's, and then to all ours.

"We have something to tell you," he said.
"There's no sense in waiting."

"*Henry!*" Fairlie spat. "You promised. . . ."

"It's not right, Fairlie. We've let it go too long,"
he said, and his voice was steely and even. I had
never heard him speak so to her. My breath
seemed to stop. Whatever it was, I suddenly
wished I might die before I heard it.

"You know I've been talking about retiring," he
said. "We've decided that I'll do it early next summer, and . . . that we'll go to Kentucky."

He paused, as if waiting for us to reply, but no
one did. Camilla made a soft sound of pain but
did not speak. Fairlie was looking steadily into
the fire, her lips a tight line.

"Fairlie's given up most of a lifetime to me and
Charleston," Henry said, almost pleadingly. "It's
only fair to spend the rest of it in her place. Her

brother is selling us the family's farm, and Fairlie's going to have horses. All her old friends are there, and she's always wanted to breed flat racers."

"And what will you do?" Lewis said, his voice quiet and thick. I knew that he was near tears, or real anger. For myself, I only felt a white, ringing shock.

"Muck out the stables," Henry said, but his voice was not behind the joke. "No, I'll spend a lot more time with the flying docs, and maybe do some consulting work in Louisville. It's not far. And we'll be here every summer. We'll want to see Nancy and the kids, and of course, we can't do without you all. We'll have lots of time. That's what retirement is for."

Still, no one spoke. In the silence I could hear the crashing of walls, the pattering rain of mortar.

There was a flurry of polite conversation then, all of us murmuring our good wishes and agreeing that of course we'd see them, almost as much as we did now. I knew that no one believed it. Fairlie's eyes were fixed far away from this house on the island. I wondered if she'd ever really loved it. I wondered if I'd ever really known her.

They got up to go, and Camilla went to them and kissed both of them on the cheek.

"Nothing matters but that you're happy," she said. Her eyes were closed. I did not want to look into them. Henry's were blank.

After they had gone, we went, one by one, up the stairs to our bedrooms. There did not seem to be anything else to say. In the high old bed in the

room that had always been ours, Lewis and I
clung close together under the dusty piled quilts.
Once he started to say something, but I shook my
head against his neck, and he did not. After a
while, I think he slept.

But I did not, not for a long time. I lay still,
watching the dust-speckled path of the moon arch
over our bed and finally fade away. Camilla's
room was next to ours, and I heard no sound from
it, though I listened. I thought that I might get up
and go to her if it sounded as though she was in
distress. But the night was silent, except for the
wind and the peppering sand on the window-
panes.

I had a very strong sense of her, though. It was
almost as if I could see and feel her through the
wall, physically touch her. I felt the presence of
Camilla Curry in the next room almost painfully
clearly, Camilla lying absolutely still and silent,
alert in every atom of her being. I had the odd
sense that she was keeping watch.

The first Tuesday of the new year I was scheduled
to fly to New Orleans for a consultation trip. I was
still feeling shocked and bruised, almost physically, and did not want to go.

"Go on," Lewis said. "It'll help."

So I made my plans.

The morning of the day I was to leave, Fairlie
called me. The sound of her voice jolted me, as if
she had spoken from the grave. But it was her normal voice, rich and slow, this time full of annoyance.

"I am so mad at Henry I could spit," she said.

"He's going out of town tonight with those damned flying fuckers, and he'd promised me he'd take me to see *Tosca* at the Galliard. I'm going to run away from home. Want to come out to the island with me and spend a couple of nights? We could have a slumber party. Give each other Tonis and stuff."

It was as if she had never murdered the Scrubs with one stroke.

"I'm going out of town, too," I said, keeping my voice as neutral as I could. "Sounds fun, though. Maybe Camilla would like to go."

"No," Fairlie said. "She said she had the flu. She sounded terrible."

"Well, will you mind being alone out there? I've always loved it."

"Actually, no," she said. "It'll be good for me. I can be as sour and awful as I want to. Maybe I'll run naked on the beach. Maybe I'll pee on the fire. Maybe I'll eat worms."

I laughed a little, because she sounded so like the old, non-murdering Fairlie, and because I could see her doing it all.

"Pee away," I said. "See you when I get back."

I called Camilla. Her voice was hoarse and nearly inaudible.

"Have you got the flu?" I asked. "Fairlie said you did."

"Not really. Just laryngitis. I just didn't much want to go out to the island with her."

"Do you hate the thought of her being there? I do."

"Of course not," Camilla said. "It's as much her house as it is mine. I just don't feel like going."

"Well," I said, "take care of yourself. I'll be back in a couple of days. I'll come up."

"Do," she said. "I miss you when you go away."

The meeting in New Orleans was interminable and largely unproductive, and to add insult to injury, my connecting flight out of Atlanta to Charleston was four hours late. It was nearly three in the morning when I pulled into our court-yard on Bull Street. The downstairs windows were lighted. I frowned. I had thought Lewis would be out at Edisto.

He was sitting at the kitchen table, a cup of untouched coffee in front of him. He was in his scrubs, and he looked ghastly, white-faced and hollow-cheeked. His eyes and nose were red, as if he had been crying.

"Oh, God, Lewis, what is it?" I cried softly, running to kneel beside him.

He took both my hands in his, and squeezed them so hard that I flinched. I knew he did not notice.

"Anny . . . ," he said, then his voice died. He cleared his throat. I waited, almost totally shut down inside.

"Anny. The beach house burned. It burned tonight. There isn't anything left."

"Fairlie," I said, my ears ringing.

His voice seemed to come from a great, windy distance.

"Fairlie didn't get out," Lewis said, and began to cry.

part three

8

THE NEW HOUSE—or houses, rather—sat on a small hummock of palmettos and live oaks, looking out over sparse, winter-grayed marshes into a wide, wind-whipped stretch of steely water. Around them, as far as you could see, there was nothing but marsh, hummock, forest, water, sky. Wildness. It was beautiful, even in winter, and I knew that when the marsh greened with spring and the waterfowl and the creek's small, scuttling citizens came back, it would be spectacular. It was early February, and a low purple-and-orange sunset burned over the water and the marsh and woods beyond. The whole vista was steeped in a vast silence and stillness so profound that you instinctively whispered. Though it was creek and marshland much like that on which Sweetgrass had been built, it did not feel the same. I did not whisper at Sweetgrass. When I got out of the car with Lewis and stood looking at the three houses, I ached, suddenly and almost mortally, for the sound of the sea.

We had turned off the Maybank Highway and crossed over to John's Island from Wadmalaw Island. It seemed a long drive. I was used to the semirural landscape going to Edisto, and the banal jumble of small subdivisions, convenience stores, fast-food places, and occasional used-car lot along the highway was depressing.

Though Lewis had not told me, I knew that we were going to see a place that the others had thought might be a possible replacement for the beach house. Oh, of course not that, but a place on the water that could shelter the Scrubs. We had not spoken of it, but I knew that I for one would never again go to Sullivan's Island, never again spend time with the sight and the sound of that warm, personal sea. But that did not stop me from mourning them almost as deeply as I mourned Fairlie, and I did not think that I could like the new place. I did not say so, but I knew that Lewis could read my silences as well as my words. He didn't speak much, either, during the drive. When at last he said, "Here we are," his voice sounded rusty from disuse.

The road was graveled and pocked with winter rainwater, and though small, stark one-story brick buildings stood on either side of the turnoff, the road itself was wild and steepled with moss and branches. There seemed to be nothing on either side but the old, encroaching forest. A few of the trees wore faded orange ribbons around their trunks, but they did not intrude on the thick, chilly isolation. When we came out into a clearing and saw the houses and the marsh and the water beyond, something prickled in my mind. It seemed that something else entirely should be standing at the end of the long, stout dock that stretched forever out over the marsh before it reached the water. I could almost see it, a sort of pentimento beneath the landscaped hummock and the three graceful little tabby houses set in a semicircle on a circular shell driveway.

I looked at Lewis, my brow furrowed, and he grinned and said, "Booter's. Remember?"

And I did, suddenly: the tin-roofed pavilion where we had eaten oysters and drunk beer and danced like wild things under a white moon so long ago, the first time I had ever been out with Lewis. Now there was no flimsy lattice of sagging docks and grubby, wallowing boats, but instead the grand, silvered walkway and dock with a fretwork Victorian pavilion at the end, and three slips for boats, empty now.

I looked back up at the houses, flushed pink with the last of the sun. Thick plantings of oleanders and crepe myrtle framed them, and the great live oaks behind them made a silvery backdrop with their moss. In the spring, I knew that resurrection ferns would explode from their trunks. The houses had long, low verandas and porch swings, and I could see, just behind them, a great screened enclosure that meant a pool. A small, low tabby building beyond that proved to be a guest house. Lights glowed sweetly in the mullioned windows of the middle house.

"Oh, Booter," I said around a lump in my throat. "What happened to Booter?"

Lewis came around and opened my door, but I did not get out. I wanted to slam the car doors and wrench the car around and squeal out of this beautiful place that lay over the bones of Booter's

Bait and Oysters. A small bit of the sinew and bone of my youth was interred with Booter's.

There's less and less of us left now, I thought. Not of the people we were. It's being blown away, or burned or buried.

"Booter is in the VA hospital with Alzheimer's and emphysema," Lewis said. "He's been there a long time. Henry and Simms and I go by and see him sometimes, but he doesn't know us. I don't think he can last much longer. He sold the place and the chunk of land around it—it must be a hundred or so acres—about fifteen years ago, to some super-rich guy from New Jersey who wanted a private hunting-and-fishing place for his buddies and a getaway for his family. He got as far as these houses and the dock before he got hauled off to the slammer for insider trading."

"Who owns it now?"

"As a matter of fact, Simms does," Lewis said. "He bought it as investment property right after the guy got sent up. I think he thought he might develop it one day. But so far he hasn't. He's kept the houses and dock in good shape, but beyond that, nothing's been touched. We thought it might . . . you know . . ." His voice was so freighted with hope that I smiled and squeezed his hand.

"It's pretty, isn't it?" I said. "Not at all what you'd think a New Jersey convicted felon would build. Let's go take a look. Somebody's here already. But I'll bet you knew that."

He grinned and nodded, and we scrunched across the oyster-shell driveway and up to the middle house on Booter's marsh.

The weekend after Fairlie's memorial service all of us except Henry met at Camilla's loft and sat looking out over the cold, tossing harbor toward the island that no longer held anything for us, and talked about what to do next. From time to time, one or more of us broke off to mop at tears, and Lewis and Simms sat patting the old dogs, and looking steadfastly at the open ocean, not the island. Henry was not with us. I did not know when he would be, again.

Nobody had really wanted this meeting or this conversation, but Camilla had insisted.

"If we don't have a plan, we won't do anything, and the Scrubs will just drift apart and none of us will even have each other. I know it's too soon. I know nobody wants to talk about another place. But we need for things to go on, one way or another, and I think we need each other and the water, and I think we need to do it sooner rather than later. It will never be the same, but it might come to be something real to us. A different place for changed people, maybe, but still ours. I need the us of us. Please think about it for my sake, if nothing else."

And my heart pinched me, because Camilla literally never implored. And of us all, she had lost the most. Charlie, and her friend, and her house. I still thought of it as Camilla's house. I think we all did, except maybe Camilla.

"I think we should do it," I said, clearing my throat. "I don't think we should drift too long. What if we're not us except when we're together?"

We looked at each other and then at Camilla.

She was smiling faintly, but there was a pleading, almost painful to see, in her brown eyes. I wondered if I was the only one to have noticed that Camilla looked as though she had been starved and beaten. She seemed to have aged years in a scant week. Her candle glow was gone. I think we would have agreed to anything to ignite it again.

Within five minutes it was agreed that we would begin to look for a place on the water where we could weekend and summer, not too far from Charleston, but well away from the road and bridges that crossed the Cooper River, toward Sullivan's Island. In truth, I don't think that most of us cared much at that point where this place might be, or even what it would be like. But even if we did not want it, we needed it. That seemed enough for now.

"I might know a place," Simms said. "It could work very well. Let me take a look and let y'all know."

"Oh," Lila said. "If it's where I think it is, you'll love it."

"I doubt that," I said to Lewis on the way back to Edisto. "But I'd hate to see us just drift apart. And Camilla really needs us to be together."

"We'll at least take a look," Lewis said. "You know it can't be Sullivan's, Anny, but that doesn't mean it can't be good."

And, standing in the cold, fast-falling twilight on Booter's hummock, I looked at the shining lighted windows and smelled the sweet smoke of driftwood and cedar and heard the little slap of the river against the dock pilings, so like what I heard at Sweetgrass, and thought that perhaps, just perhaps, this might be good. Or at least, not bad.

Camilla threw the door open to Lewis's knock and we walked into a large, beamed room finished in washed cypress, with exposed cypress beams and a great river-stone fireplace, and a wall of bookshelves on either side of it. There was little furniture, but a fat denim sofa sat before the fire, and two flowered chintz easy chairs that I recognized from Camilla's Tradd Street house, and the flokati rug that Lila had given Camilla after Hugo lay before the fire on the wide, sage-painted boards of the floor. The windows were small and deep set and mullioned, but there were a great many of them on the wall facing the marsh and the river, and the last embers of the sunset flamed in the panes. The light here would be glorious, except perhaps in late afternoon, when it would swallow the room. But then you could draw the drapes. They were heavy and lined, made of rough linen in a green just a breath deeper than the floors.

Well done, I thought, swiveling my head around the room while Camilla stood smiling and with her hands folded in front of her, waiting. Whatever else it is, it's a nicely done house. Not a cottage. A house. I can't imagine sand on these floors, or oars and crab nets stacked in the corner, or old beach clogs from fifteen years back under the kitchen table. But maybe this is what and where we're meant to be now.

Camilla went out of the room to fetch drinks, and I said to Lewis, "It's nice, isn't it? But it looks like a house for grown-ups. The beach house was always for kids, even if it was for old kids."

"They didn't call it Never-Never-Land for nothing," Lewis said. "Would it be so bad, growing up?"

"Not if I don't have to dress for dinner and put on shoes."

"You don't have to dress at all," he said. "There are two other houses exactly like this, plus a guest house. We'd have one of them. You could go naked as a jaybird all day for all anybody would know. Good plan, as a matter of fact."

Camilla handed around drinks and said, "Do you think you could cut it here, Anny? There are other places we can look, of course, maybe something big enough for all of us together, like the old house. But you know, we always said we'd do this. Live like this. Maybe we should try it on for size for a year or so."

"It seems . . . oh, I don't know. Sort of *big*," I said. "Do you think we'd rattle around?"

"There has to be a place for Henry," Camilla said.

"Do you think he'll come back?"

"He'll come."

For we had lost Henry, and it felt to me like a fatal wound.

I had hardly seen him since before the fire, although I knew that Lewis and Simms had seen him on the day after that terrible night. But after that he seemed to vanish; he did not answer the Bedon's Alley telephone or the one at his office, nor could we raise him at Nancy's house. She did not seem to know where he was, and her voice was so bleared with grief that I did not have the heart to pursue it with her.

"We'll surely see him at the memorial service," Lila said, still white with shock. And Camilla, bowed by more than the osteoporosis, agreed.

"Let's let him be for a while," she said. "He always did go off by himself when something was wrong."

I could imagine nothing wronger than what Henry was facing, and agreed not to try to hover over him with offers of help and comfort. Obviously, there was neither for him, and would not be, for a very long time.

Henry was having Fairlie's remains—and none of us could bear even to speculate about what that term meant—sent to the farm in Kentucky after the service, and he would follow, and see her buried in her own earth.

"I don't know any more than that," Lewis said dully two days after the fire. He had not spoken directly with Henry since then, either, but had found a note from him under the windshield of the Range Rover in the courtyard on Bull Street. We were staying there until after the memorial service, which would be held, heartbreakingly, at Henry and Fairlie's house on Bedon's Alley. I could no more imagine it empty of Fairlie's darting, hummingbird presence than I could imagine Henry staying on in it alone. Like the others of us, my mind could cast itself no farther forward than the memorial service.

The night before the service Henry appeared at our Bull Street door with Gladys on her leash, at his heel. Both man and dog looked as if they had been boiled down to sheer bone and sinew. Henry was gray all over—face, hair, lips. Beside him, Gladys whimpered and shivered. She did not know where she was, but she surely knew that nothing good was going to come of this outing.

No, he would not come in, Henry said almost formally, or rather, oddly shyly. He did not look at us directly.

"I have an awful lot to see to, and I badly need for you all to do something for me," he said.

"Anything," Lewis and I said together.

"I want you to take Gladys, if you possibly can. I can't . . . look after her anymore. I've got her bed and blanket and food and medicine out in the car, and if you agree, I'll get Tommy and Gregory to take the golf cart out to Sweetgrass in the morning in Tommy's truck. I'd appreciate it more than I can say if you'd stay close to her, and take her around in the cart every so often. She'll love Sweetgrass, and she's used to being in the cart around water. I thought if you all, you know, found another place . . ."

"You know we'll take her. I love her," I said, starting to cry. He hugged me, briefly and hard. I could feel his heart behind his sharp breastbone, beating in great, dragging thuds. He bent and laid his chin on the top of my head, and then lifted it and looked at Lewis and me squarely for the first time.

"She's an old lady," he said. "I may not get back in time. I always thought I'd like her to live until her life gets to be a burden to her. You all know her almost as well as I do; you'll be able to tell if that happens. I hope you'll feel you can honor it."

I nodded, past words, and Lewis put his hand out and Henry gripped it hard with both his own. His knuckles were blue white.

"I'll call you," he said. "It may be a while, but I *will* call. I need . . . to be away until I can . . . well. I hope you'll honor that, too."

He bent and put his arms around Gladys and simply held her for a long time. He said something into her once-glossy ear, and then he was gone. Gladys began to whimper in earnest, and by the time I could see through my tears to kneel and take her in my arms, she was shivering hard.

We took her into our bed that night, and she lay between us, in my arms, until the shivering finally slowed and stopped. I could feel all her bones, and her faltering heart. She could not have spent many nights in her old life without the scent of Henry and Fairlie in her nostrils.

Just before dawn I could feel her begin the twitching that means deep doggy dreams, and I whispered to her: "I hope they're the best dreams in the world, and I hope I can make them all come true."

All over Charleston people were asking, "What happened? How could such a thing happen? Why was she out there by herself? Where was he?"

It's odd, I thought. It's entirely proper and natural downtown to die of illness or old age, but an accident, especially a spectacular one like this, is alarming, almost taboo. Maybe it's so in any tight-knit community. People know each other so well that what happens to the one resonates profoundly with the rest. Donne had it right. No man *is* an island. Each man is a part of the main. When the bell tolls south of Broad, it tolls for us.

"We don't really know," I said over and over in the days after the fire. I could not count the people who asked. I knew that the others were getting the questions, too. In the four days afterward, until the memorial service, I stopped going out except for essentials. I canceled a trip to St. Louis, and handled my office work from Bull Street. Lila showed no houses, and Camilla ordered her groceries from Burbage's. Our answering machines worked overtime.

For the truth was, we really did not know, absolutely and without question, what had happened that night on the beach, and likely never would. It seemed quite certain, though, that it happened exactly like Duck Portis, the fire chief on the island, and Bobby Sargent, the chief of police, thought it had. Fairlie had been curled up on the downstairs sofa before the dying fire, and had lit the kerosene heater because the night had turned bitter cold. Somehow, later, probably from a gust of the wild, booming wind that had come up off the ocean and in through the flimsy, uncaulked glass doors from the porch, the old heater had overturned. The smell of kerosene was still powerful in the charred living room, even after the water from the fire truck had saturated it. It wouldn't have taken long. The house had been a firetrap for years; we knew that. Duck and Bobby thought that Fairlie must have been deeply asleep, and died of smoke inhalation before the flames reached her. But I could tell from Lewis's haunted eyes that he did not think so. He had, after all, seen Fairlie before she was taken away. Bobby had reached him first.

Duck and Bobby and Lewis and Henry had grown up summers together on Sullivan's Island, and had authored all manner of mischief before sober manhood overtook them. When they could not find Henry, they had called Lewis at Edisto. He had gone immediately to the beach house. After pronouncing Fairlie he had tracked Henry down in West Virginia, with a team of doctors who had gone into the mountainous coal-mining country. I remembered later that I had trained the nurses who accompanied them. Lewis did not remember much of that phone conversation. He never did. We protect ourselves as best we can. Henry had wanted Fairlie to go to Stuhr's Funeral Home, so Lewis called, and rode there with her. Then he went home to Bull Street, to wait for me.

As far as Duck and Bobby could tell, the fire had started about eleven. The holidays were over and the black, blasting wind had driven most of the vacationing cottage owners home. The beach house was far down, on a jog that curved sharply right, out of sight of most of the permanent residents. It was a motorist coming home late over the great, humping bridge from Charleston who had sighted the flames and called 911.

"Why on earth was she downstairs wrapped up in an old quilt?" people asked. "There must have been five bedrooms in that old heap. Why did she light a kerosene stove as old as Methuselah when there was an electric space heater right across the room? Could she have been, you know, drinking?"

But to us, it all seemed perfectly understandable. Fairlie loved to sleep in front of the fire. She did it often when we all stayed over. Usually she built the fire up enough so that it would last her the night, but in that bone-rattling cold it would not have been enough. I could just see her dragging the old kerosene stove out of the jumbled kitchen closet, lighting it, and rolling up in the dusty quilt that covered the sofa. Fairlie had always hated the electric heater. She had thought that it was dangerous.

"They all are," she said once. "Why else do you always read about them burning down tenements and housing projects? It's never a kerosene stove."

"It's probably because even our indigent have electricity now," Lewis had teased her. "Would you willingly smell kerosene if you didn't have to?"

"I like it," Fairlie said stubbornly. "It reminds me of the bunkhouses at home. My father used to pour it on all our scrapes and punctures, too; we were always stepping on horseshoe nails."

Oh, Fairlie, I thought. If I could think that you just drifted away on a tide of warmth with the smell of home all around you, I could start to get past this. Maybe.

But I could not think that. Lewis's eyes and his silence would not let me.

"Did Henry see her?" I asked, on the evening of the day that Henry had flown in from West Virginia. He had gone directly to the funeral home. Lewis and Simms had met him there. They would not let Lila and Camilla and me go. Lewis had not even called Camilla until the middle of the morning after the fire.

"Let her sleep," he had said. "There won't be much for her for a long time."

"No. He didn't even ask to see her. I had told him on the phone pretty much how things were. She was cremated; she'd asked for that long before, after Charlie's ceremony. Henry and Nancy and the kids are going to take the urn to Kentucky. There'll be a very simple, private interment there. I don't think she's got much family left."

"She wanted to go home. He was going to go with her," I sobbed. "But, oh, Lewis, not like this."

"No, baby. Not like this."

"How was he? What did he say?"

I could not imagine what there was to be said after your wife had died by fire. I could not imagine how Henry was.

"He didn't say much at all," Lewis said, "except that if he hadn't forgotten about the opera at the Gaillard and gone out with the doctors, it wouldn't have happened. I never saw anybody in such pain. He thinks it's his fault."

"Oh, Lewis, nobody made her go out to the island," I said, weeping. "She would have been just as mad at him in Bedon's Alley. It was her choice."

But I knew Henry, and I knew that he would wear Fairlie's death like a shirt of nails until the day that he, too, died.

9

I DID NOT GO TO FAIRLIE'S memorial service. I woke up the day before in our bed on Bull Street, coughing and aching and so desperately tired that for a long while I could not get out of bed.

"Flu, maybe, or that other thing that's going around," Lewis said, dressing for the clinic in the dim, shuttered room. "Stay in bed and drink lots of water. Take aspirin. Call me in the morning."

I turned back over and burrowed under the covers. Gladys groaned in her sleep and moved up against me. She had slept with us for the past two nights, and had begun to whine anxiously when I left her sight. In truth, she was the real reason I was not going to the house on Bedon's Alley to see Fairlie off. I did indeed feel awful, but I knew it was a malaise of the heart and spirit, not the body. I simply was not going to leave Gladys.

"Oh, for goodness' sake," Camilla said briskly when I called to tell her. "She'll have to get used to being by herself sometime. You can't take her with you out of town. Why don't you bring her? She can stay in the kitchen. Or she can come stay with Boy and Girl. What will Henry think?"

But I knew that for old Gladys to be in her lifelong home without her people would be cruel past imagining. And she had never been particularly connected to the two Boykins. Henry was her polestar. Henry and now, perhaps, just a bit, me. It was, of course, a desperation allegiance, but I was not going to break it.

"It's what Henry would do," I said, sure of it. "I'll stay here and put together a little lunch for us. I know that Henry and Nancy are going straight to the airport after the service. Nobody's expecting a gathering of any kind."

"I'm going to do that," Camilla said. "I've already ordered the stuff from Ginger Breslin's. All I've got to do is pick it up this afternoon. You stay in and take care of yourself."

I felt an obscure flare of anger.

"I'm going to do this, Camilla," I said firmly. "This one time, I'm going to take care of us. I know you do it better than anybody else, but I'm doing it this time."

There was a small silence, and then she said lightly, "Well, of course you must, if you feel so strongly about it. What can I bring?"

"Nothing. Just give Henry and Nancy my dearest love."

"You know I will."

I made a pot of chili that afternoon, and cornbread. That and a salad of iceberg lettuce and Rusian dressing just felt right. It was still cold, though fair, and the wind still battered the harbor and the downtown streets. No herbed and sauced and layered things on that day. No champagne. No mesclun. Just the walloping, comforting chili and some grocery-store red and white wine, and what Lewis called the "dreaded iceberg." It was a childish meal. I ached for childhood, even the one I had had. I thought that we all would.

They trooped in just past one the next day, looking whipped and diminished, old. For the first time, at least to me, old. I hugged them as you would children who had come shivering home from school, and set them before the fire, and poured mugs of a lovely hot thing Fairlie had taught me to make long ago, saying it was an old Kentucky bluegrass recipe. Claret cup, she called it: red wine and beef consommé, lemon and cinnamon and nutmeg and a pinch of sugar. It should not have been good but it was. It warmed you down to your metatarsals. We drank a lot of it. And we talked. Gladys snuffled each of us in turn and then flung herself down at my feet.

Lewis and Henry and Camilla had spoken briefly about Fairlie at the small service with more laughter and remembrance, all told, than tears. Others had joined in; everyone had a Fairlie story. Nancy had gotten up and started to speak about her mother, and then sat back down, trembling. Camilla had put her arm around her shoulders, and for the rest of the service, Nancy wept quietly. When the young minister from Holy Cross on Sullivan's Island asked if anyone else would like to say anything, Fairlie's youngest grandchild, Maggie, only four, piped up and said, "Granny taught me how to pee in a conch shell so I wouldn't mess up the beach."

The laughter from the small group gathered on Fairlie's gilt dining room chairs, placed in curved rows around the fireplace in the big old cave of a drawing room, was instantaneous, a surf of love and delight for Fairlie. It was, Lila said, the only time Henry's expression changed. He had winced as though someone had plunged a dagger in his heart.

"But, oh, that minister," Lila said, shaking her gilt head so that her hair fanned out from beneath the black velvet band. Lila had always kept her hair a silvery ash blond; it was difficult to tell where, or if, she was graying.

"Well, he didn't know," Camilla said. "Nobody but the family and we knew that he was taking her ashes back to Kentucky. For that matter, nobody but us knew that they were planning to retire there. You can't blame him. It was a lovely thought."

"What?" I said, dreading the answer. I had wanted Fairlie's memorial to be flawless.

Just after Christmas, Creighton Mills had astounded, and, in some cases, shocked, everyone who knew him by leaving the Episcopal church and becoming a Catholic. He had since then been in semi-reclusion at the Franciscan order out at Mepkin Abbey. Downtown buzzed; an ecclesiastical scandal was a morsel of choice.

It was widely put about that Creigh had had some sort of awful secret on his conscience, and finally left the world and took the weight of it with him.

"Atonement, that's what it is," some of his elderly congregation said. But Lewis disagreed.

"I think he just got tired of being downtown's perpetual preppy priest. That habit must be pretty comfortable after all those crew-neck sweaters.

Still, I wish he'd been there for Fairlie. I know that silliness from the Book of Ruth must have hurt Henry like hell."

"*What?*" I cried.

"He talked about how Fairlie came to us in her youth and cast her lot with us," Camilla said, "and how enriched we all were that she had chosen ours and Henry's home as her own. Then he read from that passage that starts out 'Entreat me not to leave thee, or to return from following after thee. For whither thou goest I will go, and wherever thou lodgest I will lodge; thy people will be my people . . .' oh, you know. Everybody was nodding and whispering about how sweet it was, and I know Henry was simply dying. He still thinks it's because of him that she's going home in a bronze urn. This whole thing is going to kill him if he can't get past that."

There was a small silence, and then Lewis said, "You know, at least one of us is going to have to end up at Magnolia, or we'll all be put outside the city walls for the vultures to eat. Charlie in the ocean and now Fairlie in Kentucky. I don't know which is considered worse. We can draw straws."

"I probably shouldn't tell you this, Anny, but you might want to give Nancy a call before they get away," Camilla said. "I think they'll still be in Bedon's Alley. Nancy is absolutely furious with you for not being at the memorial, and nothing any of us could say changed her mind. It's shock and grief, of course, but I think it probably hurts Henry to hear it, and I'm sure you can straighten it out with no trouble."

I was as shocked and hurt as if I had been

slapped across the face. Nancy had always been her sunny, easygoing self around me; she was very like Henry in that way. That she could be angry with me was as ungraspable as it would be to learn she thought I was a child abuser, or worse.

"Of course I'll call," I said, getting up and going to the telephone in the kitchen. There was one on the table in the sitting room, but this one was out of earshot. I had no idea what I was going to say.

The telephone in Bedon's Alley rang a long time before being answered. I was just beginning to think, gratefully, that they had left for the airport after all, and then the receiver was lifted and Nancy's voice came on the line. It was flat and dull, without affect.

"Sweetie, this is Anny," I began. "I hear you're upset with me for not being with you all today, and wanted to say how sorry I am if I caused you any more pain—"

"Lewis said you weren't feeling well," her voice cut in. It had hardened into steel. "Couldn't you just have sucked it up for an hour? Everybody was talking about it. Mother always said she felt closer to you than any other woman in the goddamned Scrubs; I guess she was a fool to think you felt the same way about her."

I heard Henry's voice in the background, but hers overrode it.

"Lewis also said that you wanted to stay with the dog. Well, isn't that just wonderful? By all means, let's keep the dog happy. . . ."

I heard Henry's voice again, this time nearer, and nearly as hard as his daughter's.

"Hush, Nancy," he said. "It was just the right thing to do. Nothing could have pleased me more. Gladys was a part of your mother's heart, just like she's a part of mine. I'd appreciate it if you'd apologize to Anny."

Nancy's voice rose to a wail. I knew that she was not speaking to me.

"You care more about that damned old dog than you do us! You always did! The dog and the precious Scrubs—"

Somebody replaced the phone very softly.

I told no one.

As often happens in the Low Country, the spell of bitter February weather morphed abruptly into spring and stayed there. The air was sweet and tender with the smell of the first bloomings, and the skies over the harbor were denim blue and dotted with fluffy white Disney clouds. Afternoon temperatures crept toward the seventies, rains were mild and showery, and Charleston moved outdoors.

We moved into the three houses on the creek. Or at least Camilla did, lock, stock, and barrel, into the middle house she had been in when I first saw the creek property. She was, she said, going to spend a week or two there, and she hoped we'd join her when we could; the marshes were greening and battalions of waterfowl were back. She had seen a flight of egrets the day before that had looked like a snowstorm, settling into a huge live oak across the creek.

"Camilla, do you think you should be out there alone all that time?" I said. "It's not like Sullivan's; there's not a soul around out there for miles and miles. It's really wild country. I'm not sure I'd want to be there alone even overnight."

"I'm not afraid," she said, smiling. "I never have been, on the water. It's not like I was the only living thing out there; the marshes and creek at night are as noisy as the VFW hut on Bohicket Road. Everything in the swamp is out trying to seduce everything else."

In the end, we had decided that we could not leave her alone on the creek, and on the following weekend we brought whatever furniture we could gather and set out in a caravan down the Maybank Highway. Simms had brought a huge truck and crew from the plant, and by late Saturday afternoon, we were in.

Lila and Simms had brought most of the furniture they had moved from their Wadmalaw Island place; it had been in storage at the plant. It was lovely: big, carved pieces with the look of the West Indies about them, and a lot of airy rattan. Their bedroom had a mahogany plantation bed, overhung with sheer white cotton fabric, that I coveted. By the time the crew left with the truck, everything looked as if it had been there for years, just waiting, Lewis said, for *Architectural Digest* to get there.

Our house, on Camilla's right and closest to the water, had a few rump-sprung pieces of wicker that had not been claimed from the Battery house and a quartet of plain iron beds that had been in the children's sleeping porch at Sweetgrass. Linda and Robert Cousins, old now and withered of skin but still erect and vital, came out on moving day with a carful of wonderful old linen: sheets, coverlets, dresser scarves, napkins, tablecloths, a few thin, silky towels. They had long been folded away somewhere with camphor and lavender. It perfumed the whole house.

"They were Lewis's grandmother's everyday linens," Linda said when I exclaimed over them. "Miss Sissy was fixing to throw them out. I dug them out of the barrel and took them home and put them away. I always thought somebody might want them."

I hugged her. She smelled of the same lavender and camphor. "It will make this place home in an eyeblink," I said.

"Something needs to," she said tartly. "What you doing out here on this creek and marsh? You got a creek and marsh just like it back at Sweetgrass."

We had, in fact; I had thought about that more than once. But it seemed to me that this marsh and this creek were very different from the ones on Edisto. This was creek water, slower and darker, though almost as wide. The land on the hummock was wilder. And there were no ghosts. That was the main thing. I was done with shades and remembrances every time I rounded a corner or put a foot on a creaking stair. I would never in my life stop loving and missing Charlie and Fairlie, but I could not have borne them catching at my heart twenty times a day. I needed life and the living, and hoped that we could make it happen here.

On the first night, we had dinner with Camilla, and I thought that it would take a lot of getting used to, deciding where we would all have dinner together, or even if we would. There had been no question of that at the beach house.

We sat in candlelight at Camilla's pretty French painted table, and ate oysters Robert Cousins had dug from the bank at Sweetgrass, and Linda's she-crab soup. I had brought bread from the Saffron Bakery, and Lila had made an angel food cake, and Simms had brought wine. He did not bring champagne; he never did again, not to the creek.

Oddly, Gladys adjusted to the creek better than I would have thought. She still followed me about, or slept at my feet wherever I sat down, but she did not whine anymore, or pace, sniffing, searching for Henry. I thought that perhaps there were no ghosts here for Gladys, either. It might be as restful for her as it was becoming for me.

For we were making an entirely new context for ourselves here, and on the whole, I did not mind. If I could not have all of it, the Scrubs and the old house and the sea, then I wanted none of it. Oh, we still had each other, but we did not feel like us, at least not to me. It was hard to tell about Lila and Simms; they seemed to do the same things they had done on Sullivan's Island, without comment or apparent pangs of memory. Simms sailed; he brought the smallest of his two sailboats to the creek and moored it to the deep-water dock, and vanished into the sun every morning we were there, ghosting back in at twilight. Lila made phone calls on her cell phone to clients and the office. She had taken up painting, and spent hours on the creek or in the marsh, hatted and netted against sun and mosquitoes, painting and painting. She was not at all bad, and by the end of summer was getting quite good. Her friend Baby, who had a small gallery on Broad Street, was giving her a show in the fall. All of us had Lila's paintings in our creek houses.

Lewis took to sailing with Simms often, rediscovering the joy he had taken in it when he was newly married and living on the Battery. I remember the photograph I had seen in his office on the day that we met, of him and the dark, beautiful Sissy, on the deck of a sleek, white sailboat, with Fort Sumter in the background. He was not as obsessively competitive as Simms, but he relished it when they won an occasional Carolina Yacht Club regatta, and was talking of getting a small boat himself, to keep at the creek.

I took to the water. I had walked at Sullivan's, walked and walked, for miles, mindlessly, often with one or more of the dogs, letting the sun and the wind and sea pour over and into me until I was drunk on them. I missed walking terribly, but it was not, after all, the same here on the creek. There was only the dirt road into the property, and it was blasted with potholes and soggy most of the time with standing rainwater. And the mosquitoes were after you like F-14s the instant you went out the door. Sometimes I put on layers of clothing and thick insect repellent and took Gladys for rides in the golf cart, but even she soon learned to hate the strafing mosquitoes. But she adored the old golf cart, and often simply sat in it, dozing in the sun, like an old lady waiting for the men to play through.

When I took out the Boston Whaler or the rowboat, she often went with me, wallowing clumsily about until she found a sunny spot on the floor that suited her. In the rowboat she napped, and in the Whaler she sat beside me on the backseat, her ears flapping in the wind, her tongue lolling crazily. Once in a while she barked at a waterbird or a sunning turtle or the distant flashing white flag of a deer on a hummock across the creek, but it seemed to be more of a duty bark than anything else. I did not worry about alligators here as I would have on Edisto. Though we had heard the bone-freezing roar of a big bull somewhere far away, across the water in the night, we had seen no evidence of gator colonies, and Lewis and Simms reported none to speak of on their sails down the creek toward open water. I did not worry about gators and slow, lame old Gladys. When she was not inside, she was with me.

I would come in from afternoon hours on the water and poke my head into Camilla's house. We all did, when we returned from wherever the day had taken us. It had not been planned; it was just that Camilla was, as she had always been, the hearth at which we warmed ourselves. It seemed entirely right and natural to check in with her when we returned from our travels. Often we sat long on her porch or in the screened cage around the pool in back and talked into the twilight, and sometimes made impromptu dinners. But often we just looked in, exchanged what-did-you-do-todays, and went back to our own pursuits in our own houses.

It was a fragmented existence, that first spring

and summer. Lewis and I both still worked hard, though I had curtailed my out-of-town time drastically, and did most of my planning by telephone or e-mail. I had hired a young woman part-time, and trained her carefully, and was delighted to find that she was becoming very proficient indeed on the necessary out-of-town, face-time trips. I was in the little office on Gillon the early part of the week, at Sweetgrass with Louis on Thursdays and Fridays, and, as we had been at Sullivan's Island, at the creek house on the weekends. We seldom went to Bull Street, though I tried to look in at least once a week.

We talked often of selling it, or renting it, but I wanted, obscurely, to keep it. I simply could not give up every thread that had been woven for so long into my life.

We did not often see Camilla outdoors at the creek. The sun and mosquitoes savaged her fair skin, and she feared a fall now, as we did for her. She did garden, but very slowly and carefully; mostly she tended the common plantings and the pot garden that Robert Cousins and Simms and Lila's gardener, Willie, had put in. She was completely delighted to see us when we were there; we knew that, but she was also content during the weekdays, when she was alone. Indeed, she bloomed. Her fine, high color came back and a faint tan smoothed the lines around her eyes and lips. She had taken to wearing her hair in one long braid, down her back, and from a distance, if seen from the front, she looked like a teenager.

"What do you do out here all week?" I asked

once early on, as we sat on her porch with drinks and nibbles.

"What I always did on the water," she said. "Garden. Write. Nap. Sun. Swim a little. Wait."

"For what? For Henry?"

For a month had gone by, and we had not heard from or of Henry. He was always in our hearts, heavy under the surface. But we had not yet called Nancy, or tried to track him through the doctors' organization. It had not, after all, been so long. Give him a little more time, we said.

"Well, for Henry, sure," Camilla said. "But mainly for all of you."

Once, after we had had everybody to our house for Sunday brunch, I had gotten angry at something or other Lila had said, and she had flared up at my reaction, and things were still cool when everyone left. Lewis was surprised by the heat of my anger, and so was I; Lila's comment had been so innocuous that I could not even remember what it had been an hour after she left. I was surprised at her reaction, too. We had sniped at each other like a couple of peckish old ladies.

"We're not the Scrubs anymore," I huffed at Lewis as we cleared away the dishes. "We're just a bunch of cranky old people hanging out in tract houses."

"Well," he said mildly, "if that's what we are, let's make the best of it."

And I suppose that we did. At least, we tried. But there remained a tentativeness, a strangeness, in our togetherness, and under it all now lay a deep grief for Henry. Grief and worry that became real fear.

When two months had gone by and we still had not heard from him, we began to talk among ourselves about trying to track him down. Lila and Simms were all for it.

"Something's not right," Lila said over and over. "Ordinarily we'd have heard *something* about him, or somebody would. And if they had, it would be all over Charleston. But it's as if he's dropped off the face of the earth. He could be somewhere sick; he could—"

"He said he'd call when he was ready," Lewis said. "He asked us to honor that. I for one am going to do it. If something had . . . happened to him, we'd hear. His doctors' organization would hear. We'd know."

"At least we could call Nancy," Lila said unhappily. "He must keep in touch with her."

"He'd call us if he called her," Camilla said. "Besides, she doesn't want to hear from any of us."

"How do you know?" I said, feeling guilt start up around my heart. Had the breach I opened been extended to include all of us?

"I just know," Camilla said. "Under the circumstances, I don't think I'd want to hear from us, either."

"What circumstances?"

"You must have figured out that she thinks we cut Henry and her mother off from her. I think she thinks that if it hadn't been for the Scrubs and the beach house . . ."

I was silent. Perhaps Nancy was right.

In early May we began to hear things. One of

the doctors Henry and Lewis had been accustomed to flying with early in their tenure called Lewis to see if he'd heard from Henry. Lewis was at the clinic, and called me at work.

"I was floored," he said. "I guess I just assumed he was off on one of his flying trips with the docs in his organization. I haven't kept up with them. And maybe he has been. John hadn't been on the last three trips, and he was just now hearing about Fairlie. He's going to call around to some of the others that Henry has flown with. And some of the air-charter services they use. He said he'd let me know. Somebody's bound to have a record of him somewhere. But I have to admit, I'm really worried."

"There are things we can do, you know," Simms said that night at dinner.

It was Saturday, and we were having the first of the sweet creek shrimp, boiled in saltwater and peeled at the table. We were at our house. Shrimp juice wouldn't harm our old trestle table. Nothing would. Robert Cousins, who knew how to cast in the secret shrimp holes on Edisto with a cotton net, had brought them out that afternoon. Robert made his own nets. You could buy vastly more enduring nylon ones in every Low Country chain hardware store, but Robert thought them shoddy and somehow shameful. Lewis said he had once known how to weave the cotton nets, but it was an art that had to be practiced, and he'd forgotten. It was one thing, he said, that he planned to do with his retirement: get Robert to teach him once more to weave the beautiful, gossamer webs of cotton net, and to cast them.

It was a still night, and we could hear the tiny shrimp popping in the creek, and the plop of mullet. Camilla said they had only recently come back in force. The marsh was full green now, and so vast and deep and salt-rich that it seemed to breathe in and out like a single entity. The moon was down; it would be near morning before it rose, but the stars bloomed like chrysanthemums. The mosquitoes sang and strafed. Far out over the water we heard, or thought we did, the rolling roar of the big bull gator.

After the primal bellow had faded, we all looked at Simms. He was leaning back in his chair and had the full, suffused look on his round face that we had come to know meant the international executive had temporarily taken over. Lewis called it his evil twin. Simms could be overbearing and obsessively stubborn in this persona. None of us wanted to see the evil twin decide to go after Henry. He would pursue him like the hound of heaven.

"Such as?" Lewis said, frowning.

"You know. Phone records. Credit card records. Car rentals. Airline tickets. Withdrawals and deposits at the bank. We've got the resources at the office. I could find him in a day."

"You sound like a skip tracer," Lewis said. "We told Henry we'd honor his decision to call when he was ready, and I think we need to do it. All this sounds so goddamn furtive."

The evil twin slunk out of Simms's face, and he sighed.

"I know it. It's just that he's my oldest friend except for you all, and I'm really worried about him now. I know the frame of mind he was in when he left."

A week or so later one of the nurses at Queens, who had flown with Henry and Lewis many times, heard from a Georgia nurse who sometimes flew with the organization that there had been talk around a minuscule village deep in the forests of the Yucatán Peninsula of an American who had come in a plane with American doctors and nurses and set up a rudimentary clinic and who had stayed on when the plane flew away.

At first he had continued to treat villagers in the clinic, but then he had begun to drink away most of the afternoons and evenings, in the cantina, and had stopped going to the clinic. He stayed in a small shack on the riverbank with an Indio teenager, one of the girls at the local brothel, and did not come out except to go to the cantina. There he talked to no one, only drank, until he stumbled home late in the evening. He never fell, but he was never entirely steady, either, and the villagers, who had become fond of him when he'd first come, tacitly looked out for him. They left fish and fruit and cornmeal on his doorstep. They assumed that the teenage prostitute kept his house and cooked his food. No one knew. He had grown so thin that you could almost see through him. His beard had grown out and he shielded his eyes with dark glasses. Once, when a desperate young woman had taken her sick baby to his shack, he had begun to cry and told her that she would be better off going to the village shaman. Nobody went to him for healing anymore.

The nurse told Bunny Burford, who immediately shotgunned it around the entire medical community that Henry McKenzie had turned into a falling-down drunk and was living in a jungle hut with a fifteen-year-old whore. The news reached Lewis at the clinic a scant two hours after Bunny began her broadcast, and he was at the hospital and in her office not fifteen minutes later.

He never told me what he said to her, but when he came by my office, he was angrier than I had ever seen him, and Bunny had been called into her boss's office for a meeting with him and Lewis, and had spent the rest of the morning crying in the ladies' room. She went home without speaking to anyone.

"Lewis," I said, my heart cold, "could it be Henry? It doesn't have to be, does it? It could be anybody at all. . . ."

"It could indeed. And if that bitch says one more word about Henry I'll get her fired, so help me. Stan was ready to do it today."

His voice trailed off. He swallowed hard, and looked out my window into the little courtyard, where summer had exploded showily.

"But you think it is," I whispered.

"I think it could be."

We left the office and drove by the Bedon's Alley house, but it was shuttered and the gate was padlocked, and the palms and crepe myrtles that lifted their heads above the brick wall were dry and unkempt. No one had been there for a long time. Nancy's house on Tradd was just as silent and empty, and no one answered the phone at the house on the Isle of Palms.

"Maybe they've gone to get him," I said.

"Can you see Nancy and that husband of hers whacking their way through the jungle with a machete?" Lewis said grimly.

I couldn't.

We called everybody together at the creek that night, and told them what was being passed around Charleston. Simms yelled, "Oh, *fuck* it," and banged his fist on the table, and Lila began to cry. Camilla was silent, staring at Lewis. The candlelight flickering on her face made her look impassive and alien, a priestess at a shrine a millennium before the rise of Rome.

"I can find out easily enough where he is, if it's him at all, now that we have a start," Lewis said. "His organization surely keeps records of its flights, and who was on them when. I'll call in the morning. And if it's him, I'm going to go get him."

"I'm coming, too," Simms said. "You'll need help with him."

"With *Henry*?" Lewis said incredulously.

Simms started to argue, his face re-flushed with red, but Camilla slapped her own hands on the table. Everyone looked at her.

"No," she said. "Nobody's going after him. Don't you know it would kill him to have us see him like this—if it's even him? Either he comes to us, or he doesn't, but we do not go after him. I simply won't have it."

We stared at her. None of us had ever heard quite that note in her voice before. It was as cold as arctic core ice.

"Okay," Lewis said after a moment. "You're right. We wait and we hope and we pray."

"Yes," Camilla said, her voice gentle again. She shone in the gloom.

In late summer, Henry came home.

10

AUGUST ON THE MARSHES AND CREEKS of the Low Country is never comfortable and often hellish. The heat ratchets up until it swallows air and breath and will. No ocean breezes reach in from the barrier islands. Insects so various that no one seems to know half their names hold their national conventions here. Snakes and gators grow torpid and cross; waterbirds hunker down until late afternoon, and the marshes stink so in the hammering sun at low tide that it can make you nauseous. The wild, four-footed citizens of the marsh come out only in the hot, thick nights, and humans, on the whole, go elsewhere. Indeed, many of the beautiful old houses in downtown Charleston were built as summer homes by the wealthy owners of the rice, indigo, and cotton plantations on the creeks and rivers, to escape the pestilential swamps. The slaves who were left to tend the crops died by the hundreds of yellow fever.

But late summer here has a seduction all its own, or at least it did for me that year. The heat and humidity ran thick in my veins in a honeyed lassitude. The still, shimmering air over the marshes seemed a kind of magical scrim out of which anything at all might come gliding. There was no question of the kind of productive activity and purpose here that we pursued back in the city. Somebody once said that the two most important things ever to happen in the South were civil rights and air-conditioning, not necessarily in that order. I agreed about civil rights, but in the steaming summer days, on slow Low Country water, I wasn't sure about the air-conditioning. Living slowly and mindlessly on the summer marshes was as sensual as going naked. And I always secretly loved the ripe, brimstone smell of pluff mud.

When we were at the creek in summer, we did very little, and did it very slowly. Having an indolent streak in my deepest soul, I cherished the sweet nothingness. Lewis, still a dervish even after all the years I had known him, slowed down and was content, up to a point, to lie on the porch reading or float aimlessly in the screened-in, shaded pool. He could do it for only about a half day, and then he began to prowl, and would soon take his fishing gear and go out in the Whaler, or borrow Simms's boat and sail as far down the creek as it took to catch a little wind.

Simms and Lila did not love the marsh in summer. They came to be with us, but they did not stay on as we sometimes did, and the heat seemed to punish and cripple them. They took to leaving early to go back to Charleston, pleading business pressures. But I knew that the constant sweat bled something vital out of them. In late July Simms had a couple of men from the plant come and install air-conditioning in their house, and after that they stayed a bit longer. Lewis and I had big, sluggish ceiling fans that did absolutely nothing but stir the fetid air, but I think it seemed to us that anything more would disturb the immutable rhythm of the seasons on the marsh. It did not, however, prevent us from relishing the cool, dry air when we had dinner with Lila and Simms. Only Camilla seemed to be truly comfortable in August. She was very thin; warmth and humidity seemed to nourish her like a blood transfusion. Even I wondered at her capacity for heat. She bloomed in it, like an orchid.

My business slowed considerably in the dog days of summer, and I often came out to the creek a day or so before Lewis. He always had much to do around Sweetgrass, as I did, but in August I was simply incapable of focused action, and loved the world of the marsh and creek precisely because I could let myself, without guilt, swirl and float on its surface. Camilla was almost always there now, though she seldom went outside except to the pool cage. Lila and Simms hardly ever came that summer except for an occasional Saturday and part of Sunday. I wondered if they would come back to us in the cool of autumn, but it was a lazy wondering, without undue concern. I would care more about it in the fall. In August, what would be, would be.

The morning of the precise middle of August was already flat and white at eight o'clock, and the sheets were slick and molded to my body when I woke in the dim bedroom. I was alone, except for Gladys, who, to accommodate the heat, had wriggled down to the foot of the bed. Lewis

was still at Sweetgrass, planning to come to the
creek that evening. Simms and Lila were refriger-
ating comfortably in Charleston. I heard splashing from behind the house that told me Camilla
was faithfully doing her laps in the pool. I looked
out my window over the marsh to the creek. The
tide was full out, and the marsh glimmered poiso-
nously, like a dead fish in the low sun, and probably smelled like it. The creek had shrunk, as it did
twice a day, to a ribbon. But unlike most recent
days, its surface was ruffled. Wind. Out on the
creek, a wind blew in from somewhere.

I pulled on shorts and a T-shirt and tied my
hair back with a lace from some forgotten shoe,
and padded barefoot out of the bedroom and into
the kitchen. The air was stale and hot, but the tiles
were cool under my feet. I flipped on the overhead fan, and made coffee. As I stood drinking it
and staring out at the little dappling of wind,
Gladys came limping into the kitchen, toenails
clicking on the tile. She nosed at her food without
interest, but drank deeply from her water dish,
and looked up at me as if to say, "Just another
shitty day in paradise, huh?"

"I tell you what, Gladys," I said. "There's a
breeze out on the water. Remember breezes? Let's
take the Whaler out and find it. It may not last."

She thumped her tail. I put on a white cotton
hat and flip-flops and slathered on sunscreen and
insect repellent, and we went out into the still
morning. Whatever wind there was did not reach
the house. The humidity was like a wet wool over-
coat.

Camilla was on her front porch watering pots.

She wore a white terry beach wrap and sunglasses, and her wet hair was braided and hung down her back.

"Where are you two going?" she called out.

"Out in the Whaler. There's a breeze out there. It looks like heaven."

"Don't stay too long. Breeze or no, you could die in that sun if you broke down and nobody was around."

"We'll be back in a couple of hours," I said, and waved, and Gladys and I went down the wooden walkway to the dock, stepping skittishly on the already sizzling boards.

Gladys was so lame that I had to lift her into the Whaler, but once in she struggled up into her usual seat beside me, and I nosed the boat out into the dwindled creek. There was an avenue of water scarcely wider than a city street, but it was freckled with wind, and glinted in the sun. We picked up speed, and Gladys's ears blew back, and she gave a great doggy sigh of contentment.

I hugged her lightly.

"Don't tell me this isn't better than that phony screened pool," I said, and she grinned at me around her lolling tongue.

We followed the small wind down the creek for about an hour, until we reached the bend that I knew sheltered one of the great prehistoric shell mounds that dot the Low Country marshes. The wind began to drop and I could feel sweat popping out at my hairline.

"Enough for one day," I told Gladys. "By the time we get back, it'll be lunchtime, and then naptime. But aren't you glad we came?"

I turned the boat in a tight arc and we chugged slowly back up the creek, toward the dock. The tide was coming in, and the creek was slowly widening, spreading as infinitesimally through the marsh grass as a glacier. There was virtually no sound from the forest: no birdsong, no plop of mullet, no rustle of grass or small splash as a turtle or water snake slid into the slow water. Not even the whine of mosquitoes or the dry burr of cicada. In another month, the creek and woods would be alive with the comings and goings of its villagers, but today it was an underwater place, totally stopped and still. Gladys nodded in the sun and barked at nothing.

We were not far from the dock when her head snapped up and she raised her muzzle and sniffed feverishly. I could not imagine what she was searching the wind for. I heard nothing but the low rumble of our motor. As I cut it and glided the Whaler in toward the dock, she sprang up on the seat with a vigor that I had not seen for years, and began to bark: urgent, full-throated bronze barks that I could imagine coming from her throat years before, in the fields and woods of autumn. I hardly had us stopped, wallowing, beside the dock when she was out of the boat and running down the walkway as if she had never been stiff or lame or old. I scrambled out and sprinted after her, calling. It crossed my mind that she was having some sort of seizure, or fit.

Halfway down she misstepped, and skidded off the planks and fell headlong into the marshy black water. I did not know how deep it was here; probably not very, but the mud was thick and deep and sticky, and the grasses obscured vision. Gladys began to thrash and whine. I went off the dock after her.

The water came up only to my waist, but it was over her head. My feet sank deep into the silky, sucking mud. I could not see Gladys, only the frantic thrashing, but I grabbed for her and got her, and lifted her, still struggling, into my arms, and heaved her up onto the dock. She was coated from nose to tail with the foul-smelling mud, and I was slimed with it, too. Before I could wipe it out of my eyes, she was gone again down the dock, barking and falling, getting up, running, falling again. I caught her and grabbed her up in my arms and headed up the bank with her, trying hard to hold her still. I could feel her heart, like a trip-hammer. A vet; I would have to get her to a vet. . . .

She broke free once more and bolted toward Camilla's house. I started to follow her and then stopped.

A dusty old pickup truck stood in the center of the driveway circle, and on Camilla's porch a tall, stooped, wire-thin old man was just raising his hand to knock. He turned toward us, and my knees almost gave way with shock. Henry. It was Henry.

He saw Gladys struggling toward him, and reached her with two steps and gathered her up into his arms. She wriggled and whined and yipped with delirious joy, and lapped at his gaunt face with a frantic tongue. He held her, burying his face in her filthy coat. He raised it when I reached them. His face was as filthy with mud as

Gladys and I were, and tears cut pale tracks through it on both cheeks.

"Henry," I whispered, and began to cry, too, and threw my arms around him and Gladys. We tumbled together onto the gravel drive, man, woman, and dog, a tableau of homecoming sculpted of primal Low Country clay.

"You're the dirtiest girls I ever hugged," Henry said in a faded ghost of his old slow, sweet voice, and then we simply sat and held each other, and cried.

Presently the hammering of my heart slowed, and I lifted my head and looked at Henry. His face was white and mud stained, but he was clean shaven, and his sunken blue eyes were clear. His silvery hair fell in a tangled sheaf over his eyes. It was longer than I had ever seen it. I could feel his bones, sharp as dead branches, through the faded, mud-stained old denim workshirt that he wore. You could have counted every rib. There were still tear tracks in the mud on his face, but he was not crying anymore. His eyes had a look of great distances; I had never seen that before. Henry had always been so totally with you, so absolutely in the moment. Who was this man?

"Henry," I began, but he touched my lips with his fingers and I fell silent. Gladys was attempting to burrow herself under his arm, and he patted her absently.

"I can't, now, Anny," he said, in the cracked new voice. "I just can't. Later on, maybe, we'll talk about it, but not yet. It's like I've been living in some kind of nightmare, and everything after the fire is beginning all over again. I need to know you all are around me, but I have to start over with all this, and I need to do it alone. I need to feel it all, now. I've been drunk for a long time."

He was trembling, a fine shivering all over. I had seen it before. My mother used to do it, in the claws of a savage hangover. Many of my little clients' parents did. But his eyes were clear, and there was not that sweet, yeasty smell about him that spoke of advanced alcoholism. If he had been a drinker, he was not now a drunk. Just a frail wreck of a man.

I nodded silently, with my arms still on his shoulders. Gladys settled herself under his arm and fell silent. We were still sitting like that on the gravel drive, holding lightly to each other and not speaking, when a screen door banged and I looked up to see Camilla running down the steps of her house. I had not seen her run in years; she moved very carefully now. But on this day she ran as lightly as a girl, her pigtail flying out behind her. She wore a light, sheer flowered cotton skirt that drifted around her ankles, and a white sleeveless blouse. She was entirely the young Camilla who had laughed and danced with Lewis and Henry on the hot summer sand of the Sullivan's Island beach, long ago. Before she reached us, Henry climbed painfully to his feet and stood still, with his arms open, and she ran into them.

She held him hard. I could not see her face.

"I've been waiting for you," I heard her say. "I thought you'd come about now. I've had a pot of gumbo in the freezer for days. You can tell us about the odyssey of Henry McKenzie over a feast tonight. I'll call Lila and Simms."

Her voice was fluting with happiness, and a sort of joyful certainty. She was not, I thought, surprised to see him. With the delicate radar she seemed to employ as far as Henry went, and to an extent, Lewis, she had known he was coming, and almost when. Well, I thought, it was the three of them almost since they could walk. That kind of bond can't be broken.

She stepped back from Henry, still holding his hands, and made as if to pull him gently toward the steps, but he stood still, shaking his head.

"Cammy, no," he said in the frail voice. "Later, but not now. Right now I just need to get clean and sleep. It's been a long time since I've slept. I heard from Nancy that you all were staying out at some marsh place that Simms owned, and I remembered that he'd bought Booter's place, and I took a chance. I'm sorry to just bust in on you like this, but right now I . . . don't have any place to go. I can't go back to Bedon's Alley. . . ."

"Of course not. You've come home. We have a place waiting for you; it's been ready almost since we first came out here. It's back behind the pool. I'll show you. You take a long shower and hop in bed and we'll let you sleep till you wake up. You can't hear us from there."

"Gladys . . ."

Camilla smiled. "Of course, Gladys. We couldn't keep her out with six feet of barbed wire. Come on, now. I'll take your clothes and wash them while you're asleep, and there's plenty of food in your fridge. Did you bring any other clothes?"

"A few, in a duffle in the back of the truck. They're in pretty bad shape. I don't know what happened to all my clothes. . . ."

His voice began to fade, and the distance came back into his eyes.

"No matter. I'll sort them out," Camilla said firmly. "Come on. When you feel up to it, the rest of us will probably be around one or another porch tonight and in the morning."

She began to bustle him toward the little guest house in the palmetto forest behind the pool. I knew now why she had insisted on furnishing and decorating it just so, and stocking it with linens and silverware and dishes. She had had a window air-conditioning unit put in, too. The little house waited there all summer in the deep shade of the palms and live oaks, perfect and inviting, for guests who never came.

Instead, Henry had come. I knew that Camilla had meant it to be the home that he came to.

He held back under her gently urging hand, and looked at me.

"I've missed you," he said limply, and I began to cry again.

"You'll never know how we've missed you," I whispered. "You'll just never know."

"I hope I will, someday," Henry said, and turned to follow Camilla up the path toward a bath and food and sleep.

I called Lewis at Sweetgrass and he called Simms and Lila, and by late afternoon we were all gathered at the creek, having drinks on Camilla's front porch and talking of Henry.

"How was he?" "How did he seem?" they asked me over and over, and I could only shake my head helplessly.

"Old. Half sick. Weak. I don't know," I said. "He's not really Henry. How could he be, after what he's been through? Let's wait and see how he is when he gets his bearings."

"But did he say where . . . ?" "Did he talk about Fairlie?" "Will he be staying here?" "Is he going back to medicine?"

"I don't know," I said. "I just don't know. We really didn't talk."

"Then what did you do?" Lila said impatiently.

"Sat in the driveway with our arms around each other and Gladys and cried," I said.

"Henry *cried*?" Simms was shocked.

"If he hadn't cried, I'd cart him straight off to a shrink," Camilla said crisply. "Anny's right. We need to let him be, let him call the shots."

"But what will we talk to him about?" Lila wailed, and all at once I wanted to shake her.

"What did you ever talk about?" I said.

"Well, you know. Just stuff."

"Just stuff will do fine."

Henry slept for the rest of that day and night and most of the next day. Or at least, if he did not sleep, neither did he leave the guest house, and we saw no lights and heard no sounds. A couple of times Gladys came clicking out the slightly open front door and wandered into Lewis's and my kitchen and had a bite and a drink, but she looked at me, startled and half guilty, wagged her tail, and padded back toward the guest house.

"It's okay," I said the first time she did it. "I

know he's back. He'll want you there when he wakes up." And off she went.

In the morning Camilla tiptoed into the guest house with a pile of newly ironed clothes and a pitcher of fresh orange juice, but she did not stay.

"Still sleeping," she said. "I could hear him snoring."

"I think that's Gladys," I said. "She can blow you out of bed."

"Well, whoever, they're really sawing wood. I know you all wanted to see him, but I think it would be better, if he doesn't come out by midafternoon, if everybody went back to their own place in town. Maybe he should just ease into the group one at a time."

"That one being you," Lila said.

"You know I always stay out here part of Monday," Camilla said. "I just want to see if he needs anything. Then I'll leave him be. But I'm not going to leave him totally alone out here. Not for a while. He's going to start remembering in earnest now, and I want to be here if he wants to talk."

But apparently Henry did not want to talk. At least, not about Fairlie, or the fire, or his lost time in the Yucatán. Camilla reported at midweek that he had caught up on his sleep and was eating like a sailor on shore leave, and had begun to lose the terrible skeletal look in his face and arms. He spent a lot of time dozing in the sun or reading in the pool cage, Gladys stuck to his side like a cocklebur, and he took the little kayak that Simms had brought out into the creek and vanished out of sight in the marshes for hours at a time.

"Does he talk?" I asked, when she called.

"Oh, yes. But not about . . . all that. He talks about the land around here—apparently he and Lewis used to hang around here with somebody named Booter—and he talks about Gladys, and dogs in general, and the state of medicine today, and what's happening to downtown with the tourists and all. And he talks a lot about the old days."

"At the beach house?"

"No. Earlier. When he and Lewis and I were kids out on the island. I'd forgotten how awful he and Lewis were. He laughs a lot about that."

"So we shouldn't mention the other stuff. . . ."

"You can talk about anything else under the sun, but he's obviously not ready for that. Let him set the pace."

We all got to the creek about the same time the next Friday, at sunset, and Henry uncoiled himself from Camilla's porch swing and came loping down the steps to meet us.

"Well, if it's not the estimable Scrubs of Charleston, South Carolina, and Booter's Creek," he drawled, grinning hugely, and we all hugged and cried a little, and pounded him on the back and Lila and I kissed him. He smelled like sun and freshly ironed cotton, and, faintly, of salt and pluff mud, and his face and arms and legs were lightly tanned under a coating of new sunburn. His silvery hair was neat again, if still a little long-ish; somebody, Camilla, no doubt, had trimmed it. He wore crisp khaki shorts and a blue oxford-cloth shirt with the sleeves rolled up on his forearms, and if you did not look too long into his eyes, he was fully and truly Henry again.

"You look good, man," Lewis said, clearing his throat. "You really do. And my God, Gladys! Look at you! We ought to enter you in the Miss Charleston contest."

Gladys, capering with manic glee beside Henry and barking up at us, shone as if she had spent a day at an exclusive spa, and wore around her neck a beautiful brown and black and white cotton scarf tied like a bandanna.

"I swore I'd never do that to a dog," Henry said, "but I brought it back from Mexico for Nancy, and it was just the color Gladys is, so I gave it to her instead. Looks a million times better on Gladys. Really brings out the cheerleader in her, doesn't it? Bath didn't hurt, either."

In a way, that first conversation set the tone for the rest of the summer. We found that, after an initial awkwardness, we could talk almost naturally among ourselves and around Henry without mentioning Fairlie or the fire. Henry helped by saying, that first night at dinner, "I know you all want to know, and I want to tell you. But not yet. I've got way too much to sort out. And you'll understand that there are things I just can't talk about, and maybe never will."

We nodded, looking at him in the light of Camilla's tall white tapers. But we did not know, not really. Only Camilla knows, I thought, looking at her. She was smiling and nodding her head very slightly. When he's ready, she'll be there, I thought, and was comforted. Camilla would understand a great deal without Henry's having to say it. But Fairlie and the fire and the years at the beach house were always with him, we knew, and always with us.

For the rest of the summer, Henry stayed in the guest house, and Camilla stayed in her house. We came on weekends. It was not dissimilar to the way things had been at the beach house, except now, of course, Henry lived on the creek. Or did for the time being, anyway. He made no effort to look for a place in Charleston, and said nothing about continuing his practice, or flying with his doctors' group. I wasn't sure what he did with his weekdays; Camilla said he was out on the water a great deal, usually with Gladys, and spent a lot of time walking the fields and woods bordering the marsh. She thought that the days of solitude were when he wrestled with his demons; his eyes were often red when he came in for supper, as he always did. But at the meal, he was easy and soft-spoken, as he had always been, and often talked long to her over coffee, in the candlelight. But never of Fairlie. And never of the fire.

"He'll get around to it," she said tranquilly. "I think he's a lot nearer to it now."

He went to bed early and read late into the night, or at least Camilla thought that he did. Piles and piles of books lay about the living room when she went in to straighten up and take him his clothes and food. And his bedroom light burned late. She did not know where the books came from.

"Camilla, you've turned into Henry's maid and

cook," Lila said early in September. "He ought to kick in, or help you find somebody to do for you."

"He helps me more than anyone knows," she said, smiling. "Including him."

On weekends he was agreeable and funny and as sweet tempered as ever, and often came with us when we sailed or swam. But never with just one of us. Henry that early autumn was everyone's friend and no one's confidant. If Lewis, with whom he had always been closest, missed the lazy, bone-deep bond that the years had forged between them, he did not say so. I thought that he was simply glad to have Henry back, on any terms, as was I. In those muted bronze days of September, when the monarch butterflies came drifting in from the north and settled in shivering clumps on the trees and shrubs, and the great autumn writing spiders wove their fables in the early mornings, Henry was alone only with Gladys and Camilla.

Often, on those mornings, I would get up early and they would be sitting around the pool, dripping and bundled in towels, talking quietly. In the late afternoons, before we all gathered for drinks, Camilla and Henry and Gladys all stretched themselves in the lowering sun on Camilla's front porch. Talking, talking. Once I got up to go to the bathroom in the middle of the night and looked out the kitchen window, and saw Camilla letting herself quietly out of Henry's front door, and starting down the path to her house. I did not speak of it, except to say to Lewis once, "Wouldn't it be something if they got together? They both know what this pain is like. They might be a great comfort to each other. And they've been together so long. . . ."

Lewis looked at me oddly.

"Too much history," he said. "Way too much."

And as the slow days burned toward October, Henry seemed to me to have achieved a fragile peace that I thought might be the beginning of healing. Camilla has done this for him, I thought. He's finally talked it out to her. It was just the right thing to do. Even if the rest of us never heard the particulars of Henry's terrible odyssey, the one who could truly help him had.

Bless her, I thought. Without her he could have simply died of the infection of grief.

In late September there came a day so blue and bronze and heavy with the smell of ripening wild muscadines that I awoke with autumn literally itching under my skin. It was a Saturday morning, and Lewis had stayed at Sweetgrass to talk to an agricultural agent about his longleaf pines. I knew that the day was an anomaly; the thick heat and buzzing insects would come back with a vengeance. In the Low Country, cool weather often does not come until Thanksgiving. This day was a token, a promise to wilting souls.

It was still early when I took my bagel and marmalade out onto our porch. The sky was a brilliant cobalt vault overhead, but wisps of icy white mist clung to the shoreline of the creek. Tags of it drifted among the still-green grasses. Sound, muted and thick all summer, had a ringing new clarity; I could hear someone's boat engine far down the creek as clearly as if it had been at the end of our dock, and the thumping helicopter sound of a rising flock of wood storks far across the water was crisp and clear. I stretched luxuriously, and started to amble, bare-foot, down to the dock, simply to wrap myself totally in the morning.

Behind me there was a soft, mechanical whin-ing, and I turned. Henry and Gladys were bump-ing down the path to the dock in the golf cart. Henry raised his hand and smiled and Gladys wagged her whole back end.

"Is this a day, or what?" I said.

"This is a day," Henry said. "Gladys woke me up begging to go out in the Whaler, so I thought I'd indulge her."

"She's a good sailor," I said, rubbing the thin hair on the top of Gladys's domed head.

"Has she been in the Whaler much?" he said.

"I used to take her a lot. It's better for her than the rowboat, because she can see out."

"Well," Henry said, getting out of the cart and lifting Gladys down, "I'm glad it isn't her maiden voyage." They started down the dock, the tall, thin man and the limping old dog. Henry did not ask me to go with them. I was obscurely hurt; I don't know why.

I settled onto the bench seat in the pavilion and watched as Henry jumped down into the Boston Whaler. He reached up for Gladys, but she pulled back, turning her head from him to me and back again. You could read the confusion on her face. Finally she simply sat down.

Henry began to laugh.

"She's not about to get into this boat without

you," he said. "Come on, hop in. I won't keep us out long."

"Oh, Henry, three's a crowd. . . ."

"Get in the boat, woman," he growled, and I laughed and jumped down into the Whaler and picked up Gladys, who had come to the edge of the dock, waiting to be lifted in.

We went far down the creek, toward the place where it swirled into the larger creek, and then into the slow, dark river that went eventually to the sea. Along its path eastward the banks grew high with oyster-shell bluffs and slick clay banks riddled with fiddler holes. If you were still and silent enough, you could see the crabs in their thousands, busily cleaning their burrows and waving their great claws about. But the softest splash and the bank was empty in an eyeblink. Gladys barked dutifully, but she knew by now that she would never get her teeth and paws on a fiddler.

It was midmorning before the sun climbed high enough to touch the water. It was deep here, and opaque with the boiling, teeming strata of life that reached fathoms deep into the mud beneath its surface. It was sometimes dizzying to me to think, when I was drifting silently on the sun-dappled surface, that the creek was as close to the primal, generative stew as you could find on this present earth. Henry had slowed the motor to a soft, subterranean bumble. We had spoken very little. I was nearly mindless with contentment.

He cut the motor, and pointed across the shell banks to the marsh on the other side of the creek. It was unbroken green here, except for small islands of palmetto and elderberry brush here and there, almost to the wooded horizon line. Shell mounds, I knew; or middens, thought to be the garbage dumps of the Indians who had taken the sweet shellfish from this creek for centuries before the first white man came. Each epoch had a favorite dish, Lewis had said; some strata were oysters, some crabs, some clams and periwinkles, some river fish. I had never explored one closely.

"See that big one out in the middle of the marsh?" Henry said, and I did. It was high and rounded like a deep bowl, instead of a slightly conical hill, and larger than all the others. I had never seen it before. I had never been this far down the creek.

"Boy, the eating here must have been great," I said.

"It's not a midden. It's a shell ring. Kind of an epochal calendar, you might say. If you excavated, you'd find all sorts of things that defined the culture of the moment. Pottery shards, shells and sharks' teeth that were used for money, household artifacts, sometimes shamanistic totems. There was some big magic on these marshes. The College of Charleston has been dying to get an archeological team in here for decades, but Booter wouldn't allow it, and Simms hasn't either, so far. Lewis and Booter and I used to climb around it, and we found some pretty wonderful things, but as far as I know, nobody has ever dug it seriously. Get Lewis to take you over there sometime."

We sat in silence. A little wind smelling of brine and pluff mud and the faraway sea (Oh, the island! The island and the sea!) rose and riffled the water's surface, cooling the sweat that had popped out on our faces.

"It makes me sound like some kind of spoiled brat," I said presently, "but I don't think I could live anywhere that wasn't beautiful. The Low Country spoils us."

Henry was silent. And then he said, in a far-away voice, "When I took Fairlie back to Kentucky, I thought that, well, at least she'd be in that beautiful green place she'd loved all her life, with the farm, and the horses, and all. There was a big chestnut tree on a hill overlooking the house and barns that somehow survived the blight, and she wanted to be . . . under it. But when I got there, the pastures had all gone to seed, and the buildings hadn't been maintained, and there was red mud and sagging outbuildings everywhere. Her brother obviously hadn't lifted a finger to maintain it. He lives fifty miles away, and the horses had been sold years before. He never told her that."

He turned to look at me.

"Anny, God help me, the first thing I thought was, 'Thank God I don't have to come and live here now.' I would have, you know; I'd promised Fairlie, and I would have done it. But it would have killed me. It was all right to leave her there; her childhood Kentucky was the only world she would ever know. But I couldn't wait to back that car around and screech out of there. I've hated myself ever since, but I haven't changed my mind about that."

He was silent again. I had a great lump in my throat, but around it I said, "We love what we love, Henry. There's no reason on earth to give it up unless we have to."

He smiled, but it was a crooked smile, and I could tell by the twitching of the muscles in the corner of his mouth that it was difficult to maintain.

"Well, I do love this land. I always have," he said. "Maybe I took it for granted, but it was always my place. But, Anny, right now I don't have anywhere in it to . . . be. I can't go back to Bedon's Alley. I don't know if I ever can. The beach house . . . well. I even tried a shack on the edge of a river a thousand miles away, with a lot of tequila and a sweet little prostitute for company. None of it was a place for me. I can't leave the Low Country and I can't find a place in it."

There was so much pain in his voice that I reached over and laid my hand on his, and he squeezed it.

"What's wrong with here?" I said. "These are real houses. This is a beautiful place. People can live here comfortably just as well as in town. Maybe not forever, but for right now, why not let this be home? Camilla's almost always here now. The rest of us are here every weekend. I know there's nothing of . . . your old life here . . ."

He laughed, shortly. "That's the main reason it could work," he said. "Nothing and nobody haunts me here. You know, I came home partly to see if I could find Fairlie anywhere, but it's turning out that what I'm looking for is me."

"Well, when you find you, let us know. Meanwhile, we're all just happy to have whoever it is who says he's Henry back. It was awful, not knowing where you were. . . ."

"You're a sweetheart, Anny Aiken," he said, squeezing my hand and reaching to start the engine again. "I always told Lewis he wasn't good enough for you."

It was well after noon when we came putting up to the dock, and Camilla stood on the end of it, clasping and unclasping her hands, and smiling a forced smile.

"I wish you children would tell me when you go out," she said. "I worry about you. I imagine the most awful things when you're gone. . . ." She turned and started back up the walkway, leaning heavily on the blackthorn cane that she carried everywhere now. She seemed more stooped than I had seen her in a long time.

"I should have told her," I said guiltily. "It would be so easy for her to fall now. Somebody needs to be here when she is. I'm glad you're around during the week."

"Yeah," he said. "Listen, Anny, maybe it would be better if you didn't mention anything about our conversation to her. She's seemed kind of distracted lately. I don't want to worry her."

"You haven't talked to her about all that? I was sure you had. You ought to, Henry. She's the only one who can really know what you're going through. You know how strong she was after Charlie. She's always been our port in a storm."

He laughed. "Cammy is the consummate survivor. But she'd try to fix me," he said. "She can't stand hurt and pain without trying to fix it. She always did that. I don't need fixing. I just need listening to. Thanks for that."

When we got back to the house, Lewis was

there, and Lila and Simms's SUV, and the momentum of that beautiful bronze day flowed on.

We sat late at dinner that night. The cool, winesap air held, and the stars burned like the stars of winter. The weather forecast was for rain, followed by returning heat and humidity, and we all held on to this night almost fiercely. The sense of change was strong. I remembered other days and nights at the beach house, when change had hung in the air as palpable as fog. I shivered in my skin, and poured myself another glass of wine.

We were in Simms and Lila's dining room, which, with its dark plantation furniture and standing candleholders, had always seemed more a winter room to me, and though it was not yet cool enough, they had turned on the air-conditioning and built a fire. We teased them about the sheer decadence of that, but I think we all loved the living flame that danced on crystal and polished wood. We had had quail and hominy—"I'll choke on one more crab," Lila said—and sat now drinking wine and talking quietly. Gladys had come with Henry and lay under his chair, snoring noisily. Pachelbel poured from the little CD player. Outside, the autumnal croaking of a thousand frogs rose on the cool air, clearer now than it had been all summer.

Henry leaned forward and put his elbows on the table and said, "I made a few calls today. I thought I might find something to do with myself. I can't sit out here in the sun forever. I don't think I'll reopen the office, but maybe some on-call work, or even a few days a week at a medical center somewhere. The John's Island center is new. They were interested."

"Will you go back with the traveling doctors?" I said. I realized that I did not want Henry to go anywhere, but it was purely a selfish wish. Of course, sooner or later, Henry would need to feel useful again. He had been useful all his life. That wouldn't stop with Fairlie.

He laughed. "I don't think they'd have me on a silver platter after the last time. I am a legend among the docs of the air."

We all laughed, too, relieved. It was the first time he had spoken of those terrible weeks in the Yucatán, at least to us as a group. Another step on the journey, I thought.

"You don't want to push it," Lewis said. "A month or two more might be good. You need to get some weight on you."

"And you need to get some off you," Henry replied, and we all laughed again. Lewis's stocky frame was thickening, no doubt about it. It bothered him not at all.

"A little exercise will do it," he said.

Camilla was silent, studying Henry.

"Speaking of exercise," Simms said, "I think I've found just the boat for you, Lewis. Guy I know in Fort Lauderdale told me about it when I mentioned I might be looking. It's a Hinckley sloop, Pilot 35. Got four berths and wheel steering, and a tile fireplace. She was built in 1966, but she's been totally renovated. I know how you feel about Hinckleys, and the Pilot has one of the prettiest hulls I've ever seen. The price seems right. I thought if you were interested we might fly down sometime next week and take a look at her. He said he could get someone to bring her up the waterway for you, if you liked her."

I looked at Lewis. He had said nothing about being in the market for a boat. I knew he was loving the sailing he did with Simms, but it was odd that he had not mentioned it.

"A Hinckley," he said reverently. "I've always wanted one. I love the old ones. I went to the Hinckley boatyard in Southwest Harbor one summer, when I went to visit Mike Stewart in Maine. It was awesome. I still remember those beautiful hulls, and the smell of teak and varnish." He turned to me.

"Want to be a sailing wife, Anny?" he said, grinning.

I was obscurely annoyed, without knowing why.

"You had one of those," I said. "Surely that was enough."

Everyone laughed aloud, and Lewis waggled his eyebrows at me.

"One day out on the harbor in a Hinckley and I'll change your mind," he said. "Sure, Simms, let's go look at her. Is next week good for you?"

They settled on flying down the next Wednesday, and coming back on Saturday. That would, Simms said, give them time to sail the Pilot in many different weather conditions.

"Have a feast ready," Lewis said happily. "A home-is-the-sailor-from-the-sea feast. Lay in the champagne. Slaughter the fatted calf."

Camilla still had not spoken. Her face was grave and beautiful in the candlelight.

We went back to Sweetgrass on Sunday after-

noon, and spent the late afternoon and evening
swimming off the dock in the river. We had a
thousand things that needed doing, but the sense
of impending change was still queer and heavy
on us, and I for one wanted simply to drift in the
blood-warm waters of home. Water is eternal,
immutable.

We swam until the last light faded, and then
crawled out on the dock. The boards were still
warm from the day, but a little wind was chilling
the thick air. For some reason the mosquitoes
were taking a sabbatical elsewhere. We lay,
wrapped in damp towels, watching the ghost
moon rise in the lavender sky.

"Do you remember?" Lewis said. And I did.
The night, that first night I saw Sweetgrass, when
we had made love on this dock under the yellow
eyes of a bobcat. "Want to give it a try, old lady?"
Lewis said.

"Wait ten minutes and tell me if 'old lady' still
applies," I said, dropping my towel and reaching
out to him. His body was firm and sweet and
damp, as it had been under my hands for many,
many nights. It still made my body burn.

Afterward we lay in each other's arms, our
breathing slowing, our limbs heavy with lassitude and completion.

"It's still good, isn't it?" I said into his neck.

"It's the best."

"It always will be."

"Damn straight," he said.

I got up early the next morning. Lewis was still
asleep, deep under the bleached old coverlet that
had been his grandmother's. I made myself coffee

and an English muffin, and reluctantly pulled on my office clothes. I was flying to the University of Richmond later in the morning, to speak with the dean of the school of nursing about the possibility of making our program one of the school's elective specialties. Ordinarily I would have sent Allie, my young assistant, but this could, if effective, open up an entirely new direction for us. I needed to be there in person. I was set to stay until Wednesday night, and fly home on Thursday. In the green morning gloom of our bedroom, I thought that I had never wanted to go anywhere less than this trip.

I kissed Lewis on his forehead and he opened his eyes and blinked up at me.

"I'm going now," I said. "I'm sorry I won't be here to see you off."

"As long as you're here to see us home," he said, and kissed my knuckles, and went back to sleep.

The session at the university was profitable, but fully as tedious as all things academic, and took about a day and a half longer than it should have. I was tired when I got to my motel room on my last night there, and whispered, "Shit," softly, when I saw my message light blinking. It had blinked off and on for three days with "academic input." I almost did not pick it up, and then I did.

It was Lewis, with a message to call his hotel in Fort Lauderdale no matter how late I got in. Heart thundering, I dialed.

"What?" I said when he picked up. "What is it?"

"Bad news, babe. Double dose. Henry just called and told us. Camilla fell this morning and sprained her ankle really badly. She can't walk a step. And, Anny . . . Gladys died last night."

"Oh, *Lewis!*" I wailed, feeling tears gather in my eyes. "How? What happened? How is Henry?"

"Apparently, she just slipped away in her sleep. He found her at the foot of his bed, all curled up, her nose on her paws. He said it must have been very peaceful."

"Is he devastated?"

"Not really. He seemed sort of at peace with it. He said, 'Well, she waited for me, and that's all you can ever ask, isn't it?' He's going to take her over to Sullivan's Island and bury her just above the dune line where the beach house used to be. The people who bought the lot aren't anywhere near ready to build on it yet."

"And Camilla . . . what's going to happen to her? Oh, Lewis, I need to go straight on to the creek tomorrow. Who's going to take care of Camilla?"

"Lila's going for a day or two, and then Henry plans to take over. Cammy's being really stubborn; he wants her to go have an X ray, and she simply smiles and refuses. You can't just haul her there bodily. She says she can manage fine with her crutches, but of course she almost falls every time she gets up. Go and spell Henry for a while, and see if you can talk some sense into her. Henry says this thing could keep her off her feet for months if she doesn't get treatment."

"Oh, Lord. How will she manage?"

"She'll manage," Lewis said. "She always does."

"Have you seen the boat yet?"

"First thing in the morning. I offered to come on back, but Henry said absolutely not. We just got in from a stone-crab dinner, and I'm going to hit the sack. I'll call you at the creek Friday."

"I love you, Lewis."

"Always, babe."

I replaced the receiver and crept into bed, and lay there for a long time, crying softly for my beautiful failing friend, and for the old dog I had so loved, and for the thin, wounded man who had loved her, too.

When I got out to the creek the next afternoon, everything was still and silent, stunned into sleep by the savagely reborn sun. I looked onto everybody's porch, but saw no one, and, thinking perhaps they were napping in the heat, went into our cottage and flicked on the ceiling fan. I skinned out of my suit and panty hose before the sluggish air even began to move, and went out onto the back deck, clad only in shorts and a tee, sighing with relief. I vowed that I would do no more out-of-town trips. Not enough happened where I visited; too much happened where I left behind.

There was a languid splashing in the pool, and I squinted into the wire cage. Henry was swimming laps, slowly and easily, only his wet white hair showing when he turned his head for air. Like Lewis, like all Low Country boys, Henry was a good swimmer. The water was like air to them, another element. I saw no one else.

Henry saw me and pulled himself out of the pool. He was quite deeply tanned now, almost as he had been when he was much younger, in the days of the beach house, and it seemed to me that some of the cruel hollows around his bones had filled in. I went into the cage to meet him.

"Bad two days, huh?" I said, slumping beside him onto a canvas lounge.

"Bad," he agreed. "I've seen worse, but bad."

"Henry, I'm so sorry about Gladys. It just breaks my heart to think about it."

"Don't feel that way," he said, and his voice was as peaceful as Lewis had said it was. "She was a great old lady and she gave everybody who knew her a lot of pleasure. I want all of you to remember the good times with her, and the goofy ones. She was, above all, a funny dog."

"Well, at least it was a good way to die. In your sleep, with the one you love best nearby."

"I'd settle for it," he said.

We sat quietly for a time, listening to the rustle of marsh grass and the little waterfalls of bird-song out on the hummocks.

"I've always been afraid that when she died you wouldn't have any more reason to stay with us," I said.

"No. In a way, it's better. There's literally nothing left now of . . . the time before, but us. This place is different. I don't see Fairlie here. I won't see her now, every time I look at Gladys. I'm going to have to make a life out of this because I don't have anything left of the old one. Might as well start now."

"We all hoped you'd like the creek for itself," I said softly.

"I do. It's beautiful. And I practically grew up out here, you know, bumming around with Lewis and Booter. All the associations are good ones."

"I'm glad. Is Gladys . . . have you . . . ?"

"This morning, very early. The sun was just coming up. There was nobody around. She has a pretty place; one of the few things the new people have left on the property is that huge myrtle right on the dune line. I put her there, under it. It'll flourish like the green bay tree, and they'll never know it's Gladys."

"Was it awful, seeing the island and the beach again?"

"No. I was afraid it might be, but it wasn't. There's nothing left of us there. They've dozed the lot absolutely flat and are landscaping it all to hell, and judging from the amount of framing and supplies lying around, it's going to be four stories tall and have Palladian windows. It's going to cost a mint, and look like every other house on the beach now. In a way, that's comforting. I'd hate thinking the old house was out there, just waiting, with none of us going back."

I felt a lump in my throat.

"Do you think about the old house and . . . everything, Henry?"

"Only fifty times a day. Do you?"

"Yes. I try hard not to, but I do. I see it like it was, though. It's sort of good to know it won't be like that anymore."

"Well, there'll always be a little of the Scrubs there now, what with Gladys under her dune. Do you remember how she used to sit in the golf cart there, watching us down on the beach, but afraid to come down, after Hugo? 'Pore pitiful Pearl,' we called her."

I choked a little. I did remember. I remembered everything.

"Tell me about Camilla," I said. "How bad is it? I've been afraid of something like this for a long time."

He frowned.

"It's bad enough. I found her lying on the pool apron when I came out after breakfast. She was dripping wet, and just about out of it with pain and shock. It was the shock that worried me. I carried her into her house and wrapped her up in blankets until her pulse picked up. The ankle itself is a mess, but it will eventually heal. Or would, if she'd go see somebody about it, get it X-rayed, a walking cast, if she needs it. If she doesn't, she could literally be crippled for life."

"Why is she being so stubborn? It's not like Camilla to worry people. The last thing in the world she'd want is to be a burden to anybody."

"You'd think so, wouldn't you?" Henry said.

"So where's Lila?"

"She's gone to get groceries and stuff. I stayed here because it would be easier for me to lift Camilla if she fell. Although she can't weigh ninety-five pounds. God, when did she get so thin?"

Presently Lila came back with sacks of groceries and boxes of wine and other liquor, and we helped her carry them into her house.

"If I'm going to be stuck out here, I'm not going to be without the necessities," she said. "I'm glad you're here, Anny. Maybe she'll listen to you about the doctor. I don't know what's gotten into her."

Camilla appeared at dinnertime, leaning on her crutch with one arm and on Henry with the other. She was paper white, almost translucent, and under the Ace bandage on her ankle lurid blue bruising stained her entire foot and ran up her leg. She was obviously in pain, but she had put on a bright Mexican print skirt and blouse, and lipstick and a little blush. On her waxen face the blush stood out like circles of color on a clown's face.

But she smiled.

"Is this crap, or what?" she said. "I have the grace of a dancing beaver."

Henry settled her at the dinner table and Lila brought out our meal. It was a cold one, light against the heat that had come seeping back: shrimp salad and avocado, and some of the last of the wonderful John's Island tomatoes. We drank a flowery Chablis with it.

After dinner we moved to the porch, and sat in the soft, black night of the Low Country. It was so dark I could hardly make out the others' shapes; only the creak of the rocking chairs told me we were all there.

"Okay, now that we have a quorum, we're going to take up this business of the doctor again," Lila said firmly. I could hear annoyance in her honeyed voice.

"You need to go, Camilla," I said. "It would only take maybe a morning; Henry can get you in to see a good orthopedic man with one phone call. Chances are, all you'd need is a walking cast. It would make you a lot more stable, and you'd get well a whole lot quicker. Much as we love you, it would be hard for Lila or me to stay with you full-time. And you remember that Henry said he needs to get back to work pretty soon. You know Henry; he'll stay as long as you need him. But a doctor could cut the time in half."

She was silent. Then, from the dark, she said, "I'll go. Of course I will. I can't bear having all of you mad at me. And of course Henry must get back into the world; I don't think he's had that truck off John's Island since he got here. It's just that . . . I haven't been back in a hospital since Charlie . . ."

My heart smote me.

"I'll take you in," I said. "And I'll stay with you every minute."

"No," Lila said. "I'll do it. Henry wants to put a ramp over Camilla's front steps, and you need to start getting things ready for the big homecoming party. Simms says the boat is a beauty. They'll have pictures to show us Saturday night."

The next morning, Lila and Camilla drove away toward the appointment Henry did indeed make for her with a top orthopedist, and he brought out lumber and a handsaw while I sat under the pavilion on the end of the dock making a grocery list.

The morning was soft and blue, and spider-webs sparkled with dew in the marsh grasses. It would, I knew, be hot by noon, but there was that telltale riffle of wind out on the creek, and the tide was in full. I yearned, suddenly, for the Whaler.

And then I thought of Gladys, and my eyes misted over.

Henry appeared at my side and thumped himself down on the bench seat beside me.

"I just plain don't want to work this morning," he said. "Let's run away. I know, I'll take you down and show you the shell ring. You really should see it, and Lewis is going to be out sailing from now on until we all fall over. You good for that?"

My heart leaped up. To be out on the morning water, perhaps to laugh, perhaps to see Henry laugh . . .

"I'll go make us some sandwiches," I said, getting up.

"Bring some wine!" he called after me.

In half an hour we were out in mid-channel, facing into the freshening wind, bubbling down the October-blue creek.

We did not speak until we were in sight of the hummock that held the shell ring. To get to it, we had to cut the engine and glide the Whaler as close to the bank as possible, then anchor it and climb over the side and wade in. Where we went ashore, the creek floor was soft and slick and plushy, and the water was a dark, thick soup. I stepped as lightly as possible, dreading what, in those old, secret waters, I might step on. Henry had said there were no sharp oyster or clam shells here, but once, out in the Whaler with Gladys, I had seen the dark, triangular shape of a great skate float beneath the boat, and my blood had run cold. It was no use for Lewis to tell me that our creek skates were harmless and even shy, nor that they made sweet, wonderful eating. Whenever I see dark, opaque water, I people it with primordial skates. I was glad indeed when we slipped and slid up the bank and trudged through the deep grasses to the shade of the shell ring.

The hummock was large enough to harbor a grove of live oaks, ancient and gnarled, with ground-skimming beards of Spanish moss. Even this late in the year they were a vivid green with resurrection ferns and interspersed with the swords of palmettos. Under the canopy of oaks, a level green-mossed floor looked as landscaped as a suburban yard. It had been, Henry said, the site of the Indian village that had made the shell ring, built there for the secluded shade and the rich creek waters and the little freshwater spring that bubbled on the far side of the green. It was as hushed as a cathedral. You wanted to whisper under those trees.

We plunged the wine bottle into the spring and set out for the shell ring. It was tall, twice our height, and Henry said that if you climbed it, you would see, in its middle, a crater, like that of a volcano.

"But we never climbed it," he said. "Nobody told us not to; it just seemed wrong. We always felt like they were watching us."

"'They'?"

"Whoever first started that ring. Whoever kept it going. I've never known. Some geologists around here reckon that this creek and the others around here are at least six thousand years old. They formed when the oceans stopped rising.

The first people who lived here could be a tribe nobody's ever heard of."

I looked up at the big, sheer wall of shells and detritus, covered now with scrubby grass and ferns and sediment laid down over uncounted ages. It was dark in the shade of the ring, and cool. We rummaged desultorily along the edge of the ring, and found shells and pottery shards, arrowheads, fragments of bowls and cups, strings of broken beads. We found one gigantic prehistoric shark's tooth; Henry said it would have been used as money, and been worth a great deal of it. We left the tooth where we found it, and the other things, too. Henry was right. There was a great and silent sense of other beings around the ring and under the live oaks. When I looked back into the green shade under them, the dappling sunlight could easily be mistaken for shadowy brown people going about the ancient, everyday business of wresting a living from the creek and the hummocks. I shivered.

"I'm hungry," I said. "Are you ready for lunch?"

He smiled down at me. "You feel it, too, don't you? That whoever was here is still here somehow."

I thought of something that I had not remembered since college.

"Did you ever read *The Golden Bough*? Sir James Frazer's huge book about myths and magic throughout the world?"

Henry shook his head.

"Well, one thing he said I've never forgotten. It goes, 'The second rule of magic: Things that were once in contact with each other continue to act on each other after the physical contact has been broken.'"

Henry looked at me and smiled.

"I hope so," he said. "So far as I know, he's right."

Did he mean Fairlie? I thought he did. I smiled back.

"Well, then, we'll always have Gladys," I said.

"So we will. And a lot of other things."

While we were eating our sandwiches and drinking the wine, the sky to the west had darkened to a deep violet. I did not notice it until the wind on the creek picked up in short, violent bursts, then fell still again. It sounded as if the creek was breathing hard.

"That doesn't look so good," I said to Henry. "You think we can beat it home?"

"Fifty-fifty, I'd say," Henry said. We gathered up our paper bags and the wine bottle and ran down the squidgy, slippery bank and into the water, and scrambled into the Whaler.

Henry laid the throttle full open and we ran for home, always just ahead of the advancing dark and the eerie wind. On the sea side of the creek, the air was yellow. As we had been on the trip downstream, we were silent. I could smell the neck-prickling stench of ozone on the cooling wind. Lightning on open water in a metal boat was not a thing to be trifled with.

The storm broke just as we were halfway down the dock, running full out for the houses. There was a tremendous flash of light, and all my arm and neck hair prickled, and then a great boom of thunder that sounded as if it was just on our heels. The planks rattled under our feet. Huge, cold raindrops began to splatter the dock, and by the time we came off it and were heading up the path to the porches, we were drenched to the skin, and laughing with the sheer relief of not being dead.

We burst, dripping, into our living room, still laughing. Brushing the wet hair off my face, I saw that the others were there: Lila and Camilla. And Simms. Only Simms. Everyone stared at us. No one spoke.

Wrongness frizzled in the air like ozone. I could not catch the sense of it. I shook my head stupidly.

"What on earth are you doing here, Simms?" I said. "Did you all come back early? Where's Lewis?"

Still nobody spoke. The room flared into brightness. Later I read somewhere that the pupil of the eye expands in times of danger, so that no detail will go unnoticed. I was blinded with fear.

Simms started to speak, but I could not hear him through the shell-like roaring in my ears, or the drowning brightness. But by then I did not need to hear his words. I knew. The space in the world that had always been Lewis's was empty, and was filling with fog and darkness. Behind me I felt Henry's hands take hold of my shoulders, hard.

They were all talking at once now, softly, faces terrible with pain, but I could not hear them. There was only the sealike roaring. The fog and darkness from Lewis's empty space were rolling toward me.

Blindly, I half-turned to Henry and said, in a small, fretful voice I did not recognize, "I don't know how to do this. Please help me. I don't know how."

I turned back toward Camilla, and thought, through the whirling darkness, that she reached her hands out to me.

"Show me how to do this, Camilla," I whispered. The darkness took me and spun me then, and it was Henry's arms, not Camilla's, that were the last thing I felt.

11

HER NAME WAS *MISS CHARITY SNOW,* after the wife of the down-easter who had had her built in 1966. I remembered what Lewis had said once about visiting the Hinckley boatyard in Maine, and thought of that first owner—in my mind, brown and crosshatched with wrinkles and the look of the sea in his eyes; a sailing man—as he stood and watched her being brought into the boatyard by the great hydraulic lift. I smelled the teak shavings and marine varnish. I thought of his joy and near reverence for this simple, perfect thing, and I wished that he had died before he had ever asked Hinckley to build him a boat.

It's strange about the death of someone you love: for the longest time it doesn't matter how they died. Or at least, that was so for me. It was days before I thought to ask what had happened to Lewis, though I knew that he must have died on the water. I found that I simply was not interested in details. It was not that I was afraid to hear them; though I knew it would be terrible to do so. It was just that I did not care. What difference could it possibly make?

Finally, after helping me stumble through the endless web of seemly arrangements for the genteel dead, Henry sat me down and told me how it had happened.

"You need to know, Anny," he said, his face blanched with new grief, this for his oldest and best friend. "You've been walking around like a zombie the past few days. You aren't going to be able to get past it if you don't know. It will never seem real. Trust me on this."

"Get past it?" I said in simple disbelief. "How can you possibly think I'll ever get past it?"

We were sitting on the pool apron in late afternoon. The slanted light had the patina of old gold and a hint of chill lay under the little light wind off the creek. I was wrapped in an old sweater of Lewis's, both for the leftover warmth of his body and the smell of him trapped in the mothy wool. Still, I was cold. I was always cold in those first days.

Henry had brought me a glass of wine, but I did not finish it. It made me feel sick and dull. At that moment, I would have done anything in the world to feel better. Just a little better, just for a moment. If I could do that, I thought, perhaps I could get a deep breath and go on living with the pain until it began to dull. Both Camilla and Henry had said that it would. I did not believe them; this choking thing with tentacles around my heart and its teeth in my throat seemed sentient, with an eternal life, bled from me. But they had gone through it, both of them, and though they were scarred—or at least Henry was—still, here they were. I understood, dimly, that I could learn from them. But I had no strength and no will. It seemed the most I could manage was simply to breathe in and breathe out.

But I sat still and let Henry tell me how my husband had died—or how they thought he had. It was much later that it occurred to me that perhaps I would never really know. They found Lewis's boat, and the next day they found Lewis, but there was no one to tell his story. It seemed to bother the others a great deal, but it never did me, not even now.

Simms had had a business dinner, Henry said, not looking at me as he said it, and I knew that we were both wondering if it had been with one of his women.

What bathroom was it this time, Simms? I thought, without heat. Just a mild curiosity. Again, what did it matter? Later Lila would shout at him, in our hearing, "What kind of goddamned business dinner could be so important that you left him to go out on that boat alone, with night coming? You knew he wasn't the sailor you are. You knew he didn't know the boat yet. . . ."

Simms had said nothing. He seemed to have aged a decade since that Friday afternoon. On the Saturday that they found Lewis, he had gone back to the Battery house and had been there ever since. It was Camilla and Lila and Henry who made Lewis's final arrangements. Lost in my sick, dense fog, I simply could not seem to make a decision.

"I'm sorry," I said once to Camilla, as she sat with her ever-present notebook, making notes and telephone calls. "This isn't at all like me. I run a complicated business. I've been taking care of people all my life. I was strictly on my own until I met Lewis, and it didn't bother me a bit."

"It's the shock," she said. "It's nature's way of getting you through the first and worst of it. It's a kind of novocaine. Don't fight it. You've got us to help, and when the pain hits, you'll need all your energy just to live."

"It didn't hit you this way, after Charlie."

She smiled, not looking up.

"None of you knew how it hit me," she said.

So I sat in my dumb torpor that afternoon by the pool, and let Henry tell me what he knew about how Lewis died.

It was late when Simms got back to his hotel room. He called Lewis's room, but got no answer. He did not worry at first; Lewis had said that he might see how the boat handled at night, but that he didn't plan to leave the well-lit marina harbor. But time passed, and Lewis did not appear. After checking the bar downstairs, Simms drove over to the marina. Lewis had taken *Miss Charity Snow* out about six P.M., the dockmaster said, and she hadn't come back. He was about to call Simms himself. Lewis had been out far too long for just a shakedown sail.

At first light the Coast Guard found *Miss Charity Snow* floating on her side, sails still taut. Lewis was nowhere to be found. The Coast Guard towed the boat in after radioing ahead to the marina. Simms got the next plane home. He had wanted to get there before I heard of it another way, Henry said.

That night, they found Lewis at the edge of the

flat surf in the John U. Lloyd State Park, not a mile below the Coast Guard and navy stations. He had, they thought, been dead at least eighteen hours. I never asked how they knew.

When the call came, Simms broke down and sobbed.

Why? I thought. It's not as if they could bring him back to life.

But I soon realized that it would have been terrible past enduring if Lewis had never been found. I don't think I would have been one of those brave, cheerful, simpleminded widows who insist that someday the lost one will return; I did not believe that. But on the night after he was found, I dreamed about the lines I had always thought so lovely from *The Tempest*: "Full fathom five thy father lies. . . . Those are pearls that were his eyes. . . ."

And in my dream Lewis rose slowly from dark water and broke the surface near where I stood and looked at me with eyes that were made of flat, nacreous pearl. Blind, dead eyes.

I woke sobbing, knowing that if I had had to contain that image within myself forever, I would have gone mad or died.

Once again downtown missed getting one of us properly planted in Magnolia Cemetery. Henry met Lewis's coffin at the airport and drove it straight to Sweetgrass, and he and Robert Cousins and the Cousins's son, Tommy, a tall young man now, dug the grave in the old family cemetery in a grove of live oaks behind the house. Ornate mossy old gravestones were tumbled about here and there, and behind them the smaller white crosses of the slaves and then the markers for the beloved dogs of Sweetgrass. The pearly gray moss made a great tent for all the Aiken dead, and I thought that the plain, beautiful slab of native marble I had chosen for Lewis would look well in the gossamer pavilion.

I had been almost physically nauseated by the thought of everyone staring at Lewis's coffin as it rode hydraulically down into the sandy earth, so Henry and Tommy lowered it in themselves, with help from Tommy's College of Charleston fraternity brothers. They spaded fresh earth over it, and Linda and Lila laid fronds of fan palms and curly willow on the gentle mound.

Except for us and a few close doctor friends and Lewis's daughters, who had come down from the East to stand, erect and removed, under this alien curtain of moss, with pluff mud heavy in their nostrils, there were few other people at the graveside ceremony. I had asked Robert Cousins, who was a lay preacher at the little Methodist church about a mile from the road into Sweetgrass, if he would say a few words, and he did, gentle, dignified words about Lewis and this land and house and how they had been friends and workers together literally all of their lives, and how Lewis's stewardship of the land would be his abiding legacy.

He told a few stories of their boyhood here, and even as tears streaked our cheeks, we laughed at the exuberant antics of the two young wild things, one black and one white, running barefoot on the marshes, and swimming buck naked in the river. In his measured words I could hear the boy

Lewis laugh, and see the man as I had first seen him, so alive that his skin could scarcely contain him. Robert spoke of how Lewis used to dance "like the devil got in his pants," and I remembered the night at Booter's oyster shack, and for the first time felt a small wisp of happiness that was gone almost before it formed. But I learned something from it. I learned that there might—just might—come a far-distant day when I would think of Lewis and smile with joy.

We bowed our heads then, and Robert led us quietly in the Lord's Prayer, and then Linda Cousins and the women who had come to sing Charlie into the sea on Sullivan's Island stepped forward and sang for Lewis, too:

I know moonlight, I know starlight; I lay dis body down.
I walk in de moonlight, I walk in de starlight, I lay dis body
   down.
I know de graveyard, I know de graveyard,
When I lay dis body down.
I go to judgment in de evenin' of de day
When I lay dis body down.
And my soul an' your soul will meet in de day
When we lay our bodies down.

There was a much larger reception in the house, with many more people who came to nibble Linda Cousins's glorious food and drink Lewis's grandfather's blinding rum punch, and, Lewis being Lewis, there was far more laughter than tears. But I did not stay very long in the big living room. I felt my knees buckle under me in midsentence to an old lady who had known

Lewis's mother and often visited Sweetgrass for house parties ("You just don't know, my dear, what gracious parties we gave for each other back then. Every little detail perfect. Adelie was a famous hostess.").

Camilla, holding herself steady in spite of her crutch and the walking cast, saw me waver and motioned to Lila, who was beside me in an instant, and led me upstairs and tucked me into the old rice bed and drew the curtains. I was asleep in a heartbeat, far too quickly to feel the agony of lying in this bed without Lewis, and Lila sat with me until long after dark, when I woke. By then everyone had polished off the food and drink and gone back to Charleston, and Henry had gone to take the twin daughters of Lewis Aiken back to their suite at Charleston Place.

"Oh, Lord, I never said good-bye," I whispered blearily, when Henry got back.

"Don't worry about it," Henry said. "Neither did they."

I had thought I would spend a few days at Sweetgrass, to see if I could find any sense of Lewis and get my bearings, but as the time for Lila and Simms and Henry and Camilla to go back to the creek neared, I felt a swift, rising tide of panic that startled me badly, and knew that I could not stay alone. Not, at least, on this night.

"No earthly reason why you should," Lila said. "You're coming back with us, and we're going to put you in the guest room for a few nights."

I started to protest, but she said, plaintively, "We need you, Anny. We can't lose you, too."

"Who are we, us old people who cannot let

each other go?" I whispered, tears that I had not shed at Sweetgrass starting.

"But who else would we go to?" Lila said. "All our life's investment has been in each other."

I rode back to the creek with Henry and Camilla. I sat in the front seat and watched the darkening woods flash by, and felt nothing but a simple, one-celled gratitude at not being alone.

In the backseat, Camilla said nothing.

On my first day at the creek without Lewis, I tried to do the things I had always done and found them impossible. If I took out the Whaler or the kayak, the creeping fear paralyzed my hands and arms and I had to struggle back to the dock. If I sat down to read on the lounge chair in the pool cage, my heart pounded and my palms sweated so that I had black newsprint all over them. If I lay down for a nap, the afternoon light swelled so with panic that my hair and clothes were drenched with sweat, and I could only leap up and trot damply to Camilla's or Henry's house, feeling mindlessly that to be alone would be to die. I tried my best to mask it at dinner, or when we sat late on one porch or another, sweatered and shawled now against the star-pricked chill of the night. My hands shook and I was sweaty all the time, but I thought that I did a pretty good job of masking it with pleasant, stupid conversation.

But Henry and Camilla increasingly stared at me with troubled eyes, and I knew that I was fooling nobody. When the great Leonides meteor shower burst the sky to silver ribbons and I could only stare blindly past it, Henry said firmly,

"Anny, you can't let this go on. I'm taking you with me when Camilla and I go for her therapy tomorrow. You need to talk to somebody; at the very least, you need some tranquilizers for a little while. I think what you're feeling is probably a perfectly natural response to all that's happened, but you're not even able to function. I'm sure we can fix that, sweetie, but let's let the pros do it."

I shook my head silently, unable to speak through the pounding fear and the scalding embarrassment that I felt. Grief had dignity, at least; this craven shivering had nothing in it of that.

I burst into ridiculous, helpless tears, storms of them. Henry got up and came around to my chair and knelt, and put his arms around me, and I sobbed into his shirt until it was sopping wet. In her rocking chair, Camilla murmured soothingly in the dark. I could not see her face.

"I can't see a shrink, Henry. I just can't, not right now," I sobbed. "Can't you give me some tranquilizers for a week or so? Maybe they'd give me enough rest to take hold of things. I've got too much to do to spend hours crying in a shrink's office. I've got to get back to Bull Street and clean up. I've got to do something about Lewis's clothes—"

"You don't have to do anything but get through this," Henry said. "I know what happens when you put it off."

So he brought me a week's supply of Xanax when he and Camilla came back from the therapist's office in Charleston the next day, and I took

one, and slept, for the first time, deeply and
dreamlessly through the afternoon.

But the next morning the fear was back like a
skulking, stalking wild thing, held a bit at bay by
the Xanax, but there underneath the surface, eating at my vitals like the little fox of the Spartan
boy. I could control it a bit better; I could be alone
for short periods of time, and I took the Whaler
out once for almost half an hour. But the fear
always came back.

In those next few days, there always seemed to
be a little cool wind on my back and shoulders,
as if there was nothing behind me but empty
space, and I found myself pausing frequently
through the day to start to call Lewis, or plan
what we would have for dinner. I looked for him
everywhere until I remembered, and the remembering was so terrible that it almost brought me
to my knees. I tried to hide it, but of course, I
could not. Tears, tears, and more tears. I hated
them and I hated myself for them, but I could not
stop them.

Camilla comforted me, as did Henry, but I
knew that it could not go on forever. Henry was
starting at the John's Island Medical Center as a
half-day consultant the following week, and
Camilla was slowly but surely being worn down
by my neediness. I could sense her withdrawal; it
made the fear spike like wildfire.

One afternoon she got up abruptly after yet
another of my weeping spells, and said, "I really
need a nap. And, Anny, dear, you need to go back
to work. It saved me, after Charlie. And you need

to go back to Bull Street. If you don't, you'll never be able to."

And she got to her feet and limped back to her own house. Henry and I sat for a while before the fire in my living room. The first true cold snap had come in the night before. Yellowed bracken and marsh grass were silvered in the morning, and the hardwoods off on the hummocks were dropping their muted leaves.

I took a deep, rattling breath, and said despairingly to Henry, "How can I go back to work or to Bull Street when I can't even be alone in a room? What's the matter with me, Henry? I have never been like this in my life; you know I haven't. I can't just hang this crap on everybody. I've already worn Camilla out."

He reached out and covered my hand with his. "It takes as long as it takes, Anny. I'm not going to leave you alone. You don't have to worry about that."

"You've got to go back to work! You're ready. It's all planned. It's a big step forward for you. I'd die if I kept you from that. I'm embarrassed to death. Look at how well Camilla handled everything after Charlie."

"Camilla is an entirely different animal, Anny," Henry said. "Her will is solid iron. She simply did not allow Charlie's death to really touch her. She never has. It's your vulnerability that will save you eventually. It will let you feel it all, go through it all. That's what this is all about. You should *not* be ashamed of it, or try to hide it."

"But Camilla is vulnerable, too, right now. She's lost another friend. She can't really walk and doesn't know when she can. I can't dump all this on her. I just can't."

He looked at me for a moment. And then he said, "Anny, Camilla Curry is the least vulnerable woman I have ever known."

"Well, but if I stayed out here, I could help her," I said stubbornly. "She needs somebody; she can't be alone right now. And it can't be you; you really *must* get back to work. I could run all the errands, do the cooking and laundry, all those other things you've been doing. I could learn to do her therapy with her. It would make me feel a little less useless. . . ."

He was staring at me with those blue, blue eyes. I saw with a pang that his eyebrows were almost completely white now.

"Maybe you should try to go back, at that. You know everybody at your office well enough so that you don't have to keep up a facade with them. Spend a night or two at Bull Street, see what happens. If it's too hard, come back to the creek at night. It's nothing to be ashamed of. I still can't go back to Bedon's."

"But what would Camilla do, with us both gone?"

"I won't go until she's on her feet. It shouldn't be too long now. Want to give it a try? Either way, I'm not going to leave you alone."

"I do not know what I would do without you, Henry McKenzie," I said.

"Anny, it is entirely my pleasure."

And so, on the next Monday morning, I dressed for the first time since the funeral in a skirt and panty hose and heels and drove into

Charleston to go back to work. As I drove past the marsh and woods along the Maybank Highway, I talked to myself.

"Doing okay," I said chattily. "Not much traffic yet. Be on East Bay in no time."

As I swept over the Stono Bridge I told myself, "This hasn't been hard at all. I can do this. I'm going to work just like a thousand other people on this highway. All I have to do is keep on doing what I've been doing. After all, I've done it a thousand times before."

I went over the Ashley River Bridge and followed the road around to Lockwood, picked up Broad Street to East Bay, and turned onto the cobbles of Gillon Street.

"Piece of cake," I said, parking in my spot in the little covered garage. I got out of my car and the fear swallowed me whole. My knees crumpled and I caught myself on the hood of the car and stood there, my head down, black spots wheeling in front of my closed eyes.

All of a sudden I was angry. Furious. Boiling with a red rage I had never known before. I snapped my head back.

"All right, goddammit," I said through clenched teeth. "You've got Lewis. You've got Fairlie. You've got Charlie. You've even got Gladys. NOW GIVE ME BACK MY GODDAMNED LIFE!"

A woman walking her dog along the waterfront park looked sideways at me and loped on. The fear and rage slowed a little; the fear did not subside, but it slunk away somewhere deep enough so that I could walk and breathe again. The rage drained away.

"Thank you very much," I said, and walked to the elevator. I had no idea who I was talking to. Not God, I did not think. Not now.

I had called to say I was coming in, and my staff was waiting for me. Standing stiff and straight, not sure what to do with their arms, not sure how to arrange their faces. I wasn't, either. This was the first time I had been, so to speak, out in the world. It took me by surprise.

"Hi, y'all," I said inanely. There were murmurs in return. Marcy came forward and hugged me awkwardly, with tears on her face.

"I am so sorry, Anny," she whispered. "I am so, so sorry." Allie came next, murmuring something similar. One by one they came and hugged me as stiffly, as if I would break under their hands, and I hugged each one back. Would this orgy of hugging ever be over? Presently, it was.

I cleared my throat and said, "I know how you all feel, and I appreciate your support more than I can say. Please forgive me if I act sort of goofy at times, or talk to myself. I'm going to get through this, but I just have to do it my way, and right now I can't talk about it. But I can talk about anything else, and you should, too. You can all say 'shit' and 'fuck' as much as you want to."

There was loosening laughter, and I smiled back and went into my office and closed the door.

"That was good," I said to whoever it was who might be listening. "I did that pretty well, if I do say so myself."

There were masses of paperwork to handle and phone calls to be answered, and I went through them one by one. See the efficient woman handle her workload?

By lunchtime I was pretty much caught up, and my energy seeped out of me all of a sudden, as if a plug had been pulled. The fear did not come, but grief did: terrible, clawing grief that doubled me over at my desk and took my breath. All of a sudden I allowed myself to look ahead of me, something I had been afraid to do before now. What I could see was, simply, more of today: endless, endless days of watching myself go through a charade of normality, with the ache for Lewis's voice and touch like a cancer in me. I saw nothing else. When I went out of my office to tell my staff that I was going home for the day, I felt a profound, humbling embarrassment. Grief is an embarrassment. I did not want anyone to see me coming, trailing my darkness like a pall on a sunny day. I knew that I did not ever want to walk into my office again. I knew that I must.

Bull Street was dear and beautiful beyond comparison to me, and awful past enduring. I looked at the mellow old brick, and the pretty fan light, and the arched carpenter Gothic windows; I walked through the first floor over the lovely old carpets from Lewis's Battery house; I climbed the stairs to the sitting room and bedroom where we had spent so many mornings, with coffee and the newspapers, and nights with television and, later, love. And I knew as well as I have ever known anything that Lewis was here. I could not touch him and he could not touch me, but we both knew the other was here. And I knew also that I could not stay with him. I could not ever look into those dead pearl eyes again.

"I'm so sorry, baby," I whispered, starting to cry again. And I ran out of the house, leaving the lights on, and got in the car and called Lila on my car phone, and spent that night with her and Simms on the Battery. I was shaking with shame when I got there, but Lila came out to meet me, and put her arms around me, and said, "It was way too soon. I thought so from the beginning. Nobody is that strong. Come on and we'll have a nice dinner and a bottle of wine, and tomorrow morning I'm taking you to see Pritchard Allen. And no arguments."

"Sometimes we call it an adjustment disorder," Pritchard Allen said. She was a sweet-faced woman a few years older than me, and had had a successful solo practice for many years. She had gone to Ashley Hall with half of the women in Charleston. I felt soothed with her, at ease.

"Acute anxiety, even fear, is not an unusual response to sense stressors of most kinds," she said. "Bereavement is supposed to be a separate syndrome, but I've never thought that. You've lost three of the people you loved most. You've lost a house that you adored. Sometimes there's some fear of separation from major attachment figures involved. You'll probably have considerable depression later on. Under the circumstances, I think I'd worry about you if you weren't scared to death half the time. Yours is probably the acute type, meaning it lasts less than six months. If it's longer, we call it chronic. Either way, we can treat it, and you can help yourself a great deal. I can give you something a little stronger than Xanax, and something to help you sleep. You shouldn't use them for more than a few weeks, but I doubt that you'll have to."

"You said I could help myself?"

"Yes. Figure out what you need. And then get it."

I felt better driving back to the creek, as if I were myself again, no matter how damaged, and was not watching some parody of me move mechanically through my life. I felt that I could sleep for twelve hours and wake in my own skin, and I did that.

But I knew that I could not yet leave the creek, not at night. Not yet. And that I would not ask myself to do so. Figure out what you need, Pritchard Allen said. And then get it. What I needed was Henry and Camilla and the creek.

Henry did not, after all, start his new position at the medical center when he had planned to. Camilla fell again, this time breaking one frail wrist. She was badly bruised and shaken, and furious with herself, and consequently with us.

"So here you are, back again," she snapped at me. Her face was white with pain.

"Here I am," I said equably. I understood that the pain was not in her wrist.

After she was in bed, I sat by the fire with Henry. He knew, though I did not tell him, that going back to Bull Street had been a catastrophe, and he did not pursue it. I was grateful, but worried about him.

"You don't have to stay here full-time," I said.

"Stay in the mornings while I'm at work, and then I'll spell you when I get home at noon. For goodness' sake, get your career going again. You're too valuable to just drop out."

"I can stay a little longer," he said. "She really needs somebody who can lift her. Look at you; you've lost fifteen pounds if you've lost one. You couldn't pick up a bag of feathers."

"I can certainly handle Camilla," I said, annoyed. "I'm staying. You're going."

"I'd really rather you didn't stay here alone right now. You've got way too much on your plate. You've got too much to sort out. You've got your own career to think about. I think the answer is to hire somebody, at least part-time. Just until she's well again."

He put the idea to Camilla while we were having drinks that evening. She went white again, as much with fury as with pain.

"I have never had hired help to look after me in my life, and I'm not about to start now. I'm appalled that you even thought of it, Henry," she said coldly.

"Cammy, Anny and I can't stay here all day. We've got to get on with our lives. You do, too. You must see that."

"All I see is that I don't need any damned hired help!"

"We'll be back here at night," Henry said sharply. "But either you get some help in here or I'm calling the boys."

"You know what they'll do! They'll haul me off to some awful place in California and I'll die there."

"Then it's a helper," Henry said. "Here or at Gillon Street. You choose."

Camilla's brown eyes filled with tears and my own stung in reply.

"I can't take the city right now," she said softly. "It's too much. We've all lost too much. I need to be . . . just with you all. I need to be here."

And so it was that, a week later, I found a notice on the bulletin board in the John's Island BI-LO, and Gaynelle Toomer came into our lives, riding a flamingo-pink Harley-Davidson 2000.

12

THE WEEK BEFORE Gaynelle came was the worst week I could remember. Later I would look back on it and think of it as the February of my life: dull, leaden, endless gray, with no hope, no sign yet, of spring. A time to simply try and not yield to death by slow, cold suffocation. The time of the shocking, tearing pain was largely past. I now believed that Lewis was gone. It remained to me to try and find a way to live with that. I could not see one, and for a time, did not try. I simply kept on in my accustomed groove, head down, as an old pony at a children's party would, long after the music has died.

I went to work in the mornings and came back to the creek in the afternoons. Henry was always there; he had insisted on staying full-time until we found someone for Camilla. None of his phone calls to the hospital or the home nursing organizations yielded anyone who wanted day-long duty on an isolated creek so far out of Charleston.

"They'd have to drive too far to buy lottery tickets," Henry said wearily. "No matter. I've got the folks at Queens looking for me."

I did the shopping and cleaning and helped Camilla, so far as she would let me, in the afternoons. I managed to get light suppers together, mostly soup now, with the winter closing down on us, and the dark falling early. We would sit by the fire afterward, always at Camilla's house, so she would not have to limp over to join us, and talk desultorily of nothing much, certainly not our three numinous dead. And not of what might come next. If anyone had asked me what my plans were, I could only have stared stupidly at them. My plans were simply to live through each day.

We did not speak much, but Camilla seemed to have found her old serenity again, and smiled at us every now and then, or closed her eyes in appreciation of the music pouring from the little cassette player. She loved baroque music. I never had, but found it soothing and softening now.

But still, it was a dull, dead, frozen time, and all of us took refuge in early sleep. I would settle Camilla into bed, and then Henry would walk me to my door, give me a brief, silent hug, and disappear out back to his guest house. For the first few nights after Lewis's death I had hardly slept at all, fearful of the horror of either dreaming of the pearl-eyed man or waking up and remembering that he was gone. But I slept now, great, dreamless, sluglike drifts of sleep. I could neither remember nor imagine the long nights at the beach house, when we had laughed and drunk wine and told scurrilous stories, and listened to the hush of the surf. Now if I woke at all, I would hear only the winter stillness of the marsh, and perhaps the hunting cry of an owl. Henry said that he had heard the bellow of the great bull gator, closer now, but I never did.

Each morning, almost always around six A.M., I awoke in tears so violent that they doubled me over and took my breath. I would stuff the bedcovers into my mouth to keep from howling aloud, and cry until I was drained and faintly nauseated. After that I had only dry eyes and the heavy dullness; but I knew the tears would come once again at dawn. It did not seem to matter much.

On the Friday of that week, I came home at noon to find Henry trying to maneuver Camilla back into her bed. She had not fallen, but he had heard her cry out and found her halfway in and halfway out of her bed, unable to move either way. She was in pain, and he was having a hard time trying not to hurt her.

"Camilla, you know you're supposed to holler if you need to get up," I said, rushing to help Henry. She felt like a bundle of feathers and reeds under my hands.

"I'll be goddamned if I'm going to call Henry McKenzie every time I want to go to the bathroom," she spat out between clenched teeth. "And if anybody comes dragging a bedpan in here I'm throwing it at them. Full."

We laughed a little. Camilla was down there somewhere, beneath the surface of this straw woman. I helped her into her bathroom and looked at Henry.

"I'm going to ask around some," I said. "I'll do it tomorrow. I've seen some work-wanted notices on the bulletin board at the BI-LO. We'll find somebody."

"I guess you can get almost anything at the BI-LO," Henry said mildly. I smiled, and thought that at one time I would have laughed.

That night at dinner, Camilla said, "Guess what they're calling us around Queens? Instead of the Scrubs?"

We looked up at her. She looked pretty that night, her long hair loose on her shoulders, a bronze silk caftan shot with gold floating around her. In the candlelight she looked like . . . Camilla.

"What?"

"The Death Squad. I hear Bunny Burford started it. It's all over the hospital by now."

"How do you know?" I said, my voice trembling.

"I keep in touch," Camilla said.

I flinched. It was true, I thought. Death followed us. We were, instead of those once-golden people, smoke-dark ones. Some of the fear that had begun to subside rose in my throat.

"I think we'll just fucking see about that," Henry said, and he got up from the table and went into the kitchen. We heard him on the telephone for a long time, though we could not hear what he said.

We heard a little later that Bunny had left Queens and taken a position as administrator at the new little Frogmore medical center. It was miles away from a town of any sort, famous for its Frogmore stew and with a still-flourishing voodoo culture and a largely rural black population. Nobody in Frogmore would care a great deal about Bunny's delicately vicious innuendos. Frogmore was not given to innuendo.

"Guess you really got her sent to Coventry," Camilla said to Henry, when we heard the news.

"Why, Miss Camilla, how you do run on," Henry said, not looking up from his crab bisque.

"Lewis threatened to do that once," I said, smiling, and then remembered that that time Bunny's poison had spilled over Henry in his grief for Fairlie, and stopped abruptly. Tears sprang into my eyes.

"I'll get the bread," I mumbled, and fled into the kitchen.

"Let her be," I heard Camilla tell Henry gently. "She's trying terribly hard. I really never realized what a child she is, in many ways. We need to take better care of her."

My tears stopped and indignation took their place. Child?

"I'd hardly call her a child," I heard Henry say, and felt a small vindication. When I came back into the dining room, my tears were long dry. I did not let Camilla see them again.

The next morning I drove up Bohicket Road until I came to the John's Island rural center. There was a small collection of buildings: a town hall, a filling station, a boiled peanut and tomato stand, and a new BI-LO store that dwarfed the surrounding countryside. I never saw many houses around the intersection, but the parking lot was almost always full of pickups and dusty SUVs, and a great many mud-spattered motorcycles. I looked at them incuriously. Motorcycles, to me, meant Marlon Brando and the Hell's Angels. I did not expect to meet either at the John's Island BI-LO.

Inside, the glaringly blue-white store was thronged with people, largely women, in blue jeans and hunters' vests and thermal sweaters, pushing carts spilling over with canned beans and frankfurters and nacho chips and dog food and beer, no doubt a weekend's sustenance for a large family. Many of them seemed to know each other, and stopped to talk, clogging the aisles with only a glance at me as I tried to maneuver my cart past. I would smile apologetically, and they would shove their carts over without looking at me, going on with their talk of K Mart bargains and country music concerts at the North Charleston Coliseum. On this morning, I suddenly ached to be one of them, ached to look forward with a simple, hungry joy to hearing Travis Tritt live in concert on a cold Saturday night.

Lila and Simms were coming out for the rest of the weekend, and I bought fresh scallops and spinach and mushrooms, and, on impulse, four dozen fresh oysters in their shells, half sunk in shaved ice. I could almost taste them slipping down, sweet and briny and almost translucent. Lewis had loved them above all other edible things. . . .

On the way to the checkout stand I remembered the bulletin board, and went to scan it. Amid the notices of boat trailers and crab traps for sale, home catering for weddings and funerals, the local junior high school production of *Amahl and the Night Visitors*, and lost hunting dogs, I found a neat note on heavy pink card stock written in lavender Magic Marker that read: "I have skills in many areas, from housekeeping to baby-sitting to cooking and chauffeuring. I can do substantial home repairs, too. My hours are flexible, and I can sometimes stay over if needed." And it listed a number.

The note was signed with a fat, tipsy lavender heart.

The heart, and the unusually literate narrative, captured my interest. I took down the number, and when I got back to the creek, I called.

The answering machine chirped, "Hi. You have reached Gaynelle Toomer. If it's about the child support, call my lawyer. If it's about the card at the BI-LO, please leave a message."

"Ah . . . this is Mrs. Lewis Aiken," I said tentatively. Child support? Lawyer? "We live in the three new houses out on the creek, and we need someone to come in weekdays, usually for about five hours, to straighten up and look after a semi-invalid. There's no heavy lifting involved, and she is not elderly, just recovering from an accident. We might be interested in some cooking, too. Please call me back."

At cocktail time, when we had all gathered in Simms's and Lila's living room for drinks around the fire, I told them about the Lady of the Purple Heart, as Henry had dubbed her.

"She sounded interesting," I said. "Quirky, sort of, but quite literate. But she hasn't called yet. Maybe we're lucky. Maybe she's a transvestite coke dealer in reality."

"Just what I've always yearned for," Camilla said.

"I'll track down somebody Monday," Lila said. "I think Kitty Gregory's maid has lots of family out near here. Maybe there's a niece or a grand-daughter or something. Was this woman black?"

"No," I said without thinking, and then wondered how I knew. But I did.

Lila frowned.

"I've never had much luck with white girls. They're always running off to go to acrylic nail school or somewhere. And Lord, all those tales of woe! Straying boyfriends, and mothers locking them out of the house, and I don't know what all."

"Lawsy, Miss Scarlett," Henry said.

Lila flushed.

"I didn't mean that as a racist thing. It's just what's been my experience."

Camilla opened her mouth to speak, but her words were lost in a burring, bellowing roar that rolled down the gravel road and up into the turn-around. The outside lights came on automatically, and we hurried to the windows to look. It sounded at the very least like a bulldozer run amok.

"Keep back," Simms said, and went to the door and opened it. We crowded behind him.

In the sucking blue pool of the mercury-vapor security lights, a great fuchsia motorcycle stood, traced with tongues of painted purple and gold flames. A young woman was just getting off it and starting for the door. She was tall and broad shouldered and flat bottomed, and had a mass of fried-looking rusty red hair and a mask of freckles. Her nose was snub and her mouth was wide, lips chapped from the wind and turned up in a delighted smile. You had to smile back, even as you goggled at her. She wore tight black stretch jeans and a black leather jacket scalloped with what looked to be pounds of metal studs, and her boots were what Lewis used to call shitkickers. She was covered with dust.

"Hey," she said, smiling at us as if we were meeting at a family reunion. "I'm Gaynelle Toomer. I lost the number on the machine, but I knew where the houses were. Booter used to be an old friend of my daddy. Lord, look at these houses, will you? Booter would drop his teeth. I'm sorry to be late; my kid's rehearsal ran over. Is one of you Mrs. Aiken?"

I raised my hand like a child in school.

"I am," I said, meekly.

Behind me, Henry began to laugh.

"Please come in," I said. "You must be frozen."

"No, ma'am. Used to it."

She looked around.

"This is pretty," she said. "Booter would think he'd died and gone to heaven. I don't think he ever had anything but a double-wide out here."

I motioned for her to sit, and she did, peeling off the leather jacket. None of us spoke for a long moment. Under her turtlenecked T-shirt reposed the most amazing pair of breasts I have ever seen. They bobbled softly under the pink stretch fabric like a pair of overripe melons, and looked to be just as large. I could tell that she was not wearing a bra. She smiled around good-naturedly, as if everyone in the room was not struck to stone by the breasts, and it crossed my mind that she was not flaunting them; she had no need to. This young woman was completely at home with her body, totally situated in her freckled skin.

I wondered how she ever got any work done, hauling those breasts around. Or how she rode a motorcycle, for that matter. Jouncing must have been a real pain.

I introduced her around. She nodded pleasantly, memorizing us. To Simms and Lila she said, "This is your house, isn't it? It looks just like you."

Lila made a strangled noise of assent, and Simms nodded vehemently, not yet able to speak. I had the distinct feeling that if he ever cornered Gaynelle Toomer in a bathroom, he would definitely not come off best.

Henry smiled his sweet smile.

"You said your family knew Booter, didn't you? He was one of my best friends when I was growing up, mine and Lewis's . . . Dr. Aiken. He . . . we lost him recently. I think Booter would be sad to know that. There wasn't an inch of this creek and marsh we didn't poke through."

"I heard about Dr. Aiken," she said. She turned to me. "I'm real sorry. He was a wonderful man. He fixed my daughter's foot when she was three, and she's doing pageants now. I knew you must be his wife from your message on the machine. You must be missing him awfully."

I nodded, smiling, blinking away tears.

"Yes. I am. It's nice to know he could help your daughter. She does pageants, you said?"

"Yeah. Little Miss beauty and talent pageants. She's a natural, if I do say so. Took to it like a duck to water. She was Little Miss Folly Beach Pier last summer, when she was six, and she's practicing now for the John's Island Junior Tomato Princess. That's why I was late. BI-LO is one of her sponsors. I'm still looking for another one; she has to have two. If y'all know any rich folks who'd like to have a part in the career of a little pageant winner, put a bug in their ear."

Lila and Simms simply stared at her. Camilla smiled her most enigmatic smile. Henry and I grinned widely. This genial emu of a woman had hatched herself a swan.

"So you knew Booter," I said, thinking of the gap-toothed, red-faced man who had danced like a lightning strike to beach music on a summer night long ago.

"All my life. My mama says she thinks she got me on the end of Booter's dock one night. There used to be some good parties out here."

"And so you're looking for some work," Lila said in her best garden club voice. Simms still had not spoken.

"Yes, ma'am. I was working at the Rural Center library, but to tell you the truth, I can make better money doing cleaning and cooking, and I enjoy it."

"What did you do at the library?" Camilla said.

"I was the librarian. I have a degree in library science."

"My dear, you don't need to be cleaning houses," Camilla said warmly. "Never waste your education."

"I don't," Gaynelle Toomer said. "I read all the time. I taught Britney—that's my daughter—to read when she was four. And I have a little night class for the other pageant children, and some of their mothers, too. But I do need the work. My no-good husband took off two years ago, and I'm raising Britney by myself. You wouldn't be sorry. I'm really good at what I do."

She looked at Camilla. "You're the lady who needs a little help, aren't you? I've done some work in a nursing home back in Myrtle Beach. You'd be easy to take care of, as little as you are. And fun, because you're so pretty."

"Oh, yes, goddamnit, I'll vote for you," Simms said under his breath, but I did not think Gaynelle was buttering Camilla up. Camilla *was* thin; emaciated, almost. And she was pretty. She smiled again, her lit-candle smile.

"It would be two houses and a cottage, just a light once-over," I said. "We'll get somebody else to do the heavy cleaning. And being a companion to Mrs. Curry when we're away. We both work, but at different times. I work mornings and he works afternoons. It would be nice if you could do whatever she needs until about four. I can take over then. Maybe you could come and fix her breakfast, and give her some lunch. I usually do dinner."

"I can do that," she said. "I'd like that. I can leave you all some dinner every now and then, if you like. I'm a real good cook. And who wouldn't want to straighten up with all these books around? It must be like heaven."

"Three houses is a lot, but Mr. and Mrs. Howard aren't here except weekends. We don't want to overburden you."

"I can do these houses with one hand tied behind me," she said. "It would be a pleasure. My rates are pretty competitive. Mrs. Aiken, I'm going to do yours free."

"Of course you're not!" I protested.

"I am. I won't take your money if you give it to me. Dr. Aiken gave my baby and me a life."

My throat tightened. You left a long shadow, Lewis, I thought.

"Do you always ride the motorcycle?" Henry said. "It's a beauty. I had an old Indian, once. I loved it."

"I never knew that," Camilla exclaimed. "Henry, when on earth did you have a motorcycle?"

"In med school," he said. "I had to sell it when I started my internship. But for those few years, there wasn't anywhere I didn't go on that Indian."

"It's a grand old bike," Gaynelle said. "One of my club has one, restored. You'll have to come ride with the club sometime. Somebody's always got a spare bike around."

"You have a club?" Henry said. His eyes glowed.

"Oh, yeah, they're all over the place. There must be twenty around Charleston alone. At the big rally in Myrtle Beach, there's usually around five hundred thousand bikers. Now that's a sight. Ours is the Bohicket club; there are twenty-something of us. You'd like us. We've got doctors and lawyers and a judge and several insurance guys. My boyfriend owns a Honda dealership. And some of the women make more than the guys. Biking isn't the Hell's Angels anymore."

"I never knew all that was around here," Henry said.

"Oh, yeah. I mean it. Come ride with us. I'll find out what the next big ride is; I think it's for the Low Country Law Officer's Family Fund. January, maybe. Meanwhile, I'll take you for a spin on the Harley whenever you like. It's custom-built for me, but I'm not much shorter than you. Next time it's sunny, I'll ride her over."

"I'd really like that," Henry said, with more color in his voice than I had heard in a long time.

"You better check with your wife first," Gaynelle said, smiling over at Camilla. "Not all wives are real fond of bikers."

"He's not my husband," Camilla said gently. "My husband died years ago. Dr. McKenzie lost his wife last winter. We sort of look after each other."

Gaynelle made a small sound of sympathy, but did not gush or hover.

"It's real nice that you have each other," she said. "More people ought to do that, instead of living alone and dying of loneliness."

We settled on a price, and when she was gone, we sat looking at each other in the firelight. Camilla and Henry and I were grinning.

"A Harley-riding librarian with boobs like the front of a '53 Studebaker and a Little Miss Tomato Princess for a daughter. What hath God wrought?" Henry said, laughing softly.

"Who can cook," I added.

"Who worked in a nursing home," Camilla said, smiling at Henry. She was obviously delighting in his delight.

"I don't know about this," Lila said. "I just don't know. How do we know she won't run off back to the library? And that motorcycle . . . Lord! *And* one of those awful little mini-women who strut around shining their behinds and singing Britney Spears. That's even her name, Britney. Why can't we just get some nice black woman who'd be grateful for the work and keep her mouth shut? This one's way too familiar. Mark my words, this woman and her child are going to end up moving in with us."

"Oh, Lila, really," I said. "She's one of a kind. I think she's fascinating. What a life to have lived, as young as she is. And she can do everything we need—"

"Let's give her a try," Simms said. It was the first time he had spoken. "And require that she wear T-shirts at all times."

Henry and Camilla and I laughed, but Lila was not amused. She glared at Simms.

"Okay, but don't say I didn't warn you."

"We'd never say that." Henry grinned.

Gaynelle was as good as her word. If it was fair, she roared up on the Harley at eight in the morning, or in the truck if the weather was bad. She made a small hot breakfast for Camilla and Henry, and for me if I was still around. She tidied up my and Camilla's houses and Henry's cottage, singing in a surprisingly pleasant alto voice with a tremolo in it that reminded me of Patsy Cline. She seemed to favor Billy Gilman; Camilla said she was learning every one of his songs by heart.

For lunch she made a salad or a light soufflé, and they waited until I got home to eat. Sometimes Henry put off going in to the clinic until after lunch. I had to admit that it was pleasant.

Gaynelle was, as she had said, a very good cook. She took to making dinners that could be reheated, and we gratefully let her, conscious that we had eaten only each other's cooking for a very long time.

Mornings and afternoons she helped Camilla bathe and dress and do her therapy exercises, and at about four tucked her into bed with a book and the CD player. Camilla usually napped. Gaynelle could have gone home after that, since I was almost always there, but she asked one day if she might stay awhile to read some books from our libraries, and I said of course.

In truth, I was glad of the company. Gaynelle's matter-of-fact recountings of her hardscrabble days—sitting for hours in Medicaid clinics waiting for this test or that doctor, always foraging for money for the truck or the bike, fretting over paying the day care center where she left Britney until five, pursuing her ex-husband through the courts for the child support that was now three years overdue—were for me a window on a world that I had hardly known existed. Well, to be honest, I did know; I remembered the tattered lives of the mothers of my small clients at the agency, but it had been a very long time since that had been real to me. Gaynelle was totally without self-pity, although often full of anger at some uncaring social agency, or "that sorry son of a bitch." I came to admire her enormously. She lived constantly on the edge, and managed in spite of the rigors and strictures to live rather well. Her casual courage sometimes shamed me. Camilla was utterly fascinated by her. To her, Gaynelle led an exotic sort of gypsy life that had little to do with reality.

"I'm going to put her in a book of some sort," she said, scribbling away one afternoon after Gaynelle left. She was writing in her notebooks more than ever now, and seemed more alive and engaged than I had seen her for some time.

I overheard Gaynelle ask her one morning, "Are you writing a book? You're never without that notebook."

"I might, at that," Camilla said, smiling.

"Put me in it?"

"I wouldn't dream of leaving you out."

At the end of November, Gaynelle came roaring up on the pink Harley on a Friday afternoon after she should have been off, accompanied by a man on a monstrous black bike with an inordinate amount of silver piping and tubing showing. It was covered with dust from the road into the creek, but you could tell it was a new bike. The man himself was small—shorter than Gaynelle—and completely bald, with a great blond beard spilling over his leather jacket and a kerchief tied around his head. He wore black goggles; it was impossible to tell how old he was. Behind him, riding pillion, a little girl in full black child-sized leather regalia waved and squealed. I could see carrot red curls spilling out of her miniature helmet and saw that her small boots were sequined. Without a doubt the boyfriend and the daughter of Gaynelle Toomer.

Gaynelle brought them up to the front door, and I opened it to let them in. The last of the low winter sun was glinting on the creek, and there

was a lurid smear in the west that promised a
spectacular sunset. Gaynelle prodded them
before her into the living room like a teacher with
recalcitrant children on a field trip. They removed
their goggles, and then I could tell that the
boyfriend was years older than Gaynelle, maybe
forty. He had mild blue eyes and a nice smile
through all the hair. The little girl was so preco-
ciously beautiful and so aware of it that she
almost made you grimace.

"This is my boyfriend, T. C. Bentley," Gaynelle
said. "Bentley Honda? And this is my little
princess, Britney, who is just as sweet and talented as she is pretty. Britney, what do you say to
Mrs. Aiken?"

The child, the mass of her red hair flaming
much as Fairlie's had done, made a stiff little
curtsy, nearly toppling over, and said, "Nice-
tomeetcha."

She tossed her head, causing her hair to fall
over one eye, and gave me a smile that was clearly
meant to be seductive. I thought she had on lipstick.

She was the sort of child who always made me
wince inwardly with distaste, but something
about her tickled me.

"Pleased to meet you, too, Britney," I said.
"What's your talent?"

"I play the juice harp," she piped.

"Britney, I keep telling you, it's a harmonica. I
don't want to hear Jew's harp again," Gaynelle
said. Britney rolled her eyes at me, and I laughed.

"Will you play for me sometime?"

"I could play now. My juice . . . my harmonica is in Mama's purse."

"Not today," Gaynelle said, smoothing the red curls. "T. C.'s gon' take us to Gilligan's tonight for fried shrimp, and you've got to get a bath and change your clothes. T. C., Mrs. Aiken is—was—married to the doctor that fixed Britney's foot."

"It's an honor to meet you, ma'am," T. C. Bentley said. "That was one fine thing he did for that little girl."

He was soft-spoken, and looked down as he spoke. A shy biker?

They were turning to leave when Henry drove up in his truck. He did not come in, and I looked past them on the porch to see what kept him. He was squatting on his haunches, running his thin surgeon's fingers over the black bike with the reverence a pilgrim would accord the grail. T. C. Bentley walked out and squatted beside him. I could see that they shook hands, and were talking, but I could not hear what they said.

"That's T. C.'s Rubbertail," Gaynelle said. "He just got it last month. It's completely restored. He loves it better than he ever will me. Looks like Dr. McKenzie kind of likes it, too."

Presently she and the child and T. C. Bentley roared away into the falling dark, and Henry came slowly into the house, looking back at their retreating dust. His cheeks were pink with cold or pleasure or both, and his silver hair fell over one eye.

"He's going to bring a bike for me and let me ride with them one day soon," he said. "God, I wonder if I remember how? He seems like a nice guy. The kid's a little minx, though, isn't she?"

"Did she put the moves on you?"

"Yep. Or what passes for moves to a seven-year-old. She's going to be a handful, if she isn't already."

"I kind of liked her," I said. "She's a tough little cookie. Takes after her mama."

Henry brought Camilla over for dinner. We were having one of Gaynelle's elegant chicken potpies, and the smell of it warming in the oven curled out into the living room as we sat before the fire. Henry told Camilla about T. C. Bentley and his wondrous motorcycle, and about riding with the club.

Camilla's serene face blanched.

"Oh, Henry, no," she said. "I can't bear to think of you tearing all over John's Island on one of those things. I'd die of heart failure if you were late coming home. You hear so much about wrecks—"

"Camilla, I rode that Indian of mine like a banshee all over three states. I was pretty good. I think it's like a bicycle; you don't really forget how."

"Henry, promise me—"

"No promises, Camilla," he said gently. "I promise to be careful, but I won't promise not to ride it."

She looked at him silently and inclined her head in assent, and then it was time to take the potpie out of the oven.

Around the end of the first week in December we found that we could no longer ignore the blitzkrieg that was Christmas. Trees were for sale at every rural crossroads. Used-car lots on James Island were forested with them. Jaycees begged for toys for tots. When I drove to work on Gillon Street, the palm trees on Broad Street blazed with Christmas lights, and in the old downtown, magnolia wreaths were blooming on every door. At the Rural Center, the Bi-Lo aisles were perilous with stacked displays of lights and balls and hideous plush toys and banners proclaiming Butterball turkeys and canned yams. Henry did not mention it, but I knew that he saw the same things. We did not talk about Christmas in Charleston proper. Camilla did not ask about it.

But I knew that it loomed in their minds, as it did in mine. The ghosts of holidays past were powerful. Our last Christmas dinner at the beach lingered on my tongue. The toasts still rang in my ears. The edgy pageant of Lila and Simms repeating their vows before the fire bloomed behind my eyes. The glorious fireworks on New Year's Eve, and then the shock of Fairlie and Henry announcing their retirement to Kentucky . . .

They started something rolling, I thought. They opened us up and let something in. The voodoo started then.

No. I wanted nothing of the holidays this year.

Apparently no one else did, for Christmas drew closer and closer, and still no one mentioned it. Say its name aloud, folklore has it, and the demon will be summoned to you.

Simms and Lila told us, on a weekend in mid-December, looking rather shamefaced, that they had decided to have Christmas in Charleston this year. Clary and the grandchildren had begged. Please, wouldn't we come and share it with them? We'd all forgotten how grand Christmas in Charleston could be.

It was a fatal rupture, and we all knew it. We looked at each other, and then Camilla said, "What I'd really love to do is stay here and have a very quiet Christmas. It's a time for remembering. Henry and Anny don't need any commotion on their first Christmas . . . alone. Why not just let us old widows and widower have one final orgy of remembering?"

I could not suppress a gasp, and I saw Henry's face redden. We stared at Camilla. It was so unlike her to be insensitive that I thought perhaps I had heard wrong. Lila and Simms nodded and looked away, embarrassed.

"We'll be sure to make it for New Year's Eve," Lila said. But I knew that they wouldn't. Their bodies might be present on the creek now and then, but their hearts had flown back to Charleston. Was it the end of the Scrubs? No. That had happened sometime long ago, while we were not looking, but there remained a powerful bond between Henry and Camilla and me. I could not put my finger on what it was.

When the Howards had gone, Camilla said, "That was awful of me. I don't know what got into me. I think I was mad at them and just wanted to sting them a little. Forgive me?"

"Of course," I murmured. Who had ever failed to forgive Camilla?

"Listen," she said a day or two later. No one

had mentioned Christmas again. "I've been so absorbed in my own wants that it never occurred to me that either or both of you might want to be with your families at Christmas. If that's so, it's perfectly okay with me. I'll rent a dozen adult videos and pile into bed with a gallon of Häagen-Dazs."

"No, I'll be here," Henry said. "Nancy and the children are going to her in-laws. I'd rather spend the day at the periodontist's."

I don't have any family, not really, not close, I did not say.

And of course, neither Henry nor I would have dreamed of leaving Camilla alone. We still had made no Christmas plans when Gaynelle came for the last time before Christmas.

"Where's your tree?" she wailed. "Where's the wreath and stuff? Where are Mr. and Mrs. Howard?"

I said, "They went home for Christmas. I guess the rest of us are just not ready for home yet."

"Isn't this home?" Gaynelle said.

I flushed with shame. Gaynelle lived from paycheck to paycheck, in a cinder-block apartment building. It must be inconceivable to her that anyone had the riches of another home to go to.

After she had left, I thought, We do have homes. We all do. And this is not them.

I said something of the sort at dinner. Camilla's eyes filled with tears. "It is for me, now," she said. "I had hoped it would come to be for both of you, like we planned. All of us together."

"Oh, Camilla," I said, reaching over and squeezing her hand. Henry smiled.

On a late foggy-gray afternoon with Christmas only two days away, T. C.'s black Rubbertail belched into the drive, followed by Gaynelle and Britney in Gaynelle's old truck. The truck wore a lopsided wreath on its grill, and the Rubbertail was strung with tinsel. The truck's bed was covered with a bright red cloth of some sort.

"Uh-oh," Henry said from the window. "Elves at eleven o'clock."

They burst into Camilla's house bearing strings of lights and ropes of glitter and fresh pine boughs smelling as if they had just been cut from the woods. Gaynelle led the procession lugging a great basket covered with a white cloth. T. C. followed, struggling with three hideous small white metallic trees, whose kindred I had seen all month at the BI-LO. Britney brought up the rear dressed in a short red velvet skirt trimmed with dingy fake fur, twirling a glittering baton and singing "Here Comes Santa Claus" in a grating, whiny treble. I remember thinking that it was a good thing she had the juice harp to fall back on.

"There's no way I'm going to let y'all sit out here by yourselves with no Christmas," Gaynelle said. "It's a hard time, the first Christmas you're by yourself. I remember how it was when Randy took off and left us, just before Christmas. I'm not taking no for an answer. You all just sit still and let us put a few things around. You'll be surprised what a difference it makes."

And so we sat, Henry and I smiling helplessly, Camilla rolling her eyes, while Gaynelle and T. C. and Britney set up the dreadful metallic trees and strung lights on them, piled fresh greens on the mantelpieces, put white electric drugstore candles in every front window, tacked a silver-and-blue metallic wreath on the front door, and hung huge, gaudy felt stockings over the hearth. Gaynelle's pièce de résistance was a plastic Nativity scene that she set up on the old William and Mary gateleg table in front of Camilla's window. Jesus, Joseph, and Mary, and the lumpen camels, were bubble-gum pink.

"Doesn't do to forget what Christmas is about," she said.

When it was all done, they settled themselves on sofa and chairs and looked around, pleased with their handiwork. As a matter of fact, I was, too. The tasteful room exploded with vulgar vitality; it reminded me of the dime-store Christmases I had scraped together for my younger siblings, all those years ago. We had loved Christmas then. I felt a powerful surge of nostalgia rising, not, surprisingly, for all the past Scrubs's Christmases but for those meager earlier ones at home.

"It's fabulous," I said to Gaynelle. "It reminds me of when I was a little girl. What a sweetie you are!"

"I picked out the trees!" Britney squealed, wriggling with excitement, and I hugged her.

"I've never seen any trees like them," I said.

They all looked at Henry and Camilla, and Henry smiled and said, "Just what the doctor ordered. It looks great."

"Really unique," Camilla murmured.

"Henry, come on out and I'll take you for a little spin," T. C. said. Sometime out in the dark of

T. C.'s first visit, they had become Henry and T. C.

"You got it," Henry said, getting up.

"Henry, not this late!" Camilla cried. "It's one thing to ride a motorcycle on a good day, but in this fog, with night coming on! Please don't be an idiot."

We stared.

Her cheeks burned with color.

"It's okay, Miz Curry," Britney piped up. "I ride with Mama all the time at night, and T. C., too. They got lights on the bikes."

Camilla shook her head and smiled. "Oh, go on out and play," she said. "I'm certainly not your mother. But would you do me the great favor of putting on a hat and scarf?"

In a moment T. C. and Henry, capped and scarfed, were out the door, and in another moment we heard the farting stutter of the Rubbertail kicking into life, and gravel spurting as it roared away. Faintly, I heard the old classic rebel yell that every Southern child learns as soon as he can talk: "Yeeeeeee-*Haw*!"

I knew it was Henry, and was glad.

I lit the fire in Camilla's fireplace and said, "I think there's some hot chocolate around somewhere. It's instant but it's better than nothing. And some biscotti."

"What's that?" Britney said.

"Italian cookies," her mother told her.

"Cookies!" Britney yelped, and ran to me and threw her arms around my waist. She tipped her curly head far back and laughed with pleasure. I had forgotten the vinelike tensile strength of a child's clutch. All the children I had ever lifted or rocked or cuddled at Outreach flooded back to me. Especially I felt the wet, wriggling body of little Shawna, she of the terrible leather boot, the day I had carried her through the warm rain and into Lewis's office. Until today, I hadn't touched many other small bodies.

Oh, Lewis, I said silently. It was a mistake about the children. At least I'd have something of you left. At least I'd have someone.

I turned and started briskly for the kitchen, Britney still attached to my thighs. Gaynelle followed, admonishing her daughter to let go. Britney did, dashing around to look at the rest of the house.

"She's crazy about you," Gaynelle said. "She doesn't usually take to people she doesn't know well, but she sure has to you. So I have a big favor to ask y'all. You can say no in a second if you don't want to."

"What is it?" I said apprehensively.

"Well, Britney wants to open her presents over here Christmas morning. I don't know what it is, maybe because she doesn't see her grandparents . . . like I said, it's perfectly okay if you say no. We've got our own tree and all."

"Well . . . sure," I said. I was not able to think of any reason we should not host Britney's Christmas morning except perhaps that none of us really felt like it. It seemed a small-spirited reason in the face of a child's joy on Christmas morning.

"I think that would be fun."

"So listen, I'll bring over a big Christmas dinner just in case you want to have yours with us at noon. That's when we always have ours. I got a big turkey all cooked, and cornbread and oyster dressing, and gravy, and collards, and mashed potatoes, and yams with marshmallows. I even made some ambrosia. It's my mama's recipe. And T. C. makes these fruitcakes every year that he soaks in bourbon and keeps under a cloth for three months. You all wouldn't have to lift a finger."

What could I say? We'd love your dinner but not you? Besides, the thought of the festival day spent with Gaynelle and Britney Toomer and T. C. Bentley, of John's Island and Bohicket Creek, made my mouth tug up in a grin. Simms and Lila would die.

"Sounds wonderful. I'll have to check, but I'm sure everybody would love it."

After they had left and Camilla and I and Henry were sitting before the fire, I told them about Gaynelle's Christmas plan.

Henry laughed out loud.

"Why not?" he said. "It's not like we were expected at the yacht club."

"Oh, my God," Camilla moaned. "All day? Really? With those motorcycles out there stinking up the creek, and that child . . . I mean, I know she's a pretty little thing and all that, but she's not exactly the sort of child you'd want to come to your grandchild's birthday party. . . ."

Henry leered at her.

"Do I detect a bit of Lady Chatterley and Mellors the gamekeeper here?" he said.

"No, you do not," she snapped. "But you do know you're going to have to go out and buy presents for everybody now, don't you?"

And we did. The next morning I took off a half

day and went foraging on King Street. I found a spangled child's tutu in a vintage clothing store for Britney, books for Gaynelle, and, in the Harley-Davidson shop on Meeting Street, bought enormous logo T-shirts for T.C., Henry, and, just for a joke, for Camilla. Henry came in from his safari laden with packages that he said one of the girls at the clinic had wrapped for him. They looked it.

"Will one of you get me some nice, crisp new bills?" Camilla said. "That's going to have to do for me."

On Christmas morning I woke very early, as I had when I was a child, and like that child, felt a faint gnawing of excitement in the pit of my stomach. I dressed and went over to Camilla's house. I would not wake her, I thought, but I'd make some coffee and a fire.

When I got there, I found the living room ablaze with Christmas tree and firelight, and the smell of coffee perking, and the ill-wrapped presents under the tree. Henry sat on the couch watching the fire. He looked up and smiled at me.

"I haven't done this since Nancy was little," he said. "It's nice. I almost feel like putting a train set together, or something."

I plopped down on the sofa beside him.

"It *is* nice. Where's Camilla?"

"Still asleep. I was very quiet."

We sat in silence for a little while, and then I said, sudden salt rising in my throat from the bottomless ocean of the grief, "Merry Christmas, Henry."

He put his arm around me and pulled my head

down on his shoulder, and said, "Merry Christmas, Anny Aiken. They say it gets better after the first one."

At nine A.M. the motorcycle and the truck burped up, and peace fled. They came in shouting, "Merry Christmas," their arms full of packages, Britney in a spangled *Little Mermaid* costume that left her skinny chicken's shoulders bare. She wriggled voluptuously, and sequins peppered the rug.

"I can live underwater," she sang.

"We ought to test that," Camilla said under her breath, but she, too, was smiling.

For an hour we unwrapped gifts and exclaimed loudly and tried them on and tossed paper and ribbon everywhere. Soon Britney was hysterical with excitement, and insisted on doing her interpretation of the original Britney Spears's "Oops! I Did It Again." It was awful beyond imagining, and we all smiled just as broadly as Gaynelle did. Finally Britney choked on her bubble gum and began to cry, and was put down for a time-out in Camilla's nunlike bedroom. I flinched for Camilla.

Dinner was loud and heavy and wonderful. Camilla had laid the table with her grandmother's linen and crystal and silver, and lit white beeswax candles. Before we began, Gaynelle nodded at T. C., and he cleared his throat and bowed his bald, shining head and said, "For this and all thy blessings, Lord, we thank thee." He had put on a blue suit for the occasion, dusted now with Britney's spangles, and when he bowed his head, he brushed the beard aside. His hands were scrubbed raw; motorcycle grease was obviously difficult to dislodge. Suddenly I loved him.

"Amen. Let the games begin," Henry said.

It was entirely a semirural Southern Christmas dinner, more familiar to me than I could have anticipated. I ate heartily, and so did Henry, and Camilla did her best. She faltered at the collards and fatback, but admired the ambrosia with fresh coconut. We all had two slices of T. C.'s tipsy fruitcake.

After dinner, Gaynelle insisted on clearing the table and putting the dishes away, and sent me and Camilla into the living room to sit before the fire. I was very tired, and could not imagine why, and Camilla was frankly nodding.

"You all need a good long nap," Gaynelle said, coming out of the kitchen with a blinking, yawning Britney in tow. "I'm going to take this crowd home. We really enjoyed being at your house."

I got up and went to her and hugged her.

"You cannot imagine the gift you gave us today," I said. "It was generous beyond words."

"You all are real easy to be generous to," she said, and led Britney out the door. Henry came into the room from somewhere, wearing a heavy sweater.

"I'm going over to T. C.'s to watch the Georgia–Georgia Tech game," he said. "He'll bring me back when it's over."

"You mean you're going out and riding that motorcycle," I said, smiling.

"That, too."

Camilla said nothing. She was asleep, with her chin on her chest.

I woke her and led her to her bedroom, and

then went back to my own house and lit my fire. I thought surely that the grief pool would open again, but it did not. I simply felt hollow. The room was warm and quiet and dim, and the fire whispered, and I fell asleep on the sofa and did not wake until I heard Henry and T. C. come growling in.

The days after Christmas were gray and chilly and seemed endless, and the stillness at the creek was utter, and we turned inward upon ourselves again. We moved quietly, and spoke softly, and slept early.

But I believe that all of us remembered that, for a short while, in this place, there was life.

13

"YOU'VE GONE COMPLETELY NATIVE," Lila said on a Sunday afternoon in late January. "I knew you would."

It was one of those winter days we get in the Low Country that make you ache with sheer lust for spring. The temperature hovered around seventy-five, and the little wind off the creek was sweet and soft. The sun teased our cheekbones.

We were sitting on the chaises on Lila's porch, drinking mint iced tea and watching Britney on the lawn sloping down to the dock, romping with Lila's diminutive Honey. She had not brought the little dog out to the creek very often; her grandchildren clamored to dog-sit when she and Simms were away, and Lila was glad of their large walled garden. Honey was a determined and witless wanderer. My most vivid memory of her still is running blindly, her nose to the ground, her feathery tail waving with mindless joy. She was a pretty thing, but fretful and snappish with most people. But she had adored Britney from first sniff, and the love affair was mutual. Ever since they had set eyes on each other earlier that morning, child and dog had been inseparable.

We were alone on the porch. Henry and T. C. had gone blustering off on the Rubbertail just after lunch. Simms had a regatta at the yacht club. Camilla was sleeping. Gaynelle was with her in her darkened bedroom with the little CD player purring out a Mozart quartet. Gaynelle had discovered classical music, and could not get enough. She played it constantly while she was with us. It made me obscurely proud, as a mother might feel when a child abandons hip-hop for the first time and listens to Bach. Gaynelle had plenty of room, deep down, to collect riches.

"Meaning?" I said sleepily, knowing full well what she meant. Gaynelle and T. C. and the child's presence today was purely social. I had called and asked them when I saw the day's promise. To be with them, I had found, held off some of the emptiness. Henry and I were usually alone with Camilla on Sunday. But today the sensual sun called for energy and laughter, even if they were not my own.

"Meaning, as you know perfectly well, that your only social companions out here appear to be your cleaning lady, a mute bald-headed biker, and a trailer-park Lolita. I heard you had them all to dinner the other night, and then went over to James Island to the movies. How do you think all your old friends feel about that?"

"How do my old friends know about that? Is Bunny back in town?" I smiled. I would not be baited; the day was too perfect.

She blushed. I didn't mind. Charleston has a radar that defies all attempts at secrecy. And we certainly had not sought that. We simply had not sought company.

"You need to remember that you have any number of friends besides Henry and Camilla and Ma and Pa Kettle. Everybody in Charleston asks me when you're coming back home. Nobody's seen hide nor hair of any of you. People are starting to talk about you three, all alone out here."

I burst into helpless laughter.

"Me and Camilla and Henry in a ménage à trois? The mind boggles. Maybe you could tell them we're contemplating suttee. No, you know that Camilla is just not well. And I'm at the office every morning of the world, and Henry is at the clinic every afternoon. If anybody wants to see me, all they have to do is walk down Gillon Street."

"It's not the same thing. You're sunk so deep in this creek, you're drowning in it. Simms and I enjoy it, too; we come lots of weekends. But we do have another life."

You didn't for a lot of years, I thought. Not like the one we had at the beach.

"I like my life," I said.

"Oh, Anny, look at you," Lila cried. "You're thin as a stick. Your hair hasn't been cut in months. To my knowledge you haven't put on lipstick since you moved out here. You don't ever go out to lunch with anybody anymore. You ought to fix yourself up some; Henry ought to get off that damned motorcycle and see some of his friends. For God's sake, he could go sailing any day of the week with Simms; Simms is always saying he doesn't have anybody to sail with—"

She stopped with a gasp. I did not look at her.

"I'm so sorry," she said. "I really am. It's just that I want you to have something else besides looking after Camilla."

We were all worried about Camilla that winter. She seemed to be dwindling before our eyes, like a woman made of sand, at the mercy of every small wind. She never complained, but she was frequently so dizzy that two people had to hold on to her, and she slept through the afternoons and evenings as if drugged. But she could not, she said, sleep at night, and indeed, every time I got up in the night and looked out my window, I saw her bedroom light burning. Henry had checked her frequently, so far as he was able, and found nothing basically wrong with her heart, but he thought she needed a full blood workup and other tests. Camilla flatly refused to go into Charleston to her internist.

"I'd be better if I could just sleep nights," she said, and in desperation, Henry brought her a supply of Ambien. But her light continued to burn in the night. And still she slept in the daylight. She looked now like a portrait of a beautiful aristocrat that had faded with age. It had been a sudden change. It seemed to me it had started just after Christmas.

"Why do you do it?" Lila said, stirring her tea with her finger. "She ought to be at Gillon Street with round-the-clock help; surely she can afford it. Either that or Bishop Gadsden. She needs to be near Queens. Henry ought to be firm with her."

I looked at her.

"Isn't that what we all swore we wouldn't let happen?" I said.

"Oh, Anny, that was so long ago! It was a kind of . . . you know, a joke. None of us ever meant for you to end up a slave. Lewis would hate it."

"I wouldn't even have been a part of you if she hadn't been the first to take me in, and with all her heart, too," I said. "She's held me up many times. She's held us all up."

Lila dropped her eyes, and I knew she was remembering, as I was, those painful days after we knew that Simms was seeing other women, when she had sat as close to Camilla as a child to its mother, and Camilla had soothed and comforted her.

Tears welled in Lila's eyes.

"I know," she said. "I just hate what's happening to you all. All of you should be getting on with your lives instead of hiding out here."

"Lila," I said, "right now this *is* my life."

Camilla came shuffling out just then, with Gaynelle supporting her. She wore a crisp cotton skirt and a white shirt, loose on her now but bright and pretty. Her hair was put up in neat braids on top of her head, and her lipstick was fresh. She smelled of her customary Caleche. I thought that she looked far better than I did.

"Lila's absolutely right," she said, letting Gaynelle settle her into a rocking chair. "I couldn't help overhearing. Anny, you really must go back home, at least during the week. I've got Henry and Gaynelle. I simply can't let myself eat you alive."

I looked down at my hands; they were clenched and white-knuckled.

"I can't," I whispered. "I just can't right now. It's such a mess I wouldn't know where to begin and . . . I don't know. I don't think I can be there alone."

"Well, that's easy enough to fix," Gaynelle said, smiling at me. "I'll come with you and we'll get it in shape in no time. I'd love to do it with you."

I took a deep breath to refuse, and then lifted my hands and dropped them.

"You're right. I need to take care of it. I'd love to have your help, Gaynelle."

"Good for you!" Lila said heartily.

Camilla smiled.

Just then we heard the Rubbertail returning, and saw the white plume of its dust. We heard shouts and laughter, too. Even Lila smiled at the sound. When the bike roared into the turnaround and T. C. and Henry got off, I suddenly saw Henry, fully saw him, for the first time in weeks. At this distance, swinging off the bike and loping toward us, on the porch, newly and faintly tanned and squinting against the low sun, he looked so much like the Henry of years ago that my heart squeezed. Apparently Camilla thought so, too; I heard her give a very small gasp.

"I'm getting a little chilly," she said to Gaynelle. "I think I'll take a nap till dinner. Lila, it was like champagne to see you. Kiss Simms for me."

Lila gave her a peck on the cheek and Gaynelle led her from the porch just as Henry came up to the steps.

"Did I run you off?" he called after her.

"Of course not. I'll see you at dinner. You look like the dust man."

The next Saturday Gaynelle and I took cleaning supplies and drove into Charleston, to tackle my house on Bull Street. Henry sat with Camilla on her porch; the weather had held and the marsh was beginning to green, very faintly. It was the second greening I had seen here. Lewis had seen it with me the first time. I squeezed my eyes shut. Time enough later for tears. Henry and Camilla were drinking coffee and laughing as we left. It made me happy to see her laugh.

We turned onto Bull Street and my heart began to hammer. Sweat popped out at my hairline. If he was here, could I bear it? Would I be afraid, as I had been the last time I came here?

If he was not here, could I bear that?

Gaynelle pulled her truck into the garden parking space and sat looking at the house, and then at me. My lovely house shone like a jewel in the green gloom of the live oaks.

"It's a perfect little house," she said. "Like a fairy tale. It looks like you. But it's hard, isn't it? You're white as a sheet. If it's too much, I can do it in a couple of hours and you can go shopping or get a latte or something. It'll be easier to come into it clean."

"No," I said. "It's my house. Mine and Lewis's. I will not be afraid of it. Let's do it."

It took us just over four hours to set the house to rights. We scrubbed, swept, waxed, vacuumed, dusted, put away the things I had left scattered when I had run from the house. I was able to do it

as long as I was with Gaynelle. She seemed to
sense that. She never left me alone in a room. As I
touched the beautiful old wood and fabric, the
china and crystal and books and bibelots that had
been the texture of our lives, I looked for Lewis,
listened for him, waited for his touch. The sense
of him had been so strong the first time. Ever
since, when I thought of him, I thought of him as
somehow waiting in this house. I was ashamed. I
should have run back here to be filled up with
him; instead I fled him, running away from a
dead man with pearls for eyes whom I did not
know.

"Lewis," I whispered a couple of times. "I'm
home. Where are you? Please let me know."

But he was not there. As we moved methodi-
cally through each room, scrubbing and airing
and polishing, I had no sense of him at all. Grief
began to rise in my throat. I realized that I had, on
some level, fully expected to find him here. But if
he had ever been in this house since I lost him, he
was gone now. From now on, I would have to
think of him under the earth at Sweetgrass. Somehow, I could not bear that.

I stifled a sob and Gaynelle put her arms
around me. "You go on out now. Everything is
ready for you when you want to come back, but
you've had enough for one day. Go sit in the sun
on that bench. I've just got to go through the clos-
ets . . . but maybe you'll want to do that later."

"No," I whispered. "Please. You do it."

And I waited while she cleared Lewis's closet,
and brought his clothes out in a couple of suit-
cases and put them into the back of the truck, and

covered them with a tarp. I did not see them
again. I asked her if she would find a good use for
them, and she said she knew just the place. I
never asked where it was.

I cried silently all the way home, and she drove
peacefully, not speaking, only reaching over to pat
my knee every now and then. I loathed crying in
public, but somehow it seemed all right with her.
By the time we pulled into the driveway at the
creek, I had stopped, and mopped my face.
Gaynelle gave me a final hug.

"You were brave today," she said, and drove
away. I trudged up the steps to my house,
drained and weary to my bones. I was, I
thought, cried out for the rest of the month, at
least.

Henry was sitting on my sofa, reading the *New
York Times* and drinking red wine. He had built a
fire and lit the lamps, and the room put out its
arms to me. Night was falling, and with it the
temperature.

He looked up at me, and then patted the sofa
for me to sit beside him. I sat.

He studied me, and then said, "Bad. I was
afraid it would be. You're braver than me; I still
can't go home."

"I can't either," I quavered. "Not yet. I found
that out today. Oh, Henry, he wasn't there."

He put his arms around my shoulder and I put
my head down on it.

"Tell me," he said.

And I did, speaking into his sweater, which I
was dampening with my tears.

I told him how vivid and *there* the sense of

Lewis had been the first time, and how I had run from him in horror.

"Henry, for weeks after he died, I dreamed about him, and I always saw him rising up out of black water, with pearls where his eyes should have been. He was dead. It's a thing I remember from *The Tempest*—'Full fathom five thy father lies . . .'"

"'Those are pearls that were his eyes,'" Henry murmured. "I studied it, too. . . ."

"And you see, I ran from him, and then when I went back, he wasn't there. I thought he would wait. . . ."

Henry put his chin down on the top of my head.

"I used to dream about Fairlie on fire," he said. "She would come toward me burning."

"But you don't now."

"No."

Faintly, we heard Camilla's little bedside bell begin to ring. I gave a great sniff and got up. It was time for dinner. I was making clam linguine.

"Thanks," I said to Henry.

"Any time," he said.

A week later Henry and I went with T. C. and Gaynelle to watch Britney's dress rehearsal for her pageant. It would not be held until May, but, Gaynelle said, Britney had been so eager for me to see her act that she had cried and cried, and so they had asked me.

"Of course," I said, smiling and thinking I would rather spend a week in a Turkish prison.

"T. C. says tell Henry he's got a spare bike, if he

wants to try it out beforehand. We can go by the lot, on the way."

Henry was exuberant, and Camilla was anguished.

"Henry, please . . ."

"Come on, Cammy. It'll still be broad daylight. T. C. will tell you how safe it is."

But when the truck came, followed by T. C. on the Rubbertail, Camilla went into her bedroom and closed the door.

"I'm really tired," she said, smiling. "You can tell me about it tomorrow."

Gaynelle's sister, JoAnne, a sturdy woman who did not come up to her sister's shoulder, had come to stay with Camilla. She was, Gaynelle said, a practical nurse, and Camilla would be in capable hands.

"Is this my baby-sitter?" Camilla said when we introduced JoAnne. But she smiled when she said it.

Henry rode off in his accustomed place on the back of the Rubbertail, and I went in the truck with Gaynelle and Britney. Britney was manic and monstrously affected; for the first time, I did not like being around her. She was fully made up, with lipstick, mascara, glitter on her cheeks and fingernails, and great circles of coral blusher on her cheeks. None of the endearing freckles showed, and her curly red hair was pouffed and sprayed into cementlike submission. She was not the tough, cheeky little girl I had found so endearing. She was a ghastly little copy of a rock star, or, I thought, perhaps a porn star. Gaynelle smiled on her fondly, and tugged at her hair, or dabbed at her makeup. Fortunately her costume was in the backseat, tenderly shrouded in plastic. Her little blue jeans and sweatshirt anchored her at least a bit to reality.

At the used-car lot where T. C.'s friend kept his spare motorcycle, we left T. C. and Henry. Henry would not let us wait.

"Go on," he said. "I'm not letting anybody but T. C. watch me till I get my sea legs, or whatever. Bike butt, maybe."

So we drove on to the consolidated middle school where the rehearsal was being held, and waited in the parking lot, Britney wriggling and whining until her mother told her to hush.

Just as the light was dying out, we heard the familiar grumble of bikes, and T. C. came sweeping into the parking lot on the Rubbertail and drew up beside us with a flourish. Behind him, Henry came putting in on a smaller, lighter bike that looked to me more like a muscular bicycle. He was helmeted and jacketed and goggled so that he could have been anybody at all, but was still unmistakably Henry, and he was grinning so widely that his teeth were the brightest thing in the gathering dusk. He swept up beside T. C., cut his engine, and swung off the bike as if he had been doing it for years.

"You see? I told you you don't forget," he crowed. "I could ride this baby from here to Key West. I didn't have a minute's trouble."

"He did good," T. C. said, nodding solemnly. "Not a bobble. I thought this light little 230 Roller might be good to get him started; a friend of mine got it for his boy. It's a good little basic machine. We can get Henry up to some serious horsepower if he wants to do it."

"I might, at that," Henry said.

"Where'd you get your Halloween costume?" I said, laughing.

"It's T. C.'s spare suit-up. Boots are a little tight, but I'd kill him for the jacket," Henry said.

"You look like a thug," I said.

"I feel sort of like one. It's a great feeling."

The pageant was just what I had thought it would be: a disjointed stampede of miniature trollops in pop-rock costumes, posturing and wriggling their meager fannies and pouting and smirking redly. Some sang, some danced, some did gymnastics, some twirled batons. Britney was the only one who played the harmonica. To me it sounded downright embarrassing, but then so did the other contestants' offerings. Henry and I, twitching with suppressed laughter, would not look at each other. T. C. smiled fondly. Gaynelle took copious notes after every performance, writing in a little notebook.

When the rehearsal was over, most of the contestants were divested of their costumes by their mothers. Britney insisted on wearing hers home. She was nearly hysterical with all the adulation. She jumped into my arms and hugged me so hard that I was imprinted with makeup and spangles, and smiled with relief that this child was still, under the icing, the child I knew.

"I was the best," she crowed. "I was the pretti-

est, too. Cindy Sawyer, that's the one that did
LeAnn Rimes, is s'posed to win, but I thought she
looked stinky. It's gonna be me!"

She started in on the harmonica, and Gaynelle
winced and reached back and took it away from
her.

"Cool your jets," she said. "You did pretty good
but you can do a whole lot better. I've made notes.
We'll go over them tomorrow."

When we got back to the car lot to drop off the
little 230 Roller and collect Henry, T. C. said,
"Why not ride back with me on the Rubbertail,
Anny? It's a warm night, and we can suit you up
in Gaynelle's stuff. I promise to go real slow."

"Oh, I couldn't—" I began.

"Yes, you could," Henry and Gaynelle said
together, and I realized that this had been
planned all along.

"Oh, why not?" I said, thinking that perhaps if
I screamed enough, T. C. would stop and let me
off. They fitted me into Gaynelle's leathers, in
which, I knew, I must look like a small bear, and I
climbed onto the seat behind T. C. My heart was
pounding out of my chest.

"Please go slow," I yelled and he nodded, and
started the Rubbertail.

It felt like a gigantic live, wild thing between
my legs, the sheer power of it shooting up my
spine and into every inch of me, down to my toes
and out to my fingertips. I clutched T. C. around
his waist and buried my face in his jacket, and we
blasted out of the lot and away. For about a mile, I
did little but try to breathe enough air into my
lungs and shut my eyes and hang on. And then,

very gradually, I began to feel the night wind on my face, and smell the wet, loamy beginnings of spring on the black, moss-hung road out to the creek, and the rhythm of the bike and the road came into my legs and hips. I lifted my head and looked around; it was like flying. There was nothing between me and the fresh, rushing night. By the time we reached the creek, I was laughing jubilantly. When I got off, my legs crumpled under me and T. C. had to catch me.

"Happens to everybody the first time," he said. "I've seen folks that couldn't walk for a day. You did great."

Henry and Gaynelle and Britney pulled into the gravel circle behind us.

"You looked like a real biker bitch," Henry said, coming up and hugging me. "How'd you like it?"

"Biker bitch? Watch your mouth, sailor. I loved it. I really did."

"Told you," Henry said.

When I told Camilla about it the next morning, she just smiled and shook her head.

"Next thing, you'll be cleaning houses with Gaynelle," she said. "And taking that child to get acrylic nails and collagen."

"Oh, Camilla . . ." I felt obscurely hurt.

"I'm sorry. I just mean that I can't abide that poor child, for some reason. She's way too old for her age. It's eerie. She's going to be burned out by the time she's twelve."

The next day, Sunday, Gaynelle asked if she could come over and borrow some books.

"Of course," I said. "Bring Britney and I'll take her out in the Whaler, if the weather holds."

There was a pause on the line, and then Gaynelle said, "I think I'll leave her home this time. She's not too fond of Camilla. In fact, I think she's afraid of her."

"Oh, surely not," I said, shocked. Camilla had never been anything but pleasant with the child, even though, as I knew now, she did not care for her.

"Well, it's funny," Gaynelle said. "She usually doesn't dislike anybody, but she knows things. She always did."

"What things?"

"Who likes her and who doesn't. Things like that."

"Gaynelle, I don't think Camilla dislikes Britney," I said. "She's just ill. You know she's not doing well."

"I don't think it's that. It doesn't matter. Not everybody likes children. And I don't think Camilla is as ill as all that. Sometimes when she's writing in that book she's just vibrating with energy. She writes like a demon."

"But you know how shaky she is on her feet."

"Yes," Gaynelle said.

The weather did indeed hold for the next week. It was easy to forget that the bone-chilling damp cold could come back. The first living things began to return: we heard peepers, and the first mullet splash, and, one night after dinner, the blood-freezing roar of the big bull gator. It sounded as though he was on the front porch.

Camilla cried out and I gasped.

"I forgot to tell you," Henry said. "I've seen his crawl, where he drags his tail up and down the bank, about a half mile down from the dock. I think he's looking for a lady. We'll soon be up to our asses in alligators. Or maybe it's the mullet he's after."

"Is he dangerous?" Camilla laid her hand over her heart. Her face was pale.

"Not unless you're a mullet or a poodle," Henry said. "They don't stray far from the water, not out here. Of course, down in places like Hilton Head and Fripp, where they've built villas all over their habitat, the gators have moved right onto patios and into swimming pools. And Chihuahuas don't last long."

"But he wouldn't come up here, to the pool or anything . . ."

"No. There's nothing up here he wants. He's got it all down in the water, and beside it."

We talked of many things, as we usually did. Dinner hours that week had been quiet and pleasant, and Camilla seemed better than in many days, and talked vivaciously to Henry about the time when they had run wild on Sullivan's Island, before graduations, before marriages, before births . . . before deaths. One evening when I got up to clear the table, she said to Henry, "Stay and talk to me awhile."

He nodded.

I felt ridiculously excluded.

"Call me when you're ready to go to bed," I said.

"Henry can do that," she said. "You go on and get a good night's sleep."

But I lay awake for a long time. The lights from Camilla's house had not gone out by two A.M. I turned over and buried my head in my pillow. The last thing I heard before sleep was the roar of the big gator, claiming his kingdom and summoning his queen.

14

THE WEATHER HELD, and we slid into February on its promise. In the Low Country, February is a long sigh of relief. It is unlikely to get really cold again, not the blossom-blasting cold of January. The great camellia trees in Charleston gardens and on the river plantations are heavy and languid with blooms, and along the roadside into the city, daffodils and forsythia burn like little fires. To me, the soft radiance of this green spring was a sword in my heart. It had been a very long time since I had spent a Charleston spring without Lewis.

"I want so badly for it to be this time next year," I said to Gaynelle once, while we two and Camilla sat watching Britney pottering about on the end of the dock. A school of river dolphins had been hanging around for a week or so, often so close that you could have reached out and touched their slick, rubbery skin. They would poke their heads out of the water and give you those cunning smiles, and a conspiratorial gaze out of the one great visible eye. They seemed so benign and sweet tempered that the urge to pet them was strong, but Henry had told us not to do it.

"They don't need to think they live here," he said. "Get too friendly with them, or feed them, and they won't move on when they need to."

"Will the alligator eat them?" Britney asked anxiously. The big bull was audible almost every night now, though not yet visible.

"I don't think so. But I don't want to tempt fate," Henry said.

So Britney, having been admonished, did not reach out to touch them. But she stayed on the dock for hours, watching, watching.

"I think they talk to each other," I said once, smiling, to Gaynelle.

"I wouldn't be surprised," she said.

Now she reached out to touch my arm fleetingly.

"I know about that," she said. "You keep thinking that it'll be better when a year has passed, and none of the anniversaries will be the first one. It wasn't as bad for me after Randy, of course. But it wasn't good, either."

"Time passes," Camilla said dreamily. "After a while all the anniversaries run together and you can't separate them anymore."

"Is it better then?" I asked.

"No," she said. And I felt a surge of shame, because I had been so drowned in my own loss that I had not, in a long time, thought that Camilla, too, must still mourn Charlie.

Britney's after-school day care center had raised its rates considerably, and I knew that Gaynelle was having a hard time coming up with the increase. So, impulsively, I told her to bring Britney to the creek for the few after-school hours until her mother's workday ended. Sometimes Gaynelle stayed later than usual, to make something she thought might tempt Camilla for dinner, or to tackle a cleaning job I had not yet gotten around to. So Britney was often with us until quite late, and a couple of times I insisted that she and her mother stay for dinner.

"Can you stand it, just a few times now and then?" I asked Camilla. "She's really settled down a good bit. I haven't heard the harmonica in weeks."

"Oh, of course," Camilla said. "Don't mind me. I'm getting so cranky that I don't even like myself. And I know you and Henry are fond of the child."

I was. And Henry, surprisingly, was delighted with Britney. I never quite knew why. He was fond of his own grandchildren and saw them often, but Britney seemed more like a daughter born very late to him. He took her with him in the Whaler when he went out, and was teaching her to fish and crab, and often she accompanied him when he went off for short trips on the 230 Roller, which T. C.'s friend had rented to him for a month or so.

"You're spoiling that child horribly," Camilla said once, smiling indulgently at him, when he came back from the clinic with a plastic bag of goldfish for Britney. "And she's already cosseted enough."

"Not in the right way," Henry said. "She knows how to priss her little ass down a runway, but she doesn't know how to be a kid."

Gaynelle was pleased by the bond between the two.

"She can learn things from him and you that I couldn't teach her," she said. "I never did like the idea that she thinks shaking her booty is the be-all and end-all."

"I've always wondered why you let her do those pageants," I said, thinking that I knew Gaynelle well enough now to voice the question.

"There wasn't much else that I could give her," Gaynelle said softly. "Oh, I taught her to read, and she's beginning to write little things that are sort of nice. But private school is out. And this is the only thing she's really wanted with all her heart. I know the pageants are trashy. I hoped she'd get bored with them. I was going to pull her out of them next year, anyway. Now she's got you and Henry and the creek on her mind more than the pageants. It's a godsend."

Henry and Britney sputtered in from a bike excursion to Edisto Beach just then, and came up onto the porch laughing.

Britney was choked with giggles, her little freckled face contorted with them. She was completely covered with dust, and the red curls were wild.

"Want to share the joke?" I said, smiling at Henry's face, sunburnt and younger by far, with his teeth flashing white through the dust, than when he had come to the creek last August.

"Henry was telling me all about how bad he and Dr. Aiken were on Sullivan's Island when they were little," she said. "They used to run through these old tunnels and stuff naked!"

"Don't go getting any ideas," Gaynelle said,

smiling at her daughter. There was no trace of the little princess in Britney now.

"I grew up on the island with them, too," Camilla said. "They were my best friends."

"Did you go naked, too?" Britney said, fascinated.

"In the house," Gaynelle said. "Now."

They went off to wash their respective faces, Gaynelle behind them, and I said to Camilla, "You know, I've wondered if Britney doesn't remind Henry a little of Fairlie. There are a lot of similarities, if you think about it."

"I sincerely hope not," Camilla said levelly. "That common child is hardly competition for Fairlie, alive or dead."

I stared at her.

"I didn't mean like that. . . ."

"Will you give me a hand, Anny?" she said, faintly. "I've got a splitting headache. I think I'll have a nap until dinner. Are they staying?"

"They don't have to."

"Oh, by all means, ask them. Henry will be disappointed if you don't."

I helped her to bed and covered her with her comforter, and turned off the lights. I had thought Camilla would come to feel differently about the child when she had been in her presence for a while; the change in Britney was apparent. But it had not happened. I would have to curtail the visits. It was not fair to Camilla to force upon her a child she found so distasteful. She was one of us, too, and she could not, as we could, simply walk away. I would suggest to Henry that he take Britney out for hamburgers occasionally, instead of having her here for dinner so often. But it was strange. . . .

"Cammy's really not well," Henry said when I brought up the topic of Britney and Camilla. "She's not herself. I'm going to get her in for a physical before this week is out, even if I have to carry her. Meanwhile, can you find something to do with Britney in the afternoons away from here? Isn't there something she might like to do?"

"I think we'll form a book club," I said lightly, and then realized that it might be a very good idea.

On a Saturday morning in late February, Linda Cousins called me.

"There's been some men from some kind of real estate company out here, looking around the house and woods," she said. "They said Dr. Aiken told them back in the fall they were welcome to come look around. It doesn't sound right to Robert and me. Would you like us to tell them to leave?"

I started to say yes, and then Henry came into the room and I put my hand over the phone and told him what Linda had said.

"Tell her not to run them off," he said. "I'm going to get out there right now and see what's going on. You know as well as I do that Lewis never told them that."

"I'm going with you."

"Anny, I know how hard it is for you—"

"It's my house now, Henry. I've been letting it

slide for too long. I don't want real estate people at Sweetgrass. Not now and not ever."

We were starting for the truck when Gaynelle brought Camilla out, dressed for the day.

"You're not going out this close to lunch," she cried.

Briefly, Henry told her what was happening.

"Anny, you really ought not to go out there. Henry can handle it."

"It's my house, Camilla," I said. "I'm grateful for Henry's company, but if anybody tells them to get off the property, it's going to be me."

We got into the truck and Henry started it up. Over the engine's noise we heard Camilla call, "Be home before dark!," and there was real anxiety in her voice.

"She's so anxious now," I said worriedly to Henry on the way to Sweetgrass. "So fretful, and so weak. And it's happened so fast. I didn't think people aged that fast."

"They don't generally. Usually you can see it coming long before there are such definite signs. I'm serious about getting her in for tests. This is getting really hard on you."

"Oh, no. No more than on you. Gaynelle makes all the difference. I just want Camilla well."

"So do I," he said. We were silent the rest of the way.

When we turned off the road and onto the long driveway into Sweetgrass, my heart lifted at the sheer underwater green of the long tunnel through the live oaks, and the splashes of wild honeysuckle and dogwood standing like stilled snowfall in the dusky green. I remembered the first day I had ever seen it. It was hard to believe all that time had passed. Out here, the marsh, the river, and the deep woods stopped time. I could just as easily be the wild-haired young woman in the too-new tennis shoes Lewis had brought here for the first time, and he could easily be waiting for me on the dock over the river, with fresh comb tracks through his wet red hair and a glass of wine for me, as he had done so many times before. I swallowed hard.

"Is this going to be okay?" Henry said.

We rounded the last curve and the house came into view, at once rooted in the earth and lifted into the air like a sail, and I nodded. This first glimpse had always borne me up in joy.

"Yes."

And after all, it was. It was easy to walk with Henry up the steps of the house, and through it, and out onto the dock, not like it had been with Lewis, never like that. But easy. I kept putting out all my sensors for him: in the beautiful, light-paneled library, in the dim upstairs bedroom where I had last seen him, at the end of the dock, where we had made love and swum naked in water as warm as blood. Where we had seen the bobcat. And I did feel him near, I thought: a diffuse, enveloping sense of him. But he did not walk hungrily just behind me, as he had done on Bull Street. I thought that he must be truly at rest here, and said so to Henry as we stood beside Lewis's grave in the deep live-oak grove. The stone I had ordered still had not come, but the ferns Linda and I had transplanted were flourishing, and the little white azalea was in bud.

"Why wouldn't he be? This is paradise," Henry said. "I always thought Fairlie and I might get something like this. Lewis always said he could find us a place. . . ."

We were both silent. I remembered what he had said about seeing Fairlie's family farm for the first time. I knew that he did, too.

There had been no other car in the driveway except Linda Cousins's Jeep when we arrived. Linda, in the kitchen as she always seemed to be, said that she had gone out and called to the real estate people that if they'd wait, Dr. Aiken's wife was on her way, and shortly after that they had left.

"We knew they weren't up to any good," she said. "People do come down the driveway sometimes and stop and look at the house, but they don't get out and prowl around. I'm going to get Robert to get a security gate with an alarm put up out at the road. If it's okay with you."

I agreed that we should do it, and thought, not for the first time, that I really had to make myself get more involved in the day-to-day running of Sweetgrass. You could walk out of the little house on Bull Street and lock the door, and be fairly sure all would be as it had been when you returned. But not this vast plantation. It needed day-by-day tending, and I was deeply grateful to the Cousinses for staying on, as I had asked, and overseeing the property. But I could not let the load get too heavy for them. Both were old now, older than Lewis, older than Henry, though they were still active and vital.

"I need to get you some help out here," I said. "I've let it drag on too long. I'm going to start looking right away. Henry will help me."

I looked up at him, and he nodded.

"Well," Linda said, "if you could use him, I think Tommy might like to do that. He's getting married . . . did I tell you? No? To a premed student at MUSC, Jennie. We're crazy about her. She loves this place, and of course Tommy grew up out here, and they were thinking that if they could buy a little piece of land from you, they'd like to build a house on the river down near us. She'd keep on at school, of course, but Tommy thinks now that he wants to go into some sort of land management or conservation work. He'd be good at it, I think. He's followed his dad around out here ever since he could walk. And he's been keeping an eye on the longleaf crop, and talking to the extension agent when he thinks he needs to. He didn't want to presume, but we knew you weren't up to that yet, and it's been a pleasure for him to keep up with things. So I said I'd ask you—"

"Oh, yes, please!" I cried before all the words were out of her mouth. The plantation had been heavy on my heart in the time since Lewis's death. I knew that Linda and Robert could manage the house and grounds, but the vast longleaf plantings that were the plantation's cash crop needed constant nurturing, and were beyond my ken.

"I can't tell you how relieved I am," I said to Linda Cousins. "It's like I've been given a gift. Tell

Tommy I'll have Fleming Woodward—he's our lawyer—call him this week, and we'll set it up. Oh, to have it go on with you all . . . Lewis would love that."

"So would we," Linda said, and hugged me.

We ate the velvety cold asparagus soup she had made for our lunch, and walked back out on the dock one more time before we left.

"Lewis and I saw a bobcat here the first night he brought me out here," I told Henry. "Right over there. Lewis said not long before . . . not so long ago that he saw tracks again right on this spot. It couldn't be our bobcat, of course, but I've always liked to think one of his offspring didn't want to leave the river, either."

"Probably got fifteen grandchildren by now," Henry said comfortably. "Anny, can I ask you what you intend to do with Sweetgrass? Ultimately, I mean. You said you were okay for money, but I know you don't want to let it just sit here and deteriorate. . . ."

"No. I think I'm going to deed the whole thing to the Coastal Conservancy, with the stipulation that whoever is in the big house, and the Cousins and their kin—like Tommy—stay for their lifetimes, if they like. Lewis always wanted to see this stretch of the river safe from development."

"It's just what he'd do himself," Henry said warmly. "Want me to call Fleming Woodward about that, too?"

"Well," I said hesitantly, "it probably ought to be me."

Henry began to laugh.

"Of course it ought to be you. What was I thinking? But can you really afford to do all that? You don't need money from the sale of Sweetgrass?"

"I'm fine," I said. "Besides the trusts for the children and bequests to Robert and Linda, and a separate trust to maintain Sweetgrass, it all came to me. There was more than I thought. Lewis was good with his money. I know that the lovely and talented Sissy had a go at my inheritance, but Fleming blew her out of the water and only told me about it later. People have been doing my work for too long. I don't want to start to dislike myself."

"No. Don't do that."

It was just dark when we pulled up to the turn-around in front of the creek houses. I was drowsy and satiated, as if I had had a heavy meal, but I knew it was simply relief at finally getting Sweetgrass in order. It had the feeling of a long-put-off job well done.

"Where is everybody?" Henry said, and I looked at him. His fair brows were knit. I looked toward the houses. Mine and Simms and Lila's were dark, but Camilla's blazed with lights, as it should have, of course. But then I saw that the front door stood wide open, and that Gaynelle's truck was gone.

Henry and I were out of the car and into her house before the doors had slammed shut.

There was a Post-it note stuck on Camilla's screen door.

C. fainted in bathtub and cracked her head open, it read. *I'm taking her to Queens emergency. Please come.* It was signed *G.*

Henry called ahead and barked orders to the

nurses' desk and we drove back down the dark, moss-tunneled road toward Charleston in silence, and at a speed I would not care to repeat again. As we went over the West Ashley bridge, with the great hospital complex shining ahead in the night like a lightship, I said to Henry, "Let's decide something now. I think it would kill her to move her, either back home or to some kind of facility. Later, maybe, she can go to Gillon Street with some help, but for a few months, let's try our best to keep her at the creek, and let's stay with her. That vow we took means everything to her. I'd like to promise her we'll stay, if she's not too bad. Obviously, if she's seriously hurt or ill, we can't. But can we try?"

He looked over at me, his thin face lit green in the light from the dash.

"Are you willing to give up that much more of your life?"

"What else have I got to do?" I said. "Sooner or later I'll have to make some long-range plans, but one of the things I've loved best about the creek is that nobody pushes me. It's like being a kid just after school's out, with a whole, endless summer before me. Do you remember that sense of limitless time and space?"

"Best thing about summer," Henry said. "Okay. If we can, let's give it till fall. We can tell her that. It should ease her. I know she's been afraid we'd go off and leave her. She talks about it a lot."

"Will you mind just letting things drift for that long?"

He grinned. "You bet I won't. Lila has been trying to get me paired up with some nice lady for weeks now. I'll bet she's asked me to dinner ten times. I'm scared to move back home."

I laughed a little. It was true. An eligible bachelor in Charleston is worth his weight in Georgian silver. Never mind his age or circumstances. If his provenance is downtown, he can eat dinner out for the rest of his life, providing he is compos mentis. I've even wondered sometimes if that requirement was cut in stone. Some of Charleston's greatest and most engaging eccentrics come very close to mania, and they do just fine if they have a decent tux and know whose dining room they're in.

"Nobody is after me," I said. "Should I be hurt?"

"'Thank the living God that made you,' as the guy says in 'Gunga Din.' Besides, I think you scare the ladies of Charleston."

"Why on earth would I do that?"

He looked over at me.

"You're a thoroughly nice woman, Anny. And a pretty one, even if you don't think so. And now you're a rich one. Are you kidding? They're scared those quote 'eligible bachelors' will be after you, instead of their cousin from Columbia, or their best friend who just got a divorce. They'll be overjoyed to hear that you're staying out at the creek."

"So we're agreed," I said, as he pulled up before the Queens emergency room. His face was closed again.

"We're agreed," he said.

Camilla was still in the emergency room when

we got there. The hospital waiting room was full of tired, silent people. Gaynelle sat among them. She jumped to her feet and ran to us when we came in.

"What have you heard?" Henry said.

"They've still got her in some little room back there," she said. "Nobody will tell me anything. I feel just terrible about this; she asked for a cup of tea, and I made it and came back, and she was lying half in and half out of the bathtub, unconscious, bleeding like a stuck pig from her forehead. I didn't know she wanted a bath. She was in bed writing in her book when I left her to make the tea. If anything bad is wrong with her, I'll never forgive myself."

"Whatever it is, it is assuredly not your fault," Henry told her. "She knows to call you when she wants to go into the bathroom. Let's just see."

He disappeared into the warren of cubicles through the swinging door of the ER, and Gaynelle and I sat down to wait. In the lurid fluorescent glare, she looked bone weary, and older than I had ever seen her. I probably did, too. I took her hand and squeezed it.

"You can't read her mind," I said. "Nobody can do that. You know how she hates being dependent. She probably thought she could manage a bath by herself. . . ."

Gaynelle's head was tipped against the sofa back, and her eyes were closed.

"I'm not leaving her alone again," she said. "I'm going to be with her every breath she draws."

"You think that's good for her? She hates to be hovered over."

"It's good for all of us," she said.

Henry came back presently and sat down with us.

"It's not too bad," he said. "At least the cut isn't. The ER doc took a couple of stitches, and she's had X rays and an MRI. There's maybe a little concussion, but nothing to worry about. I'm admitting her, though. This time she's getting the full workup. Tab Shipley's writing the order now. She wants me to stay with her; she's really shaken up, so I think I will. You all go on back home. I'll come give you a report in the morning."

"When will you sleep?" I said.

"In the on-call room. In an empty room. In the linen closet. You learn your intern year to sleep anywhere. I'm going to knock her out, and she'll sleep till morning. I'll have plenty of time to rest."

Gaynelle and I didn't talk much on the drive home. Once she said, "I wish he'd stay in the room with her."

"Why on earth? She surely isn't going anywhere in that hospital room."

"You never know," Gaynelle said.

Henry came home in time for breakfast, just before I left for work. Gaynelle had come in, even though I had told her to sleep in while she could. She had made French toast, and Henry fell on it like a starving man.

"She's awake and fairly comfortable," he said. "Her head hurts and she's several different colors of purple, but her vitals seem okay. They'll get the blood work and the other stuff done today. Depending on what we find, I might be able to bring her home tomorrow or the next day. I'm worried about her bones. In the X rays they looked as porous as screen wire."

The test results came back, and had Henry stern-faced.

"Blood work's okay, though she's a little anemic. That probably causes some of the dizziness. Her heart rhythm is a little slow. Her blood pressure is low. But it's her bones that worry me. Her ankle and wrist aren't healing at all like they should, and there's a big area on one sacrum that looks like Swiss cheese. She could break a hip just by turning over in bed, and that would be the end of living out here. She knows all that. I made her promise that from now on it's going to be a wheelchair. I don't want any pressure on those bones. She's not happy, but I think she knows it's the only way she can stay at the creek. I promised her we'd all stay, like we agreed, so long as she behaves. Gaynelle, do you think you can manage her in a wheelchair? We can easily get some more help out here."

"I'm sure," she said. "In a way, it'll be easier. I won't have to worry so much about her pussyfooting around places she shouldn't be."

Camilla came home two days later with a shiny folding wheelchair accented with dark blue leather, a carful of flowers, and a black eye that covered half her face. It was lunchtime, and we had asked Lila to come and share a light celebratory meal. She had arrived with a great armful of white lilies and Honey in her carrier, and she and I were sitting on Camilla's porch, while Britney and Honey chased each other on the lawn, drinking orange blossoms and turning our faces up to the blessed sun.

It was a diamond day, when even the light trembles in glittering shards. The tiny new green leaves glittered, the light chop on the creek was like dancing tinfoil, and the sky was so blue that it hurt to look at it. The fresh smell of damp loam and pine from somewhere came in on the wind. When Henry got out and unfolded the wheelchair and helped Camilla into it, we all cheered, and she smiled the old enigmatic, V-shaped Camilla smile. Britney came dashing up to her and laid a bouquet of early tulips on her lap.

"Mama got them for me to give you," she said shyly.

"Thank you, dear," Camilla said. "Tulips are my favorite."

Britney squirmed with pleasure and dashed off after the little dog, who was yipping frantically on the bank of the creek.

"Bring her closer to the house, Britney," Lila called. "I don't like her being so close to the water. Not with that gator around."

"I've never seen the gator around here, Miz Howard," Britney said.

"Just do it, Brit," Gaynelle said briefly, and Britney did.

I had bought Camilla a new lavender cashmere cardigan, and we draped it around her, over her housecoat, as we sat on the porch for lunch. She looked revived, reborn, pink flushed in spite of the garish bruise that made us all wince.

"This is heaven," she said, closing her eyes and breathing in the sweet breeze. "Why would anybody want to be anywhere else?"

"Except maybe that gorgeous loft of yours, or

Anny's perfect little jewel of a house on Bull Street," Lila said. "And as for Henry, with that wonderful old pile on Bedon's Alley—"

"It's decided," Camilla said. "We're staying. Except if I can persuade Anny to go home and just come on weekends. She's a pretty young woman still. She ought to be somewhere there's companionship and a little fun—"

"I'm staying," I said. "End of discussion. Don't you think I love it out here, too?"

Camilla studied me, and then smiled and nodded.

Gaynelle brought out trays of shrimp salad and tomato aspic and fresh-baked cheese straws, and we had a wonderful, light trifle with fresh berries for dessert. After coffee, Henry went out and scooped Britney up from the lawn and carried her off, squealing and giggling, for a ride in the Whaler.

"Did you put Honey in the house?" Lila shouted after her.

"Yes, ma'am," Britney called, and they glided slowly out of sight down the creek. Camilla wanted a nap, and Gaynelle settled her and went into my kitchen, where she had made lunch, to wash up. Lila and I went out to the end of the dock and sat in the sun, swinging our legs.

"This reminds me a little of the island," Lila said. "When we'd sit out on the dock and wait for the guys to come in from sailing. Does it you?"

"No," I said. "That's one reason I can stay here. It's just itself. It's not much a part of any other time in my life."

She nodded in understanding.

"But you do think about the beach?"

"Oh, Lila. Every day. Every day."

"You've been braver than I could ever be," she said, and squeezed my hand.

"I've got a good support team," I said.

She turned to face me.

"People are asking me if there's anything, you know, between you and Henry. I mean, being out here all the time and all . . ."

"Lewis was it for me, Lila," I said, annoyed. I didn't want Charleston's ceaseless speculations to stain the creek for me.

"Besides," I said, "I thought it might be Henry and Camilla. I mean, Lewis said they were so close before Charlie came along. . . ."

"Well, they were. Almost joined at the hip. We were all surprised, but Charlie came, and that was it. But he's been gone a long time."

"Lewis once said there was just too much history between them," I said, and she nodded.

"That can happen."

After a while a brisk little wind came up, and we grew chilly. We got up and ambled toward our houses, agreeing to meet for lunch one day soon, after my half day at the office. I was suddenly stunned with sleepiness, and wanted a long nap. Lila said she had to get back to Charleston. We hugged briefly, and I turned into my walkway and went inside my little house. It was cool and silent. My lids were heavy.

When it came, Lila's scream literally made the hair at the back of my neck stand up. It was almost an inhuman sound, an animal howl. I dashed for her house, my heart pounding in my chest. Gaynelle came out of the kitchen, running.

Lila stood on her front porch, tears streaming down her face.

"She left the door open," she sobbed. "The front door was wide open when I got here. Honey isn't anywhere; I've looked all over. It's been at least two hours. She's gone down to the creek, I know she has. I told that child to close the door, and she said she had. . . ."

We looked for Honey until dark. When Henry brought Britney in from the creek, Lila came screaming down on her, and Gaynelle stepped in front of her daughter. Henry put his arms around Lila, and led her to her porch. We could hear Camilla calling agitatedly from her house, "What's the matter? What's wrong?" Gaynelle, tight-mouthed, sent the sobbing Britney inside, and joined the search. We scoured the creek and the marsh, and Henry even took out the kayak, so he could be closer to the water and the bank. But there was no sign of the little white dog. Neither was there any sign of the gator.

Lila wanted to stay the night and look, but Henry convinced her to go home.

"We'll keep looking," he said. "We've got the security lights. She's probably gotten lost, or she's hiding. Don't you remember how Sugar used to hide when she thought you were going to take her home from the beach?"

"It's not the same thing," Lila sobbed. "I know Honey is gone. I just know. I want an apology from that child, and then I don't ever want to see her anywhere near my house again."

Gaynelle came in from ministering to Britney.

"Miz Howard, she says she's sure she closed

the door. She double-checked. You know how much she loves that little dog. I've never known her to be careless that way."

"Just keep her out of my house," Lila said. Her face was red and swollen; her eyes were sealed shut with grief.

"She's not likely to want to go in it," Gaynelle said levelly.

"And I'm waiting for an apology."

"Well, you're not getting one from my daughter. If she said she didn't do it, she didn't," Gaynelle flared.

The two women stood glaring at each other, and then Lila, still sobbing, went home. Gaynelle took her stricken daughter home. Henry and I went in to check on Camilla. She was sleeping, so we went out again. We searched with flashlights until midnight, we called and called and called. But we never saw Honey, and nobody ever did again.

The next weekend Lila and Simms left for a month in the Grenadines, which, Simms said, was some of the best sailing in the world.

"They won't come back," Camilla said bitterly at dinner the night that they left. "Not to the creek. I know Lila. I knew we might lose them. But I never thought it would be over the cleaning woman's juvenile delinquent."

Henry and I looked at each other, but we did not speak. Neither of us really thought Britney had left the door open, but we did not know what precisely had happened, and in any event, it was not the time to challenge Camilla about it. We all felt the loss of Lila and Simms and the little dog deeply. First, let the healing begin.

15

BRITNEY WOULD NOT COME BACK to the creek. No matter how we coaxed, and offered Whaler excursions and swimming afternoons and hamburger suppers on the grill, she dug in her heels and set her small mouth and refused.

"What's wrong?" Henry and I asked Gaynelle over and over. "She must know we don't blame her about Honey. And you've told her, haven't you, that she won't have to see Lila again? We miss Britney so much. She's a breath of life in this place."

"I've told her all that," Gaynelle said. "It doesn't do any good. She won't come and she won't talk about it. She cried for a long time after that day, but she doesn't do that now. She just seems . . . sad. She loved that little dog. And nobody has ever talked to her the way Miz Howard did."

Gaynelle herself had lost some of her insouciant sparkle, though none of her energy and competence. I thought that she was thinner, too. Her shorts hung loose on her now, and you could see her ribs plainly under her cropped T-shirt. The weight loss made the astonishing breasts even more so. Somehow, the sight of them, jutting bravely out over Gaynelle's ribs, made me sad.

Pain flared in Henry's eyes. Then it was gone. His face was back to the noncommittal mask he had worn lately. I knew that he was very angry with Lila, and puzzled about the little dog. But mostly, he missed Britney. His missing her hurt me.

"What does she do after school now?" I asked, when Britney first refused to accompany her mother to the creek.

"JoAnne takes her," Gaynelle said. "It's all right. She's got a girl only three years older than Brit. It's a big gap, though. I don't think either one of them particularly wants to be friends. I've found a new pageant school for her, on James Island. This woman has run pageants for thirty years, and she knows what she's doing. She takes only about five girls at a time. I was really pleased to get Britney in. Miz Delaporte works them like mules, five afternoons a week, but Britney's learning all the tricks. Miz Delaporte says she's a natural."

"Will you let us pay for it?" I said, horrified at the thought of Britney back on the wheel of a pageant mill, but knowing better than to say so. "It could be a birthday present from Henry and me."

"Mr. Howard sent me a check," Gaynelle said, not looking at us. "He was very generous. I'm using that. It's only fitting."

Henry and I looked at each other, but said no more.

Camilla never commented on Britney's absence. Gaynelle was, with Camilla, her usual sunny self. She very seldom let Camilla out of her sight, and then only when one of us was near. But she did not stay for dinner anymore, and T. C. did not come often now.

"I miss you all," I said. "I feel like we've lost family. I don't think I could stand it if you were unhappy with us now."

"No. You *are* family. And I'm not going to leave. Not while Miz Curry needs so much help."

"I know," I said. "It's like she's quit fighting. She lies in that bed all the time now, except when we have her up in the chair and at meals. I hate to see it. Her strength and will have always been the things that held us up."

"I don't think she's lost the will," Gaynelle said. "She's tearing those notebooks up. I went to pick up one that had slid off the bed, and she was down my throat like a missile."

"I hope that's true," I said. "She's pretty frail when she's with us. Of course, that's usually at the end of a long day."

In mid-February Henry took me on the back of the bike over to Gaynelle's sister JoAnne's house. It was a Saturday, and Britney was free from pageant school. Gaynelle was with Camilla. She insisted on coming to the creek when I told her what we wanted to do.

"It would do Brit a world of good," she said.

And it did. When she heard the putting of the bike, Britney was out of the little cement-block house like a shot, and into Henry's arms before he was off the bike.

"I thought you would come," she sang, hugging me as well as Henry. "I told Aunt JoAnne you would. I told T. C., too. You want to see my new pageant routine?"

"No," Henry said. "I want to take you and Anny over to Stanfield's and get some ice cream."

"*Yes!*" she cried, giving him a high five.

We drove over to the ice-cream parlor in JoAnne's borrowed car, and sat out at cement tables under an umbrella eating ice cream. I had mint chocolate chip. Henry chose cherry vanilla. Britney dug into a banana split and got most of it down before we were done with ours. Her grin was chocolate rimmed.

"Why won't you come back to see us, Brit?" Henry said, finally and gently.

After a moment she averted her eyes and said, "I'm afraid Honey is going to come floating up on the bank while I'm there, or half of her. And Miz Curry doesn't want me there."

I flinched in pain at the image of the little dead dog. I knew the feeling. Hadn't I fled my own dead husband when I still thought that he walked with pearls for eyes?

"Sweetie, that's not true about Camilla. And in any case, I don't think you'd ever see her. She sleeps most of the time now."

"No, she doesn't," Britney said stubbornly. But that was all she would say.

So we continued to see Britney at home or at her aunt's, and late in February Henry took her a tiny Maltese puppy, and I think she was the happiest child that I have ever seen.

"I'm going to name her Henrietta," she caroled, clutching the wriggling puppy to her skinny chest. "And I'm never going to let her go outside. Not ever."

With only weekends to visit with Britney, we had a real dilemma about keeping Camilla company. Gaynelle solved it. She insisted on coming half days on Saturdays, while Camilla usually slept, so that we could have time with the child. We had argued with her.

"You'd have literally no life but us," I said. "We can alternate Saturdays. I can go one week and Henry the next. I can't have you putting your life on hold just for us."

"You have no idea how happy it makes Brit," she said. "I'd work twenty-four/seven to keep her this way. And I don't want you by yourself with Camilla, Anny. It takes a strong ox like me to lift her. You don't weigh as much as a dandelion now."

That night I took off my clothes and looked at myself in the bathroom mirror. I could not remember when I had done so. I could see my ribs, and, faintly, my hipbones, sights I had never seen before. I looked like somebody else entirely.

"Would you know me now, Lewis?" I whispered. "What if you didn't?"

It was an unsettling thought, and so I pushed it out of my mind. I did not look again.

On the last Saturday in February, Henry was up early, and prodded me out onto my porch. He was grinning broadly. Before I could ask what he thought was so funny, the familiar grumbling roar of bikes came down the sand road, and T. C. and Gaynelle came sweeping up to the turnaround, rooster tails of gravel pluming up behind them. T. C. rode the Rubbertail, and Gaynelle her pink Harley.

"School's in session," T. C. called jovially, as if he had seen us only yesterday rather than weeks ago.

"Henry, today is the day you learn the Rubbertail. And Anny, *you* are soloing on Henry's 230."

"*No!*" I squealed.

"Yes," Henry said implacably.

After a few wobbles, Henry proved to be a natural on the big, throbbing bike, and roared off down the road to the highway alone, trailing his own huge cloud of dust. I, on the other hand, was utterly inept. The little bike wobbled and spat and bucketed, and I cringed and dragged my feet and killed the engine over and over. But finally I made a wobbling circuit of the turnaround, and seemed to get the feel of the laboring little engine through the seat of my pants, and by the time Henry roared back in on the Rubbertail, I was cruising at a good enough clip so that the wind stung my face and my hair streamed back.

"Way to go!" Henry cried, swinging off the Rubbertail and giving me a high five as I dismounted the 230, my legs buckling profoundly.

"I knew you could do it!" Gaynelle called from the porch. I looked her way. She was standing behind Camilla on the shade-dappled porch, waving her clasped hands Rocky-like over her head. Camilla, in a new green-striped cotton caftan, and sunglasses, did not wave, but she smiled.

"The flying Snopeses," she called, and my face burned. I wondered if anyone caught the allusion to William Faulkner's bestial backwoods tribe. I looked at Gaynelle and saw that she had. Well, of course, Gaynelle read everything. Her mouth thinned, but she said nothing.

"Go on and do one more round," she called out. "Camilla and I are making her mother's crab cakes for lunch."

"She never leaves Camilla alone," I said to Henry. "How did we get so lucky?"

"I don't know," Henry said. "But it eases my mind a lot."

Late that afternoon, as I was getting dressed for dinner, having showered away about a pound of road dust, I reached for the heavy gold bracelet that Lewis had given me for our first anniversary, and could not find it. Since I rarely took it off, I was puzzled and then, after a thorough search, faintly alarmed. I remembered having taken it off before getting on the motorcycle, but I could not remember where I had put it.

"Has anybody seen my gold bracelet?" I said at dinner. "I took it off this morning, but I don't remember where I put it down. You all keep an eye out, will you?"

There was a long silence, and then Camilla said, softly, "I'm missing some things, too. That little signet ring that was my grandmother's, and a pair of emerald earrings Charlie brought me from somewhere or other. I suppose we shouldn't be surprised. . . ."

My head jerked up and I stared at her. In the candlelight, her face was serene. Her long eyelashes shuttered her eyes.

"What do you mean, Camilla?" I said.

"Nothing, really. Like you, I could easily have misplaced them," she said. "I wasn't even going to say anything, but when your bracelet went missing, I thought . . ."

"If you were thinking Britney, you know she hasn't been at the creek for three weeks," I said.

"I know," Camilla said, still softly, still not raising her eyes.

"If you mean you think . . ."

She raised her eyes, finally. But she did not speak.

"Never in a million years," I said. "Not ever. I hope you aren't thinking of talking to her about it. Because if you are—"

"Of course I'm not," she said indignantly. "We owe her everything. And I never really thought that, anyway. It was just funny, both of us losing things so close together."

"Then maybe we'll find them close together."

"I feel sure we will," Camilla said.

We said no more about the jewelry, but after I had settled her in bed and turned off her light, I went out onto my little back deck and sat in the chilly spring night, wrapped in Lewis's old terry robe, trying very hard not to think about the unsettling conversation. I absolutely refused to let the faintest bladelike leaf of doubt sprout in my mind.

When I finally went to bed, about two A.M., Camilla's bedroom was dark, but out in the guest house, Henry's light burned steadily.

The next weekend Gaynelle called early Saturday morning and said, "The Iron Johns and the Thun-

derhogs—that's us—are riding down to Folly
Beach this afternoon. It's nothing formal, just a
spring run. We do it with the Johns two or three
times a year. This time we're all kicking in a little
for Tim Satterwhite and his family. Tim got side-
swiped by a twelve-wheeler on I-26 and busted
his spine to pieces. He's got to have about five
operations. So we thought we'd do this one for
him. Thing is, now, T. C. and I thought you and
Henry might like to ride with us. We'll just go
down there, drink a little beer at Sandy Don's,
maybe eat some shrimp, and come on back. It's a
good introduction. Not too big, not competitive.
Everybody's friends. We won't be racing or dragging or anything. Henry would go with T. C. and
you'd ride with me. What do you think?"

It was a spectacular day after a week of bleary
spring rain, and I was literally itching to get outdoors. The three of us and Gaynelle had done little but stay in and read or listen to music, or, less
often, watch TV. Camilla had slept, slept. The
thought of sun and wind and noise and the sight
of a beach that was not our treacherous old beach
was suddenly irresistible.

I told Henry and his face lit up. Before we
could change our minds, I told Gaynelle we'd
love it.

"Pick you up around noon," she said. "Wear a
jacket and bring sunscreen."

I took Camilla in to breakfast and we told her
about the ride. She closed her eyes for a long
moment.

"Am I losing you all to a motorcycle gang?" she
said, but she smiled.

"Oh, of course not," I said. "It's just this one time. Whenever again in my life am I going to get to ride with a motorcycle club?"

"I take your point," Camilla said. "So who's staying with the old lady?"

"Don't say that," I pleaded. "You look younger than either of us. JoAnne said she'd love to come, and she's bringing her oldest daughter and her daughter's friend. You won't see hide nor hair of them. All they want to do is lie out on the dock and burn their butts in the sun. Their boyfriends are picking them up at six, and JoAnne will make you dinner, and we'll be home not long after dark."

"Sounds good," she said wryly. "JoAnne and I can continue our conversation about the time-space continuum."

Henry and I laughed. JoAnne was perhaps the sweetest woman I had ever met, but her interests lay more in the realm of reality TV.

"Tell you what," Henry said. "Tomorrow we'll take you into town to the yacht club for lunch. It's been months since you've been back in Charleston."

"Oh, Henry, I don't think so," Camilla said. "Soon, but not yet. Catch me some crabs and let's steam them for lunch."

I was vastly relieved. Lunch at the yacht club was the last thing on earth I thought I could handle. Like Camilla, I thought. Soon, but not yet.

At noon T. C. and Gaynelle roared up on their bikes, with JoAnne and her brood behind them in the truck. After introductions to the two teenage

Lolitas, who seemed only marginally able to speak, JoAnne settled Camilla on the porch.

"I made you curried potato salad for lunch," she said proudly. "My family loves it."

"We'll make it up to you," I mouthed silently to Camilla, wincing.

"You are going to owe me big time," she mouthed back.

Out on the road, dipping in and out of pools of deep shade and warm sun, I relaxed and gave myself over to the rhythm of the road and the steady, vibrating roar of the pink Harley beneath me. I was not afraid of bikes anymore, providing no one took me too fast, but except for the first night riding with T. C., I had never really and actively enjoyed them. Today was different. Today I was drunk on wind and sun and rushing air. Ahead of us, Henry turned around on the Rubbertail, where he rode behind T. C., and gave us the little fighter pilot's thumb jerk. He wore a helmet and goggles, but you could see that he was grinning hugely. I jerked my thumb in return. It was utterly unlike anything I had ever felt, this sense of being squarely and nakedly in the middle of the day.

The two clubs met in the parking lot of a Wal-Mart on Folly Beach Road. We got there a bit late, and when we pulled around to the back end of the lot, a solid mass of bikers and bikes milled about like a huge eddy on a river. Suddenly I thought of a painting I had loved when I was a small child. It was Rosa Bonheur's *The Horse Fair*, a brooding and romantic scene literally boiling with great, muscular horses plunging and rearing, their human tenders dwarfed by the beautiful giants. I used to sit for hours in my room, studying the painting in a book I had gotten from the library, trying to decide which horse I would most like to own. This reminded me of that.

We met everybody. They were cordial, if a little surprised to see such obvious civilians in the company of Gaynelle and T. C., and such elderly ones at that. Elderly to their eyes, at least; some of the bikers were middle-aged, but most were younger, men and women, supple in black leather, many with elaborate tattoos. Almost all the men wore handkerchiefs around their foreheads, and many had beards and ponytails. Almost all the women were younger, long limbed and large haired. Most were already reddened with the first of the spring sun. I liked most of them, and remembered none of their names.

It is the noise that eats you alive. The rushing air and the pulsing power under you are seductive in their own right, but it is the great roaring surf of sheer noise that consumes you, takes you totally out of yourself. There must have been no more than thirty-five or forty of us, but the huge, primal bellow of the string of bikes along Folly Road drowned out the world. I found myself in a hypnotic state that only snapped when we pulled into the parking lot of Sandy Don's.

"How many deaf members do you have?" I asked Gaynelle.

"Shoot, you ought to hear 'em when we rev 'em. You stomp the brake and rev it; blow you right to Miami. Of course the cops will be on you like ducks on a June bug."

Sandy Don's was a rambling, sagging, weathered gray shingle building on stilts, canting toward the sea, over the beach just below the Holiday Inn and the huge newish pier. You could tell it had been there a long time. Weather and time had eaten many of its shingles, and its stilts were slick and green with the twice-a-day pounding of the ocean and encrusted with barnacles.

"It used to be way back on the beach," Gaynelle shouted at me, "but the beach is eroding real fast, and nobody thinks Don's will be here much longer. Lots of beach houses have just gone into the water."

If anybody on Folly Island had had plans to lunch at Sandy Don's on this day, they would have been disappointed. The parking lot was solid with bikes, some parked, some just coming in. Bikers milled around in the lot and climbed the rickety steps into the restaurant. From inside, the Shirelles and the ubiquitous Billy Gilman boomed out over the parking lot and the beach. We climbed the stairs behind Gaynelle and T. C., stinging fiercely with windburn and to all purposes deaf, staggering on rubber legs.

Down on the beach I could see early sunbathers and surfers. The tide was far out, and a few children and dogs splashed at the edge of the flaccid surf. A searing bolt of pain ran through me: for a moment I saw the children of Sullivan's Island, and our own dogs. I saw Henry, ahead of me, falter, and knew that he saw the same thing. But then the children and dogs of Sullivan's Island were gone in the blinding afternoon glare, and only the generic children and dogs of all beaches remained.

There were tables on the deck, but the sun was savage and T. C.'s head was already magenta. My own cheekbones burned, and Henry was red of face, except where his goggles had left twin rings of white. Gaynelle had only turned a darker reddish tan and gained a million new freckles. T. C. found a table in the dim, cool, farthest recesses of the restaurant and we retreated there. Pretty soon the big room was thronged with bikers, all shouting and laughing and dumping bills into the helmet one of them passed. The jukebox thumped and pounded, and pitcher after pitcher of ice-cold beer appeared magically on tables, including ours. Ordinarily I did not care much for beer, but this was cold to the point of pain, wonderfully wet in dust-parched throats, and I drank it greedily. At some point in the afternoon, platters of fried shrimp and oysters and onion rings materialized on the tables, and more beer. We ate; I know we did, but I could not remember much about it later except that I had eaten myself nearly sick. Later on, as if at a signal, everybody got up to dance. I remember little of that, either, except the joyous abandon of dancing in a crowd to music that my feet knew by themselves, growing looser and looser and more supple with each song. I danced with a great many people, but I danced most with Henry. He did a loose, elegant shag, and I had a sudden, disjointed image of him and Fairlie, shagging in the surf of Sullivan's

Island on an August day. I pushed it away, and
that moment became the present moment again.

"I didn't know you could shag like that,"
Henry said, during a brief stop for beer.

"Lewis taught me," I said. "Oh, Henry, you
know what? He taught me out at Booter's! It was
the first date I ever had with him."

"There's nothing new under the sun," Henry
said solemnly, and swung me up to dance again.

"This is wonderful," I said to Gaynelle and T.
C., back at the table. We were all breathing hard.
"Are bikers' meets always so much fun?"

She laughed. "Shoot, this is nothing. You ought
to see Myrtle Beach at Bike Week; five hundred
thousand of us, for a week. And Daytona, my
God; a million bikers strong and something going
on every second of the day and night for ten days.
Some people don't sober up until about Waycross,
on the way home."

"What kind of things?"

"God, where to start? Races and competitions
and contests and drawings and live bands everywhere, and beer, and booze, and dancing, and
every kind of outfit you can imagine, and every
kind of custom bike . . . it's incredible. Maybe
we'll go next year."

"Yeah," put in T. C. "Henry would like the
burn-out pit—suck, bang, and blow for the unini-
tiated . . . and the wet T-shirt contests, and especially the ladies' wrestling and boxing and tattoo
contests. We could try Anny out in the coleslaw
wrestling competition, or maybe cornflake
wrestling. There's lots of options."

I laughed so hard that I could not get my breath, and Henry thumped me on the back.

"Coleslaw wrestling; that's for me," I said, and hiccupped. "Is it what it sounds like?"

"Yep. Great big pits full up with coleslaw out behind a couple of clubs. Ladies wrestle in them. There's one lady from Omaha who wins every time. We figure she sleeps in mayonnaise. By the second day, under the sun, that coleslaw is pretty ripe."

I collapsed in giggles again, and Henry rose.

"I need to get Cinderella home," he said. "Would it be okay if we headed out?"

"Sure," Gaynelle said, looking at her watch. "My God, it's nine o'clock. I told JoAnne we'd be back by dark. Let me run call her and we'll get on the road."

Somewhere in the sweet, chilly dark on the ride home, I sobered up. Beer rose nastily in my throat, and my face and arms burned fiercely, but I felt wonderful, light and free and young. I knew that I would feel dreadful the next day, and cared not a whit. I reached up to shout in Gaynelle's ear, and found that someone had tied me neatly to her waist with a length of soft rope. That struck me as so funny that I was off again. I was still laughing when Gaynelle and T. C. stopped the bikes at the foot of the driveway to the creek houses. We would walk the rest of the way so as not to wake Camilla.

I stumbled in the darkness, and Henry took my hand.

"I feel like your father is going to be waiting for me with a shotgun," he said.

"An empty Jim Beam bottle would be more like it," I snickered.

JoAnne was sitting on the top steps with her basket and the apparently endless afghan she was knitting. The back of Camilla's house was dark, but one lamp burned in the living room and in the light of it, JoAnne smiled.

"She's been asleep for two hours," she said. "Did my baby sister treat you right?"

"It was fabulous," I said.

Henry walked her to the truck, saw her off, and then came back.

"Want a cup of coffee?" I said halfheartedly.

"God, no. Bed for me. I'll take you up on the coffee in the morning, though."

We walked through my dark house, bumbling and bumping against things, laughing softly.

"Coleslaw wrestling," Henry snorted. "Suck, bang, and blow. 'O brave new world.'"

I laughed again and was still laughing when we reached my back deck. Henry would cut around the pool and up the path to the guest house.

We stood for a moment on the deck, looking up at the low crystal stars over the creek. The big dipper burned and burned.

"Want a light?" I said.

"Nope. I can see."

He paused, and then bent and kissed me, a soft, short, sweet kiss. I could feel that his lips were chafed from the sun and wind. He stepped back and looked down at me.

"Good God, I haven't kissed a date good night since med school," he said. "Should I apologize?"

"No," I said, feeling queer and detached from the night around us.

He turned and gave me a brief wave, and disappeared up the path. I stood still, thinking nothing at all, just being.

From the dark of the pool cage, I heard Camilla's voice.

"Henry," she called softly, "did you have a good time?"

Oh shit, I thought. I wonder if she saw? That would surely change things.

"How did you get out here?" I heard Henry say sternly.

"I came in the chair," Camilla said. "The deck's level with the house. I'm getting good at it."

"Hold on while I come and see you back to bed," Henry said from the dark. "This is not funny, Cammy."

I turned around and went into my house, and was asleep before I got my jeans off.

But after all, everything was unchanged the next morning. And on Monday morning Gaynelle came just as usual, and told Camilla about the ride to Folly Beach.

"These two are naturals," she said. "I'm going to get them to bike week in Daytona next year."

"Yeah," Henry said. "Tell her about the coleslaw wrestling."

Gaynelle did. Camilla laughed, the laugh of a young girl.

Henry came home from the clinic in the middle of the next week and said, "Susie called me at the office today. Tomorrow's her eighth birthday.

She's having a party, and she says all she wants is
for me to come and spend the night and make her
happy-face pancakes for breakfast. Nancy veri-
fied it. I think I'll go. I can't put it off forever."

"Of course you'll go," Camilla said warmly.
"And high time, too. Bring us some birthday
cake."

As he was leaving for the party, Henry said,
"Gaynelle is coming to spend the night. She
insisted on it. And I think it's a good idea.
Cammy, if you're going to be so rambunctious
with that chair, I insist that there be three of you.
We can't have you breaking a hip."

"Oh, Henry, really!" Camilla snapped. "I don't
ever get to spend much time alone with Anny
anymore. I promise not to even go to the bathroom by myself."

But Henry was adamant, and at sunset
Gaynelle drove up in the truck, bearing covered
dishes and a flowered gift bag.

"Lemon chicken and fresh asparagus," she
said. "And T. C. sent you some champagne. He
said even a hen party ought to be elegant."

"Tell him he's a sweetie," I said, hiding a smile.
T. C. and champagne? Michelob was more like it.

Camilla smiled, but said nothing.

Dinner was delectable. We ate until the platter
was empty, and the candles on Camilla's pretty
table had burned low. Then Camilla turned to
Gaynelle.

"Now," she said, "I want you to go home. You
do enough for us. Dinner was past delicious. But I
want to catch up with my old friend, and there's
no need for you to stay. We'll talk a little about old

times and drink T. C.'s champagne, and she'll tuck me in, and that will be that."

"No, ma'am," Gaynelle said formally. "I promised Henry."

Camilla's temper shattered. I had seen it happen so seldom that I gasped.

"I mean it, Gaynelle," she hissed coldly. "I insist that you go home. It's still my house. I can still live my own life. I WILL NOT BE BABY-SAT ANYMORE!"

She was so upset that I said, "Please, Gaynelle. You can certainly use the night off and I can certainly handle things for one night. You must see how very hard it is for her to always be fussed over. I mean it, now. Scoot."

"All right," Gaynelle said, with no inflection. "Give me a call if you need me. The cell phone is always with me."

"Thanks dearly," I said as she left, and hugged her. She hugged me back, hard.

"You take care," she said.

Back inside, I wheeled Camilla into her living room and helped her into a deep chair and lit the little apple-log fire that was laid. She stretched and sighed deeply and smiled.

"That wasn't very nice," she said. "I'll apologize tomorrow. I just get so . . . tired of it all. It never stops."

"Of course you do," I said warmly. "It's nice to have you to myself for a while."

We sat for a space of time, staring at the whispering blue flames. Then Camilla said, "Do you think we'll lose Henry to Charleston?"

"Not at all," I said. "Not in the near future, anyway. He doesn't want to go back to town. And besides, he promised."

"What about you? Do you ever miss it?"

I thought about it, and was vaguely surprised.

"Sometimes," I said. "Not the things you'd think, the things Lewis and I used to do. Just Charleston things. I miss walking on the Battery on a windy winter day. I miss rooting around King Street. I miss the horses. I miss the bells of St. Michael's, and the sunset at the end of Broad Street, over the palm trees. I miss the pluff mud."

She laughed.

"You've got plenty of that right here."

"Pluff mud ought to be filtered through wisteria and gasoline and horse poop," I said. "Sometimes I miss the sense of neighborhood. Not that I ever really knew many of my neighbors on Bull Street. But I knew they were there."

"Are you lonely out here?" she said.

"Never. Not for a minute. I can get all the Charleston I need anytime I want it. No. This is home for me now."

"You're sure of that?"

"You know I am. I promised, too."

She sighed, and said, "I know you did. I just have to keep picking at it, to see if you've changed your mind. I guess I still think you might. . . ."

"Not a chance," I said, and got up and went over to her, and kissed her cheek.

She put her hand up to my face, lightly.

"I've always loved you, Anny," she said.

"And I've always loved you. And I do love you. And I will love you. Now, how about some of that champagne?"

She looked up at me. There were tears in her eyes, but she smiled.

"I would absolutely love some," she said.

I brought the champagne and two of her Waterford flutes, and poured us both a frothing fluteful.

"This is like old times," I said, and held up my glass. "To us. Still the Scrubs, by God."

"Still the Scrubs," she said, smiling. I knew neither of us believed that, but it was comforting to say it.

It was, in fact, a comforting night. Peaceful. Full of the old, easy affection we had felt for each other from the beginning.

"I'm glad we had this time," I said. "We'll have to make it a regular date."

"Second that," she said, sipping her champagne. "Oh, listen, I forgot. I've got something for you. I came across it today and thought about you. Will you go look on my bedside table and bring me that little tissue-paper package?"

I did. When I came back, she was still staring at the fire, her champagne barely touched.

"Open it," she said, and I did. Inside the nest of colored tissue paper lay a choker of tiny, matched pink pearls.

"Oh, Camilla!" I cried. "They're lovely. But I can't—"

"I'm never going to wear them," she said. "I never have, really. Daddy bought them for me when I made my debut, and I wore them that night, to please him, but pink makes me look like old cheese, and my neck's too long for such small pearls. They'll be beautiful on you. Please let me do this."

I smiled, feeling tears start in my own eyes.

"I'll put them on right now," I said, and did.

"They look perfect," she said. "Let's toast the final, happy disposition of Daddy's debut pearls. It sounds like a limerick, doesn't it? Drink up."

We drained our glasses. The champagne was cold and lovely. I wondered who had chosen it.

"Want some more?" I said, pouring a second glass.

"No. I'm nodding as it is. Just tuck me in and have another before you go to bed. I'll guarantee you sweet dreams."

I wheeled her into her bedroom and helped her into the white silk nightgown that was laid out, and watched as she slipped under the covers.

"'Good night, sweet princess,'" I said, kissing her forehead. "'Flights of angels sing thee to thy rest.'"

She turned her face into her pillow.

"And you to yours," she whispered. I turned off her lamp and went out of the room.

I did have another glass of champagne, but it wasn't the same without Camilla, so I corked the bottle and put it in her refrigerator and let myself out, thinking that it would undoubtedly go flat overnight, but would make a good sauce for cold salmon. I trudged up the driveway to my own house, suddenly so tired I could hardly put one foot in front of the other.

It must have been the emotion, I thought, smiling to myself, sliding between cool sheets and turning off my bedside lamp. "That was a real love fest. She was Camilla again. Maybe, just maybe, we've gotten her back."

I wanted to think some more about that, but sleep seized me suddenly and bore me down, fathoms deep, where dreams lay.

Even in the middle of it, I knew that it was a dream, but that did not spoil the sweet reality of it. Reality is often more vivid in that kind of dream because the dreamer knows he must soon leave it whether or not it is a happy dream. This was a very happy one.

I was in a house by the water. Not one of the three new ones, but the one we all owned together, the big, old rambling 1920s cottage on stilts down at the un-chic western end of Sullivan's Island. It was the first one that I knew; Lewis took me there the summer we were married, and I loved it as much in that first instant as I did in all the years we went there. I never said that to the others, because it sounded somehow presumptuous, as if an outlander were laying claim to something he had not yet earned. And even though they enfolded me and took me in as one of them from the first, I knew that I was indeed an outlander. It was Lewis they loved, at least then.

In the dream it was winter, and there was a cold wind howling down the beach and scouring the gray-tan sand into stinging swirls. I knew how they would feel on my skin if I went out onto the beach: like particles of diamonds, almost bringing blood. I usually did not mind that, but this time I was glad to be inside the big living room. It was warm and lit and almost tossing in the wind, like the cabin of a ship. All the old lopsided lamps were yellow with light, and a fire burned in the fireplace at one end, spitting because the shed out back never quite kept the wood dry. At the other end, where the staircase angled up over the junk closet, the big old space heater whispered and glowed deep red. The air in the room smelled of wood smoke and kerosene and damp rugs and salt. In my dream it seemed the palpable breath of the house to me, and I breathed it in deep draughts. It gave life.

"I know this is a dream, but I don't have to wake up yet, do I?" I said to Fairlie McKenzie, who lay on the couch under a salt-stiff old blanket, by the fire, reading. Her bright hair spilled over the tattered sofa pillow in a cascade as red as the fire embers. Fairlie always seemed to me a creature of light and fire; she shimmered with it, even lying still.

"No, not yet," she said, smiling at me. "There's no hurry. The guys won't be back for hours. They never are when they're surf-casting. Sit down. In a minute I'll make some tea."

"I'll make it," Camilla Curry said from her card table beside the space heater at the other end of the room. She was copying something from a big book onto a yellow legal pad, her face and hands in a pool of light from the bridge lamp. I seldom saw Camilla without a pad and pen. She always had projects that seemed to engross her utterly, and the rest of us never quite knew what they were.

"This and that," she would say in her soft drawl. "I'll let you see when I'm done." But her projects were always works in progress, because we never saw one.

"Let me," I said, grateful to be a useful part of the tapestry of the dream. Camilla, even in the dream, was bowed with osteoporosis, as she had been for a long time. Somehow it did not distort her fragile, fine-boned handsomeness; I always thought of her as ramrod straight. Lewis said she always had been, until the cruel disease began to eat her bones. We never spoke of it, but we all tried to spare Camilla undue physical stress when we could. She always saw through us, always hated it.

"You girls stay still. You get so little time out here, and I'm here most of all," she said. "I like to fiddle around in the kitchen."

Fairlie and I smiled at each other at the "girls." I was nearly fifty and Fairlie was only a few years younger than Camilla. But Camilla was mother to the group. She always had been the one to whom you went to find something, learn something, confess something, receive something. We all knew that her role was self-chosen. Even the men followed the unspoken rule. Camilla made you want to give her the most you could of what she needed.

She got up and floated straight as a hummingbird into the kitchen. Her shoulders were erect and her step as light as a girl's. She sang a little song as she walked: *"Maybe I'm right, and maybe I'm wrong, and maybe I'm weak and maybe I'm strong, but nevertheless I'm in love with you. . . .'*

"Charlie says it's a sappy song, but I love it," she called back over her beautiful shoulder. She had on a sheer blouse and a flowered skirt, and wore high-heeled sandals. Because it was a dream, it made perfect sense for her to walk like a girl, to be dressed in the clothes of her girlhood, for Charlie to be alive. All of this made me even happier.

"Camilla, even if it's a dream, I want to stay," I called back after her. "I don't want to go back."

"You can stay, Anny," her plummy voice called from the kitchen. "Lewis isn't coming for you yet."

I curled up on the rug in front of the fire, beside Fairlie on the sofa, pulling soft old cushions down to make a nest. I wrapped myself in the faded sofa quilt. The fire burned blue with damp, but gave off a steady heat. Outside the wind gusted and rattled the winter-dried palms and peppered the windows with staccato sand. The panes were crusted with salt. I stretched out my arms and legs to their farthest length and felt my joints pop, and the heat seep into them. I looked over at Fairlie to watch the firelight playing on her face. Twilight was falling fast; the men would come stamping in soon, letting cold, wet wind eddy in with them, rubbing their hands.

"Don't bring those smelly fish in here," Fairlie would say from the sofa. "I'm not cleaning fish today or any other day."

And because it was a dream, Lewis would be there along with Henry, as he always had been, and would say, as he always said when he came back from an expedition on which I had not accompanied him, "How's my lazy girl?"

I closed my eyes and slid toward dream-sleep before the dying logs, happiness prickling like lights behind my lids. In the kitchen the teakettle began to whistle.

"There's plenty of time," I murmured.

"Yes," Fairlie said.

We were quiet.

The fire came then . . . .

16

I AWOKE TO A WASH OF CORAL LIGHT on the ceiling, and thought that it was either very early, just at sunrise, or late, at sunset. I could not seem to think which one lit the ceiling like this. I reached out for the bedside travel alarm Lewis had given me, and found that moving my arm even a little was agony. I tried to sit up, and that hurt even more. I held up my arm, insofar as I could, and saw that it was wrapped in gauze. My other arm was, too, up to my elbow. I could not think what to do about this. I felt as if my head was enclosed in a plastic bubble.

"Try not to move much," Henry's voice said beside me. "I'll give you something for the pain if it's too bad. You can sit up a little now. How do you feel?"

I turned my head on the pillow to look at him. He was sitting in the little slipper chair I had bought on King Street. So I was on Bull Street, and the warm light came from my bedside lamp. Night, then. Henry was slouched in the chair, his long legs stretched straight out, his hands jammed into the pockets of a tweed jacket. He looked ghastly, flayed, at the edge of death. My heart flopped in my chest like a gaffed fish.

"What's the matter with you?" I tried to say. "What's the matter with me?"

But only a froggy croak came out, and my chest and throat bloomed into fierce, scorching pain. I fell silent and simply looked at Henry, waiting. From inside the safe, airless bubble, I knew that Henry would tell me the story. Henry would fix the pain.

He reached over and took my bandaged hand gently in his. "Do you know where you are?" he said.

I nodded. Then I spoke again, forgetting the scorching pain.

"Henry, I had the most awful dream," I croaked. "There was a fire—"

"Shhh," he said. "Stop trying to talk. There *was* a fire, Anny. At the creek. You have some superficial burns; they'll hurt for a while, but they'll heal soon. But you inhaled an awful lot of smoke before they got you out, and you've had some pneumonia. I just brought you here last night."

I stared at him. "Creek?" I mouthed. "When? How?"

"You've been in and out of consciousness for a week. Mainly we kept you sedated to keep you from coughing and tearing up your throat and lungs. You had some suction. I'm not surprised you don't remember. I'm afraid your house is pretty much gone. I'm sorry."

"Camilla's house?" I mouthed.

"It's fine. Just a little smoke damage. But, Anny"—and he took my other hand, so that he

held both of them—"Anny, Camilla is dead."
Tears sprang into his eyes and he looked away.

From the hermetic confines of the bubble, I
stared at him. What was he talking about? A thousand days of Camilla danced outside the bubble:
Camilla far down the beach, her hair flying, dogs
milling and leaping around her. Camilla laughing
in candle- and firelight. Camilla reaching out to
me from under the umbrella, the day I met her.
Camilla on the dune line, her old raincoat a blowing gray cloud around her. Henry was wrong. I
would soon find that he was.

"I don't believe you," I croaked, and the pain
flared again.

He shook his head. "Listen to me, Anny. She
was in your kitchen. She was lying on the floor
behind the island. Gaynelle didn't know she was
there, so she didn't go back for her when she
pulled you out, and the fire and rescue people
didn't know, either. When Gaynelle checked on
her in her house and found her missing, she told
the firemen and they went back in. The fire was
almost out then, anyway. It was smoke inhalation,
not fire. She didn't look at all bad."

Why couldn't I make my head work? What was
Camilla doing in my kitchen? How could she
have gotten there without my hearing the cum-
bersome chair? I remembered putting her to bed. I
remembered coming home dead tired and getting
into bed and falling asleep immediately. I remembered the dream of the beach house, and the fire
at the end of it. . . .

But I could not remember anything else. Why
could I not remember being in a fire? None of this

was making any sense. I felt mindless with fatigue.

My face must have been piteous, because he leaned over and pushed the hair off my forehead, and sat back down in the little chair, his long frame dwarfing it. I thought that I had never in my life seen a man so tired.

"I'm going to tell you all of it," he said. "We'd thought we'd tell you just the bare bones for now, but I can see that that's not going to do. Don't try to interrupt. I don't think I can do this but once."

Gaynelle came into the room then. I gave her what must have been an idiot's meaningless smile. I wondered why I could feel nothing. Well, of course, it was the plastic bubble. Sylvia Plath had written about the bubble: *The Bell Jar*. I was pleased to know what it was, this feeling of unassailable isolation from the world.

She kissed my forehead and straightened the bedclothes, and sat down on the little love seat across the room.

"I asked Gaynelle to join us," Henry said. "She's staying with you till you get on your feet. She's the one who saw the fire and pulled you out. If it hadn't been for her, you most assuredly would not be here. The fire was terribly hot and fast. She has some things to add, too."

He took a deep breath, and went on.

"Your blood tests showed a pretty substantial amount of sedative. Ambien, I'm almost sure. You wouldn't have waked up, I don't think, not until it was too late. We think Camilla put it into your champagne; you must have left the room at some point. We're testing the glasses from her kitchen now. I don't doubt what we'll find."

The pink pearls, I thought. She asked me to go and get the pink pearls. How silly they both were. She had given me a loving gift.

"And after you were asleep, we're pretty sure she went over to your house and started the fire. They found a gasoline can and a lighter in the kitchen."

We were all silent for a moment. This was beyond pain. It was like hearing a piece of fiction read aloud.

"She could walk," Henry said in the dead monotone. "She could all along. Gaynelle saw her do it once. After that, she watched Camilla as closely as she could. You know that she wouldn't leave you alone with her. Gaynelle caught on long before I did."

"I should have told Henry at the very beginning," Gaynelle said miserably from across the room. "But it just seemed so . . . crazy. I doubted my own eyes. I thought I would just watch, and together we could keep you safe. When I heard that she shouldn't walk anymore, and had to have the chair, I was relieved. But I guess I never really believed that. I'll never forgive myself."

"That makes two of us," Henry said.

"Her hip was broken," he went on. "I think it just collapsed under her in your kitchen. That happens a lot with osteoporosis as bad as Camilla's. She must have been on her way out of the kitchen when it broke. She surely called out, but you couldn't have heard her. Jesus, those last moments before the smoke got her . . .

"Well, anyway, Gaynelle was outside in her truck. She never went home. She was watching, and when she saw the smoke, she called 911 and then went in after you. When they got you to Queens, she called me. By the time I got there, the pneumonia had a good hold. It happens fast after being in a fire. Basically, we just pumped you full of antibiotics and kept you sedated until you could be moved. I knew you wouldn't want to wake up in the hospital. And I wanted you close enough so I could look in on you. This seemed like the best choice."

I nodded serenely. Everything he said made perfect sense. The universe seemed its old, orderly self when Henry spoke. It was when he stopped that pain as huge and relentless as a great white shark bumped its snout against the plastic bubble. But then it swam away. I knew that it could not get in. Nothing could.

"Okay, here's the really bad part," Henry said.

I shook my head fiercely, but he nodded his.

"Let's get it all out, Anny. Otherwise the infection of it could kill you.

"We're pretty sure now that Camilla set the fire at the beach house. No one can really prove that, but there's good enough evidence for me. It was Fairlie she was after then. This time it was you. I don't know if I'm ever going to be able to live with that."

"Why?" I said, through the bubble. "Why?" Couldn't they hear how absurd they sounded?

I promptly choked. Henry gave me an injection.

"It isn't going to knock you out," he said, "but

it's going to calm you down some. You simply *cannot* keep on talking. Otherwise I'm going to take you back to Queens. Okay?"

I nodded.

"All right. This part of the story goes way back. Lewis told you that I used to go with Camilla. And I did. We'd been together since childhood. We weren't engaged, but we both knew that would be the next thing. It had always seemed the right progression, the path to the simple, affectionate marriage and life that I thought I always wanted. Neither of us had ever dated anybody else, not really.

"And then I met Fairlie, and everything changed in an instant, and there was just no question anymore of who I belonged with. I told Camilla the next night, sitting in a car out at Lowndes Grove. It was Lila's debut party; I remember that.

"I never in the world expected the reaction I got. I knew it would hurt her; I hated that. But to go on as we'd been would have been intolerable and unfair. I saw a part of her I had never seen in the twenty-odd years I knew her. She cried and screamed until she lost her breath and almost passed out. I just held her until she stopped, but then she started up again. I had a buddy in the Queens ER, and I went by and got a sedative for her, and by the time I took her home, she was out on her feet.

"I had to wake her mother and father, and I had to tell them. They got Camilla upstairs, and I gave them the rest of the sedative for her, and she finally went to sleep. I waited until they came down. It was one of the worst nights I've ever spent. I really thought her father was going to shoot me. By dawn we'd worked it out: we would tell everybody that Camilla dumped me, and I only got interested in Fairlie afterward. A rebound love affair, if you will."

He smiled without any humor. It was more a rictus of pain.

"Even Fairlie halfway believed that, although I told her later what had happened," he said. "She never told anybody else. I really don't think anybody knew. By the time Camilla met Charlie, right after that, it was all over Charleston that Camilla had ended our relationship and that I was nearly prostrate with grief. And I played the role, or at least I never refuted it. Guilt over Camilla has been with me all those years. I'll never forget her face the night I told her. I hated the lie, but living it made it possible for her to stay in Charleston. Back then, that kind of thing mattered a lot more than it does now.

"So for a long time we went along just fine; Camilla was warm and affectionate with me, and a good friend to Fairlie, and Charlie adored her. Nobody questioned that. You remember those years. They were idyllic. Who could possibly have thought differently? After a while it just seemed natural to me. I had you all and Fairlie, and Camilla was happy with Charlie. Something that could have been very bad had ended well. We were the Scrubs.

"And when Charlie died, Camilla was the perfect widow. God, who didn't admire her strength and courage? She held the Scrubs together; it could have been the start of our breaking up. She held us together with her sheer love. She did that until that New Year's Eve Fairlie and I told everybody we were going to retire to Kentucky. And when the chance came, that night when I forgot about the opera and Fairlie got mad at me and went out to the beach house, she took it. Camilla had been content to let things perk along, until she knew we were leaving for good. She had to move then. And after Fairlie was gone, she helped Lila find the houses at the creek, and she literally held everybody together until I came stumbling in from the Yucatán, half dead, and she could look after me. She knew I couldn't have gone anywhere else. Not at the time. And she took wonderful care of me. Do you remember?"

I nodded my head up and down vigorously, like a good child being taught something in school. I did remember. Camilla had literally held Henry up and put him back together. Okay so far. I could follow this story as well as anybody. I felt proud of myself.

"So she was content with the life we all had. It seemed as if we might last at the creek. And then Lewis . . . was gone, and you were alone, and it was obvious that I was fond of you. She couldn't have thought it was anything but the same fondness I felt for all of us, but neither could she abide any sort of feeling on my part at all that didn't center on her. She did her best to talk you into moving back to town. She had all her accidents when we two were away together somewhere. She got really ill when we took to riding with Gaynelle and T. C. And she just couldn't stand it that I was so fond of Britney. Gaynelle is sure it was Camilla who opened Lila's door and let Honey out. And as for the jewelry she intimated that Gaynelle had taken, they found it in her desk drawer, after the fire. It's been Camilla all along, and I never saw it, and when I think that maybe I could have prevented this, it makes me sick."

There were tears running down his face now. They traced silver through the white stubble on his face. Henry seemed to have aged ten years. Hard years.

"How could you know?" I rasped, shaking my head at him when he tried to shush me. "How on earth could you have known? How do you know now?"

Gaynelle came over and sat on the edge of my bed. The room was dark except for the circle of warm amber light from the lamp. In it, her face was dry and furrowed and as narrow as a fox's. There were more than two casualties in this terrible, unimaginable thing.

Henry put his head back and closed his eyes, looking, simply, dead and embalmed. It occurred to me that Henry literally might not be able to bear this. The fear of that nibbled at the edge of the bell jar, but did not come in.

"I found her diaries, or whatever they are," Gaynelle said. "And I sat down and read right through the ones she had with her. These started when Mrs. McKenzie died, but I think there must be others that go back to when her husband had his heart attack and she realized she was free. I'm not a bit ashamed that I snooped. By that time I was getting a real funny feeling about her. I'd seen her walking when she was supposed to be in the chair, remember. And I absolutely know that she cut her own head and crawled into the bathtub the day you and Henry went out to Sweetgrass and stayed gone so long. I found the soap dish she did it with. It still had blood and hair on it. I should have gone straight to Henry the day I read those damned books. But God . . . it just sounded so crazy. I thought at first she was writing fiction."

Dread iced my stomach and heart. I knew that she was going to tell me what was in the notebooks Camilla had always kept, and I knew that it would change my life dreadfully and forever. I turned my head away from her and shut my eyes.

"No, stay with it," Henry said. "It makes everything clear. It will wreck you if you don't understand."

But I still did not open my eyes.

"Every page was like a page in a diary," Gaynelle said. "Like what happened to her that day. They were calm and reasonable and even funny sometimes; she's a good writer. Was. The thing is, none of that stuff happened. It was all about what she and Henry had done that day. About what they had for breakfast, and what they did during the day, and where they went, and what she made for dinner, and about . . . how they made love every night. She even wrote two or three times about their wedding. It was the biggest and most beautiful wedding Charleston had ever seen; nobody since had come close to it. It was about their children, too. Not her boys, hers and Henry's children. They were perfect, a combination of the best of both of them. By the time I finished reading, I knew how they had grown up, and where they went to college, and who they married, and all about the grandchildren. She talked about all Henry's honors at the hospital, and the books she published, and the plantation they had out on the Edisto River. And every night, the big love scene. *Every* night. There was not a single mention of any of the rest of you. Not her husband, none of you. Oh, God, I should have told Henry that day . . . but somehow I just couldn't believe it."

"Don't beat up on yourself," Henry said wearily from the chair. "I'm the one who should have seen it."

I don't see how, I thought mildly. Who would have believed this about Camilla? I don't think I do. Not at all. She told me that night that she loved me. She gave me every chance to say I wasn't staying; she had tears in her eyes . . . who could doubt that? I think she did love me. Just maybe not as much as she did Henry. Just not enough. I can understand that. . . .

"Who knows about it?" I choked out.

Henry shook his head. "I don't know. Nobody's supposed to know about the notebooks, but I had to give them to the police. Otherwise they'd have been sniffing around you. It was your house, you know. The books cleared up a lot of unanswered questions about . . . Fairlie, I guess, but there was no use reopening that. It wouldn't have changed anything. The chief said they'd be put into a closed-case file, but this is Charleston. Could be nobody knows, could be half the city does. There's certainly been enough talk about it.

Too much happening over and over to the same people. The same people who'd always been a closed corporation. It's irresistible. I think Simms squashed some of it; Freddy Chappelle at the *Post and Courier* is a great friend of his and after the first news item, there hasn't been another word about it. TV has let it alone, too. Nobody has confronted me about it, but Gaynelle's gotten a lot of flack, and I expect you'll get plenty when you're up and around. So many people have called Lila that she got an unlisted number. She doesn't know it all yet, by the way; tell her if you want to."

"Did Lewis know?" I managed. It was like eating fire, but the pain stayed outside the bubble.

"I don't think so. He may have sensed something, but I don't think he really knew. He wouldn't have gone off to Fort Lauderdale and left you there if he'd known. He'd surely have figured it out if he'd been around the last few weeks, though. Although, when you think about it, if he'd been around, none of it would have happened. It would still be just pages in those unholy books."

"I'm glad he didn't know," I whispered. "Are you going to tell Lila and Simms?"

"I'm not going to tell anybody. I'm not going to stay in Charleston, Anny. I can't. I just can't be here anymore. If I could change anything, I'd stay, but I can't, and I have to be somewhere I can get out of my own head. You're well cared for. I can go now."

"Where?" Gaynelle said. I watched them peacefully. Sense; it all made such good sense.

"I don't know. Maybe somewhere with the

docs. Maybe . . . oh, God, I don't know. I'm sorry to fade out. I just know I can't breathe this air anymore."

"Was she crazy?" Gaynelle said. "She just about had to be, didn't she? But she seemed so normal. . . ."

"I don't know what 'crazy' means," Henry said heavily. "Obsession, maybe. But it really doesn't make any difference, does it?"

He gave me another shot then, and kissed my cheek and said that he would see me before he left. I knew that he wouldn't. Beyond the bell jar the world swayed perilously, but it held. I slid again toward sleep, as I must have been doing for days now, and the last thing I thought before it claimed me was, It was Camilla who held us together after all. Maybe just not in the way we thought.

The bell jar held firm for several weeks. I ate Gaynelle's wonderful meals, and slept and slept, and watched endless television. I seldom went downstairs; we had a small set in the upstairs library, and I watched there, lying stretched out on the sofa, covered with a quilt of Lewis's mother's. I did not light the lamps, and I did not let Gaynelle open the curtains to let in the late spring light. Wisely, she did not push me.

People called and she answered the phone and told them I was fine, but resting. People dropped by and she answered the door and said that I was resting, but would look forward to seeing them soon. The first week or so the door and telephone bells rang almost constantly, but ultimately I proved to be uninteresting prey, and soon they tapered off. I was glad. The noise had blasted into my TV shows.

I got addicted to several daily reruns—*The X-Files*, *The Twilight Zone*, *Jag*—and grew fretful when anything interrupted me while I was watching them. I did not watch CNN, and never the local stations. March segued into April, and April into early May, without my really knowing it. Gaynelle was wonderful. Anyone else would have prodded and cajoled and threatened to get me up and around again but she had an exquisite sense of the time it took to begin to heal. Only once did she say anything to me about my self-imposed isolation.

"I guess I ought to put this all behind me and get on with it, huh?" I said idly one evening, flipping through *People* magazine. Gaynelle bought me armsful of magazines, and I read them avidly. But never the news weeklies.

"I don't imagine you'll ever be able to put it behind you," she said. "But you'll probably want to get on with it sooner rather than later."

But that was all she did say.

Inside the bubble I was warm and safe and endlessly sleepy. I tried to tell Gaynelle about the bubble, and how it comforted me.

"Shades of Sylvia Plath," she said, and I smiled. I had forgotten once more how avidly she read. "And look where it got her," she added.

I really don't think I thought much about Henry, or even about Camilla. I knew that I would have to, someday, but not now. Not now. I could think now of Lewis, though, and sometimes I talked to him.

"You don't blame me for staying holed up for a little while longer, do you?" I said. And, "Good Lord, Lewis, I was watching TV last night and they said it was the first day of May. You know that thing we all used to sing out at the beach: 'Hey, hey, first of May, outdoor screwing starts today?' And remember that one May first that we did? Out at Sweetgrass. I had pine needles in my butt for days."

I did not realize at the time that I was speaking aloud.

Britney was staying with her aunt's family, and was absorbed with pageanting and taking little Henrietta to obedience classes. Gaynelle saw her many nights and one day most weekends, while JoAnne came to stay with me. We watched the Fox network together, religiously. Gaynelle said that Britney was wild to come and see me at Bull Street, but I just smiled vaguely.

"Not quite yet. Soon though."

Marcy came one day, and hugged me and cried, and said not to worry about Outreach. Camilla's sons had gratefully sold the building on Gillon Street to Simms Howard just before they took Camilla to California for burial, and he was redoing the loft, but had said that Outreach could stay in our part of the building as long as we wanted, at the same rent. Once I would have wondered caustically who Simms was redecorating the loft for, but it did not occur to me now.

"That's awfully nice," I said. Marcy chattered

desperately on a bit, and then went home. I found
The Big Chill on a cable station and settled in to
watch it with Gaynelle.

Linda Cousins called from Sweetgrass to say
that everything was going well, and Tommy was
doing wonderfully with the longleafs, and not to
worry about anything.

"Isn't that sweet?" I said.

Lila came and gave Gaynelle a copy she had
had made of the photo of the Scrubs on their first
day at the beach house, the one on which we'd
sworn, and copies of other photos of all of us, in
the water, on the dunes, romping with the dogs,
eating by candlelight. Gaynelle had been afraid to
give them to me at first, afraid that they would
shatter my fragile balance, but when I finally saw
them I only smiled with dim pleasure.

"Oh, look, Gaynelle. Don't we all look young,
though? And that's Gladys; you know, I told you
about Gladys."

It was like looking at photographs in a biogra-
phy of someone you knew rather well, but not
intimately.

Gaynelle cut my hair, and it hugged my head in
a cap of rough curls.

"You look eighteen," she said.

And she brought me some new jeans and T-
shirts from Target, because mine had grown loose
and shabby. I wore little else those days.

"You need to get out in the sun and get those
legs tanned," she said. "You've got pretty legs."

"Soon," I said. "I promise I really will, soon."

* * *

In what felt to be the middle of a night in early June, Gaynelle came into my bedroom and shook me awake.

"You've got a visitor," she said, grinning. "Get up and get dressed. Put on some long pants and a sweater. I put some over there on the vanity bench for you."

"Gaynelle, it's not even morning," I whined. "Just tell whoever it is to come back sometime during the daytime. God, what do people *think*?"

"GET UP AND PUT ON THOSE CLOTHES!" she shouted. "I MEAN IT! RIGHT NOW!"

I was so startled that I did what she said. Very faintly, the thin eggshell glass of the bell jar cracked.

Downstairs Henry was waiting for me in the sitting room. He was tanned the color of saddle leather, and had the beginnings of a silver beard. His hair was longer than I had ever seen it, and there were new sun creases in the corners of his blue eyes. He wore jeans, a black leather vest, and boots. I simply stared.

"Hello, Henry," I said finally. "Good Lord, look at you. You look like *The Wild One*. Where's your raccoon?"

"Hi, Anny. Want to go for a little ride?"

My head was spinning.

"Sure," I said. "Whatever."

We walked down the path through the garden and out to the curb. It was very dark; the faux gaslight in front of my house had gone out.

"You look nice with your hair like that," he said.

"Thank you. You look pretty spiffy yourself."

Neither of us mentioned the time of night.

At the corner of Bull Street and Wentworth, he stopped under the streetlight and looked at me.

"Aren't you going to ask me where I've been?"

"Do you want to tell me?"

"You're damned right I do. I've been in Iowa with T.C. We went out to a big bike meet. I rode with them all the way. It was . . . wonderful."

"You rode to Iowa on a motorcycle?" I said stupidly. Through the crack in the bell jar, something very like laughter began to seep in, fizzing.

"I goddamned well did," he said. "On this."

We turned the corner, and the light struck a huge, bulbous motorcycle parked at the curb. It shone blackly in the light. It looked like an archaic Cretan drawing of a bull.

"It's an Indian," he said. "They just started making them again. I bought it in Iowa. T. C. thinks I'm crazy, he says there are too many kinks in this model, but there haven't been so far. I worship this lady. Come on, Anny. Get on."

"Get on?" I was aware of how stupid I sounded.

"Get on the bike behind me. I'm going to blow some of the stuffing out of your head. It's time, Anny. It's long past time."

"How did you know about the stuffing?"

"Because I had it, too, until we got halfway to Iowa. And Gaynelle says you haven't even been out of the house. We're starting now. Get on."

I did. The big bike had a wide, deep seat, and I fit easily into it. I wrapped my arms around Henry's waist and put my face against his vest, and simply sat, breathing in leather and gasoline and June and Henry.

"This is nice," I murmured.

"You ain't seen nothing yet," he said.

The bike roared into life. I had simply forgotten the sound. My head pounded with it. I had not heard a noise this loud since the ride to Folly Beach. It seemed a lifetime ago. Well, it had been. An enormous giggle like a hiccup rose up out of my stomach and burst to the surface like swamp gas.

We threaded our way over to Hasell and turned onto East Bay. The wind was cool and heavy with Confederate jasmine and oleander. I kept my eyes shut, clinging to Henry. The giggles kept bubbling up. I could not see whether there was much traffic on East Bay, but I had no sense of it. The bike murdered the silence.

"Where are we going?" I called to him. It did not seem important.

"Damned if I know. Maybe to Daytona, to the famous coleslaw pit. Maybe to the IHOP for breakfast. Maybe just around in circles. You pick."

"I want to go to Sweetgrass," I said, and suddenly knew that I did, more than anything. I ached for Sweetgrass and the river and the new green marsh.

"Sweetgrass it is. There's one thing I want to do first, though."

"What?"

"Show you."

We bowled down to the Battery. The grand old houses were all dark, sleeping. Off beyond White Point Gardens I could see the first delicate shell-pink flush of dawn on the harbor. Against my face, Henry's vest smelled rough and masculine and somehow contentious. I giggled again, and opened my eyes.

Midway down the Battery, Henry hit the brakes and gunned the motor. The howl from the Indian broke the world apart. The bubble flew into a million shards. I threw my head back and yelled.

"Yeeeee-HAW!"

Behind us, on the High Battery, window after window bloomed into furious light.

ACKNOWLEDGMENTS

You will not find the beach house, nor the dunes it sat upon, on Sullivan's Island, though you might still find a few old houses like it. And there is not, as far as I know, a cluster of small tabby houses on a wide creek on John's Island. But to me, Charleston and the Low Country are a state of heart as well as of fact, and it is that which I have tried to evoke.

Moreover, none of the people in this book live anywhere but in my own mind. If there are similarities to flesh and blood Charlestonians, I hope they are comfortable ones.

My thanks again to Duke and Barbara Hagerty, who have shared some of their most treasured place names, and who are, to me, the heart of Charleston still. Thanks, too, to Nance Charlebois, who got me hooked on Harleys and coleslaw wrestling. And all thanks to the dedicated people who work to protect the beautiful Gullah language and culture.

And finally, as always, to the A team: Heyward, Martha, and my beloved longtime agent and editor, Ginger Barber and Larry Ashmead. Thanks for the memories, guys.

"One doesn't read Anne Rivers Siddons's
books; one dwells in them."
Chicago Tribune

Step into the world of
ANNE RIVERS SIDDONS
with these novels

— Fox's Earth —

"Beautifully calculated to keep
the pages turning at a fast clip!"
Washington Post Book World

"A lusty southern saga . . . passionate
and perverse . . . psychologically
astute and excellently written."
Cosmopolitan

At Fox's Earth there was no room for love, no
room for desire. There was only room for fear.

Ruth Yancey is only a small child the first time she
lays eyes on the magnificent, three–storied Georgia
house called Fox's Earth. The daughter of an impover-
ished and cruel mill worker, she knows that someday
she will not only live in such a house, but will make it
her own. And once she becomes Ruth Yancey Fox, she
does, achieving total domination over all those under its
roof. Or rather, all the women.

For decades Ruth rules with tyranny by way of evil
manipulation. And always, her cache of closely guard-
ed secrets and acts of cruelty grow. Eventually, even
Ruth realizes that, ultimately, those lies will have to
come out. . . .

—Homeplace—

"Anne Rivers Siddons . . . writes with such astonishing lyrical beauty that you will want to read it aloud to everyone you ever loved."
Pat Conroy on *Homeplace*

"Powerful, sensitive . . . You won't want to miss *Homeplace*."
Atlanta Journal & Constitution

After twenty-one years Micah (Mike) Winship is making the big move—she's going home for a visit. She hasn't been back since 1963, when her father threw her out, but now he is dying and asking for her. And although she is armed with her successful journalism career and the strength found after her divorce, she is nearing forty and her sophisticated urban lifestyle is falling apart.

Heading home, Mike is unprepared for a past that has lain in wait for her—one that includes an old love, a spoiled sister, and a plot to seize her family's land. And in trying to understand her long-forgotten self, she learns at last those lessons best learned early about love and loss, family and forgiveness, and the undeniable need for a place called home.

—Hill Towns—

"She creates a passel of characters
her fans will find reassuringly familiar,
and then sends them far out
of their ken—to Italy."
Kirkus Reviews

T his truly compelling novel is a magnificent kaleidoscope of the emotions that we most cherish—and fear. Showcasing the rare talent of Anne Rivers Siddons at her finest, *Hill Towns* probes deeply into the multiple meanings of love and relationships, as seen through the prism of one woman's life.

As a small child, a single event irrevocably changed the life of Catherine Gaillard—and rendered her unable to leave her cloistered mountaintop town in Tennessee for the next thirty years. Her devotion to her husband, Joe, and her desire to forever put this incident behind her propel Cat on a life-changing voyage to Italy.

Making their way across the Tuscany countryside in the company of newly married friends and an exuberant painter and his enigmatic wife, Cat and Joe feel the fabric that holds their marriage together—so carefully woven together at home—begin to unravel. The once-carefree trip turns into a journey to the very heart of their relationship . . . and the ultimate test of their love.

"Siddons fans will be enthralled . . . [an] emotionally gripping novel."
Kirkus Reviews

Elegant Kate, walking a tightrope over an abyss of lies . . . sensitive, sensible, self-contained Cecie . . . Ginger, the heiress, sexy, vibrant, richer than sin . . . and poor, hopeless, brilliant Fig—they came together as sorority sisters on a Southern campus in the '60s. Four young women bound by rare, blinding, early friendship—they spend two idyllic spring breaks at Nag's Head, North Carolina, the isolated strip of barrier islands where grand old weatherbeaten houses perch defiantly on the edge of a storm-tossed sea. Now, thirty years later, they are coming back to recapture the exquisite magic of those early years . . . to experience again the love, the enthusiasm, the passion, the pain, and the cruel betrayal that shaped the four young girls into women and set them all adrift on the . . . Outer Banks.

‑‑ *Colony* ‑‑

"An outstanding mutigenerational novel . . ."
New York Times

When Maude Chambliss first arrives at Retreat, the seasonal home of her husband's aristocratic family, she is a nineteen-year-old bride fresh from South Carolina's Low Country. Among the patrician men and women who reside in the summer colony on the coast of Maine, her gypsy-like beauty and impulsive behavior immediately brand her an outsider. She, as well as everyone else, is certain she will never fit in. And, of course, she doesn't . . . at first.

But over the many summers she spends there, Maude comes to cherish life in the colony, as she does the people who share it with her. There is her husband, Peter, consumed with a darkness of spirit; her adored but dangerously fragile children; her domineering mother-in-law, who teaches her that it is the women who possess the strength to keep the colony intact; and Maine native Micah Willis, who is ultimately Maude's truest friend.

This brilliant novel, rich with emotion, is filled with appealing, intense, and indomitable characters. Anne Rivers Siddons paints a portrait of a woman determined to preserve the spirit of past generations—and the future of a place where she became who she is . . . a place called *Colony*.

—Low Country—

"Lush, lyrical."
Boston Globe

"Compelling . . . Siddons is a pro at capturing
the humanity in her characters."
Austin American-Statesman

Caroline Venable enjoys the blessings of upper-
class Southern life: money, prestige, a powerful
husband—and a predictable and stifling routine of
luncheons, parties, and dinners with her husband's
wealthy friends and clients in his land-development
conglomerate.

To escape, Caro drinks a little too much. But her true
solace is the Low Country island her beloved
Granddaddy left her—a breathtaking oasis where a band
of wild ponies runs free. When Caro learns that her husband must develop the island or lose the business, she is
devastated. The Low Country is her heritage—and what
will happen to her enchanting horses? Yet saving the
island could cost her everything—for it means con-
fronting pain and shattering long-held illusions about
her life, her marriage, and the woman she really is.

—Peachtree Road—

"Sweeping."
New York Times Book Review

"*The* Southern novel for
our generation."
Pat Conroy

Headstrong, exuberant, and independent, Lucy Bondurant is a devastating beauty who will never become the demure Southern lady her mother and society demand. Sheppard Gibbs Bondurant III, Lucy's older cousin, is too shy and bookish to become the classically suave and gregarious Southern gentleman his family expects. Growing up together in a sprawling home on Atlanta's Peachtree Road, these two will be united by fierce love and hate, and by rebellion against the narrow aristocratic society into which they were born. Anne Rivers Siddons's classic novel vividly brings to life their mesmerizing, unforgettable story—set against the dramatic changing landscape of Atlanta, a city destined for greatness.

"Ms. Siddons uses brilliant characterization,
riveting suspense and a touch of myth to
create a truly remarkable novel."
Richmond Times Dispatch

"A multilayered, multifaceted novel
that defies you to put it down."
Los Angeles Times Book Review

Fleeing a disastrous marriage and an abusive husband, Andy Calhoun and her frightened young daughter, Hillary, head for the small town of Pemberton, Georgia, "in search of banality" and calm. Instead, she finds herself caught up in the intrigues of the elite old families of Pemberton. Just as she begins to assimilate into her new world of horse racing and society dinners, she meets Tom Dabney, the wild prodigal son of Pemberton society who lives in a magical house out in the woods. An exuberant poet who worships the wilderness, Tom both fascinates and repels Andy. Rumors about Tom's strange pagan rites hint at possible madness, and Andy resolves to keep herself and her daughter away from him. Nevertheless, against her better judgment, Andy finds herself becoming immersed in his life and his strange, mystical world.

When he discovers his precious woods are being threatened by the waste from a nearby nuclear power plant Tom declares open war on the enemy, and Andy must choose between her life with Tom and the more sane one she left behind—if Pemberton society will take her back.

"An absolute gem . . . a rare
and wonderful book."
Richmond News Leader

Everyone loves Maggie Deloach, one of the most popular girls on campus, with everything going for her. An impeccable lineage. Picture-perfect looks. The best sorority, and the best fraternity boy's pin. The ultimate Southern belle, Maggie knows what the rules are and is willing to play by them. No surprises are waiting in her future—but neither are any dissapointments.

Then, amid the stifling heat of an Alabama summer, everything changes. There is talk of a racial revolution brewing, one that surely should not touch her protected world . . . but somehow does. There is growing sexual awareness that she knows should shock her . . . yet does not. There is a single act of defiance and courage that will forever alter the way others think of her . . . and how Maggie thinks of herself.

"Siddons's prose is so fluid, graceful,
and lovely, that after diving in,
the reader is carried along effortlessly
and with great pleasure."
Library Journal

The year is 1961, and Peyton is thirteen. Her mother died when she was born, and although her widower father assures her it wasn't her fault, Peyton believes it really was. When she learns that her mother's young cousin, Nora Findlay, will be arriving in Lytton, Georgia, that summer to mind her, she is not pleased at the prospect of sharing her life and her father with a stranger. But Nora has a certain something about her—she laughs a lot, and she smokes and she seems to have done just about everything fun there is to do in this world. She is unlike any grownup that Peyton has ever known, and she reads a lot—and takes Peyton's dreams of becoming a writer seriously. Pretty soon, Hamilton Bayliss, Peyton's father, who has been on his own and reserved since her mother died, is humming while he shaves. The whole household seems revitalized with Nora's energy, and when she takes a job teaching at the local high school, it seems that she might stay on in Lytton forever.

But something is troubling Nora—something more than the snide comments of some of the neighbors, who don't take kindly to her freethinking ways. Rather, it seems to Peyton that something from Nora's past is upsetting her, and as much as Nora has tried to run away from the life she led before coming to stay with Peyton and Hamilton, it seems that she cannot keep far enough from a shocking truth that will stun the residents of this small, segregated town, and forever change the life of young Peyton.

—Up Island—

"Siddons at her best."
USA Today

If there was ever a woman who knew what was important, that woman was Molly Bell Redwine. From childhood, Molly was taught by her charismatic, demanding mother that "family is everything." But in what seems like an instant, Molly discovers that family can change without warning. Her husband of more than twenty years leaves her for a younger woman, her domineering mother dies, and her Atlanta clan scatters to the four winds. In a heartbeat, Molly is set adrift. Devastated by her crumbling world, Molly takes refuge with a family friend on Martha's Vineyard, where she tries to come to terms with who she really is. After the summer season, Molly decides to stay on in this very different place, renting a small cottage on a remote up-island pond. As Molly's stay up island widens the distance between her and her old life in Atlanta, she lets go of her outworn notions of family and begins to become part of a strange—and very real—new family. As the long Vineyard winter closes in, she braces herself for the search for renewal, identity, and strength, until the healing spring finally comes.

"A literary meteor shower . . . One great
read, it moves quickly, brings you to laughter
and tears, builds suspense, and tells a hell of
a great story beautifully."
Detroit News/Free Press

Merritt Fowler is a natural caretaker—of her
physician husband, Pom; her lovely, fragile
daughter, Glynn; her erratic younger sister, Laura; even
her destructive mother-in-law. Exhausted and confused,
Merritt no longer knows who she is or what is important to her. She only knows that she is searching for
something.

When a family argument sends Glynn running from
her Atlanta home to her Aunt Laura in Hollywood,
Merritt feels compelled to follow. On impulse, the three
women take off in Laura's red Mustang convertible, bar-
reling up the wild coast from the Palm Springs desert to
the Santa Cruz Mountains outside San Fransisco—
earthquake country. There, in the protective shade of the
great redwoods, Merritt, Glynn, and Laura struggle to
see if the widening fissures between mother, daughter,
and sister can be healed as they search for the bedrock of
strength and courage that can save them.

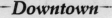

"Siddons draws her ensemble cast
with confidence and panache."
Kirkus Reviews

The year was 1966. And for Atlanta, the country, and one woman making her way in a changing world, nothing would ever be the same.

Set in the cusp of the country's great social movements, in the year before love turned to anger and peace to militancy, *Downtown* is the story of Smoky O'Donnell, her career, and her heart.

When Smoky arrives in Atlanta in 1966, after an airless lifetime back in Savannah, she is at once thrilled and chastened by this dazzling, hectic, young city on the move. Her new job as a writer with Atlanta's *Downtown* magazine introduces her to many unforgettable people, including three young men who will change her life in ways she never thought possible.

Smoky's choices, and her ultimate decisions, create a tender, joyous and powerful story of the end of innocence—both Smoky's and America's—at a time when traditional values are in question and the air is laden with possibilities.

Full of masterful characterizations, probing insight, and lyrical prose for which Anne Rivers Siddons is justly acclaimed, *Downtown* is another stunning achievement from an extraordinary writer.

"Haunting."
New York Post

Their love would never be the same.
Colquitt and Walter Kennedy enjoyed a life of lazy weekends, gathering with the neighbors on their quiet, manicured street and sipping drinks on their patios. But when construction of a beautiful new home begins in the empty lot next door, their easy friendship and relaxed get-togethers are marred by strange accidents and inexplicable happenings.

Though Colquitt's rational mind balks at the idea of a "haunted" house, she cannot ignore the tragedies associated with it. It is as if the house preys on its inhabitants' weaknesses and slowly destroys the goodness in them—ultimately driving them to disgrace, madness, and even death.

Anne Rivers Siddons transports you deep into the heart of a neighborhood torn apart by a mysterious force that threatens their friendship, their happiness and, for some, their very existence.

*And Anne Rivers Siddons's new hardcover,
available now*

—Islands—

Anny Butler is a caretaker and a nurturer—first, for her own brothers and sisters, and then as a director of an agency devoted to the welfare of children. What she has never had is a real family. That changed when she met and married Lewis Aiken, an exuberant surgeon fifteen years older than Anny. When they wed, she finds her family in a group of Charleston childhood friends who are inseparable, who are one another's surrogate kin.

Instantly, upon meeting them at the old beach house on Sullivan's Island that they co-own, Anny knows that she has found home. They vow, instead of going into assisted-living facilities when the time comes, to locate a place where they can live together by the sea.

Bad things begin to happen: a hurricane, a fire, deaths—but still the remaining friends cling together. They are nurtured and bolstered by Camilla Curry, the heart and core of their group, and always the healer. Anny allows Camilla to enfold and sustain her. They move to a new island retreat, the beginning of their long-awaited life together. And Anny must learn that everything is not as it seems, that some loves carry a secret and terrible price . . .

NEW YORK TIMES BESTSELLING AUTHOR

ANNE RIVERS SIDDONS

ISLANDS
0-06-103205-0/$7.99 US/$10.99 Can

In a rambling island cottage in the Carolina Lowcountry, a woman will discover that family has many meanings . . . and that some loves carry a secret and a terrible price.

NORA, NORA
0-06-109333-5/$7.99 US/$10.99 Can

When twelve-year-old Peyton McKenzie's cousin takes a job teaching the first integrated honors class at the local high school, it becomes clear that something is troubling Nora.

LOW COUNTRY
0-06-109332-7/$7.99 US/$10.99 Can

Caroline Venable's true solace from her predictable and stifling life is the Lowcountry island her beloved Grandaddy left her. And when she learns that her husband must develop the island or lose his business, she's devastated.

UP ISLAND
0-06-109921-X/$7.99 US/$10.99 Can

After her husband of more than twenty years leaves her for a younger woman and her domineering mother dies, Molly Bell Redwine takes refuge with a friend on Martha's Vineyard.

FAULT LINES
0-06-109334-3/$7.99 US/$10.99 Can

Three women: mother, daughter, and sister struggle to see if the widening fissures between them can be healed during a trip up the California coast.

Available wherever books are sold
or please call 1-800-331-3761 to order.

AuthorTracker
www.AuthorTracker.com

ARS 1004

(((LISTEN TO)))

🔥 HarperAudio

New York Times bestselling author

Anne Rivers Siddons

Islands CD
0-06-055458-4
Performed by Dana Ivey
6 hours / 5 CDs
$29.95 ($45.95 Can.)

Nora, Nora CD Low Price
0-06-059442-X
Performed by Debra Monk
6 hours / 5 CDs
$14.95 ($22.95 Can.)

Islands Unabridged Cassette
0-06-055459-2
Performed by Dana Ivey
15 hours / 10 cassettes
$39.95 ($59.95 Can.)

Nora, Nora Unabridged Cassette
0-69-452345-3
Performed by Kate Reading
12.5 hours / 9 Cassettes
$39.95 ($59.95 Can.)

Islands Cassette
0-06-055457-6
Performed by Dana Ivey
6 hours / 4 cassettes
$25.95 ($39.95 Can.)

Nora, Nora
Large Print
0-06-019718-8
$25.00 ($39.00 Can.)

Islands Large Print
0-06-054545-3
$24.95 ($38.95 Can.)

Low Country Low Price Cassette
0-06-057747-9
Performed by Debra Monk
6 hours / 7 Cassettes
$14.95 ($22.95 Can.)

Colony Low Price Cassette
0-06-059039-4
Performed by Judith Ivey
3 hours / 2 cassettes
$9.99 ($14.95 Can.)

Outer Banks Low Price Cassette
0-06-055666-8
Performed by Kate Nelligan
2 hours / 3 Cassettes
$9.99 ($14.99 Can.)

Available wherever books are sold, or call 1-800-331-3761.

🎯 AuthorTracker

HarperAudio 🔥 HarperLargePrint
Imprints of HarperCollins*Publishers*
www.harperaudio.com

Don't miss the next book by your favorite
author. Sign up now for AuthorTracker by
visiting www.AuthorTracker.com

ARSA 1004